Reviewers and readers love FLAVIA!

As **CHIMNEY SWEEPERS** **COME** *to* **DUST**

#1 pick for Library Reads
#1 *Maclean's* bestseller
#3 *New York Times* bestseller
#6 Indie bestseller
#7 *Publishers Weekly* bestseller

"Exceptional . . . [The] intriguing setup only gets better, and Bradley makes Miss Bodycote's a suitably Gothic setting for Flavia's sleuthing. [Flavia's] morbid narrative voice continues to charm."

—*Publishers Weekly* (starred review)

"Eleven-year-old Flavia de Luce, perhaps contemporary **crime fiction's most original character**—to say she is Pippi Longstocking with a Ph.D. in chemistry (speciality: poisons) barely begins to describe her—is finally coming home."

—*Maclean's*

"[*As Chimney Sweepers Come to Dust*] maintains the high standards Bradley set from the start. . . . Another treat for readers of all ages."

—*Booklist*

The DEAD in
THEIR VAULTED ARCHES

"Outstanding . . . In this **marvelous blend of whimsy and mystery,** Flavia manages to operate successfully in the adult world of crimes and passions while dodging the childhood pitfalls set by her sisters."

—*Publishers Weekly* (starred review)

"Oh, to be eleven again and pal around with irresistible wunderkind Flavia de Luce. . . . A splendid romp through 1950s England led by the world's smartest and most incorrigible preteen."

—*Kirkus Reviews* (starred review)

"Think preteen Nancy Drew, only savvier and a lot richer, and you have Flavia de Luce. . . . Don't be fooled by Flavia's age or the 1950s setting: *A Red Herring* isn't a dainty tea-and-crumpets sort of mystery. It's shot through with real grit."

—*Entertainment Weekly*

"**Delightful** . . . The book's forthright and eerily mature narrator is a treasure."

—*The Seattle Times*

"Bradley's characters, wonderful dialogue and plot twists are a most winning combination."

—*USA Today*

"This is a classic country house mystery in the tradition of Agatha Christie, and Poirot himself would approve of Flavia's skills in snooping and deduction. Flavia is everything a reader wants in a detective—she's smart, logical, intrepid and curious. . . . This is a **refreshingly engaging** read."

—*RT Book Reviews*

"This is a **delightful read through and through.** We find in Flavia an incorrigible and wholly lovable detective; from her chemical experiments in her sanctum sanctorum to her outrage at the idiocy of the adult world, she is unequaled. Charming as a stand-alone novel and a guaranteed smash with series followers."

—*Library Journal* (starred review)

"Bradley masterfully weaves a ghoulish Yuletide tale. . . . The story breathes characters full of charisma, colour and nuance. . . . Bradley gives **a thrilling ride.**"

—*The Globe and Mail*

A **RED HERRING** *Without* **MUSTARD**

"Bradley's third book about tween sleuth Flavia de Luce will make readers forget Nancy Drew."

—*People*

"Bradley's award-winning Flavia de Luce series . . . has enchanted readers with the **outrageous** sleuthing career of its precocious leading lady. . . . This latest adventure contains all the winning elements of the previous books while skillfully establishing a new and intriguing story line to explore in future novels. . . . Fans will be more than pleased."

—*Library Journal* (starred review)

"Bradley's latest Flavia de Luce novel reaches a new level of perfection. . . . These are **astounding, magical** books not to be missed."

—*RT Book Reviews* (Top Pick)

"It's **hard to resist** either the genre's pre-eminent preteen sleuth or the hushed revelations about her family."

—*Kirkus Reviews*

"There is period detail, as well as deft portraiture of the entire de Luce family and friends, in this character-driven series. . . . *The Dead in Their Vaulted Arches* moves the series in an **exciting** new direction. Flavia will surely remain as brilliant and stubbornly contrary as ever."

—*Library Journal*

"Young chemist and aspiring detective Flavia de Luce [uses] her knowledge of poisons, and her indefatigable spirit, to solve a dastardly crime in the English countryside while learning new clues about her mother's disappearance."

—National Public Radio

SPEAKING FROM AMONG *the* BONES

"The precocious and irrepressible Flavia **continues to delight.** Portraying an eleven-year-old as a plausible sleuth and expert in poisons is no mean feat, but Bradley makes it look easy."

—*Publishers Weekly* (starred review)

"Bradley's Flavia cozies, set in the English countryside, have been **a hit** from the start, and this fifth in the series continues to charm and entertain."

—*Booklist*

"An excellent reminder that crime fiction can **sparkle with wit, crackle with spirit and verge on the surreal** . . . Flavia, once more, entertains and delights as she exposes the inner workings of her investigative mind to the reader."

—*National Post* (Canada)

I AM HALF-SICK *of* SHADOWS

"**Every Flavia de Luce novel is a reason to celebrate,** but Christmas with Flavia is a holiday wish come true for her fans."

—*USA Today* (four stars)

"Whether battling with her odious sisters or verbally sparring with the long-suffering Inspector Hewitt, our cheeky heroine is **a delight.** Full of pithy dialog and colorful characters, this series would appeal strongly to fans of Dorothy Sayers, Gladys Mitchell, and Leo Bruce as well as readers who like clever humor mixed in with their mysteries."

—*Library Journal* (starred review)

"[Flavia] remains irresistibly **appealing** as a little girl lost."
—*The New York Times Book Review*

The WEED *That* STRINGS *the* HANGMAN'S BAG

"Flavia is incisive, cutting and hilarious . . . **one of the most remarkable creations in recent literature.**"
—*USA Today*

"Bradley takes everything you expect and subverts it, delivering **a smart, irreverent, unsappy mystery.**"
—*Entertainment Weekly*

"The real delight here is her droll voice and the eccentric cast. . . . **Utterly beguiling.**"
—*People* (four stars)

The **SWEETNESS**
at the **BOTTOM** *of the* **PIE**

**THE MOST AWARD-WINNING BOOK
OF ANY YEAR!**

As CHIMNEY
SWEEPERS COME
to DUST

...

BANTAM
NEW YORK

As CHIMNEY SWEEPERS COME to DUST

A Flavia de Luce Novel

ALAN BRADLEY

◆ ◆ ◆

2016 Bantam Books Trade Paperback Edition

Published in the United States by Bantam Books, an imprint of Random House, a division of Penguin Random House LLC, New York.

BANTAM BOOKS and the HOUSE colophon are registered trademarks of Penguin Random House LLC.

As Chimney Sweepers Come to Dust was originally published in hardcover in the United States by Delacorte Press, an imprint of Random House, a division of Penguin Random House LLC, in 2015. "The Curious Case of the Copper Corpse" was originally published in a digital edition by Bantam Books, an imprint of Random House, a division of Penguin Random House LLC, in 2014.

LIBRARY OF CONGRESS CATALOGING-IN-PUBLICATION DATA
Bradley, C. Alan
As chimney sweepers come to dust : a flavia de luce novel /
Alan Bradley.
pages ; cm — (Flavia de Luce)
ISBN 978-0-345-53994-6 (pbk.) — ISBN 978-0-345-53995-3
(ebook) 1. De Luce, Flavia (Fictitious character)—Fiction.
2. Boarding schools—Canada—Fiction. I. Title.
PR9199.4.B7324A9 2015
813'.6—dc23
2014029962

Printed in the United States of America on acid-free paper

randomhousebooks.com

6 8 9 7 5

Book design by Diane Hobbing

To Shirley, with love and gratitude

Fear no more the heat o' the sun,
Nor the furious winter's rages;
Thou thy worldly task hast done,
Home art gone, and ta'en thy wages:
Golden lads and girls all must,
As chimney sweepers, come to dust.

—WILLIAM SHAKESPEARE,
Cymbeline (IV.ii)

As CHIMNEY
SWEEPERS COME
to DUST

...

PROLOGUE

IF YOU'RE ANYTHING LIKE me, you adore rot. It is pleasant to reflect upon the fact that decay and decomposition are what make the world go round.

For instance, when an ancient oak falls somewhere in the forest, it begins almost at once to be consumed by invisible predators. These highly specialized hordes of bacteria lay siege to their target as methodically as an army of barbarians attacking an enemy fortress. The mission of the first wave is to break down the protein forms of the stricken timber into ammonia, which can then be easily handled by the second team, which converts the smelly ammonia to nitrites. These last and final invaders, by oxidation, convert the nitrites into the nitrates that are required to fertilize the soil, and thus to grow new seedling oaks.

Through the miracle of chemistry, a colossus has been reduced to its essentials by microscopic life forms. Forests are born and die, come and go, like a spinning penny flipped into the air: heads . . . tails . . . life . . . death . . . life . . . death . . . and so on from Creation to the farthest ends of time.

It's bloody marvelous, if you ask me.

Left to the mercies of the soil, dead human bodies undergo the same basic 1—2—3 process: meat—ammonia—nitrates.

But when a corpse is swaddled tightly in a soiled flag, stuffed up a brick chimney, and left there for a donkey's age to char and mummify in the heat and the smoke—well, that's an entirely different story.

·ONE·

"BANISHED!" THE WILD WIND shrieked as it tore at my face.

"Banished!" the savage waves roared as they drenched me with freezing water.

"Banished!" they howled. *"Banished!"*

There is no sadder word in the English language. The very sound of it—like echoing iron gates crashing closed behind you; like steel bolts being shot shut—makes your hair stand on end, doesn't it?

"Banished!"

I shouted the word into the tearing wind, and the wind spat it back into my face.

"Banished!"

I was standing at the heaving prow of the R.M.S. *Scythia*, my jaws wide open to the gale, hoping that the salt spray would wash the bad taste out of my mouth: the taste that was my life so far.

Somewhere, a thousand miles behind us over the eastern horizon, lay the village of Bishop's Lacey and Buckshaw, my former home, where my father, Colonel Haviland de Luce, and my sisters, Ophelia and Daphne, were most likely, at this very moment, getting on nicely with their lives as if I had never existed.

They had already forgotten me. I was sure of it.

Only the faithful family retainers, Dogger and Mrs. Mullet, would have shed a furtive tear at my departure, but even so, they, too, in time, would have only foggy memories of Flavia.

Out here on the wild Atlantic, the *Scythia*'s bow was hauling itself up . . . and up . . . and up out of the sea, climbing sickeningly toward the sky, then crashing down with a horrendous hollow booming, throwing out great white wings of water to port and starboard. It was like riding bareback on an enormous steel angel doing the breaststroke.

Although it was still early September, the sea was madness. We had encountered the remnants of a tropical hurricane, and now, for more than two days, had been tossed about like a cast-off cork.

Everyone except the captain and I—or so it seemed—had dragged themselves off to their bunks, so that the only sounds to be heard as one reeled along the pitching, rolling corridors to dinner were the groan of stressed steel and, behind closed doors on either side, the evacuation of scores of stomachs. With nearly nine hundred passengers on board, it was a sobering sound.

As for me, I seem to be blessed with a natural immunity to the tossing seas: the result, I supposed, of seafaring ancestors such as Thaddeus de Luce, who, although only a lad at the Battle of Trafalgar, was said to have brought lemonade to the dying Admiral Nelson, and to have held his cold and clammy hand.

Nelson's last words, actually, were not the widely reported "Kiss me, Hardy," addressed to Captain Thomas Hardy of the *Victory*, but rather, "Drink, drink . . . fan, fan . . . rub, rub," whispered feverishly to the wide-eyed young Thaddeus, who, although reduced to tears at the sight of his mortally wounded hero, was doing his best to keep the great man's circulation from crystallizing.

The wind ripped at my hair and tore at my thin autumn coat. I inhaled the salt air as deeply as I dared, the sea spray running in torrents down my face.

A hand seized my arm roughly.

"What the devil do you think you're doing?"

I spun round, startled, trying to wriggle free.

It was, of course, Ryerson Rainsmith.

"What the devil do you think you're doing?" he repeated. He was one of those people who thought that the secret of gaining the upper hand was to ask every question twice.

The best way of dealing with them is not to answer.

"I've been looking everywhere for you. Dorsey is *beside* herself with worry."

"Does that mean there are now two of her to put up with?" I wanted to ask, but I didn't.

With a name like Dorsey it was no wonder he called her "Dodo"—or at least he did whenever he thought they were alone.

"We were afraid you'd fallen overboard. Now come below at once. Go to your cabin and put on some dry clothing. You look like a drowned rat."

That did it. It was the last straw.

Ryerson Rainsmith, I thought, *your days—your very hours—are numbered.*

I would go to the young and handsome ship's doctor, whom I had met at supper the night before last. On the pretext of an upset tummy I would beg a bottle of sodium bicarbonate. A healthy dose of the stuff—I smiled at the word "healthy"—slipped into Rainsmith's invariable bottle of champagne would do the trick.

Taken on a full stomach—no worries about that where Ryerson Rainsmith was concerned!—sodium bicarbonate combined with effervescent alcohol could be deadly: first, the headache, which seemed to grow by the minute, followed by mental confusion and severe stomach pain; then the muscle weakness, the thin stools like coffee grounds, the tremors, the twitching: all the classic symptoms of alkalosis. I would insist on taking him out on deck for a healthy walk. Forcing him to hyperventilate in all this fresh, invigorating air would speed up the process—like sloshing petrol onto a fire.

If I could manage to raise the pH of his arterial blood to 7.65, he wouldn't stand the chance of a snowman in Hades. He would die in agony.

"I'm coming," I said sullenly, and followed him at the speed of a sleepy snail, aft across the rolling, pitching fore-deck.

Hard to imagine, I thought, that I had actually been handed over to this rancid slab of humanity. Hard to forget, though, how it had come about.

It had all begun with that awful business about my mother, Harriet. After ten years of being missing in the mountains of Tibet, Harriet had returned to Buckshaw in circumstances so painful that my brain was still forbidding me to think about them for more than a few seconds at a time; any longer than that, and my internal censor snipped my thread of memory as easily as Atropos, that dreaded third sister of the Fates, is said to snip the thread of life with her scissors when our time has come to die.

The upshot of it all was that I was to be packed off to Miss Bodycote's Female Academy, Harriet's old school in Canada, where I was to be trained to assume some ancient and hereditary role of which I was still kept mostly in ignorance.

"You shall simply have to *learn* your way into it," Aunt Felicity had told me. "But in time you shall come to realize that Duty is the best and wisest of all teachers."

I wasn't quite sure what she meant by that, but since my aunt was rather high up in this mysterious whatever-it-was, she was not to be argued with.

"It's something like 'The Firm,' isn't it?" I asked. "The nickname that the Royal Family call themselves."

"Somewhat," Aunt Felicity said, "but with this difference: Royalty is permitted to abdicate. We are not."

It had been at Aunt Felicity's insistence that I was packed up like a bundle of old rags and tossed onto a ship to Canada.

There had been protests, of course, at my going alone, notably from the vicar and his wife. Then there had been some talk about having Feely and her fiancé, Dieter Schrantz, accompany me on my transatlantic journey, but that idea was scotched on the grounds not only that it would be improper, but also that Feely's position as organist at St. Tancred's was classified as an essential service.

At that point Cynthia Richardson, the vicar's wife, threw her own name into the hat. Although Cynthia and I had had our ups and downs, we had recently become great pals, an unexpected twist in my life I was still finding hard to believe. Away from her husband, Cynthia was brimming with fun: a girl again, in spite of herself. The vicar would have been horrified at the amount of tea the two of us sprayed out in hysterical laughter upon the slate floor of the vicarage kitchen.

But then, alas, Cynthia's name, too, was taken out of the running. Like Feely, she was too important to be released. Without her, there would be no church calendar, no church bulletins, no flowers for the altar, no home visits, no Girl Guides, no clean cassocks and surplices, no meals for the vicar . . . the list went on and on.

I knew she was disappointed: She told me so.

"I should have liked to see Canada," she told me. "My

father, as a young man, worked as a log driver—a river pig—on the Ottawa River. Instead of fairy tales at bedtime, he used to tell me horrific stories of the loup-garou—the werewolf of the Canadian woods—and of how he once gave a good dunking to Ole Bull and Big Jacques Laroque in the log-rolling contest at the Rapides des Allumettes, both on the same morning.

"I had always hoped that I would one day be able to lace on a pair of spiked logger's boots and have a go at it myself," she added wistfully. "Now I suppose I shan't have a chance."

I could have wept at the sight of her sitting there at the vicarage kitchen table, her eyes staring damply into her past.

"The Altar Guild is likely just as dangerous," I said brightly, hoping to cheer her up, but I don't think she heard me.

That same afternoon, Aunt Felicity announced that the problem was solved: She had heard from Miss Bodycote's Female Academy that the chairman of the academy's board of guardians, who had been summering in England, would be setting sail for home in September.

He had been shooting for a few days with one of our neighbors, Lord Crowsborough, and it would be no trouble at all, he said, to drop by and pick me up—as if I were an empty milk bottle.

I shall never forget the day that he arrived at Buckshaw—an hour and a half late, I might add—in his borrowed Bentley. He had leapt from the car and dashed round to the offside to open the door for Dorsey, the queen of Sheba, who unfolded herself from the machine like a stork from an eggshell and stood blinking in the September sunshine as if she had just been startled awake from a hypnotic trance. She was wrapped in a dress of turquoise silk, with a matching scarf on her head and far too much magenta lipstick on her mouth. Need I say more?

"Oh, Ryerson," she cooed, gazing at our ancestral home. "It's all so quaint—so tumble-de-dump. Just as you said it would be."

Ryerson Rainsmith, in a summer suit the color of cold coffee and curdled cream, stood looking round in a self-satisfied manner with his thumbs tucked into his yellow waistcoat, drumming his fingers on his ample stomach. I was reminded of a partridge.

Father, who had gone to the front door to greet him, stepped out onto the gravel sweep and shook hands.

"Colonel de Luce, I presume," Rainsmith said, as if he had just solved some great mystery. "I'd like you to say hello to my wife, Dorsey. Come and shake hands with the squire, my dear. It's not every day you'll get such an opportunity.

"Ha ha ha," he added mirthlessly. "And this must be our little Flavia!"

On paper, the man was already dead.

"Mr. Rainsmith," he said, shoving a damp hand into my face.

Dogger had once warned me to be wary of any man who introduced himself as "Mr." It was an honorific, he said, a mark of respect to be bestowed by others, but never, ever, under any circumstances, upon oneself.

I ignored the extended hand.

"Howdy," I said.

Father stiffened. His eyes narrowed. I knew what was going on in his head.

My father was from an era when gentlemen were taught that politeness was everything, that the only sure way to lose out to the Philistines was to lose your temper and admit that they had wounded you. His years in a Japanese prisoner-of-war camp had perfected his ability to remain, in the face of insult, as silent as a standing stone.

"Please come in," he said, gesturing to the open door. I wanted to give him a swift kick in the trousers and at the same time I wanted to hug him. Pride in a parent often takes strange forms.

"What a quaint old hall!" Dorsey Rainsmith said. Her voice was as sharp as elderly cheese and her words echoed back unpleasantly from the dark paneling of the foyer. "We have the same trouble with cracking varnish in our *salon* back home in Toronto, don't we, Ryerson? Smithers, our handyman, says it's from either excessive heat or excessive cold."

"Or age," I suggested.

Father pierced me with a transparent look, but I knew what he meant.

In the drawing room, without being asked, the Rain-smiths subsided into the coziest seats, while Father and I perched on the edge of the remaining chairs.

After an interval timed to perfection, Dogger appeared and offered tea. I could see that the Rainsmiths were impressed.

"Thank you, Dogger," I said. "And please convey our thanks to Mrs. Mullet."

It was a game Dogger and I played: a game with rules so subtle that no one outside our immediate family could ever hope to grasp them.

"Not at all, Miss Flavia," Dogger said. "It is our very great pleasure to be of service."

"Yes, thank you, Dogger," Ryerson Rainsmith said, out of his depth but paddling madly to keep his head above water.

"And also your Mrs. Mullet," his wife added.

Dogger gave them a three-percent smile and vanished in the way he does.

After a while, Daffy and Feely came into the room, pretended to be bereft at the thought of losing me, chatted in a maddeningly polite fashion with the Rainsmiths, then drifted off to their respective books and looking glass.

But there's no sense in raking through the ashes of that dismal afternoon.

It was decreed that the Rainsmiths would be my chaperones on the voyage to Canada, where they would deliver me up safely to the doorstep of Miss Bodycote's Female Academy.

"Chaperones?" Daffy said when they were gone. "'Cicerones,' you mean. That's the proper word for it. Flavia on the Grand Tour—just think! I hope you appreciate it, you lucky chump. I'd give anything to be in your plimsolls."

I threw a handy tennis racket at her, but I missed.

* * *

I missed Daffy in a very different way as I trudged up the sloping deck in the footsteps of Ryerson Rainsmith. Daffy, at least, was my own flesh and blood and could be defied without permanent damage. Ryerson Rainsmith, by contrast, would remember this moment for as long as he lived. He would still be telling his putrid grandchildren about it when he was no more than a shriveled pudding in a wheelchair.

"And there she was—there I found her," he would tell them in a cracked, quavering voice, "standing on the first six inches of the ship's bow with the waves breaking over her head."

He spoke not a word until we were belowdecks, tottering like walking toys along the heaving passageway toward the Rainsmiths' stateroom. He had obviously forgotten ordering me to change into dry clothing. Or perhaps he had decided to deliver me up damp to his wife.

"Take my advice," he said in a conspiratorial whisper, as if we were suddenly old pals. "Don't rile her."

He rapped at the door with his knuckles before opening it and motioning me to go ahead of him.

By the way Dorsey Rainsmith looked at me, I might have been a cobra shoved into her face.

"Look at you!" she said. "Just look at you!"

It is an order often given to girls of my age with little thought given to how difficult it is to carry out, actually.

I crossed my eyes very slightly, but if she noticed, it went over her head.

"Where have you been?" she demanded.

"On deck," I said.

"Why?"

"Fresh air."

"You might have fallen overboard. Did you never think of that?"

"No," I said truthfully. I might also have been hit on the noggin and killed by a falling albatross, but I didn't say so.

What was it about this woman that grated so violently on my nerves? I'm generally a very tolerant sort of person, but there was something about Dorsey Rainsmith that rubbed me in the wrong direction.

I think it was the way in which she reduced her husband to less than a comma.

There is a word my sister Daffy uses whenever she wishes to be particularly cutting: "obsequious." It might have been coined expressly to describe the behavior of Ryerson Rainsmith whenever he was in the presence of his wife: fawning and cringing to the point of nausea.

I looked at him standing at the door of the stateroom as if in fear of her, almost afraid to come in. He had delivered me up to her in the way a cat presents a dead bird to its owner. He was waiting for a pat on the head—or perhaps a bowl of cream.

But he didn't get one.

"What are we going to do with you?" Dorsey sighed, as if the weight of the entire British Empire were upon her shoulders.

I did what I was expected to do: I shrugged.

"Dr. Rainsmith is very disappointed with you," she said,

as if he weren't in the room. "And Dr. Rainsmith cannot tolerate being disappointed."

Dr. Rainsmith? He had introduced himself as *Mr.* As chairman of the board of guardians at Miss Bodycote's, he must be a doctor of education, or maybe of theology. Well, I certainly wasn't going to address him by any fancy titles.

"Go to your cabin and change into dry clothing. And stay there until you are sent for."

Go to your room. The classic response of someone who is fresh out of ideas.

Checkmate! Hallelujah! Game, set, and match!

I had won.

Next morning, I was standing on the railings at the starboard bow, waving my hat into the wind and singing "A Life On the Ocean Wave" to cheer myself up, when, from the corner of my eye, I noticed Ryerson Rainsmith. The instant he spotted me, he sheared off and went astern.

Which pretty well set the tone for the rest of the voyage.

A couple of days later, as we approached the harbor at Halifax, Dorsey told me to wipe my nose. That was my first glimpse of the New World.

At Quebec City, we disembarked. A Canadian customs officer in black suit and cap asked me the purpose of my visit.

"Penal colony," I told him. He raised his eyebrows, gave the Rainsmiths a sympathetic shake of his head, and stamped my passport.

Only then—at that very instant—did I realize how far from home I was. Alone in a foreign country.

Unaccountably, I burst into tears.

"There, there," said Ryerson Rainsmith, looking not at me, but rather at the customs officer. The words came out as "They-ahh, they-ahh," and I realized, in spite of my tears, that the farther west we traveled, the more pronounced his fake English accent was becoming.

"The little English girl is homesick," the customs officer said, kneeling down and dabbing at my eyes with an enormous white handkerchief.

No great detective work there: He had already examined our passports and knew that I was not their child.

What was he up to, then? Was this close-up inspection part of his routine search for contraband?

For just an instant I flirted with the idea of faking a faint, then calling aloud for a restorative shot from one of the six bottles of Gordon's Gin that—among other things—were hidden under the false bottom of the Rainsmiths' steamer trunk.

Don't ask me how I know that: There are a few things in my life of which I am still not proud.

"Chin up!" the customs officer said, lifting my face with a folded finger and looking into my eyes. He smiled at the Rainsmiths. "I have one just like her at home."

Somehow I doubted it, but I forced a weak grin.

But what an inane remark! Even if he had a hundred daughters at home crying into a hundred silken handkerchiefs, what did I care? How could it possibly matter?

One of the things I dread about becoming an adult is that sooner or later you begin letting sentimentality get in the way of simple logic. False feelings are allowed to clog the works like raw honey poured into the tiny wheels of a fine timepiece.

I have observed this again and again in adults with whom I am acquainted. When all else failed, a good old cry was guaranteed to get them off the hook. It was not just instinct: No, it was more than that. It was something to do with the oleaginous chemical essences given off by a crying human: some supersensor in the nose designed to detect the altered hormone and protein levels in the emotional weeping of humans—and of the human female, in particular.

I had been thinking of producing a paper on this fascinating subject—*Tears and the Test Tube*—but had been forced to shelve the idea when I was flung, without ceremony, out of my ancestral home. The very thought of being cut off from my late uncle Tarquin's splendid chemical laboratory, with its gleaming glassware, its lovely old Leitz microscope, its rows upon rows of bottled chemicals and pretty poisons, was enough to reduce me to tears again, so that I was right back where I started.

It had been in that quiet room, by the light of its tall casement windows, that, with the assistance of Uncle Tar's notebooks and library, I had taught myself chemistry, and by so doing had set myself apart forever from the rest of the human race.

No matter that I had been a mere child when I began. I

was now twelve, and remarkably proficient in juggling what Uncle Tar had once called "the crumbs of the universe."

"I'm sorry," I said. "I was overcome. Forgive me."

The trance was broken. The moment had passed and we were back again in the cold, cold world.

The customs officer got to his feet, and looked hastily round to see that no one had observed his momentary weakness.

"Next!" he shouted as he scratched his chalk mark on our luggage.

As Ryerson Rainsmith queued for tickets in the railway booking office, I helped myself to a map and timetable from a handy rack. The distance from Quebec City to Toronto, I saw, was five hundred miles: more than half the distance from Land's End to John o'Groats.

It was going to take about nine hours, and we would not arrive in Toronto until late—eleven o'clock in the evening.

Dorsey Rainsmith had fortified herself with a paperback novel from the news agent's kiosk: *Vengeance Is Mine*, by Mickey Spillane. She tried to conceal it in a folded copy of the *Montreal Gazette*, but not before I had a chance to see the cover illustration: a man in trench coat and floppy hat lugging in his arms what appeared to be a dead blonde, whose white silk dress was rucked up to somewhere in the neighborhood of her tonsils.

I recognized the title as a quotation from the Bible: a

quotation I had several times mulled over myself as I planned various schemes to teach my sisters a lesson. Slashed across the book's cover were adverts for other volumes by the same author, such as *I, the Jury* and *My Gun Is Quick.*

There was something vaguely but deeply satisfying about these titles, but I couldn't quite put my finger on it.

"All aboard!" the conductor shouted.

I was learning quickly. Back home in England, trains had guards while buses and trams had conductors. Here in Canada, the guard was a conductor, and the carriages, called cars, were built with seats on both sides of a center aisle, rather than having compartments, each of which opened directly onto the platform.

It was like falling asleep and awakening as Alice in *Through the Looking-Glass.* Everything was larger than life and everyone drove on the wrong side of the road.

One could easily see why they called it the "New World."

At last, the train jolted into motion and we were on our way. I was made to sit facing the Rainsmiths, as if I were in the dock at the Old Bailey facing a pair of sour old magistrates.

After about fifty miles of blessed silence, Ryerson Rainsmith decided to become instructive. He unfolded a railway map and began reading aloud the names of each town through which we should next be passing. "Val-Alain, Villeroy . . . Parisville . . . St. Wenceslas . . ."

I stifled a yawn.

But on and on he droned, all the way from St. Léonard

de Nicolet, St. Perpétue, St. Cyrille, St. Germain, St. Eugene, St. Edward, St. Rosalie, St. Hyacinthe, St. Madeleine, St. Hilaire, and St. Hubert to St. Lambert until I could have screamed. I tried for a while to fake sleep, but it was no use. He would lean across and shake my arm as if he were a terrier and I a rabbit.

"Geography ought to be fun, Flavia," he said. "Why can't you engage yourself?"

Dorsey hardly removed her nose from the pocket bloodshed. She looked up only once to ask, "What does 'the Dutch act' mean, Ryerson?"

He went white. His face looked as if his brain were wrestling his tonsils. "Little pitchers," he said after extracting a handkerchief from his vest pocket and wiping his face.

Dorsey went back to her book as if she hadn't heard or cared.

I could have told her that it meant suicide, but I didn't feel like it.

Ryerson resumed reading aloud names of the places we would pass through later in the day, but this time he added the mileage and times from the printed schedule.

By the time we reached Central Station in Montreal, I was a gibbering jelly.

Fortunately, we had to change not just trains but stations, and my self-appointed tutor was kept so busy for the next four hours condescending to taxi drivers and bullying railway booking clerks and porters that my ears were able to take a rest.

Then, all too soon, we were off again.

"Westward ho!" I wanted to shout.

I could scarcely wait to arrive in Toronto—not so much to reach my destination as to be rid of this man I had come to think of as the Marquess of Mouth.

We swept along in comfort—except for Ryerson—beside the broad St. Lawrence River, which was studded with as many islands as there are stars in the sky, some with stone cottages perched in solitary and splendid isolation.

I would leap off the train at the next stop, I decided. I would swim to one of the hidden islands where I would become a modern Robinson Crusoe. Canada was a wilderness of wildernesses. They could never find me.

"Look there, Flavia!" Ryerson said, pointing to a castle of what looked like gray limestone. "That's the Kingston Penitentiary."

"Where *you'll* wind up if you don't behave yourself," Dorsey said, glancing up from her bloody thriller.

I hadn't the foggiest idea what a penitentiary was, but it sounded as if it described my present situation to perfection, and for a few precious moments, I imagined myself sheltered within the high walls of that bleak and stony stronghold, safe from the Rainsmiths.

The hours trudged by with chains on their ankles.

Outside the train's windows, Canada rushed past, as if on a rotating turntable. It seemed to me to be composed of a remarkable amount of water.

And then it was dark, and all I could see in the window was the reflection of the Rainsmiths. Dorsey had fallen asleep, her neck twisted awkwardly, as if from the end of a rope, her mouth hanging open in a most unpleasant but satisfying manner.

I pretended she was the murderess Edith Thompson, whose violent drop was said to have caused John Ellis, the public hangman, to commit suicide.

A filament of drool appeared at the corner of Dorsey's mouth, swinging with the motion of the train like an acrobatic spider on a thread. I was trying to decide whether this spoiled or enhanced the hanged-woman effect when Ryerson touched my arm.

I nearly leaped out of my skin.

"Toronto soon," he whispered, so as not to disturb his sleeping wife.

He didn't want her awake any more than I did.

I turned to watch the lighted windows that were now sliding by outside in the darkness: windows in which dozens of mothers cooked in dozens of kitchens, dozens of fathers read newspapers in dozens of cozy chairs, dozens of children wrote or drew at dozens of tables, and here and there, like a candle in the wilderness, the lonely blue-gray glow of a little television screen.

It was all so unbearably sad.

Could things be any worse?

·TWO·

IT WAS RAINING IN Toronto.

Low clouds, reddened to the shade of inflamed intestines by neon advertising signs, glowered above the towering hotels. The wet pavements were a soggy crazy-quilt of swimming colors and running waters. Trams sparked in the damp darkness, and the night air was sharp with the acrid smell of their ozone.

Dorsey Rainsmith was not yet fully conscious, and she stood blinking on the curb beneath the umbrella her husband was holding, as if she had just awakened to find herself on an alien and most unpleasant planet.

"Taxis are busy tonight," her husband said, looking up the street and down. "There's bound to be another soon." He wigwagged his arms frantically at a lone taxicab passing on the wrong side of the street, but it splashed on, oblivious.

"I don't see why Merton couldn't have met us," Dorsey said.

"His mother died, Dodo," Ryerson said, forgetting I was there. "Don't you remember? He sent us a telegram."

"No," she said, going into one of her Grand Pouts.

Ryerson was gnawing fiercely at his lower lip. If a taxicab didn't come along in the next two minutes he was going to need stitches.

"I shall order flowers tomorrow," he said, "for *both* of you."

Galloping Galatians! Was that an insult? Or had my ears deceived me?

Dorsey turned a slow, cold, reptilian eye upon him, but just at that moment, a taxicab splashed to a stop at the curb.

"Ah! Here we are," Ryerson said brightly, rubbing his hands together—or wringing them, I'm not sure which.

The Rainsmiths climbed into the backseat and I was left to sit up front with the driver.

Ryerson gave their home address.

"We'll put you up for the night, Flavia," he said. "It's too late now for Miss Bodycote's. Well past their 'lights-out.'"

"We'll do no such thing," his wife said. "We haven't a room made up, and with Merton indisposed, I can't possibly cope. Take us directly to Miss Bodycote's Female Academy, driver. We'll wake them up."

And that was that.

In the driver's rearview mirror, I could see Dorsey Rainsmith mouthing silent but angry words at her husband.

The streetlights, seeping in through the taxi's watery windows, made Ryerson's face look as if it were melting.

Miss Bodycote's Female Academy was on a cul-de-sac just off the Danforth.

It was not at all what I had expected.

Tall houses loomed up on both sides of the street, crowded cheek-to-cheek, their windows alight and welcoming. Standing in darkness among them in its own grounds, Miss Bodycote's was a vast shadow in their midst: taller, larger—a couple of acres of stony darkness in the rain.

I was to learn later that the place had once been a convent, but I didn't know that as Ryerson yanked angrily at the bell of what appeared to be a porter's lodge, a sort of Gothic wicket set into one side of the arched front doorway.

Down a long flight of stone steps on the street, Dorsey waited in the taxi as I stood beside her husband on the step. Ryerson pounded on the heavy front door with his fist.

"Open up," he shouted at the blank, curtainless windows. "This is the chairman."

"That ought to fetch them," he muttered, almost to himself.

Somewhere inside, a dim glow appeared, as if someone had lighted a candle.

He shot me a triumphant look, and I thought of applauding.

After what seemed like an eternity, but which was probably in reality no more than half a minute, the door was edged open by an apparition in nightgown, thick spectacles, and curlers.

"Well?" demanded a creaky voice, and a candle in a tin holder was raised to light and examine our faces. And then a gasp. "Oh! I'm sorry, sir."

"It's all right, Fitzgibbon. I've brought the new girl."

"Ah," said the apparition, sweeping the candle in a broad arc to indicate that we were to step inside.

The place was a vast, echoing mausoleum, the walls pitted everywhere with pointed, painted nooks and alcoves, some in the shape of seashells, which looked as if they had once housed religious statuary, but the pale saints and virgins, having been evicted, had been replaced with brass castings of sour-faced, whiskered old men in beaver hats with their hands jammed into the breasts of their frock coats.

Apart from that, I had only time enough to register a quick impression of scrubbed floorboards and institutional varnish disappearing in all directions before the flame blew out and we were left standing in darkness. The place smelled like a piano warehouse: wood, varnish, and an acrid metallic tang that suggested tight strings and old lemons.

"Damnation," someone whispered, close to my ear.

We were in what I presumed was an entrance hall when the electric lights were suddenly switched on, leaving the three of us blinking in the glare.

A tall woman stood at the top of a broad staircase, her

hand on the switch. "Who is it, Fitzgibbon?" she asked, in a voice that suggested she fed on peaches and steel.

"It's the chairman, miss. He's brought the new girl."

I could feel my temper rising. I was not going to stand there and be discussed as if I were a mop in a shop.

"Good evening, Miss Fawlthorne," I said, stepping forward. "I'm Flavia de Luce. I believe you have been expecting me."

I had seen the headmistress's name on the prospectus the academy had sent to Father. I could only hope that this woman on the stair *was* actually the headmistress, and not just some lackey.

Slowly, she descended the stairs, the startling white of her hair standing out round her head in a snowy nimbus. She was dressed in a black suit and a white blouse. A large ruby pin glowed at her throat like a bead of fresh blood. Her hawk nose and dark complexion gave her the look of a pirate who had given up the sea for a career in education.

She inspected me up and down, from top to toe.

She must have been satisfied, because she said, finally, "Fetch her things."

Fitzgibbon opened the door and signaled the taxi driver, and a minute later, my luggage, soggy from the rain, was piled in the foyer.

"Thank you, Dr. Rainsmith," she said, dismissing the chairman. "Most kind of you."

It seemed short shrift for someone who had lugged me across the Atlantic and halfway across Canada, but perhaps it was the lateness of the hour.

With no more than a nod, Ryerson Rainsmith was gone and I was alone with my captors.

Miss Fawlthorne—I was quite sure now that it was she, because she hadn't contradicted me—walked round me in a slow circle. "Do you have any cigarettes or alcohol either on your person or in your baggage?"

I shook my head.

"Well?"

"No, Miss Fawlthorne," I said.

"Firearms?" she asked, watching me closely.

"No, Miss Fawlthorne."

"Very well, then. Welcome to Miss Bodycote's Female Academy. In the morning I shall sign you in properly. Take her to her room, Fitzgibbon."

With that, she switched off the electric light and became part of the darkness.

Fitzgibbon had relighted her candle, and amid flickering shadows, up the staircase we climbed.

"They've put you in Edith Cavell," she croaked at the top, fishing a set of keys from some unspeakable crevice in her nightgown and opening the door.

I recognized the name at once. The room was dedicated to the memory of the World War I heroine Edith Cavell, the British nurse who had been shot by a German firing squad for helping prisoners escape. I thought of those famous words, which were among her last and which I had seen inscribed upon her statue near Trafalgar Square in London: "Patriotism is not enough. I must have no hatred or bitterness toward anyone."

I decided at that instant to adopt those words, from now

on, as my personal motto. Nothing could have been more appropriate.

At least for now.

Fitzgibbon placed the candlestick on a small wooden desk. "Blow it out when you're ready for bed. No electrics— it's past lights-out."

"May I light a fire?" I asked. "I'm actually quite cold."

"Fires are not permitted until the fifth of November," she said. "It's a tradition. Besides, coal and wood are money."

And with no more than that, she left me.

Alone.

I will not describe that night, other than to say that the mattress had apparently been stuffed with crushed stones, and that I slept the sleep of the damned.

I left the candle burning. It was the only heat in the room.

I would like to be able to say that I dreamed of Buckshaw, and of Father, and of Feely and Daffy, but I cannot. Instead, my weary brain was filled with images of roaring seas, of blowing spray, and of Dorsey Rainsmith, who had taken upon herself the form of an albatross, which, perched at the masthead of a storm-tossed ship, screamed down at me wild cries of bird abuse.

I fought my way up out of this troubled sleep to find someone sitting on my chest, pummeling me about the head and shoulders with angry fists.

"Traitor!" a voice was sobbing. "You filthy dirty rotten traitor! Traitor! Traitor! Traitor!"

It was still well before sunrise, and the faint light that leaked into the room from the streetlamp was too dim to make out clearly the features of my attacker.

I gathered all my strength and gave a mighty shove.

With a grunt and a thud someone fell heavily to the floor.

"What the dickens do you think you're doing?" I demanded, snatching the candlestick from the desk. As a weapon—in a pinch—it was better than nothing. The guttering flame flared up.

Breath was sucked in. It sounded surprised.

"You're not Pinkham!" the voice said in the gloom.

"Of course I'm not Pinkham. I'm Flavia de Luce."

The voice gulped. "De Luce? The new girl?"

"Yes."

"Oh, sheep shears! I'm afraid I've made an awful boner."

There was a rustling sound and the overhead light was switched on.

There, with what Daffy always described as "strangle eyes" blinking in the glare, stood the most remarkable-looking little person I had ever seen. Long lizard legs clad in baggy black woolen stockings protruded from the dark blue skirt of a rumpled school uniform. Her body—almost an afterthought atop those remarkably long, bandy legs— was like a flattened lump of dough: a gingerbread man carelessly made.

"Who the deuce are you?" I demanded, taking the upper hand.

"Collingwood, P. A. 'P. A.' for Patricia Anne. Gosh, I hope you're not too cheesed off with me. I thought you were Pinkham. Honest! I'd forgotten they moved her into Laura Secord with Barton because of her nightmares. Special dispensation."

"And what did Pinkham do to deserve such a beating?" I wasn't going to let her off easily.

Collingwood colored. "I mustn't tell you. She'd kill me."

I fixed her with the famous cold blue eye for which we de Luces are noted—although mine tend more toward violet, actually, especially when I'm riled.

"Spill it," I said, raising the candlestick in a menacing manner and taking a step toward her. I was, after all, now in North America, the land of George Raft and James Cagney—a land where plain talk was understood.

Collingwood burst into tears.

"Oh, come on, kid," I said.

Come on, kid?

My ears couldn't believe what my mouth was saying. A couple of hours in Canada and I was already talking like Humphrey Bogart. Could it be something in the air?

"She ratted on me," Collingwood said, wiping her eyes with her school tie.

They really *did* talk like that here. All those afternoons with Daffy and Feely at the cinema in Hinley had not been wasted after all, as Father had claimed. I had learned my first foreign language and learned it well.

"Ratted," I repeated.

"To the head," Collingwood added, nodding.

"Miss Fawlthorne?"

"The Hangman's Mistress, we call her. But don't let on I

told you. She's done the most unspeakable things, you know."

"Such as?"

Collingwood looked over both shoulders before replying. "People disappear," she whispered, pinching her fingertips together and then, like a magician, with a quick gesture, causing them to fly open to reveal an empty hand. "Poof! Just like that. Without a trace."

"You're pulling my leg," I said.

"Am I?" she asked, her eyes huge and damp. "Then what about Le Marchand? What about Wentworth? What about Brazenose?"

"Surely they can't *all* have vanished without a trace," I said. "Someone would have noticed."

"That's just the thing!" Collingwood said. "No one did. I've been making notes. Pinkham caught me at it. She ripped the book out of my hands and took it to Miss Fawlthorne."

"When was this?" I asked.

"Last night. Do you think they're going to kill me?"

"Of course not," I said. "People don't do things like that. Not in real life, at any rate."

Although I knew perfectly well that people did. And, in my own experience, more often than you'd think.

"Are you sure?" Collingwood asked.

"Positive," I lied.

"Promise you won't tell," she whispered.

"I swear," I said, for some unfathomable reason making the sign of the cross in the air.

Collingwood's brow wrinkled. "Are you an RC?" she asked.

"Why?" I said, to stall for time more than anything. As a matter of fact, she had hit the nail on the head. Even though we appeared outwardly to be practicing Anglicans, we de Luces had been Roman Catholics since Rome was little more than seven picturesque hills in the Italian wilderness. The soul, Daffy says, is not necessarily where the heart is.

"As a matter of fact, yes," I said.

Collingwood whistled through her teeth. "I thought so! We have next-door neighbors back home in Niagara-on-the-Lake—the Connollys?—they're RCs, too. They make those same fiddles with their fingers that you just did. It's the sign of the cross, isn't it? That's what Mary Grace Connolly told me. It's a kind of magic. She made me promise not to tell. But listen! What are you doing here? Miss Bodycote's is—"

"I know," I interrupted. "So high Anglican that only a kitchen stool is required to scramble up into Heaven."

Where had I heard that? I couldn't for the life of me remember. Had Aunt Felicity told me? Surely it wasn't Father.

"You mustn't let on, though," Collingwood said. "They'll skin you alive."

"We Catholics have been martyrs since the invention of the flame," I said. "We're quite accustomed to it."

It was a snotty thing to say, but I said it anyway.

"Your secret's safe with me," Collingwood said, sewing

her lips shut with an invisible needle and thread. "Wild horses couldn't drag it out of me."

The last sentence came out sounding like "Wye-oh oh-ffef goodem agim ow momee."

"It's not a secret," I told her. "Actually, we're quite proud of it."

At that instant there was a terrific pounding at the door: a wood-splintering banging so loud that I almost kissed a kidney good-bye.

"Open up!" a voice demanded—a voice I had first heard only too recently, but one I knew too well.

It was Miss Fawlthorne.

"Turn out the lights!" Collingwood whispered.

"It's no use," I whispered back. "The door's unlocked anyway."

"No, it's not. I locked it when I snuck in."

She crept across the room on tiptoe and threw the switch. I blew out the candle, and we were plunged into darkness.

Well, almost. After a few seconds I could see that there was still a certain amount of light falling into the room from the street outside.

"What am I going to *do*?" she asked me. "We're not al-lowed in others' rooms after lights-out. I'll be blacked."

I looked round the room in the strange dim glow of the electric twilight. Other than the obvious bed and clothes-press, there was nowhere to hide, unless she could squeeze herself behind the wallpaper.

I'll give Collingwood this, though—she was quick. With a single bound, she was on the hearth, crouching under the mantel, and somehow clawing her way upward. The last I saw of her was those long lizard-like legs, clad in black, standing tiptoe on the firedogs, then vanishing up the chimney.

I wouldn't have believed it if I hadn't seen it with my own eyes.

Desperation is capable of wonderful things.

"Open up!" the voice said again. "I know you're in there."

Another knock—more thunderous than the last—shook the door. If the first one hadn't awakened the entire academy, this one surely must have.

Dozens of girls must be sitting bolt upright in their beds, sheets pulled up to their chins, their eyes wide in the darkness.

The dead silence that followed was even more terrifying than the knock.

"Open this door at once!" Miss Fawlthorne demanded. "Or I shall have Mr. Tugg come up and take the hinges off."

I padded across the room, gave the key a twist, and pulled the door open. "What is it?" I asked, blinking and rubbing at my eyes. "Is there a fire? I was asleep."

"It's no use, girl," Miss Fawlthorne said. "The lights were on in this room. Someone was talking in here."

"I was having a nightmare," I told her. "I expect it's being away from home, and so forth. I quite often talk in my sleep."

"Do you indeed," Miss Fawlthorne said. "And do you also switch on electric lights in your sleep?"

"No," I said. "But I didn't know where I was when I woke up. I was disorientated."

It's a bold girl who tries out a new word when she's being grilled, but I was desperate. "Disorientated" was an excuse Daffy had once used when Father had caught her pinching Christmas pudding from the pantry.

"*I was disorientated,*" she had claimed, and Father had believed her. Actually *believed* her!

I shot a quick glance behind me as I switched on the electric light, and the room was bathed in a harsh glare.

"No lights!" Miss Fawlthorne said, reaching past my face and switching them off again instantly. "'Lights-out' means lights out, you stupid girl."

That did it. As with Ryerson Rainsmith's calling me a drowned rat, it was the straw that broke the camel's back. A week away from home and my list of people to poison was already up to two—three if you counted the insipid Dodo.

From somewhere about her person, Miss Fawlthorne produced a packet of paper matches. She struck one gravely and, without taking her eyes from mine, lit the candle. It was rather a neat trick of eye-hand coordination.

"Now, then," she said, her gaze fixing me like a butterfly pinned to a card in a specimen box. "To whom were you talking?"

I could see that we were going to sit here until the sun came up or until I answered. It was obvious that Miss Fawlthorne was that kind of person.

"Myself," I admitted, looking away. "I'm afraid I sometimes talk to myself when I'm upset. It's one of my greatest faults. I'm trying to train myself not to do it."

I was wasting my breath, and I knew it even before the words were out of my mouth.

Miss Fawlthorne was now looking round the room slowly, her head rotating like an owl's. I wondered idly if, after a certain number of degrees, it would snap and fall off.

I rather uncharitably hoped that it did.

I didn't dare glance at the fireplace. Doing so would surely give Collingwood away. I kept my eyes humbly on my feet.

"Look at me!" Miss Fawlthorne commanded, and I slowly lifted my gaze to meet hers.

I was on the verge of tears; I could feel it.

The next words out of her mouth shocked me to the core.

"Poor, dear, lonely, unhappy Flavia de Luce," she said, lifting my chin with a forefinger and gazing fondly into my eyes with a wry smile.

What was I to think? She might as well have slapped my face. If she had, I'd have known how to handle it.

But this unexpected compassion caught me completely off guard. "Scuppered," I believe is the nautical word. I didn't know how to respond.

As I was raising my eyes to hers, my supernaturally acute hearing—a trait I had inherited from Harriet, my mother— detected a scraping noise in the chimney. Even without looking round, I knew that soot was falling into the hearth. To a trained ear, the sound is unmistakable.

Miss Fawlthorne—praised be all the saints!—had not noticed it. Her hearing apparatus was considerably older than mine and blunted by time.

I was offering up a silent prayer of thanks for my deliverance when there was a sudden rush of sound and cold air. Something came rocketing down the chimney and exploded into the room with a sickening thump.

The candle blew out and we were plunged instantly into darkness.

Miss Fawlthorne—and I must give her credit for this—had the candle burning again in seconds. She must still have had the matchbook in her hands.

Collingwood lay sprawled on the carpet, her face and hands as black as any Welsh coal miner's, her open red mouth and white eyes giving her the appearance of some fiend who had just been vomited up out of the pit.

Beside her, what appeared at first to be a charred log was still rolling slowly toward us, unfurling as it came, like a roll of dropped lavatory paper, the sooty and discolored Union Jack in which it was wrapped.

I must state here that I have no fear whatsoever of being in a room in the dark with a corpse. In fact, quite the contrary. The little shiver I experience is one of excitement, not of fear.

As the bundle rolled, the skull became detached and tumbled to a stop at my feet.

At the core of the bundle was a blackened and desiccated human body, and I knew, even before it came to rest, that it had been dead for some time.

Quite some time.

·THREE·

THERE WE WERE, THE four of us: me, Miss Fawlthorne, Collingwood, and the corpse, all equally motionless.

It was one of those moments our Victorian ancestors called a *tableau:* a frozen pose with none of us moving so much as a muscle; a moment when time stood still; a moment when eternity stopped to take a deep breath before rushing on and sweeping us with it into a future that could never be undone.

Then Collingwood began to cry: a long, low, drawn-out sobbing that threatened to become a howl.

Miss Fawlthorne went white in the candlelight. Of the four of us, only the corpse and I were calm.

I could hardly wait to have the electric lights switched on so that I could have a good gander.

I have seen numerous dead bodies in my lifetime, each more interesting than the last, and each more instructive. This corpse, if I was counting correctly, was number seven.

Even by the sparse light of the guttering candle, I had already decided, because of the slight frame and thin wrists, that this one was almost certainly female. The sooty skull and the horribly grinning jaws gave her the look of a freshly unwrapped mummy.

Tarred by time and the chimney into a smoked kipper.

Although that might not seem like an appropriate thought, I must be truthful: It was what I was thinking at the moment.

First reactions are not always ones we can later be proud of, but I knew from personal experience that there would always be time, before I was questioned, to concoct a more charitable version to make myself look good. That's the way the human mind works.

At least, mine does.

Time had resumed, but still crawled as it tends to do in such circumstances. Miss Fawlthorne seemed to be moving across the room as slowly as a stick insect on a twig in a nature film. After an eternity, she switched on the lights.

"Collingwood!" she demanded, in a voice that was far too quiet to be comforting. "What have you done?"—while Collingwood, black as Old Frizzle, her arms wrapped round her knees, had begun rocking herself back and forth on the hardwood floor, giving out a wail which I believe is called "keening": a hair-raising howl that arises from some ancient banshee part of our brain.

It was hardly human.

If this were the cinema, someone would slap her face and reduce her to civilized sobbing, but I hadn't the heart.

I dropped to my knees and cradled her in my arms.

"Fetch some water," I heard my mouth ordering Miss Fawlthorne. "And brandy. Quickly! She's going into shock."

Miss Fawlthorne began to say something, but thought better of it and strode out of the room.

I yanked a quilt from the bed and threw it round Collingwood's shoulders.

I covered the cadaver and the skull with a sheet—but not before having a jolly good gander at the grisly remains.

With Miss Fawlthorne gone, here was a Heaven-sent opportunity. I knew that I would have no second chance.

The body was, as I have said, smoke-blackened. The flag in which it had been wrapped had acted as a container in the same way—or so it is said—that banana leaves are used by natives of some of the far-flung outposts of the Empire (such as India) to bake fish.

The detached skull was as black as a bowling ball, bizarrely bare of hair and skin. The curled fingers of both hands were pulled up to where the chin should have been, as if Death had caught its victim sleeping. Clutched loosely in one of them was what appeared to be a small, tarnished medallion.

I nestled it in my handkerchief and pocketed the thing immediately—before Miss Fawlthorne could return. All hail to the gods who had sent me to bed fully clothed!

The garments in which the body was clad were too tangled and smoky to identify. They might once have been a pauper's rags—or the robes of a fairy-tale princess.

Death by cooking is not beautiful.

Or had she met her end by some other means? Or perhaps in some other place?

Like a police photographer, my mind began taking an efficient and methodical series of mental snapshots: close-ups of the skull, the blackened teeth, the hands, the feet (which were bare except for a single scorched woolen sock, half off).

I peeled it back an inch or two from the shrunken ebony ankle, and saw by the inner surface that it had originally been red.

This examination was not made any easier by the fact that Collingwood had now begun howling like an air raid siren, her voice rising and falling unnervingly.

"It's all right," I kept telling her, all the while keeping my eyes on the dead body. "Everything is all right. Miss Fawlthorne will be back in a jiffy."

Did I imagine it, or did Collingwood now begin to ululate—as Daffy would put it—all the louder?

Quite frankly, she was getting on my nerves.

"Put a cork in it!" I said. "You're drooling."

As anyone with older sisters will tell you, there's no quicker way to make a female dry up, no matter her age, than to point out that she has slobber on her face.

So I was not surprised, then, when Collingwood hiccupped to an abrupt halt.

"What . . . is . . . that . . . *thing?*" she asked, hauling her-

self on her bottom as quickly as she could across the floor
and away from the sheet-draped body.

"It's a bird. Rather a large one. A stork, I believe. Or
perhaps an ibis."

I'll admit this was a bit of a stretch—even for me. It had
been quite obvious that the blackened skull didn't have a
long curving beak. But then neither had the mummified
birds I had seen in the Natural History Museum. Their
beaks had been bandaged to their breasts both for neatness
and to make things easy for their long-dead embalmers.

"How would a stork get trapped in the chimney?"

"Happens all the time," I said. "During deliveries. They
just don't report it because it's too depressing. Some sort of
unwritten agreement with the newspapers."

Collingwood's mouth fell open, but I will never know
what she was about to say, since at that very instant Miss
Fawlthorne returned with a glass of water and a decanter of
what I assumed was brandy.

"Drink this," she ordered, and Collingwood obeyed at
once with remarkably little fuss, finishing off all of the former and a good slug of the latter.

"I fear she's awakened the house," Miss Fawlthorne said,
glancing first at her wristwatch and then at me. "No matter, I suppose. The police shall have to be called anyway.
Not that—"

There was a knock at the door.

"Who is it?" Miss Fawlthorne demanded.

"Fitzgibbon, miss."

Miss Fawlthorne sprang to the electrical switch like a

sudden gazelle. "We mustn't set a bad example," she whispered. "Lights-out means what it says."

Again we were wrapped in darkness.

But for no more than a few moments. Then a match flared and Miss Fawlthorne touched it to the candle's wick.

"Come," she called out, and the door opened.

At first, I saw only the round reflections of Fitzgibbon's spectacles, floating as if weightless in the air. She took a single step forward into the room—then froze—and all at once, miraculously, she was surrounded by a sea of pale, disembodied female faces peering over her shoulder.

Oddly enough, the thought that sprang to my mind at that instant was the famous passage in which Saint Luke is describing the Nativity. As best I can recall, it goes something like this: "And suddenly there was with the angel a multitude of the heavenly host praising God, and saying, 'Glory to God in the highest, and on earth peace, good will toward men.'"

(Although the Bible, of course, at least in the *King James Version*, for some reason known only to its translators and to the king himself, has no quotation marks.)

Even now, I can still see the white faces of those cherubim and seraphim, suspended eerily in the shadows behind the frozen Fitzgibbon: the students of Miss Bodycote's Female Academy.

My classmates.

This was my first glimpse of them—and theirs of me.

"Begone, girls!" Miss Fawlthorne commanded, clapping her hands several times, smartly.

And like puppets being jerked offstage in a rather sinister Punch and Judy, they vanished.

"Take Collingwood to her bed," Miss Fawlthorne instructed Fitzgibbon. "She's had a bad shock."

Did she think *I* hadn't?

Like a reluctant robot, Fitzgibbon hauled Collingwood to her feet and led her to the door, quilt and all.

"It was quick of you to have thought of the sheet," Miss Fawlthorne said when they were gone, shooting me a piercing look above the candle's flame. "You have made an excellent start, Flavia.

"Except for allowing Collingwood in your room," she added. "Both of you must be punished, of course."

I might have pointed out, I suppose, that Collingwood had come into the room uninvited and that since I was asleep at the time, I could scarcely have prevented it. To say nothing of the fact that, being newly arrived, I had not been informed of the stupid rule.

But I kept my bun trap shut.

It is decisions like this, for better or for worse, which make you who you are.

Instead, I stooped to lift the corner of the sheet.

"No! Don't! Please!" Miss Fawlthorne snapped, and I let it fall.

What harm could there possibly be in having another squint? But I knew in that moment that there would never be another chance.

Generally, when you discover a body, you have the luxury of close examination before the police are called in to trample the scene like cows at a picnic. But not always—and this was going to be one of those times. I had seen all that I was going to see. Whatever the physical evidence, it was already in my head.

Besides, I should have thought Miss Fawlthorne might want to learn as much as she could about the cadaver that had, until recently, inhabited her chimney.

Or did she know already?

I stood primly by, allowing her to regain control.

"I suppose I shall have to report it," she said for the second time, almost as if thinking aloud—as if she were being forced into it. Perhaps she was thinking of the academy's reputation. I could already see the headlines:

Carcass Cooked in Chimney
Body at Miss Bodycote's
Girls' School Aghast!

If the newspapers here in Canada were anything like the ones back home, we could be in for a jolly couple of days.

"But you must be absolutely exhausted!" she said, and until that moment I hadn't thought about it. Six days at sea and another on the train—to say nothing of the fact that it was now the middle of the night . . .

Miss Fawlthorne's words were hypnotic. I was suddenly yawning like the Cheddar Gorge, my eyes full of grit.

"You can't sleep here, obviously," she said, waving a hand at the sheet-covered form on the floor. "I shall put you up in my sitting room."

I had a fleeting vision of Miss Fawlthorne nailing my

severed head to the wall as if I were a mounted trophy: some wild animal that she had shot in Africa, or in the Arctic wastes.

"Come along, then," she said, leading the way by candlelight.

The electric lamps remained switched off.

At Miss Bodycote's, a rule, I could see, was a rule was a rule. Daffy would have been delighted with my insight.

I would never have thought it possible, but I missed my sister. She had been the lemon on my fish, the vinegar on my chips, I realized with a sudden pang, and that without her, life from now on was going to be less tasty. It was an odd thought to have at that particular moment, but then, life itself was odd. At least mine was.

Get a grip, Flavia, I remember thinking. *Steady on.*

We were now walking along a paneled corridor, Miss Fawlthorne leading the way.

"This is our Old Girls' Gallery," she said, raising the candlestick so I could better see the long rows of black-framed photographs that lined the gallery on either side.

Tier upon tier they rose up round us, flickering in the candlelight: faces of every size and shape imaginable, and again I thought of the hordes of angels.

Well, I had been told that Miss Bodycote's had strong ties with the church, hadn't I?

Even so, it hadn't prepared me for the sight of all these scores of black-framed souls, each one staring directly down at me—and none of them laughing—as if they were some solemn heavenly jury and I the prisoner at the bar.

"And here, of course," Miss Fawlthorne said, "is your mother."

She should have warned me. I was not prepared.

Here was Harriet, in her black frame, gazing levelly out at me with such a look . . .

In that young face—my face!—was everything that needed to be said, and in her look, all the words that she had never had the chance to speak.

Directly beneath Harriet's photograph was a small wall sconce, and in it was a spray of heartbreakingly fresh flowers.

Suddenly I was quaking.

Miss Fawlthorne put a hand gently on my shoulder. "I'm sorry," she said. "I didn't think. I ought to have prepared you."

We stood for a moment in silence, as if we were the only two left alive in that catacomb of the dead.

"She is much honored here," Miss Fawlthorne said.

"She is much honored everywhere," I said, perhaps a little too sharply. I realized, almost as I said it, that there was a certain resentment in my words. I had caught myself by surprise.

"Are they all dead?" I asked, pointing to the portraits, partly to change the subject and partly to show that there were no hard feelings.

"Good lord, no," Miss Fawlthorne said. "This one went on to become a swimming medalist . . . this one, Nancy Severance, a film star. Perhaps you've heard of her. This one the wife of a prime minister . . . and this one . . . well, she became famous in her own way."

"That's what I should like to do," I said. "To become famous in my own way."

That was it in a nutshell, and I was pleased that I had finally realized it.

I did not want to be Harriet. I wanted to be myself.

Flavia de Luce. Full stop.

"And who is this?" I asked, pointing to a striking and rather enigmatic-looking girl who gazed out at us with hooded eyes.

"Mrs. Bannerman is still with us at Miss Bodycote's," she said. "You shall meet her tomorrow. She is our chemistry mistress."

Mildred Bannerman! Of course! She had been charged and acquitted—a number of years ago after a sensational trial—of the murder of what the *News of the World* had called "her wayward husband."

It was claimed by the prosecution that she had poisoned the blade of the carving knife with which he cut up the Christmas turkey.

It was an old trick but a good one: Parysatis, the wife of Darius II of Persia, in the third century B.C., had murdered her daughter-in-law, Stateira, in precisely the same way.

By applying the poison to only the outer side of the blade, and serving Stateira the first slice, she was able to dispatch her victim and yet eat from the bird herself with little or no risk.

It was called "having your turkey and eating it, too."

By great good fortune and an even greater defense attorney, Mildred Bannerman had been spared the hangman's noose, and indeed, had been portrayed to the jury as the real victim of the crime.

And just think: In no more than a few hours I would be meeting her!

We moved on through an endless maze of darkened corridors until, after what seemed like an eternity, Miss Fawlthorne produced a set of keys.

"These are my rooms," she said, flicking on the lights.

Presumably the rules didn't apply to her.

"You may sleep on that couch," she said, pointing to a black leather monstrosity with a pattern of stitched dimples. "I shall bring you a blanket and a pillow."

And with that, she was gone, leaving me standing in the middle of her sitting room: a room that reeked of cold, silent unhappiness.

Was I picking up vibrations from the Old Girls who had been punished here for switching on a light after curfew? Or worse?

I remembered the words that Daffy had read aloud from *Nicholas Nickleby*, the words of the schoolmaster, Wackford Squeers: "Let any boy speak a word without leave, and I'll take the skin off his back."

But no, girls were not caned, Daffy had told me. They were reserved for the more exquisite tortures.

Miss Fawlthorne was back with a pillow and a tartan motoring blanket. "Sleep now," she said. "I shall try not to disturb you when I return."

She switched off the light and the door closed with a chilling click. I listened for a key in the lock. But even with my acute hearing, there was nothing more than the sound of her retreating footsteps.

She was going to her study to call the police: That much seemed certain.

I was straining my brain to think of ways I might contrive to be present in Edith Cavell at the moment the sheet was removed and the body revealed.

Perhaps I could wander in, rubbing my eyes and claiming a history of sleepwalking; or that I was in desperate need—due to some hereditary tropical disorder—of a glass of cold water.

But before I could put either of these plans into action, I fell asleep.

I dreamed, of course, of Buckshaw.

I was riding my bicycle, Gladys, up the long avenue of chestnuts. Even in the dream I was thinking how remarkable it was that I could hear a skylark singing and smell the trampled chamomile of the defunct south lawn. That and the decay of the old house itself.

Dogger was waiting at the front door.

"Welcome home, Miss Flavia," he said. "We have missed you."

I rode past him, into the foyer, and up the east staircase—which goes to show how ridiculous dreams can be: Although I had ridden down the stairs, I had never, ever been guilty of riding *up* them.

In my chemical laboratory, an experiment was in busy

progress. Beakers bubbled, flasks simmered, and various colored liquids flowed importantly to and fro in twists and coils of glass tubing.

Although I couldn't remember the purpose of the experiment, I was full of excitement at the outcome.

I would write it up in my laboratory notebook: from *Hypothesis* to *Conclusion*, all neatly presented so that even an idiot could follow each step of my brilliant thinking.

The chemical journals would come to fisticuffs over the rights to publish my work.

And yet there was an indescribable sadness about this dream: the kind of sadness that comes when the heart and the brain do not agree.

Half of me was filled with joy. Half of me wanted to weep.

When I awoke, a bell was ringing somewhere.

· F O U R ·

MY EYES REFUSED TO open. It was as if, as I slept, someone
had glued them shut.

"Hurry up," Miss Fawlthorne's voice was saying. "The
bell has already gone."

I looked up at her from bleary sockets.

"Your uniform is on the chair," she said. "Put it on and
come down for breakfast. There's a ewer on the table.
Wash your face. Brush your teeth. Try to look presentable."

And then she was gone.

How could anyone be so changeable? I wondered.

The woman's moods appeared to be connected to some
inner weathercock that swung wildly round with every
wind. One moment she was almost tender, and the next a
harridan.

Even the mercurial Daffy—from whom I had learned

both words—was no match for these cyclonic changes of character.

The cold horsehair stuffing gave out a groan as I sat up and levered myself to my feet. My back was sore, my knees were numb, and I had a crick in my neck.

I already had the feeling that this was not going to be a red-letter day.

I forced myself to crawl into the school uniform Miss Fawlthorne had laid out for me: a sort of navy blue wool pinafore dress with a pleated skirt, black tights, white blouse, and necktie—the latter striped diagonally in the school colors, yellow and black. A navy blazer completed the horror.

I winced as I examined my reflection in a silver tea service that stood on a side table. Hideous! I looked like someone in one of those baggy bathing costumes that you see on Victorian postcards.

I pinched a sugar cube and washed it down with a swig of slightly soured milk from the creamer.

Curse this life! I thought.

And then I remembered the dead body upstairs and I cheered up at once.

Had the police come in the night? Surely they must have, by now.

I was hardly in a position to ask, but there is no law against keeping your eyes peeled and your ears open, is there?

* * *

I had been worried that I would be stared at, but no one gave me so much as a second glance as I came tentatively down the staircase and paused on the landing. From some far corner of the house came the sound of a distant regiment of girls, all talking and laughing at the same time.

I won't say that my blood ran cold, but it distinctly cooled. I was not at my best with hordes: a fact that I had not entirely realized until the day I was sacked (unfairly) from the Girl Guides.

My case had been debated from the vicarage kitchen all the way up to the solemnly paneled council chamber of the Girl Guide Imperial Headquarters in London.

But it was no use. The die, as someone or another had said, was cast.

I recalled with bitterness the moment that Miss Delaney ripped my badges from my sleeves as the troop was made to chant in unison: "*Shame! Shame! Shame! Shame! . . . Shame! Shame! Shame! Shame!*"

I knew suddenly how the children of Israel must have felt when they were cast out by the Lord.

Farewell to the Scarlet Pimpernel Patrol! And farewell to their motto, "Do good by stealth." I had done my best to fulfill that commandment, but it was hardly my fault that things had gone so badly wrong.

Fate loves slight miscalculations, the vicar had told me later, and it was true. I would not likely ever live it down.

"Better hustle your bustle," someone said, touching my arm—a short, stocky girl with black-framed spectacles.

I almost jumped out of my skin. My nerves were edgy.

"Sorry," she said. "Didn't mean to startle you, but at Bod's, punctuality is paramount. Translated into English, that means if you're late for breakfast, they'll nail your hide to the barn door."

I nodded acknowledgment and followed her down the stairs.

At the bottom, I stuck out a hand. "De Luce, F. S.," I said, sticking to the formula Collingwood had used.

"I know," the girl said. "You're quite notorious."

I followed her into the Great Hall, a vast raftered expanse of dark hanging timber; a medieval cowshed with trestle tables. The hubbub was deafening.

A couple of harried-looking servers in white were ladling great gouts of porridge into bowls.

I took a seat at the end of one of the long tables and tucked in.

As I ate, I looked discreetly round the room, pretending not to. As a new girl, it would be impolite to stare. Not that I really cared.

It was important, though, not to draw attention to myself.

There was a possibility that whoever had killed the cadaver in the chimney was in this very room at this very moment.

I would need to begin my investigations from scratch.

I looked round the hall for Collingwood, but she was nowhere in sight. Perhaps she had been excused to recover from last night's ordeal.

Because most of the girls had their heads in the feed troughs, it was not easy to examine their faces. I noticed though that even as they ate, they were still talking rapidly to one another from the corners of their mouths, which made it difficult to read their lips as I had trained myself to do. Besides, I didn't want to stare.

It wasn't too much of a chore to guess the sensational topic. The buzz and thrill of bad news was heavy in the air.

An older girl, two tables away, elbowed her neighbor in the ribs and pointed at me with her chin. When they saw that I had noticed, they both looked away quickly.

The faculty, all of them women, sat on a raised dais at one end of the hall, overlooking the grazing girls.

At the center of the high table sat Miss Fawlthorne, her head inclined, talking with pinched brows to a youngish-looking woman whose short black hair was as tight as a bathing cap.

There are rare and precious moments, when one is a stranger in a room, that one can examine its inhabitants with little or no prejudice. Without knowing so much as their names, it is possible to form an assessment based purely upon observation and instinct.

Even at a glance I could tell that the faculty of Miss Bodycote's Female Academy had one thing in common: They were all dead serious. There was no frivolity: no laughter and no lipstick.

Even as they ate, they spoke quietly to one another as if they were a panel of grave judges with all the weight of justice on their shoulders.

Could one of them be a murderess?

As a simple exercise, I set myself to deduce their teaching specialties.

The woman at the far right, with short steel-gray hair, was almost certainly the French mistress. She had that Cupid's-bow mouth with the raised corner and peculiar but slight twist of the outer nostril that can come only from speaking French from the cradle. No Englishwoman could ever possibly form those shapes with her mouth while talking. I knew that from my own close observation of Mrs. Lennox—Chantelle Lennox—who lived next door to the vicarage in Bishop's Lacey, and who had been brought back to England as a sort of war trophy by her husband, Norman.

She was from Montmartre, pronounced through the nose.

Next at the table was a hatchet-faced individual with high cheekbones and an air of solitude about her, who seemed to exist in her own aura, almost as if she were surrounded by an invisible bell jar.

Sad, I thought. *Lonely and unpopular*.

My first thought was that, judging by her face alone, this should be Mildred Bannerman, the acquitted mariticide. (A useful word meaning "husband killer" that Daffy had taught me: a word unknown, it would appear, not only to the shrillest of the tabloid newspapers, but even to *The Times*.)

But no—just yesterday I had seen a schoolgirl photo of Miss Bannerman in the Old Girls' Gallery. She could not possibly have aged into such a hard-looking creature.

My eyes moved on along the table, and there, on Miss Fawlthorne's right, sat a sweet-faced pixie: the youngest teacher of the lot—was this the girl from the photograph? She appeared still not much more than my sister Feely's age, which was eighteen.

She must be older than she looks, I thought.

Not wanting to stare, I watched her from the corner of my eye, reveling in the very thought of breakfasting with a killer. Mildred Bannerman—at last!

The others were unremarkable: a mere assortment of noses and chins, eyes and ears plucked from a sack and tossed together at random.

"Welcome to Bods," said a voice at my ear.

It was the girl whose hand I had shaken on the stair.

"Van Arque," she said. "We've already met. I've been more or less put in charge of you until you're on the rolls. I'm a monitress, by the way."

She looked slowly round the room as if she were keeping an eye out for predators. Satisfied for the moment that we were safe, she turned her attention back to me. "Say, you don't have a cigarette on you by any chance?"

"No," I said. "I don't smoke. Are you allowed to? In here?"

Van Arque made a honking noise through her nose. "Of course not. We use the third-floor kybo."

"I beg your pardon?"

"The kybo. The bog house. The four-flusher. The holy tabernacle—"

"The crapper, you mean," I said.

"The crapper! Ha! That's a good one!" she hooted, choking on her porridge.

She was seized with a spasm of coughing and her face grew red. Her hands flew to her throat. Her breathing had become a loud, wheezing gurgle.

I knew instantly that some mass of the glutinous stuff had lodged in Van Arque's windpipe—and that she was in real danger.

Her face was already darkening.

I leapt to my feet and began pounding her furiously on the back—with the flat of my hand, at first, and then with both fists.

I couldn't help noticing that everyone round us—even the faculty—seemed stuck to their chairs. No one, besides me, had moved a muscle. The room had gone silent.

Suddenly—and unexpectedly—Van Arque coughed up a disgusting clot of porridge and spat it noisily out onto the floor.

"Are you all right?" I asked.

She was now sucking in great, grateful breaths of fresh air, her shoulders heaving. Her color was improving by the second.

She grimaced.

"No," she croaked, "but I must go on . . . It's trad. Monitresses are not allowed to be ill."

I looked at her in disbelief. Was she joking?

"If we catch so much as a sniffle, they put us to death."

She could see I didn't believe her.

"It's true," she whispered. "They have an abattoir. There's a secret door behind a cupboard in the infirmary."

"With bloody meat hooks hanging from the ceiling," I said, catching on.

Practical jokers can recognize one another as easily as bees from the same hive. Van Arque and I had far more in common than I had realized.

"Exactly!" she said. "Meat hooks and racks of butcher's knives. And they feed the mulch to the chickens."

"Or what's left of it after making the porridge," I said, shoving a large spoonful of the stuff into my mouth and chewing it with relish.

Van Arque sucked in a breath and her eyes went as big as saucers. "Oohhh!" she said. "How disgusting!" and I knew that I had made an impression.

Van Arque picked up a table napkin and gave my mouth a couple of dabs, as if I were dribbling porridge.

"Shhh!" she said, covering her own mouth as she faked a small additional cough. "Druce is watching us. She reads lips."

Much as I wanted to brag about my own achievements in that department, I made a quick decision to keep a few tricks up my sleeve. It is sometimes better to let science be thought magic.

Two tables away, the large girl who had elbowed her neighbor in the ribs—this must be Druce—was staring openly.

She was the only person in the hall looking at us. Everyone else was studiously looking away, as Anglicans invariably do when faced with group embarrassment. It was a trait I had noticed even as a child, which, as nearly as I could puzzle out, was somehow connected with the famous ostrich-and-sand reaction. Roman Catholics, by contrast, would have been clambering over one another for a front-row seat.

"Let's get out of here," Van Arque said. "I need some fresh air. Come on. We've got a few minutes before the next bell."

As we pushed back our chairs, I turned deliberately toward Druce and, as if I were talking to Van Arque, clearly pronounced the word "flap-dragon."

It was my favorite word from Shakespeare: not as long as "Honorificabilitudinitatibus," which preceded it in *Love's Labour's Lost*, but enough of a workout to let Druce know that when it came to lip-reading, she was not dealing with someone who was wet behind the ears.

"You're sure you haven't got a cigarette?"

We were leaning against the stone rim of a neglected goldfish pool in a small courtyard behind the laundry.

"No," I said. "I told you. I don't smoke. It's a filthy habit."

"Sez who?" Van Arque demanded, squinting like Popeye and taking up a boxer's stance—squeezing her biceps to make them bulge. I knew she was joking.

"Never mind," she said. "Here comes Fabian. She's always good for a fag. Fabian! Over here!"

Fabian was a tall blonde who looked as if she came from Finland: a pale, cool Nordic type, who wore rather too much face powder, as if she had a lot of spots to hide. I wondered if she, like me, was exiled from her homeland.

"How much?" Fabian asked, holding out a single cigarette. She didn't even need to be asked.

"A nickel for two," Van Arque said.

"Three for a dime," Fabian countered, and the deal was done.

"It's highway robbery, that's what it is," Van Arque said, lighting up when Fabian was gone. "She's only been here a year and she's already as rich as Croesus. She pays seventeen cents for a pack and makes three hundred percent profit. It isn't fair."

Nickels? Dimes? I knew that cents were roughly equivalent to pence, but beyond that, Canadian currency was a veiled mystery.

Why had I ever been sent away from the land of the sixpence—the land of half-crowns, ha'pennies, florins, farthings, and shillings, the land of decent coinage, where everything made sense?

How could I possibly learn to survive in such a pagan place, where trams were streetcars, vans and lorries were trucks, pavements were sidewalks, jumpers were sweaters, petrol was gasoline, aluminium was aluminum, sweets were candy, a full stop was a period, and cheerio was good-bye?

A towering wave of homesickness broke over me: a wave even greater than the Atlantic gales through which I had safely sailed; greater than anything I could ever have possibly imagined.

I put a hand against the stone wall to steady myself.

"Are you all right?" Van Arque asked anxiously.

"Yes," I said weakly. And then again, more strongly, "Yes."

It was only the thought of this curious creature who

stood so casually beside me, smoking, that gave me strength. If Van Arque could go from choking to joking and smoking in the wink of an eye, then surely so could I.

"Morning, ladies," said a voice behind me, making me jump. I whirled round to find what I took at first to be a weasel in a shabby trench coat: a thin young man with an alarmingly pale, pinched face and an unconvincing mustache.

"Students, I take it?" he asked. "A couple of Miss Bodycote's beauties?"

"Go away," Van Arque said, pulling a nickel-plated whistle from her pocket, "before I call the police."

"Hey, take it easy. Don't do that," he said, dredging a damp leather wallet from the depths of the wreckage that was his raincoat. He flipped it open and held out what appeared to be some kind of official identity card.

"Wallace Scroop," he said, offering it. "The *Morning Star*. Mind if I ask you a few questions?"

"We're not allowed to speak to reporters," Van Arque said.

"Listen," he went on, ignoring her. "I've heard this place is haunted. It's an old convent, you know . . . ghostly footsteps in the night—all that sort of thing. I thought it would make an interesting story. You might even get your pictures in the paper."

"There are no such things as ghosts—or haven't you heard, Mr. Scroop? Any footsteps in the night at Miss Bodycote's are caused by too much lemonade at the school carnival—not by phantoms. Now please go away."

"If I did," Scroop said, "my editor would wring me out

like a dishcloth. Come on, girls, have a heart. Let's be honest. What do you know about the body that was carted off to the morgue last night? Someone you know, maybe? Listen, I could make it worth your while."

I glanced at Van Arque, but she didn't seem surprised at the news. Without further warning, she jammed the whistle between her lips and blew a long, ear-piercing blast. For a fraction of a second, Wallace Scroop looked as stunned as if she had slapped his face. And then, with a couple of surprisingly coarse words, he was gone.

"Creep," Van Arque shot after him, but he was already too far away to have heard her.

Somewhere indoors, a bell began to ring.

"Curses!" Van Arque muttered. "Wouldn't you just know it?"

She tossed the cigarette down and ground it out beneath her heel. "Come on," she said. "We've got to go. They've put you in the fourth form—at least for the time being. As I said, Miss Fawlthorne told me to oversee you until she gets round to the formalities. She's got rather a lot on her plate at the moment—or so she says."

"I should say she has!" I volunteered, wondering if Van Arque's had been one of the cherub faces floating in the darkness. "Did *you* see what happened in Edith Cavell last night?"

I hated myself as soon as I had said it. I am not ordinarily a gossip, but some inside force was suddenly making me spit out information like a clockwork ticket dispenser.

Was I automatically sucking up to Van Arque because of my inferior position as a new girl? I surely hoped not.

"No," she said. "But I heard about it. That's for darn sure!"

I said nothing. I have learned to use silence as a jimmy to pry information free. Or did I keep my mouth buttoned because I was still nauseated from that tidal wave of home-sickness? I shall never know.

But whatever the reason, I held my tongue.

And it paid off. Van Arque couldn't resist demonstrating her superior knowledge.

"The guff has it that Miss Fawlthorne found you standing over a dead body in Edith Cavell, and Collingwood in hysterics. I told you—you're notorious. Now hurry up before they skin us and use our guts for snowshoes."

·FIVE·

As we made our way along the dark passage that led from the back entrance to the Great Hall, the bell clanged again.

"Oh, corn!" Van Arque whispered in the sudden silence that followed. "Now we're in for it. We'll be blacked."

"Blacked?" I said. Collingwood had used this term, but I still had no idea what being "blacked" involved, although I must say it didn't sound like much fun. I had visions of being painted with boot polish, like the vicar as Othello in the parish play. It seemed rather an extreme punishment for missing a stupid bell.

As if by chance, another bell sounded: this one closer and less loud.

"It's the doorbell," Van Arque said.

As sometimes happens when you're in a pinch, Fate offered up a free spin of the wheel, and I took it.

Rather than following Van Arque, I veered across the hall and opened the door.

There, with his finger still on the electric bell button, stood a tall and excessively slender man. He had the long face and long fingers of a carved medieval saint and the body of a long-distance runner.

A younger, shorter man in a dark blue uniform stood sturdily to one side, his feet apart and his hands clasped—I assumed—behind his back. He might as well have had "ASSISTANT" stamped across his forehead with indelible ink.

"Yes?" I asked, taking the upper hand.

Behind me, Van Arque sucked in a noisy breath at my boldness.

"Miss Fawlthorne," said the medieval saint. I could tell already that he was a man of few words. Rather like Gary Cooper.

"Ah!" I said. "You must be the police."

It was, of course, a dim-witted thing to say, and yet at the same time, precisely right.

The tall man nodded, almost reluctantly. "That's correct," he said. He was giving nothing away.

"I'm Flavia de Luce," I said, sticking out my hand. "And you are . . . ?"

"Inspector Gravenhurst."

"Ah!" I said, as if I had been already half-expecting that to be his name.

He gave me a quick but firm handshake. I could see that he was sizing me up even as our hands went up and down.

"And Sergeant . . . ?" I said, taking a chance. Surely an

inspector's right-hand man would be a sergeant of one kind or another.

"LaBelle," the sergeant said, not correcting me.

"I shall tell Miss Fawlthorne you wish to see her," I said.

The inspector nodded, stepping inside and looking round the Great Hall with keen interest, taking in every detail with his penetrating gaze.

I liked this man already.

"By the way," I said, turning back toward him. "I'm the one who discovered the body."

This was not precisely true, but it was my only chance of becoming involved in the case. I resisted the powerful urge to tell him that this corpse was not my first: that in fact, cadavers were my calling card.

Modesty, though, prevailed.

The inspector brightened immediately.

"Indeed?" he said, and I liked him even more. Pity, though, that he wasn't a member of the legendary Royal Canadian Mounted Police. That would have made things perfect, but it wasn't likely his fault. His height had probably exceeded some idiotic and arbitrary physical requirement.

"Van Arque," I said, surprised by my own boldness, "run upstairs and tell Miss Fawlthorne the inspector's here." I resisted adding, "There's a good ducks."

Van Arque's mouth fell open.

"Van Arque's a monitress," I explained to the inspector. "She has first dibs on fetching the head."

It was the right thing to say. Van Arque squeezed off a proud smile and was off up the stairs like a galloping rocket.

"You're English," Inspector Gravenhurst said.

"Yes," I replied. My accent alone made me stand out among these Canadian girls like a—

"Been over long?" the inspector asked.

"Since last night," I said. "Well, yesterday, actually."

How I loved talking to this man! What a breath of fresh air it was to converse with someone who didn't natter endlessly on and on like a village spinster.

I wanted desperately to tell him about Inspector Hewitt, my great friend back home in Bishop's Lacey, but there would be time enough for that later. I would find a plausible way of dragging my dear inspector and his goddess wife, Antigone, into the conversation at a more appropriate time.

There was a clatter behind me on the stairs as Van Arque came scuttering quickly down, followed at a much more solemn pace by Miss Fawlthorne.

Blast them! I had barely got started. Well, there was nothing for it now but to play along. I clasped my hands daintily at my waist and went all submissive, staring up attentively at Miss Fawlthorne as if I were a beagle waiting for her to throw the ball.

"Thank you, Flavia. You are dismissed. Take her along to the fourth, Van Arque."

I couldn't help myself. I curtsied.

Van Arque tugged at my arm, and I had time only to flash the inspector a fleeting—but dazzling—smile.

"You'll pay for that, you know," Van Arque said when we were far enough along the corridor.

"Pay for what?" I asked.

She didn't reply and on we marched.

* * *

"I've brought the new girl, Mrs. Bannerman."

Van Arque paused, holding open the door.

I nearly swooned as the teacher turned round: She was, of course, the sweet-faced pixie! The elflike creature who looked as if she would be more at home perched on a fox-glove leaf, sipping dewdrops from a fairy thimble.

"Come in, Flavia," she said. "We've been expecting you."

Flavia? Did the murderess (acquitted) Mildred Bannerman know my name?

I'm afraid that, for the first time ever in my life, although I may have been speechless, my heart was singing.

"Come in, Flavia," she repeated, and I entered in a zombie trance.

Needless to say, I was the center of attention, which I loathe being. The girls all stared at me openly and I made a point of staring just as openly back. I was as curious about them as they were about me.

Who, for instance, was this girl with the needle-sharp nose and the hole in her stocking? And who the plump one with the pleasant face and fingernails bitten to the elbows? Who was the girl staring so intently at me from the farthest corner of the room? If I didn't know better, I'd have sworn she had some ancient grievance.

And who was the girl that, in the middle of a room bubbling with curiosity, was so studiously ignoring me? I made special note of this one, recording her details in my mental notebook: small mouth, small nose, and hooded eyes; long black hair and a general air of self-importance, as if she were a wealthy tourist shopping in a bazaar swarming with ragged beggars.

After marking up what I took to be an attendance sheet, Mrs. Bannerman left the room to take a chemistry class with the fifth form, and was replaced by the gray-haired woman I had spotted at breakfast. I was right—she *was* the French mistress.

The girls all stood as she entered the room, and I went along with it.

For the next hour, Miss Dupont—I found out later whom she was—twittered away at the class, asking what seemed to be useless questions and nodding wisely at the useless answers. I didn't understand a word of their palaver but, because she addressed each girl by name, the time wasn't entirely wasted.

"*Flav-ee-ah,*" she said at last, mispronouncing my name and then rattling off a string of gibberish. I studied my fingernails, pretending I hadn't heard.

"*Elle est très timide,*" she remarked to the class, and everyone laughed except me.

I felt like a chump.

What a jolly good idea it had been for my ancestors to forsake France in the days of William the Conqueror, I thought; otherwise, I, too, should have been brought up speaking through my nose.

And what utterly useless rot these girls were made to rehearse!

"*The niece of my gardener has given me a blue handkerchief.*"

Who has left Grandmother's best photographic album in the garden in the rain?" (What a silly-sounding word *"pluie"* was: like the outcome of too many hot beans on toast.) *"Run for the doctor, Marie—Madame has suffered a gastric explosion."*

I only know these things because Van Arque told me later what had actually been said.

Pitiful!

I won't bother with the rest of that morning, except to say that it was uncomfortable. As I have said, I hate being the center of attention, and yet at the same time I can't tolerate being ignored.

How I longed for a brisk knock at the door, and for someone to announce that Inspector Gravenhurst wished to consult with me.

Not that he would put it that way, of course. No, he would be much more discreet than that.

"Inspector Gravenhurst presents his compliments," they would say, *"and begs that Miss de Luce favor him with her assistance."* No, *"her* valuable *assistance."*

Or "invaluable *assistance."*

Were things still done that way in Canada? Somehow I doubted it. Even in England nowadays, in my experience, the police were more likely to send you off to fetch them a cup of char or, when they finally came to their senses, to wring you dry as a dishrag before collaring all the credit for themselves.

Life wasn't fair. It simply wasn't fair, and I meant to make a note of it.

Before I left home, Aunt Felicity had presented me with a small leather notebook and a miniature propelling pencil, the latter cleverly concealed in a gold crucifix which I wore round my neck.

"Even a barbarian will think twice before meddling with *that*," she had said.

The crucifix itself was altogether quite remarkable, modeled, Aunt Felicity told me, on the idea of the Trinity, three-in-one: Father, Son, and Holy Ghost.

And so it also contained, besides the pencil, a small but powerful magnifying glass that swung out from inside the cross, and a surprisingly complete set of lock picks.

"For quiet Sundays," she had said, giving me what I would have sworn was a glacially slow, lizardlike wink.

It wasn't until after dinner that the call actually came. I was walking with Van Arque toward the hockey field when the police sergeant, LaBelle, appeared as if from nowhere. Had he been lying in wait behind the laundry?

"The inspector wants to see you," he said, his words reeking of cigarette smoke.

Just like that. No niceties.

I gave Van Arque a helpless shrug and followed the sergeant indoors.

"Big place you've got here," he said as we climbed the stairs to Miss Fawlthorne's study. "Roomy but gloomy."

And he was right. Miss Bodycote's Female Academy was a shadowed maze: a place in which daylight never strayed far from the windows. It was a place designed not to be lived in, but to be prayed in; a place whose narrow zigzag corridors were meant, perhaps, to confound the Devil.

"All that ever escapes a convent," Daffy had once told me, after reading a rather sensational book about a nun's life, "is the prayers and the smoke."

Which brought me back to the body in the chimney.

I had been kept so busy I had scarcely been able to give it more than a moment's thought.

Who was she? How had she died? How long had she been hidden in the chimney?

And—most tantalizing—how and why had she come to be wrapped in a Union Jack?

We paused at the door of Miss Fawlthorne's study. The sergeant's knuckles were raised as if to knock.

He stood for a moment, examining me from head to toe.

"Watch yourself, kid," he said, adjusting his tie as if it were an uncomfortable noose.

And then he was tapping timidly at the door.

"Ah, Flav-ee-ah," Inspector Gravenhurst said, mispronouncing my name in precisely the same way as Miss Dupont had done.

Miss Fawlthorne sat quietly at her desk as if she were merely a guest.

"It's Flavia," I told him. "The first syllable rhymes with 'brave' and 'grave.'

"And 'forgave,'" I added, in case he thought I was being frivolous.

He nodded, but I noticed he had not begged my pardon.

"Now, then," he said. "Tell me about your discovery."

It was obvious that he had not yet interviewed Collingwood; otherwise, he would already have heard her some-what different version. Better to face up to my fib right away and get credit for honesty.

"Actually, it was someone else, I think, who found the body. What I meant was that I just happened to be there."

"I see," he said. "And who might that have been?"

"Collingwood," I said. "Patricia Anne."

From the corner of my eye, I noticed that Miss Fawl-thorne had stopped whatever she was doing and looked up from her desk.

"She was having a nightmare," I said. "Walking in her sleep. She tried to climb up the chimney. I was trying to keep from waking her. I've heard that sleepwalkers can die of shock if they're awakened too suddenly."

I was proud of myself! Here was a sign of my great com-passion, an excuse for fibbing to Miss Fawlthorne, and a plausible account all rolled up neatly into one tidy tale.

Three-in-one again: a holy trinity of truth, righteous-ness, and quick thinking.

"And that's when the, ah . . ."

"Body," I supplied.

"Er, yes, the body, as you say—was dislodged from the chimney."

"No," I said. "That didn't happen until after Miss Fawl-thorne came into the room.

"I didn't know it was a body at the time," I added.

"Because you were in the dark," the inspector remarked matter-of-factly.

By the lord Harry! I had to give the man credit: He was as sharp as a tinker's tack. It was obvious he had already interviewed Miss Fawlthorne and heard her version of the night's happenings.

"Yes, that's right," I said. "Miss Fawlthorne's candle blew out and we were left in the dark."

"For how long?"

"Oh, not long at all. A couple of seconds, I should say. Miss Fawlthorne lit a match almost immediately."

"What kind of match?"

"A paper match. The ones that come in a booklet. They give them away in places like the Savoy, and so forth."

The inspector glanced at Miss Fawlthorne, who nodded to confirm my statement.

"And then?"

"Well, it was just then that Collingwood fell out of the chimney, and the body right behind her. She must have jarred it loose. Like a chimney sweep—or a pipe cleaner," I suggested.

I knew as soon as I spoke that I had gone too far.

"Flavia!" Miss Fawlthorne exclaimed.

"I'm sorry, Miss Fawlthorne," I said. "It's just that with the amount of soot and tar—"

"That's quite enough," she said. "Inspector, I'll not have my girls exposed to such questioning. They have, after all, been entrusted to my care."

My girls! She already thought of me as one of her girls. In some odd, but unknown way, that made all the difference in the world.

"Quite right," the inspector said. "It's clear that Flavia here"—he pronounced it correctly this time—"has seen enough."

Whatever did he mean by that?

"You've been very helpful," he said. "Thank you. You may go now."

I looked at Miss Fawlthorne, who gave her assent.

Although I got to my feet, I lingered at the door (an art of which I have made a particular study, and one which is greatly underestimated by amateurs) long enough to hear him say, "Now, then, Miss Fawlthorne: I'd like a list of everyone who has been in and out of this building within the past twenty-four hours."

In the corridor, I wondered: Why twenty-four hours? The body had been in the chimney for ages and ages. That was as plain as a pikestaff.

Surely the inspector's next step wouldn't be to demand a list of everyone who had crossed the threshold of Miss Bodycote's Female Academy for the past quarter century?

But wouldn't a list such as that include the name of my own mother?

A cold chill gripped my spine.

·SIX·

VAN ARQUE WAS WAITING at the bottom of the stairs.
Had she been listening at the door?

"Jumbo wants to see you," she said.

"Jumbo?"

"The head girl. Her name's June Bowles, actually, but
you must always call her Jumbo, or she'll have your eyeballs for earrings."

"I see," I said.

"You darn well won't if she does it!" Van Arque cackled,
clapping her hands together with animated joy, as if she
had just made the world's greatest witticism.

"What does she want to see me about?"

"You'll see."

All these "sees" were having a nauseating effect on me.
In fact I was becoming positively "see-sick."

"She's in Florence Nightingale," Van Arque said, jabbing with a forefinger at the ceiling, so up the stairs we trudged—the same stairs I had just come down.

It was like living on a treadmill.

Florence Nightingale was at the far end of Athena Wing. The various wings at Miss Bodycote's, I was to learn, were named after goddesses, the rooms after heroines, the houses after female saints, and the WCs after defunct royalty.

"She's in Boadicea," meant that the person in question was communing with nature in the little closet behind the kitchen, while Anne of Cleves and Jane Seymour were two of the loos on the upper floors.

Florence Nightingale turned out to be a rather grand study that overlooked the hockey field.

Van Arque knocked and entered without waiting for an invitation.

"Here she is, Jumbo," she said. "The new girl. Her name is de Luce—Flavia."

Jumbo turned slowly away from the window, waving a hand idly to disperse the few wisps of tobacco smoke that still hung in the air. The room reeked of the stuff.

Diana Dors in a tunic, was my first thought.

Jumbo was what the cinema magazines would have called breathtakingly gorgeous. She was tall, blond, and statuesque in the way that Britannia is statuesque.

Carved in marble is what I mean. Cool . . . calculating . . . and perhaps a little cruel.

I was awash in impressions, some of them favorable—others not so.

"Cigarette?" the sculpture asked, offering me a pack of Sweet Caporals.

"No, thank you," I said. "I'm trying to give them up."

It was an excuse I had used before, and it seemed to work.

"Good for you." She smiled. "It's a revolting habit."

She selected another for herself, setting fire to it with ceremonial flourishes of a small silver lighter that looked like a miniature Aladdin's lamp, and inhaling deeply.

"Vile," she said again, the word issuing from her mouth in a cloud of acrid smoke.

She looked for a moment like a Norse goddess: or perhaps one of the Four Winds pictured in the corners of the ancient maps, puffing a cold blue blast from the Pole.

"Blow, winds, and crack your cheeks! Rage! Blow!"

For an instant I was transported back to Buckshaw, sitting in the drawing room with Father, Feely, and Daffy, listening to *King Lear* on the BBC Home Service during one of our compulsory wireless nights.

And then, just as quickly, I was returned to Miss Bodycote's.

It was disconcerting. My head was spinning, and it wasn't just from the cigarette smoke.

"Catch her, Van Arque!"

Those were the last words I heard.

I was crumbling.

Into a deep, hollow, and horribly echoing well.

*   *   *

I opened my eyes and immediately wished I hadn't. Shards of light from the window pierced my eyes like needles of bright glass.

I squinted and whipped my head to the other side.

"Steady," said a voice. "It's all right."

"Here, drink this," said someone else, and the hard rim of a glass was pressed against my lower lip. I sipped, and a warm liquid slipped down my throat.

Almost at once a heat began diffusing through my guts, as if my heart had caught fire.

I pushed the glass away, still blinking blurrily in the harsh light.

"Pfagh!" I said, wiping my mouth with the back of my hand.

"It's only brandy," said the voice, which I now recognized as Jumbo's. "You fainted. It'll do you good."

"It's not brandy," I heard myself saying, as if an automaton had inhabited my body. "Brandy doesn't have potassium bisulfite in it—or sulfurous anhydride."

My taste buds and olfactory system had detected them. I was sure of it.

Both of those chemicals, I knew, had been approved thirty years ago by the Holy Office for use as sterilizers, preservatives, and antioxidants in Communion wine.

And, as in Rome, so in the Anglican High Church.

Someone had pinched this stuff from the chapel.

It was no more than common sense.

"Very good!" Jumbo said as she came swimming slowly into focus. "We'll need to be more discreet, Gremly."

Gremly turned out to be a pasty-faced little girl with fish lips and a servile stoop.

"Agh," Gremly said with a guttural gurgle, as if she were handmaiden to Dr. Frankenstein. Was she laying it on with a trowel, or was this her normal way of communicating?

"You gave us a fright," Jumbo said. "We thought for a minute you'd bought the farm."

"I beg your pardon?" I asked.

"Bought the farm. Bit the dust. Snuffed it, et cetera. Girls your age do that sometimes, you know. Constitutional weakness. Undiagnosed heart mumble. Poof! Just like that!"

"Not me," I said, struggling to get up. "I'm as strong as an ox."

I could hear my own voice echoing weirdly, as if it were coming from another room.

Jumbo pushed me down again with a forefinger. I was powerless.

"Relax," she said. "You're among friends."

Was I? I looked from her face to Gremly's.

My uncertainty must have been obvious.

"Friends," she repeated. "Of course you are. You're the daughter of Harriet de Luce, aren't you?"

My silence was my answer.

"She's worshipped here as a saint, you know. Haven't you seen her shrine in the hall?"

I gulped and looked intentionally back at the bright window as the tears welled in my eyes.

"The light—" I said.

"We were all sorry to hear about your mother," Jumbo said, touching my arm. "Damnably sorry. It must have been especially tough on you, poor kid."

That did it.

I leapt to my feet, dashed from the room, and fled blindly to the little chamber at the end of the hall, which I would later learn was called Cartimandua.

There I barricaded myself in one of the two cubicles, sat down on the WC, and had a bloody good knock-'em-down, drag-'em-out howl.

When I was finished, I honked into a wad of lavatory paper, washed my face, and freshened up with strategic dabs of carbolic hand soap.

What a week it had been!

Even the last few minutes alone had been shocking. I had broken at least three of the Ten Commandments—the "Thou shalt nots" of British girlhood: I had cried, I had allowed alcohol to pass my lips, and I had fainted.

I examined my blurry image in the hanging glass.

The face that stared dimly—but defiantly—back at me was a hodgepodge of de Luce: a grab bag of Father's features, Aunt Felicity's, Feely's, Daffy's—but above all, Harriet's. In the harsh glare of the flickering overhead lightbulb, it reminded me—but only for a moment—of one of those topsy-turvy paintings by Picasso we had cocked our heads at in the Tate Gallery: all pale skin and a kaleidoscope mug.

The recollection of it made me grin, and the moment passed.

I thought of the faded, flyblown wartime posters that still hung in Miss Cool's confectionery in the high street of Bishop's Lacey: "Get a Grip," "Chin Up," and "Best Foot Forward."

I took a deep breath, squared my shoulders, and gave myself a smart regulation salute in the mirror.

How proud Father would be of me at this moment, I thought.

"Soldier on, Flavia," I told myself in his absence. "Soldier on, de Luce, F. S."

Van Arque was lurking anxiously in the hall. "Pip-pip?" she asked.

"Pip-pip," I told her.

"You've made a friend," she said as we walked slowly down the stairs. I was still not up to dashing.

"Oh?"

"Jumbo thinks you're the cat's pajamas," she said. "And not just because you're Harriet de Luce's daughter. She's invited you to Little Commons tonight."

"Little Commons?"

"In her room. After lights-out. Just a few of her chums."

I should have known.

It is difficult to look interested when you're asleep, but I had developed a useful technique at St. Tancred's, during some of the vicar's excessively long sermons on Saving Faith, which I was now able to put into practice.

First, I would lock eyes with the teacher, nodding now and then in agreement with whatever she was saying. I might even pretend to be taking voluminous notes.

I would next plant my elbows firmly on the desktop and rest my forehead on my cupped hands, as if I were meditating on the profound wisdom of her words.

In that way, I could catch forty winks undetected, twenty at a time, trusting in faith (there it is: faith again!) to wake me up if I were spoken to directly. But in fact, it never happened. In all of recorded history, a teacher has never been known to question a thoughtful pupil.

Was it deceitful? Well, yes, I suppose it was, but to my mind, all's fair in love and education.

Although I hadn't learned a thing by the end of the day, I had at least slept a little, so that when the last class ended (mathematics, incidentally) I was feeling surprisingly refreshed.

By suppertime, the novelty of my presence was beginning to wear off among the girls. Nearly all of them had exchanged a word or two—almost always touching my arm as if I were some sort of talisman to be rubbed—and those who didn't had at least stopped staring.

In spite of the jolly companionship, I could hardly wait to be alone. Bedtime couldn't come soon enough.

"Are you all right?" Van Arque asked. It was becoming a ritual.

"Yes," I told her.

I made my excuses: fatigue, travel, irregular meals, lack of sleep, and so forth.

I did not mention my real reason for wanting to be

alone, which was that I desperately needed solitude for my mind to be at its best: to come to grips with the sudden and gruesome (but fascinating) appearance of the body in Edith Cavell.

Like Mr. Gradgrind in *Hard Times*, I wanted Facts— nothing but Facts. Even though that schoolmaster was a fictional character invented by Charles Dickens, I fancied I could hear his dry voice droning in my head: *"In this life, we want nothing but Facts, sir; nothing but Facts!"*

The facts I wanted were these: (a) Who was the deceased? (b) Why was she stuffed up the chimney? (c) Who had put her there? (d) Had she been murdered? (e) If so, how? And, of course, (f) By whom?

Hadn't Collingwood mentioned a number of girls who had gone missing?

I needed room and solitude to think.

"If you'll excuse me," I said, "I think I'll get to bed early."

"But it's only six o'clock!" Van Arque protested.

"I know," I said, "but my brain thinks it's midnight. It's still on Greenwich Mean Time, you see. I expect I'll catch up in a day or two."

It was the best excuse I could come up with on the spur of the moment, but Van Arque accepted it without question.

"Run along, then," she said. "I'll call you in time for Little Commons."

I nodded eagerly, as if I could hardly wait, and made my escape.

*   *   *

But I could not sleep. Even though the body had been removed and the room swept, swabbed, and dusted, I found myself tossing and turning, wrestling with my sheets and pillow as if they were crocodiles and I had been plucked from the burning sands of Egypt and flung into the Nile.

I tried to imagine what the police were doing, but theorizing without any real information was agony.

I tried counting sheep, but it was no use. Sheep bored me.

Then I tried counting bottles of poison:

> Ninety-nine bottles of arsenic on the wall (paper),
> Ninety-nine bottles of arsenic,
> If one of the bottles should happen to fall (paper),
> There'd be ninety-eight bottles of arsenic on the wall
>   (paper).
> Ninety-eight bottles of arsenic on the wall (paper) . . .

Were the bottles of arsenic actually pictured on the wallpaper, or had each roll been soaked in the stuff? Arsenical wallpaper, I remembered, colored with the poisonous pigment Scheele's Green, had killed Napoleon, among others, and was sadly no longer manufactured.

Had Scheele's Green once been used on wallpaper in Canada, as it had in England? Had the girl in the chimney been poisoned by sleeping in a contaminated room? Had the stuff in which she had been wrapped been Union Jack wallpaper? Surely it would have burned . . .

Even as it was thinking these thoughts, my mind realized that it was exhausted—running in senseless circles. I needed sleep and I needed it desperately.

I jerked awake.

It was dark in the room and someone was knocking—scratching, actually—at the door.

"Flavia!"

I was being called in a hoarse whisper.

I remembered at once that I had locked the door as a protection against being pummeled again in my sleep by Collingwood.

I jumped out of bed still tangled in the wreckage of my bedsheets and hopped to the door.

Van Arque stepped back, startled, when she saw me.

"Were you asleep?" she asked.

"No," I said. "I was just resting my liver."

"Well, never mind," she told me. "Get dressed. Quickly. Have you forgotten Little Commons?"

To be truthful, I had.

"No," I said.

I dashed about trying to make myself decent as Van Arque waited outside the door.

Still, I felt like a scarecrow as we crept through the darkness toward Florence Nightingale.

Van Arque produced a slip of paper from somewhere and, slipping it into the crack under the door, began to move it slowly from side to side.

I saw at once that it was a silent signal, and far superior to knocking.

In a moment the door was opened slightly and we were beckoned inside.

Jumbo and a group of about half a dozen girls—one of whom was Gremly, and another the tiny blonde with a round face who had been elbowed in the ribs by Druce at breakfast—were sitting on the floor in a circle round a single candle, which danced and guttered madly as we came into the room.

"Shift!" Jumbo whispered, and the circle enlarged itself to make room for us.

"Welcome, Flavia Sabina de Luce," Jumbo pronounced.

I couldn't think of anything to say, so I smiled.

"It is a tradition at Miss Bodycote's Female Academy for each new girl, by way of introduction, to tell us a story. You may begin."

To say that I was unprepared would be an understatement.

Tell them a story? I didn't know any stories—at least not any that I could repeat to a group of girls.

"What kind of story?" I asked, hoping for a hint.

"A ghost story," Jumbo said. "And the bloodier the better."

Seven flickering faces leaned in closer, all eyes intent upon mine, except Gremly's, who kept hers shielded with an upraised hand, as if protecting herself from a hostile sun.

What a Heaven-sent opportunity! Wallace Scroop, the lubricious newspaper reporter—"lubricious" was a word I had learned from Daffy, but hadn't, till now, had an opportunity to use—had suggested that Miss Bodycote's Female Academy was haunted. And now, here was a chance to bring up the topic without seeming to be either childish or gullible.

But the only ghost story I could think of on the spur of

the moment was one that Feely and Daffy had told me
when I was quite small: a story that had terrified me so
much that I had almost shed my skin.

It was called "The Old Woman and the Pimple."

It went like this—

·SEVEN·

"IN THE VILLAGE OF Malden Fenwick, in England," I began, "not far from Buckshaw, my family's ancestral home"—it was important, I knew, in order to draw them in, to supply credible details—"stands the ancient church of St. Rumwold. It is dedicated to the infant who, immediately after being born, is said to have cried out three times, 'Christianus sum! Christianus sum! Christianus sum!' ('I am a Christian'), requested baptism, delivered a sermon, and died when he was three days old."

A little murmur ran through the group as the girls looked uneasily at one another.

"In the north transept of the church is a chapel containing the tombs of a crusader and his various wives and children, and, to one side, built into the wall, is a most peculiar stone carving.

"This is the thirteenth-century effigy of a prosperous

local miller named Johannes Hotwell, or Heatwell—the inscription is now much worn and not easily legible. There, on his back, he lies among the crusaders, his eyes open, his stone nose pointing to the overhead vaulting as if scanning the heavens for some signal from the painted stars. In his marble hands he clasps what seems at first to be a sack of flour, but which some insist must be, because of its ornamental nature, a hot-air balloon—although it can't be, can it? since the hot-air balloon was not yet to be built by the Montgolfier brothers for another five hundred and thirty years."

I paused to let this sink in. I was telling the tale in, as best as I could remember, the same words in which my sisters had told it to me.

I could tell that my listeners were taken in.

"Johannes, being of an overbearing mind, had, in spite of his father's warning, married young. 'Tend your mill,' the old man had told him time and again, 'and leave wyves to such as be smytten.'" All of this can be found in a little booklet sold near the font by the ladies of the Altar Guild.

"In spite of his father's warning, Johannes had, as I say, taken to himself a wife: a shrewish spinster from the next village who knew a good thing when she saw it.

"It was not long afterwards that Johannes's pimple appeared.

"At first, it was no more than a tiny red spot between his shoulder blades, as if he had been bitten by an absent-minded gnat. But as time passed, it grew and grew into a fat, pus-filled pimple: an angry red blemish on his back.

"Rather like a dormant volcano," I added, "with a cap of snow, or pus, on its upper peaks."

"Ugh!" one of the girls said.

"His wife begged him to let her burst the thing. 'It may be thought a wytch's sign,' she told him.

"But he would have none of it.

"'Leave it, wife,' he had told her, 'for though it be but a pymple, it be myn own,' and she knew her place well enough to leave the thing alone.

"At least, while he was awake.

"But one night, she couldn't sleep for worrying about what might become of them. Surely when her husband stripped off his jerkin to take the first ceremonial May Day dive into the millpond, someone would spot the pimple. They would be aghast!

"Word would get round. Gossip would see to it that the villagers would stop bringing him their custom. They would begin carting their grain to Bishop's Lacey, instead. She and Johannes would come to ruin, while others prospered.

"All of this and more ran through her mind as she lay awake, the moonbeams streaming in through the casement window as if it were broad daylight, illuminating her sleeping husband's back—and its lurking purple pimple.

"She reached over and took the thing between thumb and forefinger—"

Jaws dropped round the circle of girls.

"It was almost too easy. With an audible *pop!*"—I made the sound with my finger in my cheek—"the thing broke, and the pus came out. She urged it along a little, coaxing it until there was nothing left in it but blood.

"Her husband stirred, gave a long sigh, rolled over, and began to snore.

"Next morning, he complained of a scratched back. 'You must have rolled against the wattle,' she told him, and he said no more about it.

"But as time went on, the pimple began to fill again, even more red and angry, if that were possible, than before.

"As she had done the first time, the miller's wife waited until a Saturday night when he was sleeping off a second (or perhaps third) pot of ale, and then she broke it again, this time with more confidence—almost joyously.

"It surprised her that, rather than being fearful, she now actually enjoyed popping the pimple.

"As the years went by, the purple pimple bloomed, each time bigger and more livid than the time before. It was, she thought, as if Hell itself were filling the thing with foul and sulfurous matter thrown up from deep down in the inferno that was her husband, Johannes.

"The miller's wife found herself looking forward—almost impatiently—to the next swelling of the infernal bag, which had now become a cyst. She could hardly wait, each time, for its slow and weary filling.

"And then one night the miller died. Between the beef-steak and the beer. Just like that!

"He keeled over at the table and was dead before his face hit the floor.

"The old woman was filled with mortal fear! Had she

killed him with her incessant and secret tampering? Would he still be alive, eating roast beef and parsnips, if she had left well enough alone?

"Would she be taken by the high sheriff and hanged for her crime?

"And so she kept her silence and told no one about the pimple, or what she had done, and a few days later, the miller was laid to rest in the transept of St. Rumwold, under the lid of a massive slab tomb, with his name and dates carved upon the lid.

"Time passed, and the village began to forget him, as villages do with things that are always under their noses.

"But Johannes's wife did not forget him. Oh, no—quite the contrary!

"She lay awake nights, thinking not of her husband, but of the excrescence which was quite possibly still growing between his shoulder blades—even in the grave. With no one to empty it, she thought, the thing would go on filling. She thought of it there in the darkness of his coffin, growing and growing and growing—untended. Neglected.

"She thought of it as hers.

"And to be truthful, she missed it. Missed squeezing the thing. Missed hearing it pop.

"She could hardly bear thinking about it. It was quite clear what she should do.

"And so on a moonless night, the old woman crept quietly through the sleeping village and made her way by a roundabout route along the riverbank to the church.

"Inside, she blessed herself, said a dozen Our Fathers and two-dozen Hail Marys, and, with a stout iron poker she had brought from her own hearth concealed in her shawl, pried open the lid of the tomb."

I paused in my tale to look round me. The candle flame was perfectly smooth and still. No one was breathing.

Even Jumbo's mouth was agape. "And . . . ?" she whispered in a husky voice, the word rising in wisps at the end like smoke from a wooden match.

"There in his stone box lay the miller, just as she had last seen him. In fact, he appeared to have changed hardly at all. Had he been miraculously preserved, as some saints were said to remain, forever incorrupt?

"Or—and the hair on her head rose as she thought of it—*was he still alive?*"

Again I paused for my words to have their effect. One of the girls on the far side of the circle had quietly begun to sob.

"It was not easy, but she . . . rolled . . . him . . . over," I said slowly, "and hauled up the hem of the shroud . . . in which all but his head had been wrapped."

The silence was by now unbearable. I let it lengthen, watching the reaction of each of them.

"And there . . . there was the gigantic pimple, swollen by now to the size of a pomegranate—and much the same livid color, as if it were full of blood!

"The wife's hands shook as she reached for the thing . . .

"And as she reached there came a sudden hollow groan!

" 'No-o-o-o-o-o-o!'

"—as if the miller's corpse were protesting, as if he wanted to keep this treasure for himself, to take away into eternity. A ruby made of skin.

"In spite of her fear, the old woman leaned even closer. It would take only a moment and then she would be gone, her duty done. *I shall leave it to the Lord*, she thought, *to say if I be right or wrong*."

The seven faces around me had now gone as white as socks. They had ceased breathing. Save for the flickering candle, time was suspended.

"And then, slowly . . . carefully . . . she placed her fingers upon the swollen thing . . . gave it a squeeze, and—

"BLAZOOEY!"

I shrieked the word as loudly as I could, grabbing the arms of the girls each side of me.

Jumbo screamed gratifyingly.

Girls clung to one another in fright.

Gremly fell on her face and pulled her dressing gown over her head, moaning.

"What happened?" someone cried.

I waited for a long moment before I replied. "The damned thing burst," I said matter-of-factly.

"And the hot-air balloon?" Jumbo asked, making a remarkably quick recovery. "What about the hot-air balloon?"

"Oh, that," I said. "That was added to his effigy later by the miller's wife as a sort of allegory."

"Allegory?" Gremly croaked.

"As a civilized way of indicating to posterity that the stomach gases of the deceased had exploded, as sometimes happened in those days. It was the best excuse his wife could come up with on short notice."

There was a scraping sound outside in the hall, and something banged.

"Shhh!" Jumbo said. "Someone's coming! Lights out."

She blew out the candle and we all sat stock-still in the dark.

There was a knock at the door.

"What's going on in there?" a voice demanded. It was Fitzgibbon.

We held our collective breath, some of us with hands clapped over our mouths and noses.

We huddled there together in the dark, paralyzed at the thought of what would happen when light was restored and time resumed.

"It's all right, Matron," Jumbo called out after what felt like an eternity, putting on a sleepy drawl. "I was having another of those horrid nightmares. I shall be all right in the morning. Good night."

She was a girl after my own heart.

There was a muttered response, and then footsteps shuffled away in the hall, their sound fading.

"Some story!" Jumbo said when the danger had passed. She laughed lightly, as if she had to; as if it were part of a ritual.

She lighted the candle again, and our faces flared up out of the darkness, the whites of our widened eyes as large as the polar caps.

But something had changed. We were not the same girls we had been just minutes before. In that shared eternity of fright, and in some strange and indefinable way, we had

102 · ALAN BRADLEY

suddenly all become sisters. Sisters of the candlelight—
and sisters of something else, also.

"Fetch the board, Gremly," Jumbo ordered, as if a sudden decision had been made, and Gremly, scrambling to
her feet, vanished into the shadows.

A moment later she was back with a flat red box. She
opened it and, with surprising tenderness, placed a wooden
playing board on the floor at the very center of our circle.

It was a Ouija board.

I was quite familiar with the game. Daffy and Feely had
dug a similar one out of a cupboard at Buckshaw and had
terrorized me for a time by raising the ghost of Captain
Cut-Throat, a malicious spirit from the days of piracy on
the high seas, who had ratted on me at every opportunity.
The captain had informed my sisters, by way of the moving
tablet, that I had stolen perfume from one of them (true: I
had taken it for a chemical experiment involving the essential oils of civet musk) and that it was I who had caused
a certain book to vanish from beneath the pillow of the
other (also true: I had nicked Daffy's copy of *Ulysses* because it was the perfect thickness to prop up the broken leg
of my bedside table).

Letter by letter, word by word, and interspersed with his
beastly "Har! Har! Har!," the dead captain had caused the
planchette to creep across the board on its three little legs,
laying bare, one by one, some of my best-kept secrets—
including several of which I was not very proud—until I
happened to notice that the old sea dog misspelled the
word "cemetery" with the ending "a-r-y"—in exactly the
same way as Daffy did in her diary!

I couldn't help smiling now as I recalled how sweet—and how swift!—my revenge had been upon my smug sisters. Daffy, in particular, had been afraid to close her eyes for a month.

"All fingers on!" Jumbo commanded, and we all pressed the first two fingers of each hand onto the heart-shaped wooden pointer. It was a tight fit.

Someone giggled.

"Shhh!" Jumbo said. "Show the spirits some respect." She closed her eyes and took a deep breath. "O spirits," she said, "we bid you come among us."

There was a nervous silence.

"O spirits," she repeated, her voice a tone higher, "we bid you come among us."

I remembered from my sisters' use of the Ouija board that, like the characters in fairy tales, the spirits needed to be told everything three times.

I could easily relate to that.

"O spirits," Jumbo said again, this time in a whisper, "we bid you come among us."

Something electric was in the air. The hair at the back of my neck was already standing on end as it did when, in my laboratory, I rubbed an ebonite rod on my woolen jumper and waved it behind my head.

"Is someone here?"

With startling speed, the cursor jerked to life and began to slide. Across the board it flew, without the slightest hesitation, and stopped at "Yes."

Jumbo had opened her eyes to take a reading. "Who are you?" she asked in a conversational tone.

There was no reply and she repeated her question two more times.

Now the cursor was on the move again, sliding silkily to and fro across the board's smooth surface, picking out letters, one by one, pausing only briefly at each before moving on to the next.

D—A—R—K—H—E—R—E, it spelled out.

"We understand," Jumbo said, snapping her fingers. "We light a light for you."

Snap!

She had obviously done this sort of thing before.

"Is that better?"

The cursor scurried across the board and stopped at the word "YES."

"Do you have a message for someone here?"

"YES."

For just an instant, my blood ran cold. Could this be the ghost of my mother, Harriet? She had, after all, once been a student at Miss Bodycote's. Perhaps a part of her was attached to the place forever.

In truth, I hoped it wasn't Harriet. I had received from her once before a message from beyond the grave: a message telling me that she was cold and wanted to come home.

I didn't think that I could bear another.

Please don't let it be Harriet!

As uncharitable as that might seem.

Get a grip, Flavia! I thought, and not for the first time.

"Who are you?" Jumbo asked, three times and slowly. "What is your name?"

It came in a rush. The pointer scuttled back and forth across the board like a panicked lobster.

L—E—M—A—R—C—H—A—N—D

Gremly, who had been writing down the results with the stub of a lead pencil, gasped. "Le Marchand!" she cried.

It was the name of one of the girls who, according to Collingwood, had gone missing from Miss Bodycote's.

I looked round the circle of blanched faces. It was obvious from their haunted eyes that each one of them had already made the connection.

"Oh, my God!" someone whispered.

I have to give Jumbo credit. She was on to it like a terrier on a rat.

"We are prepared for your message."

I noticed that even at a moment so tense as this, Jumbo spoke to the spirit in a grammatically correct manner. Again, she repeated her words three times.

The pointer fairly flew across the board.

O—N—E—O—F—Y—O—U—K—N—O—W—S—M—Y—K—I—L—L—E—R

"One of you knows my killer!" Gremly gasped, reading aloud the words she had just scribbled down.

With a sweep of her hand, the tiny blonde across from me sent the planchette flying to the far corner of the room.

"Enough!" she said. "This is stupid."

"Steady on, Trout," Jumbo said. "If you've busted the thing, it's coming out of your pocket money."

Trout. So that was her name.

I looked round the circle.

One of the girls—on my left—had made a puddle.

·EIGHT·

ANYONE WHO HAS EVER played with a Ouija board has pushed.

I can practically guarantee it.

Let's admit it: You've pushed, I've pushed—everyone has pushed.

The opportunity is simply too good to pass up.

Initially, someone else in the circle had been doing the pushing, and for a few minutes, even I had wavered. Wavered? No, more than that: I'll admit that the first message shook me. But then rational thought had returned, and I realized that I'd just been handed a rare gift from the gods.

From that point on, it had been yours truly, Flavia de Luce, guiding the planchette.

One of you knows my killer.

Sheer inspiration on my part!

The results had been even more gratifying than I'd

hoped. Trout had been shocked into scattering the board and its runner, and the girl to my left had lost control of her bladder.

I needed to make her acquaintance at the earliest possible moment.

"Oh, dear!" I said, going all solicitous and helping her to her feet. I noticed that no one else made a move. I would have her all to myself.

I led her along the hall to the WC called Cartimandua, which would be a safe haven for an interview, I thought. Although it was forbidden for any girl to be in another's room after lights-out, there was no law against two of us answering the call of nature at the same time.

"My name is de Luce," I said, as the tiny creature retired into one of the cubicles. "Flavia."

"I know who you are, well enough," she said, her voice echoing oddly from the room's glazed surfaces.

"But I don't believe I know yours," I said.

There was a hollow silence. And then her name came, almost in a whisper.

"Brazenose. Mary Jane."

Brazenose? It couldn't be! That was the name of one of the missing girls.

Le Marchand, Wentworth, and Brazenose—or so Collingwood had told me.

Surely there couldn't be more than one Brazenose in such a small establishment as Miss Bodycote's?

Or could there?

"Was she your sister?" I asked gently.

A torrent of sobs from the cubicle provided the answer.

"Come out of there," I said, and surprisingly, she obeyed. The cubicle door clicked open and a moment later, this poor, pale, damp little chick was enfolded in my arms, weeping woefully into my shoulder as if her heart would break.

"I'm sorry," I told her, honestly meaning it, and for now that had to be enough.

The possibility that the body in the chimney might be her sister must not—at least for now—be put into words. I hardly dared even think the thought for fear that she would somehow read my mind.

But perhaps she had realized it already.

Brazenose was hanging on to me as if she were a ship-wreck victim, and I a floating log. And who knows? Perhaps she was.

Perhaps I was, too.

What remarkable bonds we form, I thought, as she clung to me. *And what very odd ones*.

She seemed reluctant to break away—reluctant to have to look me in the eyes.

"Better wash your face," I said at last. "In case they call a snap Holy Communion service."

That fetched the ghost of a smile.

"You are a very peculiar person, Flavia de Luce," she said in a dampish voice.

I made a deep bow, heel to instep, sweeping an imaginary cavalier's feathered hat toward the floor with one hand.

As Brazenose was scrubbing her face at the sink, the door opened and Fitzgibbon came into the room.

Was she surprised to see us? I couldn't tell.

"You're up late, girls," she said. "Is everything all right?"

"Yes, Matron," Brazenose said in a surprisingly strong voice, and I, as a newcomer not expected to know any better, merely nodded.

"Well, then, off to bed with the both of you," Fitzgibbon said. "No lights, mind."

We whispered to each other as we went along the hall.

"Don't believe the Ouija board," I told her. "It's a gyp. Someone in Jumbo's room was spelling out the words."

Brazenose's eyes were like lanterns in the darkness. "Are you sure?" she breathed.

"Yes," I told her. "It was me."

Half an hour later, as I lay in bed, unable to sleep, I wondered about what I had said.

Were points given out in Heaven for a half-truth?

I remembered from long-ago sermons at St. Tancred's that lying lips are an abomination to the Lord, but that those who act faithfully are his delight. But how did God feel about those who merely fiddled the facts?

It was true that I had been in control of the board toward the end of the séance, but not at the beginning. It was not I who had spelled out that spine-chilling name, Le March-and.

Who, then, had been the culprit?

The only possibilities were those other girls, besides myself, who had placed their fingers on the Ouija board's planchette. These were Jumbo herself, Gremly, Van Arque,

Brazenose, Trout, and the other two whose names I had not learned.

Druce, of course, had not been present. That let her out.

It was clear that I needed to find out at once the identities of those other two girls.

Whom should I ask? It seemed obvious: the girl who was presently most obligated to me.

Dear little Brazenose.

Had I been wrong to confide in her? Had I put myself at risk by taking a chance?

Well, for better or for worse, I had done so. And now I needed to grill this girl at length.

It had been too late to begin tonight, and I had already risked—not once but twice!—being abroad after lights-out.

It would have to wait until morning.

With that decided, I rolled over and slept like the log in the proverb.

I don't think that I shall ever forget, as long as I live, the sounds of Miss Bodycote's Female Academy coming to life in the morning.

First would come the clanking of the pipes and steam radiators, sounding for all the world like armored knights having a practice joust with playful young dragons, who gurgled and hissed more to show off than anything else.

Then the distant tobacco-coughing of the mistresses and—I'm sorry to say—some of the more forward girls, which seemed to me were most of them.

Next was the synchronized flushing of the WCs. Some-where a gramophone would start up as one of the sixth-form girls exercised her senior's rights: The sounds of Mantovani's "Charmaine" would come slithering down the staircases like liquid honey, pooling stickily on each floor before oozing on down to the next. This would be fol-lowed by "Shrimp Boats Are A'Comin," "Mockin' Bird Hill," "On Top of Old Smokey," and "Aba Daba Honey-moon."

To ears such as mine, brought up on the BBC Home Service, it was like living in a grass hut among savages on a desert island.

Voices would call to one another and sudden laughter would ring out, followed by the scuffing of shoe leather on floors and stairs and, drifting in through an open window from the street outside, the clopping of the elderly automa-ton horses that drew the various bread and milk wagons from door to door.

In the distance, on the Danforth, the streetcars would clang their impatient *ding-ding!* at foolhardy motorists and pedestrians.

How very different it all was from the seclusion of Buck-shaw.

It was then, in the mornings, that homesickness would rise in my throat, threatening to choke the very life out of me.

Hold on, Flavia, it shall pass, I would tell myself.

I was doing that this morning, hanging on to the man-telpiece for dear life when suddenly, and with no warning, my door flew open.

It was Miss Fawlthorne.

"Report to me after gymnastics," she said abruptly, scanning the room with a professional eye, and then she was gone.

Damnation! I'd been hoping she'd forgotten about my promised punishment, but it was obvious she had not. Collingwood would be there, too. We would go to the stake together like a yoke of Christian martyrs.

Would I have time to question her—even as we burned?

Gymnastics was humiliating. The class was being held out of doors today, on the hockey field, and we were made to dress in plimsolls and bloomers that would have been laughed off the beach even in Victorian Blackpool.

We exercised to shouted commands:

"Heels: Raise! Sink!

"Right knee upward: Bend!

"Right knee backward: Stretch!

"Knee: Flexion! One! Two! Three! Four!"

The games mistress was the hatchet-faced individual with the short gray hair, the one I had spotted at breakfast. She stood off to one side, commanding us with a shrill whistle.

Phweeep-phweeep-phweeep! "Cheerfully now!"

"Cheerfully!" Gremly grumbled through gritted teeth. "Yes, Miss Puddicombe. No, Miss Puddicombe. Three bags full, Miss Puddicombe."

From this I gathered that the games mistress's name was Miss Puddicombe.

Puddicombe by name, Puddicombe by nature, I thought, even though I knew it didn't make any sense.

But in times of torture, even a defiant thought can serve as a soothing salve.

I had just finished changing from bloomers to tunic when Jumbo stuck her head in at the door.

"Headmistress wants to see you," she said. "Better shift your carcass.

"And, oh," she added, smiling sweetly, "you'll keep mum—if you know what's good for you."

Miss Bodycote's was like that, I was to learn: the slap in the face with a velvet glove, the sting in the smile, the razor blade in the butter.

Just as in real life.

"Come in, Flavia," Miss Fawlthorne said in reply to my knock.

I squeezed through the barely opened door.

"Sit down," she commanded, and I obeyed, perching myself on the edge of a leather divan.

"First things first," she said. "You will recall, no doubt, that I promised you punishment?"

"Yes, Miss Fawlthorne," I said. "I'm sorry, I—"

"Tut!" she said, holding up a restraining hand. "Excuses are not legal tender at Miss Bodycote's Female Academy. Do you understand?"

I didn't, but I nodded anyway, imagining a red-faced

magistrate in a horsehair wig glaring down at me from his elevated bench.

"Rules are rules. They are meant to be obeyed."

"Yes, Miss Fawlthorne. I'm sorry."

The old, old formula. It had to be played out, step by meticulous step, according to some ancient ritual.

Perhaps I should have business cards printed to hand out, each embossed with my name and the words "I'm sorry, Miss Fawlthorne." Every time I offended I would pluck one from my pocket and hand it—

"For your punishment, I want you to write out five hundred words on William Palmer. He led, I believe, an interesting life."

It took a moment for the light to come on, but when it did, my brain was dazzled by the sheer brilliance of it.

William Palmer? The Rugeley Poisoner? Why, I could write five hundred—a thousand—ten thousand!—words on dear old, jolly old Bill Palmer with my fingers frostbitten, my wrists handcuffed, my ankles bound, and my tongue tied behind my back.

I struggled to keep from squirming. *Remember, Flavia— play the game.*

"Yes, Miss Fawlthorne," I said, putting on a hangdog look.

I could hardly wait to lay hands on my pencil and notebook.

But why? I thought later. Why would Miss Fawlthorne, as punishment, assign me such a happy task?

It was as if a sinner in the confession box, having admitted murder to the priest, were given the penance of devouring a chocolate cake. It simply made no sense.

Unless, of course, the priest was secretly a baker—or the son of a baker—who stood to profit from the transaction.

It may have been an uncharitable thought, or perhaps even a blasphemous one, but that's the way my mind worked.

You can't be hanged for thoughts, can you? I wondered.

Miss Fawlthorne was writing something in a black ledger, and I was turning to go, when she spoke again.

"You will also report to me here, personally, at this same hour, every Monday, from now on. Beginning next week."

The air went out of my lungs as if I had been run over and crushed by a cartwheel.

Permanent punishment for such a small infraction? What kind of hellhole had I been tossed into? One minute the woman was a guardian angel soothing my fevered brow, and the next a slavering executioner measuring my neck. What was one to think? What was one to do?

"Yes, Miss Fawlthorne," I said.

I flew up the stairs to Edith Cavell. I needed to be alone.

I needed room to think.

I sat huddled on my bed, knees under my chin and my back against the wall.

School was not turning out to be at all what I thought it would be.

Father—the very thought of him shot a bolt through my heart—had often lectured us on the pleasures of learning.

And—up until this moment—he had been right.

There had been no happier hours of my life than those spent alone in my chemical laboratory at Buckshaw, bundled against the cold in the ancient gray cardigan of Father's I had rescued from the salvage bin, rummaging through the dusty notebooks in Uncle Tar's library, teaching myself, little by little, atom by atom, the mysteries of organic chemistry.

The doors of Creation had been flung open to me, and I had been allowed to walk among its mysteries as if I were strolling in a summer garden. The universe had rolled over and let me rub its tummy.

But now—!

Pain.

With an abrupt shock, I realized I was slamming the back of my head monotonously against the wall. *Bang! . . . bang! . . . bang!*

I leapt off the bed and found myself marching, like an automaton, to the window.

Ever since the days of Gregor Mendel and Charles Darwin, scientists have puzzled over inherited characteristics in everything from people to pea plants. It has been suggested that cell particles called "genes" or "gemmules" carry down, from one generation to the next, a set of maps or instructions, which determine, among other things, how we might behave in any given situation.

In that clockwork walk to the window, I realized even as

I went that what I was doing was precisely what Father always did in times of trouble. And, now that I came to think of it, so did Feely. And Daffy.

The Code of the de Luces. It was a simple equation of action and reaction:

Worry = window.

Just like that.

Simple as it was, it meant that in some complicated, and not entirely happy, chemical way—and far deeper than any other considerations—we de Luces were one.

Bound by blood and window glass.

As I stood there, and my eyes focused gradually on the outside world, I became aware that, down behind the stone gate, a small red-haired girl was thrashing wildly on the gravel. Two older girls were tickling her to the point of insanity. I recognized them at once as the pair I had seen at breakfast: the lip-reader, Druce, and her thrall, Trout.

Something clicked inside me. I could not stand idly by and watch. It was an all-too-familiar scene.

I unlocked the window and pushed up the sash.

The victim's shrieks were now unbearable.

"Stop that!" I shouted, in the sternest voice I could manufacture. "Leave her alone!"

And, wonder of wonders, the two torturers stopped, staring up at me with open mouths. The sufferer, freed from their attentions, scrambled to her feet and bolted.

I slammed down the window before her tormentors could reply.

I would probably pay for it later in one way or another, but I didn't care.

But try as I might, I could not get that little girl out of my mind.

How could tickling, even though it causes laughter, be at the same time such a vicious form of torture?

Sitting on the edge of my bed, I thought it through.

I came to the conclusion, at last, that it was like this: Tickling and learning were much the same thing. When you tickle yourself—ecstasy; but when anyone else tickles you—agony.

It was a useful insight, worthy of Plato or Confucius or Oscar Wilde, or one of those people who make a living by thinking up clever sayings.

Could I find a way of squeezing it into my report on William Palmer?

Had the Rugeley Poisoner tickled his victims?

I shouldn't be at all surprised to discover that he had.

·NINE·

I HAD BARELY SAT down at my desk with pen and ink and begun to collect my thoughts about William Palmer when the door flew open and a small whirlwind exploded into the room, with hair as red as it is possible to possess without bursting into flame.

I was not accustomed to constant invasion, and it was beginning to get on my nerves.

"What's the matter with you, anyway?" the fiery one demanded, arms spinning round in the air like a runaway windmill. "What do you mean by interfering? What business is it of yours, anyway?"

"I beg your pardon?" I asked.

"Oh, come off it! What are you trying to do? Get me killed?"

Only then did I realize that this furious creature was the

same girl who, barely minutes before, had been in danger of writhing to death in the dust.

"Miss Pinkham, I presume," I said, taking a wild stab in the dark.

The windmill came to an abrupt halt. I had caught her off guard.

"How did you know that?" she asked belligerently.

"By a series of brilliant deductions with which I will not trouble you," I told her. "Plus the fact that your name is clearly marked in indelible laundry ink on a tab in the neck of your tunic."

This, too, was a shot in the dark. But since the tunic Miss Fawlthorne had issued me was marked in this way, it seemed a reasonable assumption that hers was also.

"Very clever, Miss Smarty-pants," she said. "But you'll be laughing out of the other side of your face when the Hand of Glory gets hold of you."

The Hand of Glory?

I knew that the Hand of Glory was the pickled and mummified hand of a hanged murderer, carried by eighteenth-century housebreakers in the belief that, in addition to paralyzing any hapless householder who might interrupt them in their burgling, it would also unlock all doors and confer invisibility upon them: a sort of primitive version of the do-it-all Boy Scout knife. Dried in a fire of juniper smoke and yew wood, and used to hold a special candle made from the fat of a badger, a bear, and an unbaptized child, the Hand of Glory was the answer to a burglar's prayer.

So why would the girls of Miss Bodycote's choose it as the name of some kind of ridiculous secret sorority?

Pinkham must have seen my puzzlement.

"Druce and Trout," she explained.

"Those two morons?" I exploded with laughter. I couldn't help it. "The Hand of Glory? Is that what they call themselves?"

"Shhh!" she said, finger to lips, her eyes wide. "Keep it down, for cripes sake!"

The very thought of a secret society at Miss Bodycote's Female Academy set me off cackling again. I couldn't help myself.

"Please," she said in a pleading whisper. "They'll kill us both."

"Like Le Marchand?" I asked. "Like Wentworth? Like Brazenose?"

Her face went slack with horror, and I saw at once that it had been the wrong thing to say.

"Look here," I said. "You can't allow them to go on bullying you. It's not right."

"No," she said. "But it's how things are."

"Here," she added.

Something touched my heart. This child was genuinely frightened.

"Don't you worry about Druce and Trout," I heard my mouth telling her. "You leave them to me—and let me know if they get up to any more of their tricks."

"But—you're the new girl," she protested.

I put a sisterly hand on her shoulder. I did not need to

tell her that when it came to revenge, I, Flavia Sabina de Luce, was a force to be reckoned with.

"Fear not," I told her. "Simmer down."

I think that, even then, I was beginning to formulate a plan.

Pinkham stood paused in the doorway, and just for an instant she looked like a girl in a painting by Vermeer: as if she were constructed entirely of light.

"You're a brick, Flavia," she said, and then she was gone.

I sat there for a long while, staring at the door, my mind churning.

What had I got myself into?

Then I closed my notebook and put away my pen. Justice was calling.

Palmer the Poisoner would have to wait.

The corridors of Miss Bodycote's Female Academy were, as I have said, a maze: a series of labyrinths, of twists, of turns, of offshoots. The floors went abruptly and without warning from broad planks to tiny tiles and back again, the walls from plaster to marble, and the ceilings from great galleries and soaring vaults to small, dark tunnels of ancient boards through which you needed to duck your head in order to pass.

There were no directional maps to help the newcomer. One was expected to know the layout of the place with the same efficiency as a London cabbie knows his city: the Knowledge, they call it—the names and locations of 25,000 streets, courts, closes, yards, circuses, squares, lanes, and avenues, and the best and quickest ways of getting from every single one of them to the others.

Why do my thoughts keep harking back to home and England? I wondered, as I caught my mind adrift for what must have been the hundredth time.

Here I was in Canada—the New World—with all that that implied. I was young, healthy, intelligent, curious, and chock-full of energy, and yet my mind, whenever I took my eye off it, flew instantly back like a homing pigeon to the land of my birth: to England and to Buckshaw.

It was inexplicable. It was annoying. It was entirely uncalled for.

Now I found myself at the top of a steep, narrow staircase that led up from a narrow L-shaped cubbyhole on the ground floor to an unsuspected niche behind a linen cupboard on the second, and, to be perfectly honest, I hadn't the faintest idea where I was or how I had got there.

Get a grip, Flavia, I thought, for the umpty-umpth time. It was becoming my theme song, my national anthem.

The science lab and the chemistry lab, I knew, were located in one of the wings: far enough away that the stinks wouldn't pollute the holy atmosphere. I had had a glimpse of test tubes and beakers from the hockey field, and I knew from a casual remark Van Arque had made that the science department and its attendant natural history museum were immediately adjacent.

"Science?" I said to a girl who ducked round me and went clattering down the stairs, a cardigan tied over her shoulders and a squash racket gripped in her hands.

She paused just long enough to give her head a sharp

jerk to the left, her hair coming unfastened and flying into her face, and then she was gone.

Left I went, and there it was, stenciled on the green wall at eye level in official-looking black capital letters: SCIENCE & CHEMISTRY.

The two departments seemed to occupy the entire wing. A series of doors, each with its own small window, receded into the distance in a rather odd effect that made it seem like an optical illusion. I cupped my hands and peered through the glass into the first room.

This must be the natural history museum. Not large, but remarkably complete for its size. Glass cases round all the visible walls seemed to house a cross section of all creation: birds—I recognized a stuffed specimen of the extinct passenger pigeon, of which I had seen a photograph in one of Arthur Mee's endlessly fascinating encyclopedias—butterflies, bees, moths, and other insects, all pinned neatly to cards and labeled: everything from small mammals to minerals, and from fossils to fish.

I tried the door, but it was locked.

By craning my neck, I could see hanging in a corner, on a wrought-iron stand, an articulated human skeleton. The very sight of it brought a momentary lump to my throat as I thought of Yorick, my own dear skeleton, hanging patiently back home in my laboratory at Buckshaw. Yorick had been given as a gift to Uncle Tar by the great naturalist Frank Buckland, who had not only autographed the skull but had also neatly printed on the frontal bone the playful inscription *Multum in parvo*—"much in little": a great deal in a small space—which might have been meant as something of a joke.

Beside the skeleton was a glass case in which animal skulls were displayed in neat rows, all boiled and bleached, ordered by size, and containing everything from what I guessed to be a mouse all the way up the scale to a human skull, which ended the series.

Above the case, mounted on the wall, was the enormous skull, complete with antlers, of a moose—what we call back home an elk. This, too, seemed to be meant as a joke for those in the know: "From mouse to moose." Or vice versa.

I'm beginning to suspect that, everywhere on earth, professionals in the life sciences must share with Sherlock Holmes's Dr. Watson that same vein of pawky humor. Fun, perhaps, but childish, when you come to think of it. You certainly don't catch chemists behaving like that.

Well, hardly ever.

Still, I must admit that I trifled with the idea of sneaking down to the kitchen in the wee hours of the morning, pinching some eggs, and whipping up a dish of chocolate mousse. I would sneak it into the glass display case to be discovered in the morning.

Anyone clever enough would make an immediate connection: moose . . . mouse . . . mousse.

If they didn't, so much the better. All the more mysterious.

The school newsletter would have a field day.

"Midnight Marauder Monkeys with Museum!"

But, as with so many of my best ideas, I kept it to myself, and moved on.

At the end of the hall was the entrance to the chemistry lab. I felt my breath quickening with excitement as I approached. I was now entering the domain of Mildred Bannerman: chemistry mistress ... acquitted murderess ... Faerie Queene.

I could see at once through the window that Mrs. Bannerman was busy with the fifth form.

How I would have loved to join them, shoulder to shoulder, peering through safety spectacles at the lovely liquids, jotting down penciled observations, and inhaling the vapors of boiling and deliriously happy distillations.

But it was not to be: As a lowly fourth-former I would be stuck with general science, and would probably end up dissecting maple leaves—or snails. And with my luck, they wouldn't even be my favorite cone snails, those denizens of Australia's Great Barrier Reef, the effects of whose venom are so disgusting that they can only be fully described in medical texts with plain brown wrappers.

I lingered, longingly, reluctant to tear myself away from this glimpse of Paradise.

My eyes scanned the room, drinking it in, memorizing every detail.

But wait!

What was that object on a side bench—just there, to the left?—so strange, and yet so familiar: a black box the length of a yardstick, no more than eight or ten inches deep.

A hydrogen spectrophotometer! Could it possibly be?

My heart gave a joyful leap in its cage of ribs.

Not just any hydrogen spectrophotometer, but by all that was sacred, a Beckman model DU if I was not mistaken! I had seen a photograph of one in the pages of *Chemical Abstracts & Transactions*. This baby, I knew, could see and analyze blood and poisons well into the ultraviolet portion of the spectrum.

And look—just there in an alcove!

That large vertical tube, so like a silver stovepipe, and connected by a black umbilical cable to a squat desk swarming with meters and gauges—was it not an electron microscope?

Good lord! There were barely a handful of these things in the world!

Aunt Felicity had told me outright that Miss Bodycote's Female Academy was well-endowed financially, and she had been right.

Holy Halifax, had she been right!

I realized with a start I was licking my lips, perhaps even drooling a little, and quickly wiped my mouth dry on my sleeve.

How I envied these girls on the other side of the windowed door. I'd have given half my heart—no, the whole of it—to be among them.

But I didn't dare intrude. A chemistry class was a sacred session and . . . well, you don't barge in on prayers, do you?

I was about to steal away when a voice behind me said, "What are you up to, girl?"

I spun round and nearly tripped over her. I hadn't heard her coming, and the reason for this was easy enough to spot: The hard rubber tires of her wheelchair had allowed her to float along the floor in utter silence.

I gaped, not knowing what to say. In fact, I'm afraid I stared openly at this sinister apparition.

For a moment, I thought I had bumped into Edward G. Robinson: the unnervingly froggish face and the thick lips turned down at the corners like blankets, the head too big for the squat body, the black menacing eyes under black, arched brows, fixing me with their relentless gaze through thick spectacles . . . almost as if—

"Well, girl? What do you have to say for yourself?"

I couldn't find words. I could only stand goggling at this curious wheeled creature and her fittings. Polio, I guessed, but I couldn't be sure. How I wished Dogger was here to suggest a diagnosis.

The chair was equipped with a sort of hinged shelf or desk in the front, like a baby's high chair, which was cluttered with all the necessities of a life on wheels: paper, ink, pen, letter opener, stamps, a box of paper tissues, another of throat lozenges, matches, a package of cigarettes (Sweet Caporal: the same brand that Fabian smoked), a china cup and saucer, and, incredibly, what I guessed to be a large teapot under a quilted cozy: a Brown Betty, by the size of it.

"Well? Haven't you a tongue?"

"Yes," I managed.

"Yes, *Miss Moate*," she said.

"Yes, Miss Moate," I echoed.

"I asked you what you were up to. Favor me with a reply, if you please."

"Nothing . . . Miss Moate," I said.

"Nonsense! You were tampering with the doorknob of my laboratory. I saw you."

Her eyes had never left mine for an instant, and now they were crinkling at the corners, as if she had amused herself by catching me up in a particularly clever trap.

"I—I was just looking—"

"You were spying on me! Admit it."

"No, Miss Moate. I was just looking—at the skulls."

"You have some specific interest in skulls, do you? Is that it?"

I could have been truthful and said yes, but I didn't. Actually, I was keen on skulls, but this was hardly the time to say so.

"I'd never seen a moose before," I said, letting my lower lip tremble a little. "We don't have them in England, you see, and—"

As if it were a robot appendage, her arm reached for the cozy, lifted it, and poured a cup of steaming tea: valerian, by the cheesy smell of it.

I took the distraction as an opportunity to change the subject.

"I'm Flavia de Luce," I said, as if that explained everything. Perhaps she had already been briefed on my background, and the mere mention of my name would be all that was required. "I'm a new girl," I added, almost wishing it were true.

"I know well enough who you are," she said. "You're the daughter of Harriet de Luce, and I might as well tell you, that cuts no ice with me whatsoever."

Oh! The things I could have said to her—the clever retorts I could have made.

But I held my tongue.

Was it fear?

Or could maturity be setting in?

"No, Miss Moate," I said, and that seemed to be the right reply.

Much in little.

Multum in parvo.

"I taught your mother, you know," she said, still fixing me with her gimlet eye. "And I shall teach you."

Was this a promise? Or a threat?

"Yes, Miss Moate," I said dutifully.

When you're in the front lines, you have to learn fast, even if it's only to surrender.

Or appear to.

With an unnerving squeak of tires on hardwood, her hands clawing at the wheels, she spun round on her axis and trundled herself away, growing smaller and smaller as she went in much the same way as the characters do at the end of an animated cartoon, until she disappeared in the distance.

Did I imagine it, or had I heard a little *"Pop!"* at the end of the hall?

·TEN·

I THINK IT WAS Aristotle who first said that Nature abhors a vacuum. Others, such as Hobbes, Boyle, and Newton, climbed onto Aristotle's soapbox at a much later date. But for all their collective brains, these brilliant boys got it only half right. Nature *does* abhor a vacuum, but she equally abhors pressure. If you stop to think for even a second, it should be obvious, shouldn't it?

Give Nature a vacuum and she will try to fill it. Give her localized pressure and she will try to disperse it. She is forever seeking a balance she can never achieve, never happy with what she's got.

I am not only surprised, but proud, to be the first to point this out.

There are times when my personal pressure is mounting that I crave a vacuum to counteract it. One thing was perfectly clear: I was going to get no peace and quiet in Edith

Cavell. No privacy, no time to think, no place of my own where I could come and go as I pleased.

In short, I was in dire need of a bolt-hole.

Where, I asked myself, is the one place that the inhabitants of a bustling academy are least likely to go?

And the answer came at once, as if sent down on a mental lightning bolt from Heaven. It wasn't carved on a stone tablet, but it might as well have been.

The laundry.

Of course!

The laundry was a detached hut of painted brick. A faint humming came from within and a column of steam rose from a tall brick chimney into the autumn air.

I pushed the door open and stepped inside.

The place was like Dante's *Inferno*, but with plumbing—a vast steaming cavern. The heat of the gargantuan washing and drying machines swept over me in a wave, almost knocking me off my feet, and the noise was infernal: a hissing, clanking clatter of machinery gone mad.

Why had I thought I'd ever find a quiet haven here?

Like a dark castle looming over a medieval village in a valley, an enormous boiler at the end of the single large room overshadowed the place, looming above the deep sinks, the scattered mangles and presses, the wringers and the sewing machines alike. The high roof was crisscrossed with steam pipes, all wrapped like mummies in eternal-looking bandages.

The air smelled of steam, soap, washing soda, and starch,

their odors floating uneasily upon a faint background reek of scorched bedsheets.

A little woman in a gray uniform, with her grayish-red hair in a net, was busily sorting nightgowns into two piles.

So much for solitude. I needed to change my plans this very instant.

It had been ever so long since I had last made use of my "little girl lost" demeanor, and I must say that it was like pulling on a cozy old cardigan to arrange my face and body: shoulders slightly hunched (check), hands arranged in a wringing position (check), hair tousled (check), eyes rubbed a little to make them red and watery, then widened and set to shifting nervously from side to side (check), voice up half an octave: "Hello?" "Hello?" (check), toes turned in, knees together, a touch of the trembles: check, check, and check.

"Excuse me, please, Miss." I put on my tiniest voice.

She paid me not the slightest attention.

I crossed the floor and tugged at her sleeve.

She leaped with surprising agility quite high into the air.

"Gaw blazes!" she shouted. "Who the dickens are you, and what the devil do you want?"

"Please, miss, I'm sorry," I began.

"Spit it out! Who are you? What's your name?"

"De Luce," I told her. "Flavia. I'm in the fourth form."

"I don't care if you're in the Forty-eighth Highlanders. You oughtn't to be in here. You're not allowed."

"Please, miss, I'm sorry," I said. "I've lost my best handkerchief. Miss Fawlthorne is going to kill me if I don't find it. I think I left it in the pocket of my dressing gown."

"Ha!" the woman said. "She thinks she left it in the pocket of her *dressing gaywn*, Sal. Did you hear that? *Dressing gaywn*, fancy!"

I hadn't noticed the second woman, who was operating a steam pressing-machine in a brick alcove. Her round red face stared out of a cloud of hissing steam as if she were a bodiless head suspended in midair like the Wizard of Oz.

"Dressing gaywn!" she shrieked in a voice that told me she was the junior of the two. She was trying to impress her superior by laughing too loudly at her jokes.

I knew the type all too well.

"Dressing gaywn!" she shrieked again, gasping for breath, wrapping a wet strand of hair round her forefinger and tugging playfully at it as if it were the pin of a monster hand grenade.

For a fraction of a second, my hopes were up, thinking her head might explode. But no such luck.

"I expect she means 'bawthrobe,' Marge. Ask her if she means 'bawthrobe.'"

Marge's eyes rounded on me.

"Yes, please, miss," I said. "She's right: That's what I meant."

Marge's tongue was rolling busily about inside her cheek, rooting out thoughts—or perhaps in search of something to eat.

"What color was it?" she demanded suddenly.

"Yellow and black," I said. I remembered that some of the girls at Little Commons had been wearing their dressing gowns, all of them in the school colors.

"Yellow and black!" Marge hooted. "Listen to her, Sal! Yellow and black she says!"

Sal slapped her leg and pretended to be on the verge of apoplexy. "The *hankie*, dimwit, not the dressing gown—oh, I beg your pardon, *bawthrobe* is what I meant to say."

"Please, miss, it was blue, miss," I said. "Periwinkle blue."

I would play along as if I were a serf in their little kingdom until—

"It's blue, Sal. Think of it! A *periwinkle blue* hankie!"

"Well, la-di-da!" Sal said, mincing, and they were both off again in showy laughter.

It was obvious that the girls of Miss Bodycote's didn't often come to the laundry. Marge had said as much: We weren't allowed.

All the better for my purposes.

When she had recovered somewhat from her hysterics, Marge stood staring into my eyes as if she could look clear through them into my very soul—as if she saw something that no other human being could see.

"Well, let's just have a wee look then," she said, softening suddenly. "What do you think, Sal, shall we have a wee look?"

"A wee look couldn't hurt, Marge," she said, drying her eyes on the corner of a long white tablecloth, "so long as it's just this *once*."

That did it. They were off again instantly into gales of laughter.

Marge tripped off to a large table half hidden by a partition, delicately holding up the hem of her skirt with dainty fingers, like a dairymaid who had not been given enough lines in a stage play. She and Sal began rummaging through a couple of canvas sacks, and although I couldn't make out their words, I could hear the two of them exchanging low, tittering remarks.

I took advantage of the lull to look round the room.

Overhead, crisscrossed by metal walkways, pipes, tubes, ducts, and hoses ran everywhere in an intestinal tangle of water, steam, and air. From below, it seemed like a whole vast aerial world that simply cried out for exploration.

It was like standing in Captain Nemo's submarine, or the belly of an iron whale.

Except for a large calendar advertising Maple Leaf soap flakes, and a board with a row of nails, which was partially hidden behind the door, the whitewashed walls were oddly bare. Upon the nails hung three keys, each attached to a wooden disc by a silver ring.

One of these was crudely marked in ink with the initial "M," another with the letter "S."

The third key's disc, worn smooth and oil-stained, bore an almost illegible "K."

I pocketed it without a moment's hesitation, reasoning that those marked "M" and "S" belonged to Marge and Sal. The third key obviously belonged to a person with dirty hands: not someone who worked all day with their hands in soap.

A caretaker, probably: a jack-of-all-trades whose name began with "K"—"Keith," possibly.

No, not Keith: A caretaker would never be addressed as

an equal, and certainly not by the likes of Miss Fawlthorne. The "K" must be a surname.

So it couldn't be Mr. Tugg, the handyman, for obvious reasons.

Kennedy, perhaps, or Kronk . . . or Kopplestone.

But it was useless to speculate.

At any rate, I knew that if I pinched Marge's key, or Sal's, it would be missed before the end of the day, while with any luck, the third one might just belong to someone who took it only when needed, and even then, only occasionally.

It was a risk I would have to run.

"No hankies," Marge said suddenly at my elbow, startling me. "Periwinkle blue or otherwise. So buzz off."

Buzz off?

It was obvious that whatever milk of human kindness had flowed briefly in the woman's veins had evaporated as quickly as it had appeared.

The more I dealt with adults, the less I wanted to be one.

"Thank you anyway," I said. "I'm sorry to have bothered you. And now, I mustn't keep you from your nightshirts and knickers."

And I marched out the door with my head held high.

"Yoo-hoo! Flavia," a voice called. "I've been looking for you everywhere."

It was Van Arque, of course. She was sitting like Humpty Dumpty on the short stone wall that shielded the wash yard from the hockey field, kicking her heels.

"Ah!" I said. "The ubiquitous Van Arque."

"Ubiquitous" was another word I had picked up from my sister Daffy, and it meant someone who was always everywhere, and not in a nice way, either.

"You'd better hustle your bustle," she said, vaulting down from her perch and glancing at an imaginary wristwatch. "Mrs. Bannerman wants to see you."

By the time I reached the chemistry laboratory, my heart was pounding like a pile driver. What could the notorious Mrs. Bannerman want with me?

"Come in, Flavia," she called as I hesitated at the door, trying to catch my breath.

Did she possess some kind of supernatural antennae with which she had detected my presence?

I shuffled into the lab, doing my darnedest not to gape at the wonderful equipment with which the room was filled. The electron microscope and the hydrogen spectrophotometer lurked in my peripheral vision like great dark gods that must not, on any account, be looked at—not even glanced at—directly.

"Come in, Flavia," she repeated, patting the seat of a tall lab stool.

I climbed up onto it and tried to settle myself. Mrs. Bannerman remained standing.

"Well, what do you make of us so far?" she asked.

I couldn't think of an answer, so I shrugged.

"It's like that, is it?" She laughed.

In the presence of this poisoner—yes, I'm afraid that's

the way I thought of her, acquitted or not—I had been struck dumb. Words died in my throat as if they had been steeped in belladonna and perished in my craw.

It was mortifying. I had never in my life, so far as I could remember, been stuck for words. It was as unlikely as if the Atlantic was stuck for water. And yet—

Mrs. Bannerman threw out a lifeline. "I've had a little talk with Miss Fawlthorne," she said, "and we have come to the conclusion that it would be beneficial to admit you to chemistry classes."

What!

"In spite of the fact that you are, technically, only a fourth-former."

Were my ears deceiving me? Chemistry classes, had she said?

I must have looked like a haddock, my mouth opening and closing with nothing coming out but air.

"But—" she went on.

Crikey! There's always a "but," isn't there? As sure as there's bones in a blowfish breakfast.

"But—your admission will depend on your ability to pass a proficiency test. Miss Fawlthorne tells me that she has already given you a written assignment, the result of which she has not yet evaluated. She has left it to me to administer the oral component."

I gulped. Coming from someone with Mrs. Bannerman's history, these were strong—perhaps even deadly—words.

"Are you ready?" she asked brightly.

I nodded, still stricken for words.

"Very well," she said, "now, then—"

I held my breath. In the great silence that followed, I could hear the wheels of the universe turning.

"Emil Fischer," she said suddenly. "What can you tell me about him?"

"Professor of chemistry at Erlangen, Würzberg, and Berlin," I blurted. "He won the Nobel Prize in 1902."

"And?"

"He was a genius! He demonstrated that the rosaniline dyes were derived from triphenylmethane."

"Yes?"

"He was the first to work out the formula for caffeine and uric acid. He synthesized fructose and glucose, and demonstrated the way in which the formulae of the stereo-isomeric glucoses could be deduced, which confirmed independently van't Hoff's theory of the asymmetric carbon atom, and opened the way to a study of fermentation: decomposition!"

"Go on."

Go on? I was just getting started.

"He also discovered how the chemical reactions of proteins worked in living organisms, and how caffeine, xanthine, hypoxanthine, guanine, uric acid, and theobromine all shared the same nitrogenous parent substance, purine."

"Theobromine?"

"$C_7H_8N_4O_2$. Its name means Food of the Gods."

"Is that all?"

I wanted desperately to mention the fact that Emil Fischer's father had once said, of his son, "The boy is too dumb to be a businessman; he should go to school," but I didn't want to push my luck.

"Well," I admitted, with a sheepish grin, "I have his signed photograph stuck to my dressing table, back home in England. He was a great friend of my late Uncle Tarquin."

Mrs. Bannerman smiled as she reached out and touched my hand. "You'll do, Flavia de Luce," she said.

· E L E V E N ·

So there it was. From now on, I would be taking regular chemistry classes with the fifth and sixth forms. A tricky schedule had been worked out which would allow me, with a certain amount of sprinting, to get from class to class by the skin of my teeth. It was like embarking upon a long railway journey with changes at every station and only seconds to spare between trains.

"You'll manage," Mrs. Bannerman had told me, and she was right.

As the days went on, I found myself actually looking forward to the mad dash between classes. In some vague and inexplicable way, it made me feel wanted.

My presence was required here, now, at this very moment, and then, suddenly, it was required somewhere else, and off I would bolt.

Van Arque had begun referring to me as "Lightning de

Luce," but I did not encourage it. "School nicknames stick like shite to a shoe," Daffy had once told me. "There are old men being loaded into their coffins even as we speak, whose friends, up until yesterday, still called them 'Icky' or 'Toodles'—or 'Turnips.' "

I remembered that Shakespeare had once written "That which we call a rose, by any other name would smell as sweet," but even the Great Bill himself must have forgotten the cruel and indelible labels that could be attached by fellow students. I couldn't help wondering what his own schoolmates had called him. "Quilliam"? "Shakey"?

Or even worse.

This is what I was thinking as I stood on my head in bed, my heels against the wall. I had discovered almost by accident that an inverted posture improved my thought processes because of increased blood circulation to my brain.

The few times I had to myself were those precious hours of darkness between awakening and having to get up: the only hours when I could luxuriate in being alone.

I had not forgotten the body in the chimney. It was simply that there had been no time to think about its blackened bones and clutching fingers, at least until now.

Somewhere in the recesses of my brain, a memory was shaken loose and fell with a *"clunk!"* into my consciousness.

The metal medallion! I had taken it from the corpse's hand and shoved it into my pocket.

I let my legs fall and flipped out of bed onto the floor. I reached carefully into the right jacket pocket of my school uniform, which I had left hanging—against the rules—on the back of a chair. Thank heavens Miss Fawlthorne was not here to see it.

The pocket was empty. I checked the other.

Nothing.

But wait! When the body had come tumbling out of the chimney, I was wearing the outfit in which I arrived in Canada: skirt, blouse, and jumper.

It was hanging in the cupboard.

I held my breath as I dipped my hand into the folds of my former clothing.

Thank heavens!

In an instant the little object was resting tightly in the palm of my hand.

Almost without thinking, I switched on the forbidden light. When I realized what I had done, I listened intently, putting my near-supernatural hearing to the utmost test. But the house was quiet as a country crypt. Not a creature was stirring, and so forth.

Except me.

In my hand was an object no bigger than the first joint of my thumb.

A magnifying lens would have been a godsend, but alas, alas!, I was lensless. Perhaps I could improvise with a pin-hole punched in a piece of paper . . .

But wait! I'd almost forgotten. Hadn't Aunt Felicity given me that utility crucifix? A veritable Swiss Army knife of prayer? The very tool I needed—and it was hanging round my neck!

As I reached for it, I offered up a prayer of thanks to Saint Jerome, the patron saint of spectacles.

I flicked out the pivoted glass and examined the object I was now holding gingerly between thumb and forefinger. I knew at once from its tarnished surface that it would require special handling. It would have to wait until I was alone in the chemistry lab and able to analyze it at my leisure.

The thing had a face, though—that much I could tell. And wings!

Yes—it looked *very much* like a wrapped body. It brought to mind the famous statue we had seen at St. Paul's, of John Donne, its onetime dean, who was believed to have posed for it in his shroud on his deathbed. It was also said to be the only one of the cathedral's statues that had survived the Great Fire of 1666. Even now, after nearly three hundred years, some of the soot smudges were still visible.

And like poor Donne's effigy, this little winged figure had been subjected to heat.

Coincidence?

I surely hoped not.

I was so intent upon peering through the magnifying glass that I did not hear the door open. I had forgotten to lock the blasted thing.

I did not know Miss Fawlthorne was there until she spoke.

"What is the meaning of this?"

She said it in the same, slow, cold, slippery, sinister tones that the snake must have used when speaking to Eve in the Garden of Eden.

With lightning reflexes, I slid the medallion into the

pocket of my dressing gown and wrapped it in the depths of my handkerchief.

"What have you got there?"

"Nothing, Miss Fawlthorne."

"Nonsense! What is it? Hand it over."

It was an all or nothing moment: the moment of truth, as bullfighters call it.

Or, in my case, the moment of untruth.

"Please, miss, phlegm," I said, pulling the handkerchief from my pocket and holding it out for her inspection. I arranged my features into a look of embarrassment. "I think I've caught rather a bad chill."

As added insurance I brought up from the very depths of my gizzard a convincing cough, and spat an imaginary substance into the crumpled handkerchief.

Again I offered it.

It requires a certain nerve to play at this kind of game: a kind of steely bluff combined with the innocence of a baby lily, and I must say that I was rather good at it.

"Put that filthy thing away," Miss Fawlthorne said with a look of disgust, before abruptly changing the subject. "Why are these lights turned on?"

I almost said, "I thought I was coughing up blood, and wanted to have a look," but something told me to quit while I was ahead.

"I got up early to write my report on William Palmer," I said, giving my mouth a final wipe and gesturing to my notebook and pen, which were—praise be!—lying on my desktop.

What a perfect title that *would make for one of the volumes of my autobiography when it comes time to write it:* Lying on My Desktop. *I must remember to make a note of it.*

Miss Fawlthorne said nothing, but stared at me steadily, the ruby pin at her throat rising and falling in slow, regular hypnotic waves. One breath after another.

"I cannot allow this to pass, Flavia," she said at last, as if she had come to a sudden decision. "Do you understand?"

I nodded—suddenly Miss Humility herself.

"We shall have a talk," she said. "But not here, and not now. Immediately after your gymnasium class this morning, I want you to go out for a long walk—alone—and reflect upon your disobedience. When you have done so to my satisfaction—well, we shall see."

The gymnasium was an echoing canyon with a floor on several levels. It had once been a chapel, with towering stone arches, sunken aisles, gilded organ pipes, and quaint grottoes, but now the saints and martyrs in the stained-glass windows had nothing better to look down upon than a clutter of vaulting horses, parallel bars, climbing ropes, and rings suspended on chains: remarkably like the torture chamber in a castle I had once toured in Girl Guides.

I felt even more cold and naked and doltish in the square-necked navy gym slip than I had the first time, as if I were the village idiot in a smock—or a cowering pawn on someone else's chessboard.

A shrill whistle blew as I entered and instructions were shouted. "Left arm upward . . . right arm forward . . . stretch! Right arm forward . . . left arm upward . . . stretch.

148 · ALAN BRADLEY

Head forward . . . bend . . . stretch! Head left sideways . . .
bend . . . stretch!"

I must be honest about the fact that I'm made extremely
uneasy by excessive noise, and that I do not care for
shouted instructions. If I'd been meant to be a sheep, I rea-
soned, I'd have been born with wool instead of skin.

I swarmed up a wooden ladder; dropped heavily to the
mat; gave out a little cry of agony; winced in the direction
of Miss Puddicombe, the games mistress; hooked my leg at
an awkward angle as if to check for a broken bone; mas-
saged my calf; and limped off to my room to get rid of the
clown outfit.

We'd deal with the paperwork later.

I was blessed to have been born with an excellent sense of
direction so that, even in the bath or the WC, I always
have a fairly good idea of which way's north.

Standing in the street outside Miss Bodycote's, I could
have gone either north or south but decided to strike off
north because it was my favorite direction. North lay the
North Pole, which seemed so much closer here in Canada
than it had at Buckshaw. Too far north, I knew, and you
run out of trees and into polar bears, but there seemed little
chance of that with trams—sorry, *streetcars*—clanging
away at the end of the block.

But I soon reconsidered. I was supposed to be thinking
about my disobedience, but instead I found myself realizing
that in street upon changing street of nearly identical
houses, I might well become lost. I was, after all, in a

strange city—face it, Flavia: in a strange *country*. Who knew what unsuspected dangers lurked just round the next corner?

A woman in a pink knitted hat came running out of a house whose windows upstairs were covered with bed-sheets and an unfamiliar flag.

"Are you lost?" she called out, after no more than a glance at me.

Could it be so obvious that I was a stranger?

I smiled at her (no point in aggravating the natives), turned on my heel, and went back the way I had come.

It didn't take much thinking to realize that there was much greater safety in sticking to the busier streets.

Follow the tram lines, my instinct was whispering into my ear.

A few minutes later I found myself once more in front of Miss Bodycote's, from which a buzz of busy voices floated to my ears. It was good to be outdoors. It was good to be alone.

I marched off to the south until I saw a Danforth Avenue street sign, at which point I turned my face toward the west.

It is a remarkable fact, and one not often commented upon, how hard it is to walk upon pavement after a lifetime of village streets and country lanes. Before I had gone a mile I made a pretext of stopping at what appeared to be a greengrocer's shop for a bottle of ginger beer.

"Your money's no good here, dear," the elderly woman behind the counter said after examining and handing me back my shilling. "Tell you what—I'll give you a bottle of cold pop just for the pleasure of hearing you talk. You have such a lovely accent. Go ahead, say something."

I did not like thinking of myself as having an accent: It was everyone else who had one.

"Thank you," I said. But I knew, even as I spoke, that "thank you" was not enough to pay for a drink.

"No, something decent," she said. "Give us a song—or some poe-try."

Other than a couple of comic verses about chemistry, which didn't seem appropriate to the occasion, the only poem that I could remember was one I had heard a couple of little girls chanting as they skipped rope in Cow Lane, back home in Bishop's Lacey, which seemed now like a remembered scene from a previous life.

I launched into it before shame could make me change my mind, and bolt. Striking a demure pose with my hands clasped at my waist, I began:

"*Poor Little Leo*
Was sunk by a torpedo
They brought him back in a Union Jack
From over the bounding sea-o.

Poor little Leo
He lost his life in Rio
They brought him back in a Union Jack
From over the bounding sea-o."

"That's lovely, dear," the woman said, reaching into a cooling cabinet and handing over a frosty bottle of Orange

Crush. "I had a nephew Leo once. He wasn't sunk by a torpedo, but he did move to Florida. What do you think about that?"

I smiled because it seemed the proper thing to do.

I was already on the street, strolling quickly away, when the words of the stupid rhyme came flooding back into my head: "They brought him back in a Union Jack . . ."

Why did they seem so familiar? It took a moment for the penny to drop.

Brought him back in a Union Jack—just like the body that had fallen out of the chimney!

Could there possibly be a connection?

Was someone—some unknown killer—murdering his victims according to the skipping rhymes of schoolchildren, in the way that Miss Christie has written about?

Daffy had told me about the mysteries based upon nursery rhymes, railway guides, and so forth, but was it even remotely possible that a Canadian killer had decided to copy those methods?

The very thought of it both excited and chilled me. On the one hand, I might well have part of the solution already in hand, but on the other, the killer could still be at large, and not far away.

I'm afraid I wasn't getting far with reflecting upon my disobedience. Miss Fawlthorne would almost certainly quiz me when I got back to the academy, and I'd need to have some kind of acceptable penitence prepared. But a body in the chimney isn't something that falls into your lap every day, and I needed now to give it my undivided attention. All the nitpicking at Miss Bodycote's had been so distracting that the flag-wrapped corpse had been forced to climb into the backseat, as it were.

By now I was crossing a tall limestone bridge or viaduct, which crossed a broad valley. I hauled myself up by the elbows on the rail and peered over the side at the muddy brown water that seeped sluggishly along far below. It was a long way down, and the very thought of it made my stomach feel ticklish.

I walked on, unwilling or unable to turn round and go back to captivity.

Captivity! Yes, that was it—I was the tiger caged in a zoo, longing to be returned home to its jungle. Perhaps I could escape, as tigers were occasionally reported to do in the newspapers.

In fact, I was already out, wasn't I?

·TWELVE·

PERHAPS I SHOULD MAKE a break for it. I could be well on my way to England before they even realized I was missing.

But other than the few useless coins in my pocket I had no money.

Perhaps I could ask a stranger for directions to the police station and throw myself, as a refugee, upon the mercy of Inspector Gravenhurst.

Or would he be obliged by law to take me into custody? The police station, however fascinating it might be, would be far less comfortable than Miss Bodycote's, what with the drunken prisoners in the clink, the noise, the swearing, and so forth.

I still needed to find a quiet place to sit down and think this through.

I had now reached the far side of the viaduct and was walking along a broad and busy city street.

And just like that, as if by some Heaven-sent miracle, a churchyard appeared as if out of nowhere, and I made for it at once. It was not *quite* as good as being whisked back to Bishop's Lacey, but for now, it would do.

No sooner was I safely among the gravestones than a great feeling of warmth and calm contentment came sweeping over me.

Life among the dead.

This was where I was meant to be!

What a revelation! And what a place to have it!

I could succeed at whatever I chose. I could, for instance, become an undertaker. Or a pathologist. A detective, a grave digger, a tombstone maker, or even the world's greatest murderer.

Suddenly the world was my oyster—even if it *was* a dead one.

I threw my hands up into the air and launched myself into a series of exuberant triple cartwheels.

"Yaroo!" I shouted.

When I landed on my feet, I found myself face-to-face with Miss Fawlthorne.

"Most impressive," she said. "But not ladylike, particularly."

Joy turned to terror. My heart felt squeezed in an iron fist.

I needed to get the upper hand, even if only for a few moments before this woman killed me and shoveled me into a shallow grave. Who would ever think to look in a cemetery for a missing girl? She had planned this to perfection.

But how could she be sure that I would come to this place?

"You followed me," I said.

"Of course I did." She smiled.

"But I didn't see you."

"Of course you didn't. That is because you failed to look in the right place."

My face must have been as blank as the side of a barn.

"Most people who suspect they are being followed look behind themselves. Consequently, the superior tracker is always *ahead* of her quarry. Now, then, have you done as you were instructed? Have you reflected upon your insubordination?"

"No," I said. "So you might as well go ahead and kill me."

And I might as well die defiant, I thought.

"Kill you?" she said, throwing back her head, laughing with delight and showing, for the first time, a complete set of small but perfect teeth. "Why on earth should I want to kill you?"

I shrugged. It was always better to let the killer do all the talking. In that way, you were able to gain much more information than you gave up.

"Let me tell you something, Flavia. You're right about one thing. I *might* have killed you just then. At least, I *might* have wanted to. But only if you had answered yes: only if you tried to convince me that you *had* reflected upon your disobedience. Only if you had spouted off some meaningless twaddle about how sorry you were; only if you had promised improvement.

"But you did not. You stood firm. You proved that you are indeed the person I believed you to be. You are, indeed, your mother's daughter."

It was more words than I had heard her say since we met; it was, in a way, as if the Sphinx had spoken.

A crow gave a rude "Caw!" as it landed in one of the trees, and regarded us in its hunchbacked way from the branch. How did we appear to a bird? I wondered. Two small, insignificant figures standing in a field of stones, I expect, and nothing more. I picked up a pebble and tossed it. The bird turned its back.

"Are you not at all curious about my reason for following you?" Miss Fawlthorne asked.

I shrugged again, but then thought better of it and said, "Yes."

"It is a simple one," she said. "It is because I wanted to be alone with you."

Again, a small flame of fear flickered up in my mind.

"But not for any reason you may think. The truth is that today, here and now, in this churchyard, your real training begins in earnest. You must speak of it to no one. You will appear to be, for all intents and purposes, just another schoolgirl—and a rather dull one, at that."

She paused to let her words sink in, fixing me with the same bright eye as the crow had done.

"Come over here," she said strolling across the grave-yard and beckoning me to follow. She pointed to a rather plain and unremarkable tombstone.

"'Cornelia Corwin, 1907–1944,'" she read aloud. "'Well done, thou good and faithful servant.' You'd think she was some wealthy family's chambermaid, wouldn't you—or perhaps a nanny? But she wasn't. She was one of us. Without Cornelia Corwin there would have been no successful evacuation of Dunkirk. Three hundred thousand men would have perished in vain."

She bent over and gently brushed away a dead leaf that had settled on the tombstone. "Do you understand what I'm saying?"

"Yes," I said, looking her straight in the eye.

"Excellent," she said. "We must understand each other perfectly. There must be no barrier to communications between us. Now, then—"

As she spoke, she began to stroll among the tombstones and I fell into lockstep beside her.

"Miss Bodycote's Female Academy is a house divided not by dissent, but by choice. The day girls know nothing of what goes on with the boarders such as yourself."

"The day girls are a front, you mean," I said.

"Flavia, you simply amaze me."

I glanced up at her proudly.

"You will be taught everything you need to know, but you will be taught it discreetly. You will be trained in the arts of genteel mayhem. Oh, don't look at me like that. The vegetable scraper, the cheese grater, and the corkscrew are often overlooked as effective means of disposing of an adversary, you know—even the pickle fork, in a pinch."

Was she teasing me?

"But the war has been over for ages," I said.

"Precisely so. You will discover that certain skills become even more essential in peacetime."

She saw at once the look of horror on my face.

"At Miss Bodycote's," she went on, "we encourage our girls in all aspects."

"But—" I said.

"In *all* aspects. Do you understand, Flavia?"

"What about poisons?" I asked, hoping against hope.

"Of course you'll be taught the more traditional skills," she continued, ignoring my question, "such as ciphers and code breaking, and so forth, as well as the more modern and inventive arts that are not yet dreamed of by even the most sensational of our novelists."

"My aunt Felicity told me I was to become a member of the Nide—" I began.

The Nide was the name of the hush-hush organization into which I was to be inducted, my reason for being in Canada.

"Shhh!" she said, reaching out and touching my lips. "You must never utter that word again. Never."

"But how will I know which of the boarders—"

She touched a gentle finger to my lips. "They will make themselves known to you. Until they do, trust no one."

"What about Jumbo? What about Van Arque?"

"All in due time, Flavia."

How easy, I supposed, it would have been at that moment to ask Miss Fawlthorne if she had heard anything about the identity of the corpse that had plummeted out of the chimney, and yet it was not.

A conversation between a person of my age and a person of hers is like a map of a maze: There are things that each of us knows, and that each of us knows the other knows, that can be talked about. But there are things that each of us knows that the other doesn't know we know, which must not be spoken of, no matter what. Because of our ages, and for reasons of decency, there are what Daffy would refer to as taboos: forbidden topics which we may stroll among like islands of horse dung in the road that, although perfectly evident to both of us, must not be mentioned or kicked at any cost.

It's a strange world when you come right down to it.

"You must learn not to ask unnecessary questions," Miss Fawlthorne went on, as if she were reading my mind. "It is a cardinal rule here that no girl may give out any information whatsoever about any other girl, past or present."

Her words had an eerily familiar ring. "Certain questions must not be asked," Aunt Felicity had told me, as we walked together on the Visto at Buckshaw. Now here it was again.

"You mean I need to deduce those facts myself," I declared flatly, taking care to make it a statement, rather than a direct query.

"Gold star," she said quietly, almost as if to herself, as she looked off, almost idly, into the distance.

A gentle wind stirred the leaves, and in it was a touch of coldness. It was, after all, autumn.

"There will be field trips," Miss Fawlthorne went on suddenly, "which will require a great deal of courage on your part. I trust that you will not let us down."

"Did Harriet undergo this training?" I asked.

Her silence was an answer in itself.

"I have arranged with Mrs. Bannerman to tutor you in

advanced chemistry. She assures me that your level of comprehension is far beyond expectations. You will begin work with both the electron microscope and the hydrogen spectrophotometer almost at once."

Yaroo! I couldn't believe my ears. This, truly, was Heaven with knobs on!

"And I don't mind telling you that it is entirely due to the influence, in high places, of the elder Miss de Luce that our humble establishment has been presented with the funds necessary to acquire such advanced apparatuses."

The elder Miss de Luce? Aunt Felicity! Of course!

Aunt Felicity had not taken credit for herself when she mentioned the latest scientific equipment with which Miss Bodycote's had been endowed, but now everything was suddenly, remarkably, brilliantly clear.

Miss Fawlthorne smiled, as if she were reading my mind. "So you see," she said, "in a way, if there had been no Flavia de Luce, there also may not have been, for much longer, a Miss Bodycote's Female Academy."

I'm afraid I could do no more than gape as the meaning of her words took root.

"We have a great deal riding upon you, Flavia . . . a *very* great deal."

What could I do? What could I say? The whole world had suddenly, and without warning, revealed itself to be far larger a place than ever I could have dreamed of. I was standing at the edge of a very great abyss whose further lip was so far beyond imagination that only faith could bridge the gap. It was, I suppose, the bridge connecting childhood with whatever vast unknown might lie beyond.

I know now that there is a very precise instant when one stands at that threshold at which the choice must be made: whether to remain, even if only for a while, a child, or whether to step boldly across into another world.

I did the only thing I could think of.

I seized Miss Fawlthorne's hand and gave it a jolly good shake.

"Excellent," she said. "I'm glad that we understand each other. Now, then—"

Was I imagining it, or was she now speaking to me in an entirely different tone? An entirely different voice?

"Your work with Mrs. Bannerman must, necessarily, take place in the small hours. You must not be seen to be spending an unusual amount of time in her company, although you may, of course, at your own discretion, occasionally feign stupidity as an excuse to return to her classroom for explanation or clarification after your regular chemistry class."

Feigning stupidity was one of my specialties. If stupidity were theoretical physics, then I would be Albert Einstein.

"But for now," Miss Fawlthorne went on, making a broad sweep of her arm which took in all of our immediate surroundings, "this will be your classroom. No one pays the slightest bit of attention to a woman and a girl in a grave-yard. What else can they be but mourners? What else can they be doing but grieving?"

We walked for a long time, among the tombstones, Miss Fawlthorne and I, stopping occasionally to sit on a bench in the sunshine, or to rearrange the flowers on a random grave.

At last she looked at her wristwatch. "We'd better be getting back," she said. "We shall split up and take different routes when we're four blocks from home."

Home. What a strange-feeling word.

It had been a long time since I had had one.

Home. I repeated the word in my mind. It was good.

And so we set off on the long walk . . . home.

Much of what we talked about I am forbidden to commit to paper.

·THIRTEEN·

THE ALARM WENT OFF with a muted clatter. I reached under my pillow and silenced the thing, then hauled it out and looked blearily at the time: It was three A.M.

Miss Fawlthorne had planted the clock in my bed while I was in class, just as she had promised she would. The thing was a large, self-important alarm clock with radium hands that glowed greenly in the dark, and a bell loud enough to be heard through the feathers of the pillow but not outside my room.

I stretched, climbed out onto the cold floor, and hurriedly dressed, taking great care to be mouse-quiet.

There had been several good reasons to assign me to Edith Cavell, Miss Fawlthorne had explained, not the least of which was to make possible my "Starlight Studies," as she jokingly called them; she had asked Mr. Tugg to oil the hinges, so that I was able to come and go in perfect silence.

Some of the girls had grumbled, of course, about a scabby fourth-former having her own room, but the story had been put about that for certain reasons I was not a fit roommate: flatulence, I believe, although I can't prove it.

For a time I was the butt of their jokes, but after a while they tired of it and moved on to fresher cruelties and easier victims.

Mrs. Bannerman was awaiting me in the chemistry lab. She had already drawn the heavy blackout curtains that had been installed to allow demonstration of certain experiments with light (but I must say no more), and to permit the showing of instructional ciné films in perfect darkness.

For three o'clock in the morning, Mrs. Bannerman looked remarkably fresh. Perhaps "vivacious" is more the word. Her hair was perfection, as if she had just stepped out of the salon, and she smelled of lilies of the valley. She reminded me a great deal of the young chorus girl Audrey Hepburn whom Aunt Felicity had pointed out when she took us as a rare treat to a West End theater.

"I knew her in an earlier life," my aunt had whispered.

"I didn't know you believed in reincarnation, Auntie Fee," Feely had said.

"I don't," she had replied. "Shhh."

"Good morning, Flavia," Mrs. Bannerman said brightly. "Welcome to my little kitchen. Would you like a cup of tea?"

"Yes, please," I said, somewhat flustered. The only other person who had ever invited me to tea was Antigone

Hewitt, the inspector's wife, who was now, perhaps, through my own fault, lost to me forever. She had not even turned up to bid me farewell, as I had so desperately hoped she would.

Perhaps she hadn't known that I was leaving. Had her husband not told her? But he himself might not have known that I was being banished. I might die an old woman without ever learning the truth.

All this was going through my mind as the tea steeped in the lengthening silence.

"You're looking very thoughtful," Mrs. Bannerman said.

"Yes," I told her. "I was just thinking of home."

"I do, sometimes, too," she said. "It's not always as pleasant as one expects, is it? Now, then, shall we get started?"

I was a bit shy of the electron microscope at first—reluctant even to touch it—but when Mrs. Bannerman brought up on the cathode ray screen the hairs of a louse, magnified nearly sixty thousand times, my reverent fingers were everywhere, caressing the thing as if it were a favorite pet. Wild horses couldn't have dragged me away.

"The first electron microscope in North America was built by a couple of students not far from here at the University of Toronto," she told me. "Before you were born.

"What we are now observing is the leg of a species of louse called *Columbicola extinctus*, or passenger-pigeon-chewing louse, which lived exclusively upon the body of that particular bird, which has been extinct since 1914. Why it should have been found a month ago, in the hair of a murdered clergyman in the Klondike, makes for a pretty little puzzle. Ah! I see that I now have your undivided attention."

"Murdered?" I asked.

What a peculiar feeling it was to be sitting in a locked room in the middle of the night, sharing a microscope with a woman who had herself been tried for murder. I wouldn't have thought the subject would come up so easily.

"Yes, murdered," she said. "I provide assistance to the police from time to time as a way of keeping my hand in. Although I earn my bread and butter by teaching chemistry, my professional qualifications are actually as an entomologist."

I hadn't the foggiest idea what an entomologist was, but I could already feel the look of admiration spreading across my face.

"Bugs," she said. "Including insects, spiders, centipedes, worms. I specialize in the ways in which their study may be used in criminal investigation. It's quite a new field, but also a very old one. Shouldn't you be making notes?"

I had been too entranced to do anything but gape.

"Here's a notebook," she said, handing me a red-covered secretary's dictation pad. "When it's full, ask for another. You may write as much as you wish, but with one proviso: Your notebooks are never to leave this room. They will be kept here under lock and key, but you may add to them or consult them at any time."

She didn't say "Do you understand?" and I blessed her for that.

"Now then: At the top of your first page, write this name: Jean Pierre Mégnin." She spelled it out for me

and made sure I got the accent leaning in the right direction.

"His two greatest works are *La Faune des Tombeaux* and
La Faune des Cadavres. Roughly translated, that means
Creatures of the Tomb and *The Wildlife of Corpses*. Sounds a
bit like a double-bill horror movie, doesn't it? Both are in
French. Do you have any inkling of the language?"

"No," I said, shaking my head sadly.

What had I been missing? How could such treasures
exist in a language I was unable to read?

"Perhaps Miss Dupont could give me extra tutoring in
French," I blurted.

I could hardly believe that I was listening to my own
mouth speaking!

"Excellent suggestion. I'm sure she would be, how do
you say, *enchantée*?

"Now, then, pencil ready? Mégnin discovered that those
creatures which feed and breed upon corpses tend to arrive
in waves: In the first stage, when the body is fresh, the
blowflies appear. In the second stage, the body bloats as it
putrefies, and certain beetles are attracted. As full-blown
decay sets in at stage three, and fermentation takes place,
butyric and caseic acids are produced, followed by ammo-
niacal fermentation, at which point entirely different
tribes of flies and beetles are attracted. Maggots proliferate.
And so, as you will have deduced, it is possible, by studying
the presence and life cycles of these various flying and
crawling things, to work out with some precision how long
the dearly departed has been dead and even, perhaps,
where they have been in the meantime."

Corruption? Putrefaction? Acids? This woman was speaking my language. I may not know French, but I knew the language of the dead, and this conversation was one I had been dreaming of all my life.

I had found a kindred spirit!

My brain was all aswirl—like one of those spiral galaxies you see in the illustrated newsmagazines: sparks, flame, and fire fizzing and flying off in all directions—like a dizzying Catherine wheel on Guy Fawkes Night.

I couldn't sit still. I had to get up from my chair and pace round and up and down the room like a madwoman simply to keep from exploding.

"Heady stuff, isn't it?" Mrs. Bannerman asked.

She understood perfectly the tears in my eyes.

"I think we'll call it quits for tonight," she said with an elaborate stretch and a yawn to match. "I'm tired. I hope you'll forgive me. We've made an excellent start, but you need your sleep."

How I was dying to quiz her about Brazenose, Wentworth, and Le Marchand, but something was holding me back. Miss Fawlthorne had forbidden me to ask any of the girls about another, but did the same restriction apply to the teaching staff?

As both Mrs. Mullet and Sir Humphry Davy have said, "Better safe than sorry."

And as for the little metal figure in my pocket—it would have to wait. I could hardly haul it out and begin heating it without a full confession of how I had come to have it in my possession.

Besides entomology, I was going to have to learn patience.

Back in my room, wrapped up in a blanket, I could not sleep. My head was filled with coffin flies, blowflies, maggots, and cheese skippers. The maggots were nothing new: I had thought of them often while dwelling on the delights of decomposition. Daffy had even read out to me at the breakfast table—"Knowing *your* proclivities," she had said, smirking—that wonderful passage from *Love's Labour's Lost*, where one of the characters says, "These summer-flies have blown me full of maggot ostentation."

It had caused Father to put aside his sausages, get up, and leave the room, but had given me a whole new appreciation of Shakespeare. Anyone who could write a line like that can't be too much of a stick-in-the-mud.

Dear Father. What a sad life he'd had. What a rotten hand Fate had dealt him: a prisoner-of-war camp, the death of a young wife, a decaying pile for a house, three daughters, and no money to speak of.

With Buckshaw now mine—in theory at least—some of the entanglement in which we had lived for as long as I could remember should have begun to be sorted out. But Harriet's will had raised at least as many questions as it had answered, and Father had been swept into the storm of legalities like a housefly into a tornado.

There had been some hope that a grateful government would intervene, and I had learned—thanks to my acute hearing—that Father had spoken at length with Mr. Churchill on the telephone, and for a day or two, his face had seemed a little less ashen. But nothing seemed to have come of it.

"It's exactly like *Bleak House*," Daffy had said on another day when Father had left the table without finishing his breakfast. "They'll still be jawing about the excise tax long after we all are in our graves with spiders nesting in our skulls."

And then, of course, had come the day of my banishment: the day upon which I had truly become an exile. With England and Buckshaw now more than three thousand miles somewhere across the sea, I had no way of knowing my family's fortunes.

I was alone in the wilderness.

And with that thought, I fell asleep.

Someone was chopping trees in the forest. A woodcutter, perhaps. If only I could summon the strength to scream . . .

But would he hear me? The noise of his ax was surely louder in his ears than any feeble cry that I might make. To make matters worse, a squadron of ships offshore had begun firing their cannon at some invisible enemy.

Boom! Boom! Boom!

I shoved my hands under the pillow to cover my head and banged my knuckles on a hard metal object. I hauled it out and held it up to my face.

It was the alarm clock, and its hands were pointing to twenty past eight. I had slept right through its ringing.

"Flavia! Open up."

I toad-hopped from the bed to the door, unlocked it, and stuck my head out.

There stood Van Arque, staring at me as if I were an apparition.

"Better get a move on," she said. "The Black Maria will be here in ten minutes."

Black Maria? What on earth is she talking about?

"Oh, and incidentally," she added, "you ought to know that you look like the wreck of the Hesperus."

I flew about the room, scrubbing the taste of dead horses out of my mouth with toothpaste on my finger, raking the sticky grunge out of my eyes, giving my hair a lick and a promise with the hairbrush I had purloined from Harriet's boudoir.

At last I was ready. Three minutes down and seven to go.

The bed had to be made upon pain of punishment, and what a mess it was: as if some madwoman in Bedlam had spent the night in it, tossing in a straitjacket.

Another three minutes.

As I stepped into the hall, the building fell suddenly silent, in the way the birds do in a wood that a hunter has entered.

I clattered down the stairs, making enough noise to raise the dead.

Miss Fawlthorne stood at the door, and as I approached, she swiveled and pointed with a long, forbidding finger to the outdoors, as if she were the ticket-taker for the ferryboat on the river Styx.

As if she had never seen me before.

An ominous vehicle stood in the driveway. I thought at first it was a hearse, but quickly realized that the thing was far too large. It was a bus: a matte-black bus with smoked windows and the heavy door standing open. It didn't have "Abandon all hope, ye who enter here" painted above the door, but it might as well have.

I put my foot onto the bottommost of the two steps but, because of the heavily tinted windows, and the fact that I was blinded by sunlight, I could make out no details of the gloomy interior.

"Hurry up, de Luce," someone growled, from out of the shadows.

I climbed up, the doors hissed at my heels, and we jerked into motion.

I tottered to a seat, going mostly by the sense of feel. The driver shifted through a seemingly endless number of gears, until at last he settled upon one that displeased him the least. By the position of the sun through the windscreen, I judged that we were now traveling east.

As my eyes accustomed themselves to the gloom, I looked round at some of my fellow passengers. Van Arque sat opposite, two rows back, her nose pressed against the window. Behind Van Arque, Jumbo was examining her nails as intently as if they were lost Scripture. And at the back of the bus, in the middle of the aisle, was Miss Moate, the science mistress: the woman who had accosted me in the hall.

Her wheelchair was lashed to the seats on either side by

a network of belts so that she seemed to hang suspended like a spider lurking at the center of its web.

I looked away quickly, flexing my neck in a complex set of side-to-side stretches, as if I were merely working out a morning kink.

Aside from the laboring engine, which sounded to be making much ado about nothing—a characteristic shared, I have come to believe, by all buses everywhere—we rattled along quite briskly.

We had soon broken free of the suburbs and were making our way along a two-lane macadamized motorway which snaked easily between green fields dotted with cows and hay bales. If the truth be told, it wasn't all that much different from England.

Electrical wires and telephone lines on both sides rose and fell . . . rose and fell . . . in long scallops, like the flight path of a determined woodpecker.

How far had we come? I tried to work it out in my head. The roadside speed limit signs allowed a maximum of fifty miles per hour, and a minimum of thirty in the settled areas: an average, say, of forty miles per hour.

Now, then: How long had we been traveling?

I thought back to my Girl Guides training in the parish hall when Miss Delaney had taught us to estimate time in stressful situations.

"One never knows when one may be kidnapped by Communists," she told us, "or worse," she added. "*Be Prepared* is more than just a motto."

And so we had been made to learn how to estimate time

while locked away alone in total darkness in the crypt of St. Tancred's, as well as while balancing blindfolded on a chair as a gang of girls, singing at the top of their lungs "Ging-gang-goolie-goolie-goolie-goolie watcha, ging-gang-goo, ging-gang-goo!," hurled tightly balled-up winter socks at our head.

I judged that we had pulled away from Miss Bodycote's about fifty minutes ago, and had therefore traveled, at a speed of forty miles per hour, approximately thirty-three miles. The calculation was a simple one.

It had become surprisingly warm in the bus and I was just beginning to think I might curl up on the seat for a catnap, when the bus suddenly shifted down through several octaves of grating gears and turned off into a narrow, unpaved lane.

The driver stopped, got out, and wrestled open a rusty metal gate, beside which was a ramshackle hut and a weathered sign that read: *Stop. Report to Guard.*

We crept through, the driver closed the gate behind us, and again the bus's infernal gears ground into motion.

Ahead, in the distance, lay the waters of Lake Ontario. I had seen it from the train, of course, but then it had been gray and sullen in the rain. Today, the surface glittered and twinkled in the bright morning sunlight like a vast plain of blue-green jewels, and a fleet of white puffy clouds floated slowly and self-importantly along overhead as if they were posing for a painting.

A number of tall radio masts, painted in alternating red and white sections, rose into the air ahead, seeming to sprout from a cluster of low, white, weather-worn buildings which nestled like chicks around an abandoned farmhouse of painted boards. As we approached them the road narrowed, and then ended—

Abruptly. We had come to a stop.

"Everybody out!" Miss Moate commanded in a loud voice, and I looked round to see her unbuckling her restraints. With remarkable speed she was free of her web and rolling herself toward the front of the bus. She came close to running me over.

I counted bodies as the students disembarked: ten, eleven, twelve . . .

I was the thirteenth.

"Ramp, Dawson," Miss Moate snapped, and from an under-floor luggage compartment, the driver dragged out a pair of wooden channels that he manhandled into position at the door. Miss Moate maneuvered her wheels onto them and without a glance to either side went barreling down so rapidly that she was propelled far beyond the bus and into the long grass.

But no matter. In an instant, she had seized the rims of her wheels, swiveled as neat as a pin, and was back at the door, glaring defiantly up at the disembarking students as if to say, "There! *That's* the only way to deal with the dragon polio!"

I was proud of her in a complicated sort of way.

"Line up!" she shouted, and there was something more than the sound of a drill sergeant in her voice.

"Single file—"

We shuffled.

"Right turn!"

Our shoes pivoted in the dust.

"Quick . . . march!"

And away we went in our panama hats, our pleated pin-afore dresses, our blazers, our school ties, and our tights, swinging our arms as we trudged off toward a distant em-bankment of weeping willows, looking, no doubt, for all the world like a dozen or so ugly ducklings on a forced march.

I felt we ought to be whistling some bright but defiant military tune.

·FOURTEEN·

WE WERE DIVIDED INTO two groups. The one into which I was placed—with Trout, Druce, Gremly, Barton, and an alarmingly red-faced girl I didn't know—was called, for obvious reasons, the Sixes, and the other the Sevens.

"Sixes in the shade!" Miss Moate called out. "Sevens in the sun."

"Divide and conquer," Trout grumbled. "They always do that to keep us from overpowering them."

Although she and Gremly were part of my group, they wandered off and stood under a tall elm, while Druce and her hanger-on, Trout, stood off to the other side, leaving me with the girl whose name I didn't know, alone between the two camps.

"De Luce," I said out of the corner of my mouth. "Flavia. I'm the new girl."

"I know," she whispered. "I've been dying for a chance to talk to you."

She took off her hat and slowly fanned her face to cover our conversation.

Who was she worried about: the lip-reading Druce, or someone else?

"It's about Brazenose—" she began.

"Which one?" I said quietly behind my hand, pretending to pick my nose. "Mary Jane, or—"

"Clarissa. Brazenose major. The one that disappeared."

Her face was becoming redder than ever.

"Are you all right?" I whispered.

"Of course. I've been holding my breath to make myself flush. That's why Moatey sent our group into the shade."

Here it was barely mid-morning and I'd already added a new weapon to my arsenal.

"What's your name?" I asked, even though it may have been forbidden.

She gave me a strange smile, as if to reprimand me, then said, "Scarlett. Amelia Scarlett."

You are a girl after my own heart, Amelia Scarlett, I thought. *Without even suspecting it, the whole world is putty in your hands.*

"Water!" Miss Moate called out loudly, clapping her hands, and we all turned our attention toward her. "Water is life. Remember that, girls, and remember it well. You can live without food and sunlight for a remarkably long while, but you cannot live without water. You must know at all times and in all places how to acquire water. You will be taught, therefore how to locate it, how to collect it, and how to purify it. Now, then . . ."

She glared at us, one at a time, as if daring us to contradict her, her eyes like little black searchlights. "Let us say that we require water here and now. Let us say that one of us has sustained an injury, and that boiling water is required at once for emergency surgery. Where shall we find it?"

Gremly's hand shot up. "In the radiator of the bus!" she shouted, grinning at us, pleased as punch to have guessed the answer straightaway.

Miss Moate nodded her head slowly, as if to say, "I might have known some idiot would suggest that."

"And what, pray tell, if the radiator is full of antifreeze?" she asked in a voice dripping with sarcasm. "Remember, Gremly, we live in a harsh northern climate, and not, as you seem to suppose, in the land of the bandaged pharaohs."

Some of us laughed dutifully. But others didn't. A dark image flashed on a screen in a back room of my mind— then quickly flickered out.

"The lake," Scarlett suggested. "We could bring water from the lake in buckets and boil it."

"It's seawater," Gremly interrupted. "The salt would make us sick!"

"It's not salt water," Scarlett shot back, fanning her face furiously, even more alarmingly red. "Any fool knows that the Great Lakes—"

"Girls! Girls! Girls!" Miss Moate shouted, wheeling her

chair round with surprising speed, charging into the middle of our little group—like a Roman chariot, I thought—and almost running us over.

I noticed now for the first time that the Sevens were standing in silence. It occurred to me that several of its members—Jumbo for certain, because she was head girl—had been through this exercise before, and knew perfectly well the expected answers.

Why, then, was she here? Why was she keeping quiet? Had she been ordered to? Was this whole stupid beanfest being staged for my benefit? Or for the handful of us who were the latest arrivals?

Which of us, then, were the players—and which of us the audience in this charade?

I decided to dig in my oar.

"Water may be obtained," I said, "by finding the lowest point of the terrain, constructing a condensation trap—"

My Girl Guide days hadn't been *entirely* wasted.

"Correct," Miss Moate snapped. "Bowles will demonstrate the correct technique."

Bowles? I didn't connect until Jumbo marched off down a slight slope to the west. Of course—Bowles was Jumbo's surname.

Miss Moate did not follow as the lot of us straggled off in Jumbo's footsteps.

At the bottom of a gully, Jumbo dragged a rusty garden spade from behind a tree.

"First thing to know: Be prepared," she said, and began digging. It was obvious—at least to me—that she had done this before, and at this very spot. The soil was unusually loose.

"Give us your mackintosh, Druce," she ordered, and Druce reluctantly handed over a tightly bundled waterproof packet.

"Druce is *always* prepared, aren't you, Druce?"

"Yes, Jumbo," Druce said meekly. "But be careful. My mother said she'd beat my brains out if I ruined it."

"No danger of that," Jumbo said, and everyone, even Druce, smiled as she began digging. Scarlett and I stood off to one side to watch.

"About Brazenose—" I prompted her quietly, keeping my eyes on the growing hole in the ground.

Scarlett's eyes went as wide as the dog's in the fairy tale. "I saw her last night," she whispered.

"What?"

The word flew out of my mouth before I could turn down the volume.

"Come on, you two," Jumbo said. "Stop horsing around and pay attention. This is serious. I'm not having black marks against my name because of you slackers."

Caught in the act. Think fast, Flavia.

I threw my hand over my mouth and turned quickly away. With my back to Jumbo, I rammed my middle finger down my throat and gave my uvula a jolly good prod.

The uvula is that little fleshy stalactite that hangs down from the back of one's throat, and its sole purpose, as far as I can tell, is to trigger a quick vomit when one is required on short notice, as it was now.

I spun round, took a couple of reeling steps, and threw up into Jumbo's condensation trap.

And Druce's mackintosh.

Just enough to be convincing.

"Sorry, Druce," I said, trying to look repentant. "It must have been the bus. Motion sickness, and so forth."

"Oh, you poor kid!" Jumbo said. "I'm sorry. I thought you were just clowning around. Honestly."

This was even better than I'd expected. Sympathy and an apology to boot.

I waved off her words gracefully and set off on unsteady legs for the closest tree trunk.

"Go with her, Scarlett. Fetch her a cold drink. There's a canteen in the bus."

And so it came to pass that Scarlett and I found ourselves propped comfortably under an elm watching the others clean up the contaminated condensation trap.

Which goes to show that the old saying is true: that just when things seem blackest, things often turn out for the best: the darkness before the dawn, et cetera.

"Now, then," I said, "tell me about Brazenose."

Scarlett was still gaping a little. "You're astonishing," she said.

"No more so than you, Amelia," I told her, realizing even as I spoke that, since my arrival at Miss Bodycote's, she was the only person I had dared address by her given name.

"It was you and your apoplexy that suggested it to me," I said. "No! Don't laugh—they'll be on to us."

Scarlett replied by moistening her handkerchief and

dabbing with great concern at my supposedly overheated brow.

"You fraud!" she said in a low but scandalized whisper as she added a sheen of counterfeit sweat to my forehead.

"About Brazenose—" I reminded her. "Feed me the facts."

"I saw her last night."

She paused to let the effect of her words sink in.

"Saw her? I thought she disappeared? I thought Miss Fawlthorne—or someone—murdered her. I thought she was dead."

"So did I," Scarlett said. "And so did everyone else."

For a few seconds, my mind felt like one of those fence posts you see in the news photos: posts impaled by flying straws in a tornado as easily as if they were pincushions— the sheer power of the impossible.

"Are you sure?" I asked.

"Of course I'm sure," Scarlett said, giving me the ghost of a dirty look. "I'd know her anywhere." She said this with such certainty that I knew she was speaking the truth.

"Where was this?" I asked. "And when?"

"Last night. Just after study. She was coming out of the laundry."

Good lord! This was like something out of one of Daffy's Victorian chillers, *The Lady in White* or something—the specter briefly glimpsed which then promptly vanishes.

I seized Scarlett's wrist and stopped her dabbing at my forehead, an action which had now become so mechanical that it seemed more likely to attract attention than to deflect it.

"Tell me," I said. "From the beginning. Don't leave anything out."

Fifty yards away, the two groups of girls had combined into one, and having filled in the corrupted condensation pit, were now, under Jumbo's supervision, rather lethargically digging another.

At the top of the embankment, Miss Moate had vanished from sight.

"It was just getting dark," Scarlett said. "I remembered I had left my hockey stick in the grass behind the net. Miss Puddicombe would be furious if I let it warp."

The very thought of the hatchet-faced games mistress made me shiver, in spite of the sunshine, which was now creeping under the tree as if to be with us.

"I had just come back across the field and was going round that bit of wall that sticks out beside the laundry, when the door opened. It was just dark enough that I saw the light thrown out onto the gravel path—and someone's shadow. I ducked back before she could see me. But it was Clarissa Brazenose—I'm sure of it."

"How could you tell, if she was no more than a silhouette?"

"I'd know her anywhere," Scarlett said. "Besides, she turned toward the light as she turned to switch it off, and I had a good look at her face. Honest."

Scarlett scratched a cross-my-heart promise on her blouse, and I believed her.

"And then?"

"She hurried round the laundry and into that little stone

passageway beside the kitchen. It goes clear through to the street."

"Yes, I know," I said. "Did you follow her?"

"Of course I didn't!" Scarlett scoffed. "I didn't want to be caught, remember? Besides, I was petrified. I thought I'd seen a ghost."

Here it was: ghosts again. The haunted convent.

"Do ghosts switch off lights behind themselves?" I asked. "Do they even need to turn them *on?*"

"Ha ha! Very clever, Miss Flavia de Luce. I told you this because your mother was supposedly such a brain. I thought you might be, too, but I can see that I was wrong. I wasn't expecting you to poke fun at me."

"I'm not poking fun," I reassured her. "I was merely thinking aloud. Don't be so touchy—I'm trying to help."

We were silent for a moment, each of us licking her invisible wounds. On the one hand, I did not like having Harriet slighted—not even obliquely—but on the other, I could sympathize with Scarlett, who, like me, had probably been bundled up and shipped off to school without so much as a "Fare-thee-well-and-mind-the-flypaper."

We were a couple of tender souls tossed together into a cement mixer.

"Look," I said, taking a chance and hoping I wouldn't regret it later. "We're a team, you and I."

I thought, just for an instant, of my other so-called partner, Adam Sowerby, even though I had never actually agreed verbally to a partnership with him. Adam was too secretive and, let's face it, too old to be trusted fully. At this very moment, he would be poking round some moldy, ivied ruin of an English castle pretending to be searching for seeds, yet all the while prying into Lord Somebody-or-another's activities during the war, and all for some dark master whose identity he refused to reveal, even though it could well be, in fact, my own aunt Felicity.

Complicated?

I should say so. Just the thought of it drove me crazy.

Scarlett did not reply. But what she did was this: She reached for my hand and gave it a coded squeeze: one . . . two . . . (pause) . . . three . . . just like that.

And so the deal was sealed.

"Now, then," I said. "About Clarissa Brazenose—when did you see her last? Apart from last night, I mean."

"It was the night of the Beaux Arts Ball, so it must have been June, the year before last. I'm quite sure of that because I was wearing my Cinderella dress with short sleeves and long gloves. I remember thinking how odd I must look creeping round the hockey pitch in that getup. Not that many people would see me, of course—not with the ball going on, and not with it being after dark. It must have been well after nine: twenty past, perhaps."

"The Beaux Arts Ball?" I asked.

"It's a tradition. Everyone comes to it. Faculty, staff, students, the board of guardians. Even some of the parents come as chaperones. They hand out prizes for deportment and stuff like that. I got one for washing and ironing."

"You're joking."

"No, I'm not. I'll show it to you some time if you don't believe me. It's a little silver-plated mangle."

"Thank you, but no," I said. "I'll take your word for it. Do you mean you saw Brazenose at the same spot last night as you did two years ago, just before she vanished?"

Scarlett nodded, biting her lower lip.

"But listen—why would Brazenose be in the laundry after dark? Two years ago, I mean. Why wasn't she at the ball?"

Scarlett shrugged. "Brazenose was a sixth-former and she'd been here for donkey's. She must have been sixteen. She could pretty well do as she liked as long as she didn't attract too much attention."

"Hmm," I said, my mind milling the possibilities. One would not ordinarily go to a laundry after dark. If one did, it would almost certainly be to pick up some piece of clothing that had been forgotten: an item that had not been retrieved during normal working hours; one that had been suddenly, and perhaps unexpectedly, required. Perhaps something had happened that made Brazenose want to run away.

But would a girl of sixteen, who had been at the school for ages, be likely to do that? Not unless something unthinkable had happened.

Perhaps she had gone to the laundry, not to pick something up, but to drop something off. But what could be so urgent that she couldn't leave it in her room until the next day?

"What day of the week was the ball held?" I asked.

"Saturday. It's always on a Saturday."

The laundry would almost certainly have been locked up for the weekend, which made it even more strange.

Could it be that Brazenose had crept off from the Beaux Arts Ball to meet someone?

And why the laundry? Why not the common room—or the great hall, or any of the dozens of other places where two could talk without fear of interruption?

"Did Brazenose have any particular friends?" I asked.

"No," Scarlett said. "She was rotten popular. She played badminton, squash, and tennis. She bicycled, knitted, sewed, sketched, and painted with watercolors. She was a member of the drama club and the debating society, and she was the editor of *The New Broom*—that's our school newspaper."

Was I detecting a note of resentment in Scarlett's words? And I couldn't help but notice her repeated use of the past tense. But perhaps that was unavoidable when referring to someone who hadn't been seen for more than two years.

"How did *you* feel about her?" I asked. Daffy would have been proud of me. It was the kind of bear-trap question that her beloved Sigmund Freud would have asked.

"She was all right, I suppose," Scarlett said. "She made the rest of us look bad, though."

And then she added, "In much the same way, I expect, that—"

But she cut herself off short.

"Yes?"

"Oh, nothing."

I licked the tip of my mental pencil and made a note: *Query: Brazenose resented for brains in general? Harriet and Flavia ditto?*

"And what do *you* believe happened to her?" I asked. A sudden probe without warning.

Again I thought how remarkably time can sometimes slow to a crawl: the wings of a bird in midair slowed to the speed of breakers on a beach; an arrow suspended in flight, halfway to the bull's-eye.

My mind flew back to the night of my arrival; to the flag-wrapped body tumbling out of the fireplace. To the skull detaching itself and rolling to a grisly halt at my feet.

Had Collingwood recognized what was left of the face? It seemed unlikely, given the condition of the corpse. But if she *had* . . . let's just say she *had* . . .

Had she told anyone?

We had still not heard, either from Inspector Gravenhurst or from the news reports, that the body had been identified. With all the radios that blared in dormitories in the early morning we could scarcely have missed it. Which meant either that the police were withholding the information because they were having difficulty getting in touch with next-of-kin, or that they didn't know.

And, come to think of it, I hadn't laid eyes on Collingwood since that horrific—but utterly fascinating—night.

All of this raced through my mind as I waited for Scarlett to answer.

She seemed to be having difficulty making her mouth move.

"I believe . . ." she said at last, her eyes as large and damp as peeled grapes, "I believe she—"

THWEE! THWEE! THWEE!

Three sharp blasts on a pea whistle came from the top of the embankment. Miss Moate, in her wheelchair, was making impatient "Come-here-at-once" motions with her arm.

Sixes and Sevens were dissolved as the two groups swarmed together and went scrambling up the slope. Under the elm, Scarlett and I got slowly to our feet. She put a solicitous arm round my shoulder, supporting poor, sick Flavia's weight, and we crept as clumsily as a conjoined crustacean up the embankment.

Halfway to the top, pretending to lose her footing and floundering for traction, she contrived to bring her mouth so close to my face that I could feel her breath hot upon my cheek.

"Questions," she rasped into my ear. "She asked too many questions."

·FIFTEEN·

LUNCH HAD BEEN BROUGHT in the bus and we picnicked upon pink bricks of tinned pork, boiled eggs, and Brazil nuts that looked like devil's toenails, those fossilized bivalves from the Jurassic period, all of it washed down with milk from a galvanized carrier that had stood in the sun for too long.

Druce and Trout had plopped down·on either side of me without invitation. In future, I decided, I would make it a rule not to be the first to sit. If Aunt Felicity were here, she would likely be pointing out that patience, to a point, provides choice. She probably had an elaborate mathematical formula to work out the optimum time to sit when in a group of thirteen.

How I missed the dear old girl.

I was wondering how Miss Moate, being wheelchair-bound, would fit into the equation, when I realized that Druce was speaking to me.

"I said, how does it feel to be a dog?" she repeated.

"I beg your pardon?" I asked, bristling.

"Don't make me chew my cabbage twice," she said. "How does it feel to be a dog? You know, D.O.G. Daughter of a Goddess."

Trout collapsed into the grass, cackling helplessly at the wit of her mistress.

"Ah!" I laughed, airily, I hoped. "About the same, I expect, as it does to be a D.O.B."

I left her to work it out.

Druce's face clouded, then brightened suddenly as she forced a smile. "Listen," she said, as if butter wouldn't melt in her mandibles, "I've been wanting to ask—are you one of us?"

"Us?" I summoned up and assumed Utility Mask #7: the Village Idiot.

"Yes, you know . . . *us*."

Was it my imagination, or did the word have a hiss in it?

I was aware, of course, that this might be an official test of my ability to keep a zipped lip when it came to the exchange of personal information.

"Come on," Trout blurted, "you're a boarder, aren't you? Just like us. You *have* to know."

Druce shot her a poisonous look, and Trout began furiously digging an unconscious hole for herself in the dirt with the end of a twig.

"Well?" Druce insisted.

"Well, what?" I asked. Village Idiots are not thrown out of character as easily as all that.

"Don't play the fool with me," she snapped.

If only she knew how close to the mark she was.

"I'm sorry," I said, throwing my open hands upward in puzzlement and hauling my shoulders up round my ears. "If you mean am I a pupil at Miss Bodycote's, or am I in the fourth form, then the answer, obviously, is yes. Otherwise I haven't the foggiest idea what you're talking about."

I should have left out the "obviously."

"Right, then," she said. "Just so we know where we stand."

And she matched her actions to her words by getting to her feet.

"Come on, Trout," she said. "Let's sit somewhere else. Something here stinks."

They walked with stiff necks, like a pair of Old Testament princesses, to the shade of another tree, where they sat down again with their backs to me.

"Argh," said a voice behind me. "Ignore those chumps."

It was Gremly, the gnomish girl I had seen at the Ouija séance in Jumbo's room.

She squatted beside me, plucked a blade of grass, and began to chew on it reflectively.

"I've been watching you," she said. "You're okay."

"Thank you," I told her, because I didn't know what else to say.

We sat in silence for a long moment, not looking at each other, and then Gremly spoke: "I can tell you're a person who enjoys her pheasant sandwiches."

The world stopped. My heart stopped.

Pheasant sandwiches! The very words Winston Churchill had spoken to me five months ago on the railway platform at Buckshaw Halt. The exact words my mother, Harriet, had mouthed toward the camera in the ancient ciné film I had found in the attic at Buckshaw.

Pheasant sandwiches: the secret words that identified the speaker as a member of the Nide.

"The phrase was chosen carefully," Aunt Felicity had told me. "Innocuous to the casual observer, but a clear warning of danger to an initiate."

Gremly had spoken it very matter-of-factly—almost too casually. Was she giving me a warning, or was she simply making herself known?

I tried not to appear panic-stricken as I looked round at the small groups of girls seated here and there in the grass. Had anyone noticed?

No one seemed to be paying us the slightest attention.

"I know *I* do," she prattled on, as if nothing had happened. "Quite a welcome break from your usual cucumber and soggy lettuce. Still, peanut butter and banana is my own favorite. Rather exotic so far north, don't you think?"

Could this possibly be the same creature who had crouched, mumbling over her words, at the Ouija session? If so, she was an absolute wizard of camouflage, and I was filled with admiration.

"Yes," I said with a smile, "pheasant is pleasant," and then we both tittered. Just two little girls picnicking in the sunshine, relishing all the millions of words that remained unspoken between us.

Again came the shriek of Miss Moate's infuriating whistle.

THWEE! THWEE! THWEE!

"Girls! Girls! Girls!"

Did the blasted woman do everything in threes? My mind boggled at the thought.

"Form a column—off you go. No straggling."

Her extended finger was pointing us toward the cluster of wooden huts that lay slightly to the south.

"Dah-dit-dah-dit," Gremly said, making the high-pitched sound of a ship-to-shore telegraph with her mouth. *"Dit-dah-dit . . . dit-dah . . . dit-dah-dah-dit."*

Even though I couldn't decipher the code, I understood the meaning by the tone of her voice and the rebellious look on her face.

Miss Moate shot us a sour glare, but said nothing.

At the huts, there was trouble with the keys, and the bus driver had to be sent for to open the door. As we stood waiting in the sun, Gremly raised an eyebrow almost imperceptibly and I couldn't help but grin. There are times when eyebrows speak louder than words. I knew as well as she did that either one of us could have had it open in a quarter of a trice blindfolded with both arms in plaster casts.

Two of the older and larger girls lifted Miss Moate's wheelchair across the threshold in a bizarre reenactment of the honeymoon rituals I had seen in the cinema. This time, however, there was no waiting bottle of champagne and no discreet fade-out: The inside of the hut contained not much more than half a dozen rickety trestle tables with folding chairs, a potbellied iron stove with a twisted pipe, and a bird's nest that had fallen out of the rafters.

The place smelled of ancient dust, of plaster, and of rising damp.

A strange uneasiness shimmered in the air.

For some peculiar reason I felt as Jack must have felt when, having climbed the beanstalk, he was forced to hide out, barely breathing, in the giant's kitchen cupboard. I know it sounds strange, but that's as close as I can come to describing the tense atmosphere of the place: as if something unseen were coiled . . . waiting.

Miss Moate opened several drawers of a painted counter and dragged out an enormous octopus of tangled cables, telegraph keys, and headsets, which she distributed as if they were the riches of King Solomon.

"*Dit-dit-dit-DAH!*" Gremly said triumphantly. "Didn't I tell you?"

I knew perfectly well that she was forming the letter V for Victory, the same pattern of four notes that Beethoven had used for the opening of his Fifth Symphony.

Without warning, a tidal wave of homesickness broke over me. My mind was suddenly aswim with images of Father, Feely, Daffy, and me (aged six) sitting among the hanging ferns in the study at Buckshaw, listening to those opening chords of doom on the wireless. I should have known that, as Daffy would say, they did not bode well.

But it was now too late for tears. I could never remember, in my entire life, feeling so alone. I thought I was going to vomit, and this time it would be the real thing.

I pretended to wipe a speck of rogue grit from my eye. I sat, shaken, at the table, unable to speak, and the taste of ashes in my mouth.

"In twos," Miss Moate said, and I grabbed at Gremly's hand before anyone else could do so.

We sat across from each other at a trestle table upon which someone with a penknife had carved "KILROY WAS HERE" and other things which I will not take the trouble to repeat. Jumbo handed out pencils and papers from a canvas knapsack that looked as if it had seen service during the Trojan War.

"I'll send, you receive," Gremly told me. "I've done it before. It will be easier this way." She handed me a card upon which were printed the letters of the alphabet and the numerals from one to zero:

A . —

B— . . .

C—.—.

And so forth.

I clapped the headphones over my ears, plugged them into a chipped enamel terminal box, and Gremly gave the key a couple of presses: *Dit-dit-dah-dit.*

I looked it up on the card and found that it was an *F.*

Dit-dah-dit-dit. L.

Dit-dah. A.

She was tapping out my name. This was easy.

I already knew what was coming next: the familiar *dit-dit-dit-DAH . . . V.*

I smiled to let her know I was getting the hang of it, and

picked up a pencil. Gremly gave her head an almost imperceptible shake.

Dah-dit . . . dah-dah-dah, she sent.

No. I was not to write it down.

I pressed the cold cups of the headset to my ears. No one else could hear the dots and dashes. At least I hoped they couldn't. But with six girls tapping away at the same time, it seemed impossible that anyone in the room would be able to pick out the sounds of a single key.

T—R—U—S—T . . . N—O . . . O—N—E, Gremly tapped out.

I read it at first as "*Trust noon*," but quickly realized my error.

She must have seen my puzzlement.

"*No one*," she sent again. "*Keep away from—*"

"Well?" Miss Moate said suddenly, slapping the surface of our table for attention. "How are you getting on?"

I nearly sprang out of my skin. Neither of us had heard her coming.

I tore off the headset.

"Gremly's just telegraphed my name, *F—L—A—V—I—A*," I said. "What jolly good fun!"

For an instant I considered bursting into Gilbert and Sullivan:

> "*Three little maids who, all unwary*
> *Come from a ladies' seminary*
> *Freed from its genius tutelary*
> *Three little maids from school . . .*"

But I didn't.

Miss Moate looked from one of us to the other, and without another word, moved on to lurk somewhere else.

"My turn," I said loudly. "Let me try," and we swapped sending key and headset.

"Where's Collingwood?" I tapped out slowly, picking the letters from the chart.

Gremly removed the headphones and placed them over my ears. It was an awkward way of carrying on a conversation, but it would have to do.

"Infirmary," she sent. *"Gone mad."*

·SIXTEEN·

THE SPATTER OF RAIN, which had begun as we left the huts, had now become a downpour. A pair of sluggish wipers swept sheets of water from the windshield, and it had become suddenly cold. My short sleeves were no protection and I hugged my arms against my body.

Gremly did not sit with me on the bus. Quite the contrary: She had gone far to the rear to sit in the shadow of Miss Moate, leaving me up front behind the driver, pretending to appreciate the beauty of the landscape, which was made up principally of tall elms in rainswept fields, glimpses of the lake, and the occasional wrecker's yard in which the rusting hulks of once-loved automobiles were piled like so many colossal steel ant hills.

Again the word "disorientated" flashed into my mind. It meant, essentially, having lost one's compass bearings, which is what had happened to me.

Cast out from my childhood home, banished to a strange land, and now isolated even from the low, gooselike gabble of my classmates, I was alone in the world, at the mercy of even the slightest gust of wind.

I needed to focus my mind on something outside myself—to regain the scientific view and so to resettle my soul.

But where to begin?

"Trust no one," Miss Fawlthorne and Gremly had each told me, and when you stopped to think about it rationally, that included even them.

I needed to seem to the faculty of Miss Bodycote's an apt pupil; to the other girls, an invisible bore.

There was only one way I could think of to achieve this with a minimum of fuss.

"Slowly, slowly," Fitzgibbon said, helping me up the stairs. I made my hand tremble on her arm as I tottered my way upward.

I had managed a small but convincing vomit at the curbside, which I was inordinately proud of. Miss Moate had insisted I report to the nurse—exactly as I had intended she should. A few more dry heaves on the stairs for insurance and I had won the toss, so to speak.

"Thank you, Matron," I managed.

"Don't try to talk," she said. "You didn't drink any of the groundwater at the camp, did you?"

The camp: That's what it was called.

I shook my head. "Milk only," I managed.

"Good," she said. "You've got at least half a chance, then."

Was she being what Daffy called "ironical"? Irony, she had explained, was a special class of sarcasm in which the meaning was the opposite of what it seemed. It was an art at which I had not yet become as adept as I should have liked, although it was high on my list of things to do.

Even recognizing it, though, was a major accomplishment, and I was quite proud to have possibly done so.

"The infirmary's in here," she said, leading me through a dark narrow passage that joined the front of the house to one of the more obscure wings.

At a white-painted door she jangled her keys noisily, as if she were warning someone inside that we were about to enter.

"Will the nurse be long?" I asked.

"The nurse is standing before you," she said. Spotting my bewilderment, she added, "*I'm* the nurse—or at least I was before the budget cuts. Nowadays I'm plain old Matron with three pairs of perfectly good white Oxfords lying unused in my portmanteau."

I nodded as if I understood.

"Now in your mother's time—ah, those were the days—we had a fully kitted-out dispensary and the authority to use it. Nowadays it's all Band-Aids and iodine and cod-liver oil. Shocking, but there you are. The War did something to the world, and we haven't seen the worst of it yet."

The door came open suddenly and she beckoned me inside.

The infirmary overlooked the hockey field, and would have been a pleasant enough place if it hadn't been for the rain. Curtains of green-looking water shimmered down the panes, giving the infirmary a weird glow, as if it were lit by phosphorus, which, oddly enough, made me feel more at home than I had since my arrival at the academy.

Fitzgibbon put a finger to her lips and pointed to a hanging curtain on the far side of the room. I could see, below its gatherings, the legs of a white iron bed.

"Collingwood," she whispered. "She's not doing well, poor child. I don't expect she'll be much trouble, though. She's sleeping the clock away at the moment."

As she spoke, Fitzgibbon was turning down the sheets of another bed at the far end of the room.

From a small glass cupboard between the windows, she selected a tentlike cotton nightgown that might have been worn by Wendy in *Peter Pan*.

"Put that on and climb in," she said, "and I'll see to you directly."

Like a magician producing a rabbit from a hat, she pulled a second ring of keys from somewhere about her person and, turning away, went to another glass cupboard that was tucked away in an alcove.

By the time she returned, I had flattened myself and pulled the sheet up to my chin.

"Temperature first," she said, and a clinical thermometer appeared in her hand. I noticed that it was one of the type invented in the seventeenth century at Padua by Sanctorio Santorius, but not perfected until 1867 by Sir Thomas Allbutt in Leeds: a clever device based upon the uniform expansion of mercury from a reservoir into a narrow, calibrated glass tube.

"Open up," she told me. "This will tell me if you've got a temperature."

I nodded dumbly as she shoved the thing under my tongue. I gave a little moan and rolled my eyes to look up at her appealingly.

So far, things were going precisely according to plan.

"Sorry," she said. "I know it's unpleasant, but we need eight minutes to get an accurate reading. Don't move . . . don't bite down on it. I'll be right back."

She crossed the room and went behind the curtain that hid Collingwood's bed. My acute sense of hearing told me she was fussing with the pillows and pouring water from a pitcher into a glass.

I whipped the thermometer out of my mouth and began rubbing it fiercely with the corner of the bedsheet pinched tightly between thumb and forefinger.

One of the many happy things about physics is that it works anywhere in the world. No matter whether you're in Bishop's Lacey or Bombay, friction is friction.

The red column of mercury was already beginning to climb—but not quickly enough. I could still see Fitzgibbon's legs below Collingwood's curtain, but I wouldn't have much time left.

Hold on, I thought. With its more abundant free fibers, my cotton gown might have a higher coefficient of friction than the linen bedsheet.

I put my hem to work.

That was better! As I rubbed frantically, the red column

was rising like billy-ho. It was already above 100 degrees on the Fahrenheit scale. I kept up the rubbing until I saw Fitzgibbon's feet begin moving toward the end of Collingwood's bed.

I quickly shoved the instrument back under my tongue and gave another little moan to encourage Fitzgibbon to take a rapid reading.

As she came into view from behind the curtain, I tossed restlessly.

"Easy," she said. "Don't bite down, remember? We don't want to lose you to mercury poisoning, do we?"

I should say we didn't!

Mercury poisoning was one of the most ghastly poisonings in the catalog of chemistry: the hellish burning, the itching, the swelling, the shedding of skin, the strangulation, the endless stream of saliva like a cow with pasture bloat, and, finally, the loss of bodily functions.

"No," I whispered weakly.

Fitzgibbon pulled the thermometer from my mouth and glanced at it. I could see her eyes widen.

"Mmm," she said. "A bit higher than I'd like."

I have observed that, unless it's normal, they never tell you what your actual temperature is. They'd rather leave it to your fevered imagination than tell the truth. Even dear old Dr. Darby back home in Bishop's Lacey had been evasive when I fell off the roof after my spectacular and widely tut-tutted Christmas fireworks display.

I rolled away and groaned as Fitzgibbon reached out to feel my forehead.

"I'll have the doctor look at you when he comes by

later," she said. "For now I'll give you an aspirin for your fever. Try to have a little sleep. It's remarkable what a little sleep can do."

I nodded and closed my eyes. The sooner I could get her out of the room the better. At least the doctor wasn't coming until later, by which time I would have done what I had come to do, and would be well on the way to the most miraculous recovery in medical history.

Was it wrong to be so deceitful? Well, yes, it probably was. But if God hadn't wanted me to be the way I am, He would have arranged to have me born a haddock instead of Flavia de Luce—wouldn't He?

As soon as Fitzgibbon was out of the room, I counted to twenty-three, then leaped out of bed and dashed to Collingwood's bedside. If I were caught out, I would pretend that I was delirious.

Collingwood's face was as white as the pillow, her long hair spread out round her in waves as if she were a mermaid underwater.

"Collingwood!" I whispered in her ear. "It's me, de Luce. Wake up."

She didn't stir.

"Collingwood!"

Louder this time. Although the infirmary was somewhat off the beaten track, I didn't want to attract the attention of anyone who just happened to be passing.

"Collingwood!"

I pressed my thumbnail into her upper lip, a consciousness test I had learned the hard way at a Girl Guides summer camp.

She groaned.

"Collingwood! Wake up! It's me, Flavia!"

One bloodshot eye came slowly open and stared out at me blearily.

"Wha . . ." she managed, and the smell of her breath made my blood curdle.

I recognized it at once: that acrid stab of chlorine embedded in an exotic aromatic odor—like a diamond in a dung heap.

Chloral hydrate. I'd know it anywhere. $C_2H_3Cl_3O_2$. Unmistakable.

I had once happened upon a box of the jellied red capsules in the bedside table of the vicar's wife, broken one open for a sniff, and added it to my store of chemical memories.

The stuff was, I knew, a powerful hypnotic.

If I were myself, I should have spotted at once how troubling Fitzgibbon's statement was: that Collingwood was sleeping the clock away. I could understand her being badly shocked by the body tumbling out of the chimney, but that was ages ago. How could she still be sleeping so much after all this time?

I should have thought of it sooner, but living in this *Alice in Wonderland* world had obviously blunted my usually razor-keen perceptions.

"Everything's fine," I told her, even though it wasn't.

Except for beds, curtains and windows, and a sink, the room was bare.

But wait! My eyes and my brain lighted upon the cupboard in the alcove.

In less than half a flash I was peering through the glass at the school's medical supplies. Band-Aids and cod-liver oil, Fitzgibbon had said. But there was quite a bit more than that, actually: gauze bandages, surgical cotton, tape and scissors, iodine, Mercurochrome, aspirin, mustard (for making plasters and poultices, I supposed), a folded sling, a white enamel kidney bowl, tweezers, rubber gloves, tongue depressors . . . all of it, unfortunately, behind glass.

I tried the door but it was locked. I let slip a quiet curse.

I could, in a pinch, break the glass, but that seemed a bit extreme, and besides, the noise would more than likely attract attention.

I had foolishly left my crucifix lock picks on the washstand when I scrubbed my face and neck: another proof that cleanliness, besides being next to godliness, could also be foolhardy.

A quick glance round the room showed that there was nothing from which I could quickly improvise a suitable tool. A bedspring might have served in a pinch, but there wasn't time.

My eye fell upon the glass cupboard from which Fitzgibbon had taken my nightgown. It was identical! Both white, both glass-plated. They had been bought as a pair.

I must have looked like a harpy in a tent as I flapped quickly toward the windows.

Let there be . . . let there be . . . let there be . . .

And yes . . . there *was* a key in the keyhole! My prayers had been answered.

Identical cupboards—identical keys . . . or so I hoped.

The key was cold in my hand as I flew back across the infirmary and, to my ears, anyway, the resulting *click!* was as welcome as a lost symphony of Beethoven.

In all these years it had never occurred to anyone that the key for the linen cupboard would also open the dispensary.

With not a moment to waste, I took the tin of mustard to the sink, turned on the tap, and waited for the water to run hot. I took the glass of water Fitzgibbon had poured for Collingwood, dumped it down the drain, and refilled it with warmish water.

Into this I added what I judged to be six teaspoons of the powdered mustard, which I stirred with the surgical scissors.

"Collingwood!" I whispered urgently, hauling her up with an arm behind her shoulders. "Drink this!"

Her eyes came open—both of them this time—dreadful upon mine.

"Drink," I told her. "You must!"

Somehow her lips attached themselves to the rim of the glass: like a bivalve trying to climb out of a swimming pool. She choked—gagged twice—and wrenched her head away.

All things considered, she was remarkably strong, but I was stronger.

I wedged her head back with the rim of the glass and dumped the liquid down her throat, struggling all the while.

It was not a pleasant task—something like trying to force-feed a bedridden grampus—but I persisted. In the end, I managed to get about half the stuff into her stomach, with the other half splattered equally upon myself, the bed, and the floor.

She was coughing and choking and sobbing, and through it all, her eyes blazed at me as if they were weapons.

I stood by with the kidney dish: a pillar of strength dressed in a Bedouin's tent. For just a moment I had a horrid flashback to being Balthazar in the Christmas pageant at St. Tancred's and being made to sing:

"Myrrh is mine, its bitter perfume,
Breathes a life of gathering gloom;
Sorrowing, sighing, bleeding, dying,
Sealed in a stone-cold tomb."

At first it seemed as if nothing was going to happen: the darkness before dawn, the calm before the storm.

But it didn't take long. Collingwood gave a couple of surprised hiccups, followed by a long sigh. Her face was almost placid, and then, suddenly, she gave a great gulp, her lips dragged themselves down at the corners, and up it all came.

I held her head as great gouts of the reeking stuff came gushing out of her and into the waiting kidney dish.

It was my own spur-of-the-moment vomiting at the camp that had given me the idea: that and the knowledge that a mustard-induced tossing of the cookies was the best—and perhaps only—antidote to poisoning by chloral hydrate.

Had Fitzgibbon administered a fresh dose of the stuff

under my very nose? Had she roused Collingwood enough to swallow a capsule or a spoonful of syrup, or, worse, to administer an injection by hypodermic needle?

I hadn't heard anything—but that would argue for the syringe, wouldn't it?

Why were they keeping this child asleep? Was it to guard her own sanity, or was there a far more sinister reason? Had she, for instance, seen too much? Was it because she had been caught making notes on the missing girls?

Collingwood fell back against the pillows, her face ghastly, her breathing only slowly returning to normal.

Whoops-a-daisy!

There was more where that came from. I barely had time to get the bowl into position when she was at it again.

"Sorry," she wheezed, gasping horribly.

A good sign—an excellent sign, in fact. Anyone who could apologize while puking still possessed a brain able to function at the highest levels of decency.

I patted her on the back.

"More?" I asked, solicitously.

She shook her head.

"Good!" I said, and I meant it.

I went to the window, opened it, and emptied the kidney dish outside, apologizing silently to the groundskeepers as I did so. I rinsed out the bowl at the sink and replaced it in the medical cupboard, which I locked, and returned the key to its mate.

"Stay quiet," I told her as I changed back into my school uniform. "Try to get some decent rest. But do me a favor: I wasn't here. You haven't seen me. You woke up, threw up, and suddenly you were feeling much better, understand? Don't let them give you any more medicine. If they try to, scream bloody murder—and keep it up: I shall hear you. All right?"

Her eyes were upon mine, huge now.

She nodded, and suddenly the tears welled up. I turned away. There wasn't a moment to lose.

I was almost at the door when she called out to me: "Flavia . . ."

I turned.

"The dead person in the chimney," she said, ". . . the flag . . . wrapped in the flag. I know her."

·SEVENTEEN·

THERE IS AN ELECTRIC silence that comes with shock: a silence which is intolerable yet which, in spite of that, you are powerless to break. I stood staring at Collingwood and she at me for what seemed like an eternity of eternities.

I walked slowly back across the infirmary, placing one foot in front of the other, plod, plod, plodding toward her like some relentless zombie.

"Tell me," I said, perhaps too harshly, because Collingwood burst immediately into tears.

"I can't," she sobbed, "I simply can't," and in an instant I was catapulted back to that moment she and the corpse had come tumbling out of the chimney. How shockingly I had treated her!

"Put a cork in it," I had told her, and pointed out that she was drooling, and all the while the body had been lying there before us, decapitated on the floor.

And who had harvested all the sympathy? "Poor, dear, lonely, unhappy Flavia de Luce," as Miss Fawlthorne had said, while poor, dear, lonely, unhappy Collingwood had been drugged and tossed into captivity.

Not only did it not make sense, it was rapidly becoming a nightmare.

By the time I reached Collingwood's side I was feeling more dreadful than I ever should have thought possible.

"Tell me anyway," I said, gripping her hands in both of mine, and now the two of us were quaking with tears.

"I can't," she whispered, squeezing tightly, and I saw in her eyes that she was telling the truth. In telling me that the dead body was someone she knew, she had already reached her limit. It had cost her dearly and there was, at least for the time being, nothing else to share.

What terrible kind of fear could so effectively silence the girl? Was the dead body an example of what happened to those who talked?

"What if I ask you questions?" I said, suddenly inspired. "That way you won't be telling, technically."

She shook her head and I knew that I was going to have to figure it out myself.

The sound of cheering girls in the distance indicated that the day's hockey matches had come to a close. If I were to get back to my room unnoticed, I'd better be on my way.

There's no better cover than a milling gang of rowdy winners.

I made my way back to Edith Cavell and locked myself

in. I was the fox gone to earth, and if they wanted me, they could jolly well dig me out.

I got out my William Palmer notebook, and by the simple method of turning it upside down and beginning at the back, created a new one.

The Characters in the Case, I wrote at the top of the first page, and underlined it.

I would list them alphabetically, since it was more objective.

STUDENTS

Bowles, June (Jumbo): Senior girl. Seems an all-right type. Dabbles in the occult.

Brazenose major (Clarissa): Has been missing since the night of the Beaux Arts Ball two years ago—in 1949.

Brazenose minor (Mary Jane): Frightened by the message of the Ouija board. Queries: (a) Why would she believe that the board was spelling out a message from the missing Le Marchand? (b) Was she convinced that the message "One of you knows my killer" was coming instead from her missing sister?

Collingwood, Patricia Anne: Impetuous. Keeps notes on the missing girls. Claims to have known the body in the chimney. She is now too terrified to speak.

Who is keeping her drugged? And why? Murky waters here.

Fabian: Nordic. Remote. Mysterious. Sells cigarettes.

Gremly: Jumbo's handmaiden. Tells me to trust no one. Goes to great lengths to appear cretinous but has, perhaps, the highest IQ in the entire school. (Present company excepted, of course: Mine is somewhere north of 137, so I ought to know)

Druce: School bully. Reads lips.

Pinkham: Ratted on Collingwood to Miss Fawlthorne for keeping a notebook on the missing girls. She believes Miss F. to be responsible. Must question her.

Scarlett, Amelia: Claims she saw Brazenose major coming out of the laundry LAST NIGHT (!) And yet Brazenose maj. has been dead or missing since the night of the Beaux Arts Ball of two years ago June (see above).

Trout: Druce's toady. Small, blond, and nervous. Spilled the Ouija board. Reason? Must question her.

FACULTY AND STAFF

Fawlthorne, Miss: Headmistress. Mentor and tor-mentor. I hardly know what to make of her.

Bannerman, Mildred: Chemistry mistress. Acquit-ted murderess. Wizard chemist and excellent teacher. Assists police from time to time.

Dupont, Miss: French mistress. La-di-da.

Fitzgibbon: Matron. Former school nurse. Has access to drugs.

"K": the missing key holder. Still need to find out who he—or she—is.

Marge & Sal: Laundresses.

Moate, Miss: Science mistress. Medusa in a wheel-chair, and like that Gorgon, all head and no body.

Puddicombe, Miss: Games mistress.

Rainsmith, Ryerson: Chairman of the board of guardians and despicable milquetoast, at least when it comes to:

Rainsmith, Dorsey: His wife. Enough said. Reads lurid detective stories, though.

So there it was: my cast of characters—my dramatis personae—like the heroes, the villains, and the bit players with their exits and their entrances, all listed neatly on the first page of a play by Shakespeare.

Was there a killer among them?

Of course my list did not include Inspector Gravenhurst or his assistant, Sergeant LaBelle. It was probably safe enough to discount these two as suspects, but I added them for the sake of completeness. As Uncle Tarquin de Luce once wrote in the margin of one of his many notebooks of chemical experiments: *Consider also the container.*

Wise words indeed, and ones I intended never to lose sight of.

Something was nagging at me as I read and reread the list: something just below the surface; something that remained maddeningly invisible, like the crystal ball I had once found hidden in plain sight in a running stream.

It was time to make use of a technique I had invented, which I called "word fishing." I would focus on one key word at a time, letting my mind fly wherever it might in search of associations. *Occult . . . chimney . . . Ouija board . . . cigarettes . . .*

The bell did not clang, the whistle did not blow, the penny did not drop until I got to *Scarlett, Amelia . . . laundry.* Scarlett claimed to have seen Clarissa Brazenose—or her ghost—coming out of the laundry just last night.

Although my mental fingers were tickling the belly of the thought in the same way that the late Brookie Harewood had once tickled the trout he poached on our estate, I could not quite grasp it.

Scarlett, Amelia . . . laundry.

Part of the technique of word fishing was to shift the attention somewhere else when the quarry was elusive: to think of something entirely different and then, when the unsuspecting thought nibbled again, to seize it by the throat.

And so I forced myself to think of Johann Schobert, the German composer who, with his wife, child, maidservant, and four casual acquaintances, died in agony after eating certain mushrooms which he had insisted were perfectly edible. Schobert had written the failed comic opera *Le Garde-Chasse et le Braconnier* (*The Gamekeeper and the Poacher*), from which Aunt Felicity had insisted Feely play selections on the night of my departure.

Perhaps only Aunt Felicity and I, in all the wide, wide world, knew the reason why.

And it worked!

Laundry.

The word poked its head out of its lair and I seized it. *Laundry.*

"Yaroo!" I wanted to shout.

Laundry. It wasn't that Scarlett had seen Brazenose major coming out of the laundry. No, that wasn't it at all. It was that Scarlett had been awarded a prize for washing and ironing: a little silver-plated mangle.

Had Clarissa Brazenose also been presented with a silver award: a small, tarnished little creature with wings that was, at this very moment, burning a hole in my pocket?

I reached in and fished it out, shivering a little at the very thought of where it had been and what it had been through.

I examined it again through my magnifying glass, this time more carefully.

As I had noticed the first time, it seemed to have wings and a face, but the thing was so tarnished that it was difficult to make out the details. Gruesomely suggestive, though, of a fallen angel that had struck the earth at the blazing speed of an aviator whose parachute had failed to open.

At the top of the head was a tiny perforation, as if for a string or a ring to pass through.

It had been worn round the neck! A medallion. A religious charm. An angel. No, an archangel! Saint Michael the Archangel.

The chain of deductions came as quickly as that.

Why hadn't I noticed it sooner? The folded apex of the wings extended well above the top of the head. Only an archangel had wings of such dimensions. I had seen them often enough in the moldering volumes of art with which Buckshaw was littered—a momentary pang here—and in the great stained-glass window at St. Tancred's given in the Middle Ages by the de Lacey family.

Ordinary angels, I knew, all the way down to the seraphim and frankly incredible cherubim, had fluffy swansdown wings that sprouted from the shoulders: capable enough for domestic flight but nowhere near as powerful as the eagle wings of their superiors, the archangels.

This scorched relic, which I held in the palm of my now suddenly shaking hand, had belonged to one of the missing girls: Le Marchand, Wentworth, or Clarissa Brazenose.

Which of them had worn a Michael round her neck? Which had been presented with a medallion?

It would be child's play to find out. I would pry it out of Jumbo, who, as head girl, would be most likely to know. But first I would need to catch her alone.

Fitzgibbon had not yet noticed I was missing from the infirmary—at least I didn't think she had. There had been no hue and cry, no alarms, and no search parties. No one had even bothered to come to Edith Cavell in search of poor, sick, fevered Flavia. That, in itself, was annoying, in a way.

It was not easy trying to cut Jumbo from the herd (I'm quite proud of that little jest) particularly while keeping a low profile myself. I watched for a while from the window, hoping to catch her coming from or going to the hockey field, but no such luck.

I crept to the top of the stairwell, waiting to hear the sound of her voice. I would call out to her and then dart back into my room. It was not a perfect solution, but it might be the only one.

After an hour I was growing desperate. "Desperate"— yes, that was the word. And what was the saying? "'Desperate positions require desperate measures,' as the cardinal said to the chorus girl." Daffy had once thrown this out casually, adding that it was in Dickens and that it was over my head.

It wasn't, of course. It is a fairly well-known fact that

most princes of the church have a love of theater, and it was no great stretch of the imagination to see that His Eminence may well have been offering advice from his own experience on the wearing of rich costume.

At any rate, desperate solutions were called for.

After listening at the door until there was a momentary lull in the voices outside, I crept from my room and down the narrow back stairs.

At the far end of the downstairs hall, in the shadows beside the ancient elevator, and almost at the rear of the building, was a black wall-mounted telephone which, I had been told, was to be used only in family emergencies. Like its counterpart at Buckshaw, there was something ominous about the instrument.

In the gloom, I peered at the grubby yellowed card which was mounted behind a circle of transparent material: GArden 5047.

I repeated it to myself several times as I slipped out the back door. It was only a jig and a jog to the laundry, and behind it, to the goldfish pool. At this hour, there were no smokers making use of the seclusion, so that I had the place to myself.

I sat on the stone rim as I had done before, but my reach was not long enough. I took off my shoes, peeled off my stockings, and waded in.

The water was cold—colder than I should have expected—but it was, after all, October. A couple of sluggish fish shimmied away to shelter in a cluster of stones and plants.

I plunged my arm elbow-deep into the slimy-feeling water, shivering at the thought of its chemical constituency. Due to refraction, it was not easy to judge the exact position of objects on the bottom, but with a bit of fishing I came up with a dripping coin which had a beaver on the back and the head of the king on the front. Five cents.

I dipped again . . . and again . . . resulting in a small silver coin with a sailing ship, and a larger one with a creature that I took to be a moose. Ten cents and twenty-five cents, respectively. I gathered a couple more for safety's sake, put on my stockings and shoes, and made my way furtively round the laundry and through the passageway to the street.

Minutes later, coins in hand, I was marching along the Danforth, headed toward the grocer's shop, where I had spotted a coin-operated telephone on our walk to the graveyard.

"Back again, dear?" the shopkeeper said. "Come to sing me another song, have you?"

I smiled a pale smile, picked up the handset, and dropped a coin into the slot. It fell through with an odd *ching* sound.

In a flash, the woman was at my elbow.

"Wrong coin," she said, prying open my fingers and selecting another, which she dropped into the slot.

A raw buzzing noise came from the earpiece.

"That's it, dear," she said. "Dial the number. Local call, I hope?"

I grinned, nodded, and stuck my forefinger into the round holes of the dial. It was the first time I had used a do-it-yourself telephone. At home, we had lifted the receiver, tapped the cradle to get the operator's attention, and given her our instructions.

With my tongue protruding from my lips, I dialed the number, GArden 5047, and after a maddening series of clicks and clacks, a robotic *burr*-ing began. It must have been the sound of the phone ringing at Miss Bodycote's.

The shopkeeper was still at my elbow, looking at me with bright, birdlike eyes.

"Could I have a bottle of Orange Crush?" I pleaded, running my spare forefinger round my collar. "I'm feeling rather faint."

I could imagine the telephone ringing in the hall at the academy, unheard, perhaps, in the noise and bustle of the place.

Burrr . . . Burrr . . . Burrr . . . Burrr: single, long-spaced rings, quite unlike the brisk, demanding double ring at home.

Come on! I wanted to shout. *Pick up the blasted thing!*

"Here you are, dear," the woman said, at my elbow again. She had removed the bottle cap, and tiny tendrils of carbon dioxide gas drifted lazily up into the air.

I took an enormous swig, smiled, handed her a coin, and turned my back to her.

"Hello?" a voice said at the other end of the line. "Miss Bodycote's Female Academy. Whom were you calling, please?"

It was Fitzgibbon: There was no doubt about it.

I almost choked on my drink. Gases were forcing themselves up through my vocal cords as I spoke, giving my voice an eerie sound, as if the Grim Reaper himself were belching out the name of his intended victim.

"June Bowles," I gargled in my best gaga grandmother voice. "Miss June Bowles."

There was an unnerving silence, and then Fitzgibbon said, "Please stay on the line while we locate her."

"Thank you," I gurgled.

Jumbo must have been up the Zambezi, judging by the amount of time it took to fetch her, but in reality, it was probably no more than two or three minutes.

The shopkeeper had retreated behind her counter and picked up an enormous clod of knitting at which she dug away like a woman possessed. Every couple of stitches she would look up at me with a reassuring smile and I would grin soppily back.

"Hello?" Jumbo's voice said, and I pressed the receiver tightly against my ear and turned away.

"It's de Luce," I whispered. "Flavia. I need your advice."

I had cannily concocted my message as I walked from Miss Bodycote's, and chosen my words carefully. There is no one, anywhere, on the planet who can refuse a request for advice, and I had meant to take full advantage of that fact.

"Of course," she said instantly, as I knew she would. "You're calling from the grocer's on the Danforth, right? Where shall I meet you?"

"In my room—in Edith Cavell. I'll be there in ten minutes."

"Roger Wilco," Jumbo said brightly. "It's simply too, too tantalizing. I can hardly wait."

I gently replaced the receiver.

"You're a long way from home by the sound of you," the woman said. "England, isn't it?"

I nodded, feeling somehow guilty and idiotic at the same time.

"One of Miss Bodycote's, I'm guessing," she said. "We get a few of you in from time to time wanting this and that. What's your name, dear? It's always nice to know your regular customers."

"Flavia," I said.

"Is that it, then? Just the Flavia? Couldn't afford a surname?"

"De Luce," I muttered. "Flavia de Luce."

The woman looked at me as if I were a phantom.

"De Luce, did you say?" Her eyes widened, then narrowed, the way they do when people are putting two and two together. It was obvious that she had known Harriet, but I didn't want to hear it. I was still too raw and unprepared to be constantly compared with my late mother— besides the fact that I might have compromised myself by giving away personal information to a complete stranger.

I'm afraid I did something incredibly rude: I put down the bottle of Orange Crush and bolted.

I had taken no more than two or three steps when I saw Miss Fawlthorne walking briskly toward me. Because her attention was taken by a streetcar driver who was using a long pole to reconnect the car to the overhead electrical lines, she had not yet spotted me.

I dodged into the dim depths of an ironmonger's next

door, and watched from among the ladders and hanging hoses as the head came closer.

"Miss! Oh, miss!" It was the shopkeeper from next door.

"You've walked off without your change!"

She had followed me into the ironmonger's and was beside me in an instant, prying my hand open and pressing into it two coins.

Miss Fawlthorne, thinking at first it was she who was being hailed, came to an abrupt stop in the street. After glancing quickly round in all directions, she had let her gaze follow the grocer and then fall, alas! upon me.

She paced slowly and sarcastically toward me.

"Well?" she asked, her voice hanging as coldly in the air as the Northern Lights.

"Oh, Miss Fawlthorne!" I said. "I'm so happy to see you. I'm feeling ever so much better now, and I thought that perhaps we could continue our discussions. Actually, I had just set out to see if I could find you walking in the cemetery. I'm sorry if I disappointed Miss Fitzgibbon, but fresh air was what I needed more than anything."

I had said too much. I knew perfectly well that the most effective lies are the briefest.

Miss Fawlthorne looked down at me as if through a microscope, and the longer she looked, the smaller I felt.

"I'm afraid I have an appointment," she said, glancing suddenly and nervously about.

I let my eyes flicker to where hers had been. A line of cars had stopped behind the stricken streetcar and behind the wheel of one of them was a familiar face.

It was Ryerson Rainsmith. I restrained myself from waving.

"All right," I said, as if I hadn't seen him. "I shan't keep you. I'd better get back. William Palmer and all that."

And off I marched, pausing to kick a couple of tin bottle caps off the curb and into the road with elaborate nonchalance, as if I hadn't a care in the world.

Just as well she hadn't called my bluff, I thought. Jumbo would be waiting.

At the corner, I paused and, pretending to read the street sign, sneaked a look back.

Miss Fawlthorne was sliding into the offside front seat of Rainsmith's sedan.

·EIGHTEEN·

I OPENED THE DOOR and my heart gave a sickening leap.

Jumbo was sitting on my bed leafing through my notebook. How long had she been here? How much had she read?

I had stopped at the goldfish pool just long enough to toss in the unused coins. I have one or two faults, but thievery from wishing wells is not one of them. I would return the ones I had spent at the first opportunity.

"Very interesting," she said, turning a page. "Very informative."

"Interesting?" I asked, angling to get a look over her shoulder. If she'd been reading my notes, I was scuppered.

"This stuff about William Palmer . . . a bit morbid, though, isn't it?"

"Miss Fawlthorne assigned it," I said. "Quite boring, actually."

"Remarkable research, though. How did you manage to dig up all that information?"

"Oh, I just happened to read a library book about the man not long ago. Quite informative. Some of it stuck in my mind."

She'd be horrified if she knew the truth.

"Hmmm," she said, handing back the book. "Now, what did you want to talk about? You said you needed my advice."

"Yes," I told her. "Quite frankly, I'm after your job. Not until you graduate, of course, but I have to admit that I've set my sights on being head girl at Miss Bodycote's. I need all the advice I can get."

Jumbo seemed rather taken aback.

"I think that the best way to go about it is to win as many medals and awards as possible. I've got plenty of time, of course, but if I begin early—"

"Hold on," Jumbo said. "It isn't all medals, you know."

"No," I said, "but it's a start. Solid academic work— science and so on—and a bag of medals ought to give me a chance. Scarlett told me she won one for washing and ironing."

"Do you want to spend your days like she did, hanging around with a ticket of leave for the laundry pinned to your blazer?"

"Well, no," I said, meaning yes. "But I thought you might give me some ideas on what prizes are available. I'm afraid I'm not much good at sports, but I'm rather keen on chemistry and religion."

Religion was a bald-faced lie, but it paid off.

"Ha!" Jumbo exclaimed. "Well, if it's theology you fancy, you've come to the right place. Miss Bodycote's Female Academy is so High Church that—"

"Only a kitchen stool is required to scramble up into Heaven," I finished. "Yes, I heard that somewhere."

"There's the Bishop's Medal for New Testament studies, the Tanner Award for a paper on the Old Testament prophets, the Saint Michael for church history, the Daughters of Mary for proficiency in elementary Greek and Latin, and the Hooker for hermeneutics."

"Good lord!" I said, and we both laughed.

"No one goes in for them much anymore. The Hooker hasn't been handed out since Miss Bodycote's day. But if theology's your game, washing and ironing won't give you much of a leg up."

"No, I suppose not. Have you won any of those?"

Jumbo snorted. "Not on your Nellie. Hockey's more my line. I want to win something you can drink champagne out of.

"Or at least beer," she added.

"No silver cup for the Saint Michael?" I asked, with just a hint of jollity.

"Fat chance," she said. "An inscribed Bible for most of them, and for the Saint Michael, a lump of silver on a string."

"When was that one last handed out?"

Her face went deliberately blank. Oh! for the power to read minds.

"Two years ago," she said. "Listen, I have to dash. I promised Kingsbury I'd help restring the nets. Don't want to keep her waiting too long—it's a filthy job."

"Right, then, cheerio," I said. "Oh, by the way," I added, "who won it? The Saint Michael, I mean. I thought I might ask her for a few pointers—a bit of coaching."

Jumbo's face was suddenly shadowed as if by scudding clouds: a dozen shades in as many agonizing seconds.

"No use," she said at last. "She's gone."

"Was her name Clarissa Brazenose, by any chance?" I wanted to ask, but I somehow managed to keep from blurting it out.

"Have to dash," Jumbo said, cutting short the interview.

When she had left the room I took a deep breath. Had I given myself away? Had I been too anxious? Had my little act been credible?

I drifted toward the window, meaning to watch Jumbo emerge onto the hockey field. As I did so, something on the table caught my eye.

A letter. A letter with a British stamp—addressed to me.

The handwriting was unmistakable.

I tore it open and yanked the folded sheets from the envelope.

But something stopped my hand.

This was not a letter to be read in an airless room. It needed to be taken into the open air and read under an open sky. It needed to be savored, its every word read again and again, committed to memory, and tucked away somewhere close to my heart.

I went slowly down the back stairs, probably in Jumbo's very footsteps. She must have brought the letter to my room and forgotten to mention it.

The mail at Miss Bodycote's was tucked into an array of little pigeonholes in a cubicle near the telephone. At mail call, Fitzgibbon, having put on a pair of flannel oversleeves and a green visor, would take up her position as postmistress and, from behind her makeshift wicket, hand out to each girl any letters or parcels that had been received.

There was generally no shortage of mail. The girls of Miss Bodycote's seemed well supplied with parents who showered them with newsy notes, postcards from exotic lands, and fat hampers full of vaguely forbidden fruits, sweets, jams, and crackers.

I, to date, had received nothing. After queuing day after day at the wicket, and being turned away each time letterless, I had simply given up waiting. It was painfully obvious, not just to me but to the population of the entire school, that no one on this particular planet gave a rat's whisker for Flavia de Luce.

As I rounded the corner of the laundry, I could see Jumbo in the distance, strolling toward the nets. Kingsbury's welcoming voice came booming jovially across the grass.

I changed direction at once and made my way back to the little courtyard where illicit smoking was, if not permitted, at least overlooked.

It was blessedly empty.

I sat down on a wooden bench and pulled the letter

from its place beside my heart, and with trembling hands unfolded the pages.

Buckshaw
October 7, 1951

Dear Miss Flavia,

I trust this missive finds you well, and that Canada is living up to your expectations. One seldom thinks of that vast Dominion without thinking of Crippen, the notorious poisoner and homeopathic doctor, who made his home there briefly; or of Dr. Thomas Neill Cream, that poor, doomed graduate of McGill College who dispatched his victims on both sides of the Atlantic with chloroform. Not forgetting, of course, Dr. William King (another homeopath, one must note), who was dropped through the trap not many miles from where I expect you shall be reading this letter.

But enough pleasantries.

Dear old Dogger! I could picture him seated in the fading light at the desk in the window of his little room at the top of the back stairs, bent over his paper, his fountain pen forming those neat characters, each of which, in its simple but elegant shape, put my own crabbed scribblings to shame. I vowed to begin a course of regular exercises in penmanship before the sun went down. So help me.

Dogger went on:

Gladys, you will be happy to hear, is basking in her new coating of winter oil. I have taken the liberty of applying graphite to her gears and giving her lamp a brisk buffing. With her seat covered by an old silk scarf, she looks remarkably like our own dear Queen Elizabeth.

My time in these dwindling days is much devoted to sowing sweet peas and dividing rhubarb crowns: the bitter and the sweet, so to speak. The garden in autumn, although somewhat somber, is full of hope for the year to come.

Mrs. Mullet asks to be remembered, and wishes me to convey to you the fact that Esmeralda has adapted admirably to her new home in the kitchen garden, and has become a wonderful "layer-on-of-eggs" as Mrs. M expresses it.

We remember you often, and trust you do the same of us.

Yours faithfully,
Arthur Dogger

Postscript: Miss Undine has insisted I enclose a short note, which I am not permitted to read. I do so, but with little real joy.

AD

I turned to the second sheet. Different paper . . . different handwriting. The mad, electric scrawl of a junior Genghis Khan.

Ha! I hope youre happy, Flavia. I expect you dont miss us as much as we dont miss you. Aunt Felicity says youre being finished off in Canada, and I hope shes right. That was a joke.

Your sister Ophelia pretends to like me but I know she doesnt. I can tell by the way she cant look me in the eye. Daphne is all right except for her books. I shouldnt be a bit surprised if her eyes fell out and rolled across the page fell onto the floor rolled across the room and down the hall and out the door and over the hills and far away. I wouldnt even fetch them back for her.

Yesterday I identified a Great Spotted Cuckoo (Clamator glandarius) near an old starlings nest in the little wood east of the Visto. Although it is rare in these parts it made me think of you and I said as much to Dogger. That was a joke.

I have worked out from the atlas that you are exactly three thousand five hundred and five miles from Buckshaw. Hurrah! Hurrah! Hurrah!

> *Love from your blighted cousin*
> *Undine de Luce*

I didn't realize how much her words affected me until a tear plopped onto the page and made the indelible pencil run purple.

The nerve! The bloody nerve!

Since Undine had been left by her lethal and recently deceased mother, Lena, to be brought up at Buckshaw—

"the kindness of strangers" as Daffy remarked—I suppose I should have felt more charitable toward her.

But I did not.

The very thought of the despicable Undine sucking up to Dogger made my heart peel. The thought of her racing through my hallways, poking into my rooms, and breathing the dusty air that was rightfully mine was unbearable.

It was agony.

Still, she had at least taken the time to write, hadn't she? Whereas Feely and Daffy hadn't.

Nor had Aunt Felicity.

Nor Father.

It was quite clear, as I had known from the outset, that I was an outcast.

A sudden and unexpectedly cool wind caught several dead leaves and made them scuttle across the walkway with the chill grating sound of old bones stirring in their moldy coffins in some forgotten underworld.

What use to them was the Archangel Michael, when a thousand times ten thousand archangels couldn't keep a single one of them from turning into rancid green moss?

More to the point: What use was he to me?

Or anyone else.

It was at that moment that I began to question my faith.

"I hope I'm not intruding."

I looked up to find Mrs. Bannerman staring at me in rather an odd way, her head cocked to one side, as if she were examining my soul.

Sitting there among the scuttering autumn leaves with

a tear-stained letter in my lap, I must have looked to her like Roxanne in the last act of *Cyrano de Bergerac*.

I crumpled the page and crammed it into my blazer pocket.

"News from home?" she asked.

I put on a grim smile and shrugged.

"It sometimes happens," she said, "that a letter from home can seem to be from another world . . . as if it had come from Jupiter."

I nodded.

"Is there anything in particular troubling you? Anything I can do to help?"

I thought long and hard before answering.

"Yes," I said. "You can tell me what happened to Clarissa Brazenose."

·NINETEEN·

HAD THE AIR BECOME suddenly too thick to breathe, or was it just my imagination?

Mrs. Bannerman and I stared at each other, our eyes locked, each of us unwilling—or unable—to be the first to look away.

Had I been too bold and overstepped? I knew from experience that was most likely to happen when you were most unsure of yourself.

How incredibly young Mrs. Bannerman looked in that long moment! With her hair coiled in neat, businesslike ropes, and her tastefully applied lipstick (practically invisible, as lipstick ought to be, especially when worn in defiance of regulations), she seemed, as I had noted that first day at breakfast, no older than my sister Feely. Hard to believe that this cool and composed young woman had been tried and acquitted for murder.

Then suddenly she spoke. The spell was broken. "To-morrow morning," she said. "Early. The usual time and place."

And with that, she was gone.

I couldn't sleep. The hours passed like semiliquid sludge, oozing blackly by in my darkened room. My mind, by contrast, was a racing blur of question marks: Why had we heard no news about the body in the chimney? Why had there been no reaction from the outside world?

Had the whole thing been swept under Miss Fawl-thorne's carpet? Had she somehow managed to derail Inspector Gravenhurst's investigation?

Did it go, perhaps, even . . . higher?

Or was it all a waiting game? A cunning game of cat and mouse played out on some gigantic Canadian gaming board too vast for my comprehension?

Why had Miss Fawlthorne got into Ryerson Rainsmith's car in the middle of the busy Danforth? Surely, if a board meeting had been planned away from the academy, he would have picked her up at the door of Miss Bodycote's. Could it be that they hadn't wanted to be seen? Was it possible they were having what Feely referred to as an "*affaire d'amour*," and Daffy called "a fling"?

It seemed unlikely. I couldn't imagine Dorsey Rainsmith allowing her trained-flea husband off his invisible gold-hair harness long enough to get up to any hanky-panky.

I must admit that I didn't know in any great detail how

a dalliance was conducted, but I had heard enough by keeping my ears open to build up a fairly good—and actually quite startling—idea.

Worse yet was the thought that the two of them might be bound, not by love or icky passion, but by conspiracy.

Knee-deep, I waded on through this dark tide of ideas until I staggered up onto a rocky beach and found myself standing on the west lawn of Buckshaw.

It was night, and a chill wind whickered through the bare branches like phantom horses champing upon phantom hay. Except for a single light at the window of Father's study, the house was in darkness.

I crept a little closer, taking care, for some peculiar reason, to keep out of sight.

Father sat hunched over his desk, his eyes blinkered by his two raised hands. Across from him sat a figure in black whose face I could not see. Between them, on the desktop, was a chessboard.

As I looked on from the shadows, my heart began to accelerate slowly, as if somewhere in the engine room of my intestines, some huge and unseen hand had taken hold of a large brass lever marked *Speed*, and was with great deliberation shoving it firmly forward.

The figure in black reached out and repositioned one of the pieces on the board. It seemed to be a girl in a dark costume and a panama hat.

His eyes dripping pain, Father glanced up at his adversary. After what felt like a very long time, but was in actuality only a few seconds, because of the way time is stretched like putty in dreams, his hand went out—each heartbreaking, vulnerable hair on the back of it clearly visible—and seized upon a silver figure which he slid shakily forward.

And I saw that the silver figure in Father's hand was the Archangel Michael and the pale girl in the dark school uniform was me.

I wanted to cry out but I was unable.

As if he had heard my silent scream, Father turned his face toward the window and fixed his sunken eyes upon mine.

This time I *did* scream, and I awoke clinging desperately to the pillow as if it were a life preserver, my heart pounding away like some infernal machine.

Had anyone heard me?

I strained my ears, listening for the sound of creaking floorboards or approaching footsteps.

But Miss Bodycote's Female Academy lay in silence and in darkness.

At that instant, the alarm went off, nearly causing a regrettable accident, but I seized it and thumbed the little lever to the *Off* position. The glowing face told me that it was three A.M.

Time to meet Mrs. Bannerman in the chemistry lab.

I groped my way to the basin where I picked the crusty crumbs from the corners of my eyes and gave my face a good scrubbing with the corner of a wetted towel.

There's nothing like friction to bring on rosy cheeks at short notice. I didn't want to look like death warmed up, as Mrs. Mullet is so fond of saying.

That done, I dressed and made my way silently down the stairs.

"Good morning," Mrs. Bannerman said. She already had the tea steeping. "I heard your alarm."

Had she? Or was there a hidden message in her words—a small rap on the knuckles, perhaps. I didn't know, so I shrugged.

"I was awake before it rang," I said. "But I couldn't shut it off in time."

"*Didn't* shut it off in time." She smiled.

It was going to be one of those days. I could already tell.

Once people have you in their power, it's remarkable how quickly their grip extends to all things. At first, they are merely teaching you a bit of harmless geography, and the next thing you know they're criticizing your posture or finding fault with your breath. I had noticed this about Miss Fawlthorne, and now here it was happening again with Mrs. Bannerman.

My automatic response to someone who has gone too far is to wrap myself in a cloak of coolness. Throughout history the cold blue de Luce eye has stopped many an overstep and many a runaway horse.

Mrs. Bannerman laughed. "It's no use, Flavia," she said. "It's simply no use. You look like someone whose crypt has been invaded by grave robbers. I'm sorry, but you do."

I felt my face hardening into an icy and involuntary smile.

"Your success here will depend greatly upon your ability to control your personal kinesics: what the experts are now beginning to call *body language*."

I'm afraid my curled lip gave me away.

"You see? You need to master the poker face. There might come a time when your life depends upon it."

"In case someone asks me to marry him, you mean."

I don't know where the words came from. There are times when the gods (or devils) choose to amuse themselves by speaking through our mouths, and this was one of them.

I hadn't even remotely been thinking about marriage—not for myself nor for anyone else of my acquaintance—but out it popped.

"Precisely," Mrs. Bannerman said. "I'm glad you understand."

She gave me a smile which I could not decode: a smile in which she narrowed her eyes and raised only the corners of her mouth. What could it possibly mean?

I looked at her for further signals, but she was sending none.

And then it hit me with an almost physical force: *approval*. She had given me a look of approval, and because it was the first I had ever received in my life, I had not recognized it for what it was.

As when a match is applied to a dry log in the fireplace, a slow warmth began seeping through my whole being.

So *this* was what approval felt like! I could easily become an addict.

The thought of a fireplace reminded me of the one in Edith Cavell, and the bundle that had tumbled down it and into the room. And, of course, of the missing Clarissa Brazenose.

Which was why I was here, wasn't it?

I took a deep breath and hurled myself into the unknown. "Brazenose major," I said, and waited for a response. In conversation among adults, there is no longer the need to spin out a question to childish lengths. In fact, it wasn't a question at all, was it? Rather, the mere mention of a missing person's name.

"What about her?" Mrs. Bannerman asked.

"She won the Saint Michael medal, or medallion, or whatever it's called—and then she vanished."

"Did she?"

Mrs. Bannerman's expression had not changed one iota, or, as we used to say in England, a jot.

She was watching with approval, I realized, as I learned the steps of the dance by placing one slow foot ahead of the other.

I knew, of course, that I was forbidden to ask personal questions of the other girls, but did that same restriction apply to the faculty? The only way to find out had been to ask without really seeming to.

It was all so bloody complicated.

And yet I was enjoying it.

Daffy had bored me stiff one rainy Sunday afternoon by reading aloud from the *Dialogues of Plato*, in which a gaggle of sissified young men—or so it seemed to me—had traipsed round a sunny courtyard behind their master asking all the right questions: the ones that allowed him to deliver his thunderbolts of logic to their greatest effect.

Like stooges feeding straight lines to a famous comedian, their function was to make him look good.

What a load of old codswallop, I had thought at the time, and had said as much to Daffy.

But could it be that this was how the world really worked?

The thought floored me—almost literally. I reached out and touched the edge of a table to steady myself.

"Yes," I said, trying out my new sea legs. "She did. She won the Saint Michael and vanished."

I took a deep breath, and then I said: "But she was seen last night. She's still here."

"Is she indeed?" Mrs. Bannerman said, raising an eyebrow in what might well have been mockery.

"Yes," I said. "She was seen near the laundry."

"Indeed? From which you deduce?"

I was thoroughly enjoying this: a match of wits in which questions became answers and answers questions: a topsy-turvy mirror game in which nothing was given away.

Or everything.

Lewis Carroll had been right in *Through the Looking-Glass.* Reality made no sense whatsoever.

"That she was never missing," I said, taking the plunge. "That she was never dead.

"And nor were—or are—Wentworth or Le Marchand," I added.

"Hmmm," Mrs. Bannerman said.

The perfect answer.

She poked a forefinger into the hair above her ear, correcting a single strand that was struggling to escape.

"Now, then," she said, turning to the hydrogen spectrophotometer, at which she had been working when I came into the room. "Let us discover why the feet of this luna moth, *Actius luna,* should be exhibiting traces of arsenic. It's a pretty puzzle."

And I couldn't have agreed more.

·TWENTY·

I HAVE SAID NOTHING so far about church or chapel, hoping perhaps that they would go away. Miss Bodycote's Female Academy, being hand in glove with the Church of England, or "Anglican" as it was called here in the colonies (and "Episcopal" just south of the border in the United States of America), was subject to all the ritual that one would expect: chapel every morning on the premises, conducted in what had once been the chapel of the original convent, and a church parade on Sunday mornings to the nearby cathedral for the full-strength dose of Scripture and dire warnings.

Church parade? I should have said "church straggle." It is probably easier to train a pack of hunting hounds to sing an oratorio by Bach than it is to get a gaggle of girls to go in orderly fashion along a broad avenue in full view of the public without some mischief making a mockery of the day.

The usual order of march was this: Miss Fawlthorne and the faculty in the lead, followed by the girls in order of form, the youngest first all the way up to the sixth, with Jumbo, as head girl, bringing up the rear.

Clustered round Jumbo were the usual culprits who enjoyed a jolly good smoke in the open air: Fabian, Van Arque, and a couple of other younger scofflaws who were just learning how to inhale.

Because of that, there was a great deal of coughing at the back of the column, accompanied by an unusual and dramatic amount of hawking and spitting.

Occasionally we would meet Sunday strollers, or overtake older churchgoers who were headed on foot in the same direction, who would sometimes look in horror upon what must have seemed like an outing from the Toronto Free Hospital for Consumptive Poor.

"It's the *food!*" Van Arque would choke, pounding her chest as we passed. "Nothing but tongue and beans." Which didn't explain the smoke leaking from the corners of her mouth as she spoke.

Although I was marching with the fourth form, I was able to fall gradually back in line by the simple technique of stopping twice to tie my shoelaces. I rejoined the column just as Scarlett came along.

"*Dit-dit-dit-dit, dit-dit,*" I said. "*Hi.*"

"*Dit-dit-dit, dit-dit-dit-dit, dit-dit-dit-dit, dit-dit-dit-dit,*" she replied. "*Shhh.*"

We shambled along in silence for a minute, and then I whispered, "What do you think happened to her? Braze-nose, I mean."

Her eyes were huge as they swiveled toward me. "I can't tell you," she said. "So please stop asking me."

This made no sense whatsoever. Scarlett had been happy enough to prattle on at the camp about her recent nighttime sighting of a girl who had supposedly vanished two years ago, but was now unwilling to hazard a guess as to why.

What—or *whom*—could she be afraid of?

I had no choice but to lay all my cards on the table. It was risky, but there was no other way. It was my duty.

Aunt Felicity had more than once lectured me on my inherited duty.

"Your duty will become as clear to you as if it were a white line painted down the middle of the road," she had said. "You must follow it, Flavia."

The words of my aged aunt echoed as clearly in my ears as if she were walking along beside me.

"Even when it leads to murder?" I had asked her.

"Even when it leads to murder."

Well, it *had* led to murder, hadn't it? That charred, de-capitated wretch, whoever she might have been, who had plummeted down the chimney and rolled across the floor of Edith Cavell, was certainly not a suicide.

I took a deep breath, leaned toward Scarlett, and whis-pered into her ear. "And have you, also, acquired a taste for pheasant sandwiches?"

The effect upon Amelia Scarlett was shocking. The color drained from her face as if a tap had been opened somewhere. She stopped dead in her tracks—so suddenly that Fabian, who had been walking directly behind, smashed into her, fell to her knees, and, seeing that she had ripped one of her stockings, let loose a word that is not supposed to be known to the girls of Miss Bodycote's Female Academy.

I knew at once that it was a mistake.

"Smarten up, you clowns," Jumbo said. "You'll get *all* of us blacked. Fall in at the rear."

And so it was that Scarlett and I found ourselves at the very fag end of the march, walking stiffly along in silence, shoulder to shoulder, but not knowing what to say to each other.

After a hundred yards of misery, she broke into a sprint and charged ahead until she was lost from view among the other girls of the fourth.

The rector was a frail old lamb with an enormous mop of white hair, who peered down at us from his pulpit like a lookout in the crow's nest of a ship in a stormy sea. Each of us, he was insisting, was no more than a section of scaffolding being used to help erect the greater glory of God.

I could well picture *him*, swaying slowly from side to side in his lofty perch, as a bit of scaffolding, but as for me . . . ?

No, thank you!

The very idea made me balk at the proceedings: so much

so that when he finally gave the benediction and came
creeping down to rejoin us other skeletons of steel, and the
hymn was sung, I made a great point of setting myself apart
from the proceedings by singing: "Braise my soul the King
of Heaven . . ."

Not that anyone noticed. They never do.

Except Feely, of course. From her perch on the organ
bench at St. Tancred's, my older sister was always able to
hear even the slightest improvisation on my part, and
would swing round her burning-glass gaze to put me in my
place.

I was struck by a sudden pang.

Dear God! I thought. *How I miss her!*

As if she were here, I fell back into line with the other
singers:

> "Angels, *help us to adore him; ye behold him face to
>   face;*
> *Sun and moon, bow down before him, dwellers all in
>   time and space.*"

That was just it, wasn't it? *That's* what we were: dwellers
all in time and space. Not old scraps of iron lashed together
like a Meccano set by some invisible builder—not on your
bloody life!

I looked over at Mrs. Bannerman. What did *she* think, I
wondered, of being labeled a section of scaffolding? She
had come within an ace of meeting her end on the most
dreaded bit of scaffolding in the whole wide world. A date

with the public hangman, I expect, is not one that can be easily forgotten.

And yet, here she was, head held high, caroling away, bright-eyed, and with a slight, mystical smile on her lips, as if science were her Savior.

. . . As if she knew something that none of the rest of us knew.

Perhaps she did. Perhaps—

In that instant, I understood what I must do. Of course I did: I had planned it all along.

There is a standing and unwritten order in most churches that a worshipper taken ill is not to be interfered with. One minute it's "We have left undone those things which we ought to have done; And we have done those things which we ought not to have done; And there is no health in us." And the next it's "Action stations!" as we flee, hand over mouth, to the nearest exit.

It is a good rule, and one that I had taken advantage of in the past.

Even before the last notes of the organ had died up among the rafters, I gave Mrs. Bannerman a tight, gulping smile.

"Excuse me," I managed, edging my way to the end of the pew, and then I fled.

The entire academy was here at church, and would be for at least the next hour. I turned my face toward the east and ran like a scalded rabbit.

I needed to question Collingwood without interference, and this was the time to do it. After the purging I had given her, and a good night's sleep, she should have recovered sufficiently from the chloral hydrate to be subjected to a jolly good grilling.

As I knew it would be, Miss Bodycote's was in perfect silence.

There is always something vaguely unsettling about being alone in an empty building that is not your own. It is as if, whenever present inhabitants are away, the phantoms of former owners come shimmering out of the woodwork to protect their territory. Although you cannot see these ghosts, you can certainly feel their unwelcoming presence, and sometimes even smell them: a sort of shivering in the air that tells you that you're not alone and not wanted.

Like layers of ancient paint, the older ones underlie the newer: fainter, paler perhaps, and yet, for all that, far more ominous.

What sights have been witnessed by these arching ceilings? I wondered. *What tragedies have played out in these ancient halls?*

My back sprouted goose bumps.

Up the cold, dim stairs I flew and into the infirmary, as if all the demons of hell were gnashing their teeth at my heels.

The gaunt drapes were drawn round Collingwood's bed.

"Quickly," I said in a hoarse whisper. "Get up. Get dressed. We're getting you out of here."

The curtain rings shrieked on their metal rods as I yanked back the hanging curtain.

Collingwood's bed was not only empty: It was as neatly and as freshly made as if it had been arranged for a magazine photograph.

"Well, well," said a voice behind me, and I spun round. Ryerson Rainsmith was closing the clasps of a black leather doctor's bag.

Of course! Flavia, you idiot!

Doctor Rainsmith, his wife had called him on the ship, and I had not heard because I had not wanted to hear.

It was Rainsmith who had been dosing Collingwood with chloral hydrate. And it was Rainsmith whom Fitzgibbon had been referring to when she said she'd have the doctor look in later. How could I have been such a fool not to see it?

"Where's Collingwood?" I demanded. "What have you done with her?"

"Confidentiality between doctor and patient forbids me from answering," Ryerson Rainsmith said quietly. "Besides, I'm in charge here. This is *my* infirmary. It is I who should be asking the questions."

"He's right, you know," said another voice behind me, and I spun round.

Dorsey Rainsmith had come up silently behind me.

I might have known.

Her dress was a sand-colored tent, its billows held in by a broad belt. Who knew what weapons were concealed beneath? There seemed room enough in it for racks of axes.

"You have no business being here," she said. "Why aren't you in church with the others?"

"Where's Collingwood?" I asked again. "What have you done with her?"

"She's had a very bad shock," Rainsmith said. "She requires peace and quiet if she's to make a full recovery."

I was not going to be shaken off so easily. "Where is she? What have you done with her?"

"Dorsey—" he said, giving his wife a brisk nod.

I did not wait to be seized and clapped into a straitjacket. I did what any intelligent girl would do in the circumstances: I took to my heels.

I clattered out of the room and down the stairs with the sound of falling tiles.

"Stop her, Ryerson!" Dorsey shouted, but it was no use. I was younger, faster, and had a head start.

At the bottom, I looked up and caught a glimpse of their white faces, like twin moons, staring down at me from above.

I shot them an insolent grin like the runaway pancake in the fairy tale, swiveled on my heel, and ran straight into the chest of Inspector Gravenhurst.

I nearly knocked him over.

The inspector looked even more surprised to see me than I was to see him.

How long had he been standing there? How much had he seen and heard?

It seemed obvious—at least to me—that he had come to Miss Bodycote's for a quiet Sunday morning snoop. After all, the doors were always left unlocked from dawn to dusk, and besides, who in their right mind would want to enter such a forbidding-looking fortress?

The question was this: Which of us was more embarrassed?

I was faced with a sudden choice and left with only an
instant to make up my mind: Should I blow the whistle on
the Rainsmiths for what they had done to Collingwood, or
should I keep my trap shut and take my chances on gaining
the upper hand?

Well, if you know Flavia de Luce as well as I do, you'll
know that it's a mug's question.

"Oh, Inspector," I said, and I'm ashamed to admit that I
allowed my eyelids and eyelashes to flutter almost imperceptibly. "I was hoping to see you again. Have you had any
luck identifying the body in the chimney?"

*Oh, Flavia! You puncturer of other people's importance!
What a saucy thing to say to the poor man. "Luck?" As if the
Toronto Police were only capable of solving crimes by a toss of
the dice—or by pulling lots from some plump constable's hat.*

"As a matter of fact we have, Miss de Luce," he said. "It
was front-page news in all the papers. But I don't suppose
you see them at Miss Bodycote's, do you?"

So. Wallace Scroop must have got his story after all.

Not knowing what to say, I glanced up at the two faces
that were still staring blankly down from the landing like a
masked chorus waiting to make their entrance.

The inspector, following my gaze, spotted the Rainsmiths.

"Ah, Dr. Rainsmith," he said. "Good morning. Perhaps,
as the pathologist of record, you're in a much better position than I am to answer this young lady's question?"

Pathologist? Ryerson Rainsmith the pathologist? Besides

being the academy's appointed medical doctor and chairman of the board of guardians?

How improbably bizarre. How downright dangerous!

But it was not Ryerson Rainsmith who responded to the inspector's words. In fact, quite the contrary: It was Dorsey Rainsmith, his wife, who began her slow descent of the stairs toward me.

"I shall be happy to, Inspector," she said. "You may leave it to me."

·TWENTY-ONE·

I SUPPOSE I SHOULD have screamed, but I didn't. Instead, as if in a trance, I watched as the inspector, with no more than a quick nod, vanished out the door.

Caught red-handed in an unauthorized Sunday invasion of the empty premises, he couldn't get away quickly enough.

Which left me alone with the Rainsmiths.

I didn't have many options. Since recent circumstances had resulted in my becoming a backslider in the fingernail-biting department, I had nothing to count upon for self-defense but my fists and my feet.

How I wished I had taken the time to pump Dogger for more details about the Kano system of jujitsu, which he once admitted he had studied for a time. One or two of the Deadly Blows would have come in handy just about now: a quick chop here and a clever thrust there, and it would be "nighty-night" to the abominable Rainsmiths.

But the sad truth is that I was so poleaxed at the thought of Dorsey Rainsmith—Dorsey Rainsmith!—being not only a doctor, but also the pathologist who had examined the body in the chimney, that my brain went into the kind of deep freeze that must have been experienced at the end by Captain Scott of the Antarctic.

"Huh?" was all I could manage.

Meanwhile, Dorsey was oozing down the staircase with slow, cautious steps, the way you might approach a rattlesnake that has been run over by a car and is writhing, injured, at the side of the road.

I had the most awful feeling that she was suddenly going to produce a blanket from somewhere about her abominable person and throw it over my head.

Her mouth was moving meaninglessly, but no sound was emerging.

And then I realized that she had been talking to me but I hadn't been listening.

". . . a very bad shock," she was saying.

Shock? Who was she talking about? Collingwood? . . . Or me?

Were they planning to bind me in wet bedsheets and pump me full of chloral hydrate? Was there a chimney waiting for Flavia de Luce?

It was only at that moment, I think, that my mind finally grasped how horribly far from home I was, and how off-balance and deprived of sleep. In ordinary circum-

stances I would have dealt the Rainsmiths their comeup-
pance and be already dusting off my hands—but I was not.
I was fighting for my life and I knew it.

I backed slowly away from the descending Dorsey,
matching her step for step in a deadly tango, edging ever
closer to the door.

"Wait," she said. "You don't understand."

Oh, yes, I do, Miss Knockout Drops. I understand all too
perfectly.

The average person, I suppose, does not often stop to
think about what can be done to one's body by a pair of
homicidal medical doctors. The very thought of it is
enough to make the blood dry up like the Dead Sea.

They could, for instance, remove my organs, slowly and
one at a time, until nothing was left on the dissecting table
but my two eyeballs rolling wildly about in search of mercy,
and my arms and legs.

Or they could—but enough!

I knew that I would have one chance—and one chance
only—to get myself out of this scrape.

Should I run? Attack? Or use my brain?

The decision was an easy one.

"Daddy!" I called out with a glance toward one of the
empty hallways. "Look who's here. It's Mr. and Mrs. Rainsmith."

In real life, if I had ever stooped to calling Father
"Daddy," we both of us should have shriveled up and died
from mortification. But this was not real life: It was a bit of
impromptu theater I was staging to save my bacon.

And with that vile name "Daddy" on my lips, I slowly strolled casually off with open arms toward my invisible parent who was standing, so to speak, in the wings.

"I hope your flight wasn't too tiresome?" I said loudly, once I was out of their sight.

And it worked!

The Rainsmiths, as far as I knew, had remained frozen on the staircase—hadn't moved a muscle, in fact, until sometime after I had crept quietly out the back door and made my way round to the laundry.

The key I had pinched made it a matter of less than three seconds—I counted—before I was inside that hellish temple of cleanliness (a phrase I borrowed from Daffy, who always used it to describe Armfields, the only London dry cleaners to whom Father would entrust his threadbare wardrobe—except his linens, of course, which were permitted to be washed, ironed, stiffened with potato starch, and correctly folded by no one but Mrs. Mullet in the kitchen of her cottage in Cobbler's Lane).

Again, a pang of something struck at my heart. I swallowed and looked round the cavernous laundry.

Lock the door! my brain commanded, and I obeyed instantly.

Because it was Sunday, the place was cold and clammy and—with the machines shut off, the great boilers as quiet as a pair of landlocked submarines—the whole place was as silent as the grave.

I shivered. Never in my life had I felt more of a trespasser—and that was saying a lot.

For a minute or two, I stood motionless on the same

spot, listening. But there was not a sound. Surely, even if the Rainsmiths had the nerve to follow me, I would hear their footsteps. The gravel outside the door would guarantee it.

Meanwhile, I might as well make use of the fact that I was now locked into the laundry, and probably would be for some time.

What better excuse for a jolly good snoop?

On my first visit to this hellhole, I had glimpsed briefly, through the steam, a small room in one corner—no more than a cubicle, really—which appeared to be an office.

Might as well start there.

A battered wooden desk with an ancient telephone handset and a mechanical chair with protruding springs took up most of the space. On the back wall were shelves lined with ledgers bound in linen, most of them dated on their spines with a span of years: 1943–46, 1931–35, and so forth.

I pulled open the desk drawers, one by one. Of the six, two were empty and the remaining four contained a remarkably uninteresting lot of litter: rubber stamps, ink in a pad, the moldy remains of a cheese sandwich in waxed paper, a bottle of Jergens Lotion, aspirin, a pair of rubber gloves, a rubber finger protector, pencils (broken) red and black, and two dog-eared paperbacks: *How To Win Friends and Influence People* by Dale Carnegie, and *How To Stop Worrying and Start Living*, ditto.

Not very encouraging.

But in the bottom right-hand drawer was a fat telephone directory, its curled cover jamming the sliding rail. I could not seem to free it, and could not look behind it without getting down onto my hands and knees on the unsanitary stone floor.

By bending my elbow at a scarecrow angle, I was somehow able to work my hand behind the bowed book. My fingers came in contact with something furry.

My first thought was that it was a dead mouse: one that had nibbled on the cheese sandwich, perhaps, and expired of penicillin poisoning, or anaphylaxis.

I fought down my girlish instinct to pull my hand away, or perhaps, even, to scream. I forced my fingers to close around the object and pull it into view.

It was a sock—a red wool sock. And I knew at once that I had seen its mate before.

I studied it carefully and shoved it back into the drawer. Fingerprints, I knew, could not be retrieved from most fabrics, least of all wool. But I had seen all that I needed to see, and I wouldn't want to be accused of tampering excessively with evidence.

Besides, there was no point in taking it with me for comparison when its matching mate was in the morgue.

Turning my attention to the shelf of ledgers, I took down the right-most book, 1950, its ending date not yet lettered. Obviously the current volume.

The binding gave a dusty sigh and a brisk crackle as I opened the book, and the smell of sweat and old starch came to my nostrils. These were the laundry registers of Miss Bodycote's Female Academy.

Would they be of any use in my investigations? I remembered something Mrs. Mullet had once told me when

I had made a condescending joke about her galvanized tubs: "Don't ever look down your nose at your laundry maid, miss," she had snapped in a rare show of short temper. "We knows what you eats, what you drinks, and what you gets up to in between. There's many a tale told on the scrub board."

I hadn't known what she meant, but it sounded like a handy bit of knowledge to keep up my sleeve for future reference, and now, it seemed, was the time.

I leafed through the pages of the ledger, each one ruled into five columns: Date, Name, Item, Notes, and Charge.

For instance:

Sept. 10, 1951 / Scarlett, A. / SW WL 2, BLM 2, ST 2, TUN, HNK 2, NGTN / $1.85

From which I deduced that Amelia Scarlett's parents were to be charged $1.85 for the laundering of two woolen sweaters, two pairs of bloomers (a form of undergarment I thought existed nowadays only in rude poems and even ruder songs), two pairs of stockings, a tunic, two handkerchiefs, and a nightgown.

This was a recent entry, made not much more than a month ago.

What tales would be told by the entries from a couple of years ago: in the aftermath, for instance, of the Beaux Arts Ball? Surely such an extravagant event would never pass without a few spilled glasses of punch or lemonade.

I reached for the previous volume. Inside the front cover were pasted calendars for 1947, 1948, and 1949, with various dates ticked off in ink.

Yes—here we were in June 1949, which had four Saturdays, the 4th, 11th, 18th, and 25th. The Beaux Arts Ball must have taken place on one of them. The question was: which?

There were a flurry of entries before and after the 18th: people having their clothing cleaned before the ball and mopping up afterward, or so I guessed. I could check the actual date later with someone who knew.

I leafed on through the book, more out of idle curiosity than anything. Mrs. Mullet was right: The laundry staff knew everything. Here, in remarkable detail, were the rips and the tears, the spills and the stains of everyday life. Doxon, M., for instance, had spilled hydrochloric acid on her blouse in chemistry class; Johnson, S. had ripped her tunic on barbed wire during a hare-and-hounds chase; while some clown named Terwilliger, A. had fallen downstairs with two jam tarts in her pocket. It was all recorded in horrible, laughable, fascinating detail.

As my eyes swept across the 6th of July, a familiar name caught my eye: Brazenose, C.

Clarissa Brazenose.

But wait! Hadn't she vanished weeks earlier? The night of the Beaux Arts Ball? And reappeared two years later—at least, according to Scarlett—the night before our trip to the training camp . . . the same day, coincidentally, as my walk in the churchyard with Miss Fawlthorne . . . and on the eve of my first class in the chemistry lab with Mrs. Bannerman?

Could there be a connection?

Where had she been for the past six hundred and some-odd days? For that matter, where was she now?

Assuming that Clarissa Brazenose was still alive and not a specter, it could hardly have been *her* body that had tumbled down the chimney.

Whose was it, then?

My mind was writhing with ideas like so many snakes in a pit.

For instance, I had not so far come across any entries for the teaching staff. Perhaps they were expected to see to their own laundry expenses, but was that likely? Any institution with such a great roaring steam laundry as Miss Bodycote's would surely not deny its services to the faculty.

Another reach to the top shelf brought down an unmarked volume.

Aha! This was more like it: Fawlthorne, Puddicombe, Moate, Bannerman, Fitzgibbon—here they were, the faculty bigwigs, in all their laundered glory.

I was exalted for about six and a half seconds, and then I saw that there were no informative details given, as there had been for the students. The items cleaned were simply listed, which made sense, of course, since the owners were not being charged for the service.

But what had I expected? Cyanide stains on the frock of Mrs. Bannerman close to the date of her husband's demise? It was too much to hope. Life didn't work that way—nor did death.

The only item of interest was a recurring entry for "Overalls" under the name Kelly.

At last! Here was my missing "K": that so-far invisible person who stoked the boilers—or whatever it was he or she did to require access to the laundry—whose key I had just used to gain entry to the place.

I saw at once that Kelly was subject to rips and grass stains, and once each to "tar" and "lock oil."

I was standing there with the book in my hand when, from the corner of my eye, I caught a sudden movement.

I whipped round and found myself face-to-face with a cliff of hulking flesh. Where on earth had he come from? I had locked the door behind me when I came in, and the only other access to the laundry was by way of a pair of steel doors at the back which, as I could plainly see, were locked and barred.

He must have been here all along! The very thought of it made my toes curl.

"What are you up to?" he demanded in a wood-rasp voice.

The smell of alcohol almost bowled me over.

It didn't take the brains of a Sherlock Holmes to deduce that this bruiser had been drinking behind the boilers. His red and crusted eyes told the rest of the tale: Here was a man who made the most of a quiet Sunday to have a nip and a nap. There were probably hundreds like him the world over.

"I found the door unlocked," I said, with just a trace of recrimination in my voice, a trick I had learned from Feely. I waved the laundry book at him.

"I was just looking to see if Miss Fawlthorne's number is listed. I intended to ring her up and then stand guard until she can come and secure the place. What I mean is that I've just *rung* her up, and I'm waiting for her to arrive."

The fact that it was Sunday and that Miss Fawlthorne and her entire scurvy crew and officers were away at church hardly mattered to this boozy specimen—or at least I hoped it didn't.

Alcohol is impervious to logic, my late Uncle Tarquin had written in one of his laboratory notebooks, though whether this insight was from personal experience, a specific chemical observation, or simply a bit of stray philosophy I had never been able to decide.

"No, don't do that!" the man snarled, wrenching the book from my hands. "I'm in charge here. If the dooorss's open—" He fumbled as if he couldn't think of the next word. "S'because I opened it, see?"

His vaporous breath trembled in the air, making the laundry seem more than ever like Dante's *Inferno*. I found myself waiting for lava to come bubbling from his mouth.

Here you are, Flavia, locked in a soundproof stone building with an angry, inebriated stranger who's three times your size and weight: a bruiser who, with one fist, could reduce you to a splatter of jam on the floorboards. There's no one nearby to rescue you. You're on your own—it's brains against brawn.

"You must be Mr. Kelly," I said, sticking out a hand.

The Human Mountain struggled to focus, edging his feet farther apart for better balance, his stale eyes staring.

"Miss Fawlthorne has often spoken so well of you," I added, "that I feel as if we've already met."

And then, incredibly, a great oily ham of a hand came forward and seized mine. "How do you do, miss. Edward Kelly is my name."

A wave of something swept over me, and I had a sudden

vision of this pathetic human being as a boy, standing defenseless before some schoolmaster or schoolmistress, now long dead.

"*Say 'How do you do,' Edward.*"

He shuffled his feet, then and now, and I knew for a fact that those words had never, ever, since that long-ago day, escaped from his lips.

"How do you do?" he asked again, as if I hadn't heard, the words stilted and awkward—not at home in his slack mouth.

"Very well, thank you, Mr. Kelly," I said, retrieving my hand. "It's a pleasure to meet you."

Was I pushing my luck? Perhaps, but his reaction told me I had chosen precisely the right words.

"Likewise," he said, reverting to some ancient remembered formula. "Likewise indeed."

Was he sobering a little, or was I imagining it?

"Well, then," I said, taking charge, "I can see there's no need for Miss Fawlthorne to be bothered. I expect she's already on her way, so I'll just run along and head her off at the pass. She'll be relieved to hear everything's under control."

"Head off at the pass" was a phrase I had heard in the cinema films, often used by Hopalong Cassidy or Randolph Scott or Roy Rogers, which seemed somehow more appropriate here in North America than it did back home in Merrie England, where cowboy chitchat was as scarce as hens' dentures.

I stepped to the door, Kelly tracking me with his sad eyes.

"A very *great* pleasure," I added, partly for his sake and partly for my own.

My exit was as serene and duchesslike as I could manage, and it occurred to me that this leaving people standing was becoming a habit: first the Rainsmiths and now Edward Kelly. If I kept it up, the whole planet would soon be peopled with people frozen stiff on the spot by my departures.

A shout in the distance and the sound of girls laughing told me that the academy had returned from church. The aged rector had either run out of energy or ideas, or passed away in the pulpit.

I drifted toward the hockey field, wanting more than anything to be alone. It was a lovely autumn day, the sun was warm, and I still needed somewhere to think without being interrupted.

I sank down onto my knees in the soft grass, planted my hands behind me, and fell back on them, turning my face upward toward the sky like a sunflower. No one would disturb me in such a posture, which clearly indicated someone communing privately with Nature.

I knew that hunched shoulders, hanging hair, and eyes on the ground were fairly reliable signs of a girl dejected, a girl who needed to be approached and jollied into a nice talk or a nice cup of tea; whereas a back-flung head, with eyes closed and a secret smile on the upturned face, was the signal of someone who needed to be left alone with her thoughts.

It was clever of me to have worked out such a useful tactic.

"Hello," said a voice. "May I join you?"

I kept my eyes closed and my mouth shut, hoping she would go away.

It was too late to form my thumbs and forefingers into little circles and begin loudly chanting *"OM MANE PADME HUM"* like a Tibetan lama, or the pilgrims in *Lost Horizon*.

"De Luce . . ."

I ignored her.

"Flavia? Are you feeling better?"

I allowed one eye to crack slightly open like an iguana.

It was Jumbo.

"Yes, thank you," I said, and left it at that. Most people would have felt obliged to tack on some kind of explanation, but not I.

There is a mystery in silence that can never be matched by mere words. Silence is power—at least until they grab you by the neck.

"Are you sure?"

"Quite sure, thank you."

I find there is always an electric thrill in such conversations: invisible fingers of excitement in the air, like lightning behind the hills.

"We were worried about you. Miss Fawlthorne asked me to see if you were all right."

I let my eye drift slowly shut. "Yes, I'm quite all right, thank you."

It was incredible! How long could I keep this up? Five minutes? Ten minutes?

An hour?

I heard the rustle of her starched skirt as Jumbo sat down beside me. Whatever was on her mind must be important enough to risk getting grass stains on her outfit. Her mouth brushed my ear as she folded herself into position beside me.

"We need to talk," she whispered.

Were we being watched? Were unknown eyes staring down at us from the tall, blank windows of Miss Body-cote's? To them, we would appear to be no more than a couple of tiny, distant sails in a vast sea of grass.

Why was I being so wary? And why, for that matter, was Jumbo?

I let my eyes come open slowly.

"I was thinking about the Michael Award," I said, which left things suitably up in the air.

"Past or present?"

Jumbo was no fool.

Without answering her question, I allowed myself to go all romantic. "I couldn't help wondering what it would be like to stand up there on the stage in front of all those people, being presented with a silver archangel by . . . who is it that hands out those things, anyway?"

"Dr. Rainsmith."

"Him or her?" I tried to keep the excitement out of my voice.

"Him, of course. She just comes along for the champagne tarts."

Jumbo ought to know, I realized. At the time of Brazenose major's disappearance, Jumbo would have been in the fifth form. And like Brazenose, she had been here for ages.

"What about two years ago, when Brazenose won it?"

"You need to watch your step," Jumbo said suddenly, hissing the words.

"Why?" I demanded.

It's ever so easy to be bold in bright sunlight.

"Things are not what they seem," she said.

I wanted to tell her that I'd been aware of that fact for as long as I could remember, but I resisted the urge.

"You're wading into real danger," Jumbo continued, "without even realizing it. You're already in over your head. Scarlett has tried to warn you, and so has Gremly."

I sat quietly, not wanting to break the fragile cobweb of power I had created with my semi-silence. Outwardly, I was no more than a serenely stubborn girl sitting on a sunny lawn with her nose in the air.

But what could Jumbo mean? How could I possibly be wrong in my deductions to date? I couldn't be—I was sure of it.

Until, that is, a horrific thought sprang into my mind: What if Miss Bodycote's Female Academy, besides our secret schooling in codes and ciphers and the black arts of science, trained certain of its students in the act of murder? What if each of them—of us!—was required, as some kind of horrific graduation ritual, to kill a human being?

What if Miss Bodycote's Female Academy, claiming to be a girls' school so High Anglican that only a kitchen stool was required to scramble up into Heaven, was, in reality, a school for assassins? An Academy for Murder and Mayhem?

Was that what Jumbo was trying to tell me?

·TWENTY·TWO·

FLAVIA DE LUCE, MURDERER.

This was not a thought that came out of nowhere. I suppose it had been simmering away in a covered pot in some subterranean kitchen of my brain for quite some time.

My mind flew back several years to the night Daffy was reading *The Private Hangman*, a black-jacketed thriller in which Special Agent Jack Cross, alias X9, wreaked vengeance upon the enemies of His Majesty's Government by such unsubtle means as boiling their blood with high-powered radio waves, binding them eyeball-to-eyeball with a giant squid, extracting a confession from a traitor who was lashed to one of the screws of an about-to-be-launched destroyer whose crew he had betrayed, and, in the last few pages, removing (with the corkscrew attachment of a Boy Scout knife, a handy weapon that he was never without) the eyes of the notorious spy Baron Noël van den Hochstein.

The latter scene had brought Daffy bursting in wide-eyed terror into my bedroom and into my bed at three o'clock in the morning, having turned on the electric light and lit an entire box of candles, all of which she insisted be left burning until well after sunrise.

At the time, I'd have hooted down anyone who suggested that I myself might one day inherit the mantle of Jack Cross, X9—the Private Hangman—but now I wasn't so sure. In this topsy-turvy world, anything seemed possible.

And yet, until now, it had never occurred to me that I might be required to kill.

My mother, of course, had been a member of the mysterious Nide, of which Aunt Felicity was chief. That much I knew, as well as the fact that there were others around me who might or might not be full-fledged agents. Gremly, for instance, who had given herself away by asking if I enjoyed my pheasant sandwiches. How I longed to quiz her, to learn more not only about her associations, but also about my own.

And yet it was forbidden. It had been made quite clear to me that one must not, under any circumstances, ask questions of any girl at Miss Bodycote's about herself, or about any other girl: a rule which, when you stopped to think about it, made a great deal of sense. It was the only way in which those of us who were chosen for a life of service could keep our secret doings from the others. Those at the academy who were not involved—the day girls—were really no more than cover for those of us who were.

They, in a way, were the drones, while we were the queens.

That much I had worked out on my own.

It was all part of a Grand Game, in which we were merely players. The rules were unwritten, and needed to be deduced by each of us: an enormous maze through which each of us must make her own way, in total darkness, by trial and error.

How beastly clever it all was!

What if the whole thing was no more than a magnificent piece of theater staged solely to test me? What if everyone but me had been handed their parts?

But, no, the drugged Collingwood was all too real. The fear I had seen in her haunted eyes was impossible to fake.

"You're very quiet," Jumbo said. It was so long since either of us had spoken that I'd almost forgotten she was there.

I looked her straight in the eye. "I know we're not permitted to ask personal questions," I said. "But what about *impersonal* questions? Neither of the Rainsmiths is a student. Am I allowed to ask you about them?"

That in itself was a risky question. I was keenly aware that Jumbo, as head girl, must not be compromised; that she must not be asked to break a rule.

The British Empire—even in Canada—had not been built by sneaks.

Like the sun after a rain, a warm smile was already stealing across Jumbo's face.

"Excellentemento!" she said. "Top marks. Of course you are."

I felt as if I had just won the Irish Sweepstakes.

By her comment about the champagne tarts I already knew that Jumbo did not care for Dorsey Rainsmith: that in terms of a sympathetic soul, I already had one foot in the door.

"What have they done with Collingwood?" I asked sneakily.

"They" being the Rainsmiths, and therefore fair game for a question.

"Took her away in an ambulance," Jumbo replied. "Before sunup. I saw it from my window."

"But where?"

"God only knows," Jumbo said. "All I can say is that Miss Fawlthorne and Fitzgibbon went with her."

I felt as if I'd been punched in the solar plexus.

Miss Fawlthorne!

But it made sense, didn't it? I'd seen her climbing into Ryerson Rainsmith's car on the Danforth. Nothing could be clearer than the fact that they were hand in glove.

"What are we going to do?"

Squinting, Jumbo raised her eyes slowly to the heavens—to the fat cumulus clouds that drifted lazily along in the painfully blue sky.

"Nothing," she said.

"Nothing?" My response was as quick as the return of a served tennis ball.

"Nothing. There are more things in Heaven and Earth, Horatio, than are dreamt of in your philosophy."

"Meaning?"

"Whatever you take it to mean."

How infuriating! How utterly—

I was tempted for a moment to give her a defiant glare, but I managed, by looking away, to keep it mostly to myself.

"You remind me of my sister Daffy," I said.

"Excellent," Jumbo replied, and with that, she got to her feet, brushed off her skirt, and without a backward glance, strode quickly away toward the rear of the school.

A kind of sadness descended upon me as I watched her walk away: a kind of sadness that was half happy and half not, which is very difficult to describe. I suppose I'd had great hopes that we would, against all odds, become great chums, and that the secrets of the universe, and of Miss Bodycote's Female Academy, would be unrolled like some great map, at no cost, for my inspection.

But it was not to be. I was me . . . she was she . . . and the world was the world—as I had rather sourly suspected all along.

I thought of the words Daffy had once recited in the drawing room as a gift for Father's birthday:

"No man is an island, entire of itself; every man is a piece of the continent, a part of the main; if a clod be washed away by the sea, Europe is the less."

I could not entirely agree with dear, dead old John Donne. I had never felt more like an island in my life.

I was the clod washed away by the sea.

I got up from the grass, my lip trembling, and began to walk—anywhere—away from the school.

Quite frankly, I was sick and tired of being held hostage by my emotions. I needed to take a stand with my feet rooted firmly in science, rather than in the dribblings of some lurking, self-important gland. At bottom, when you got right down to it, it was all chemistry, and chemistry should be miraculous, not miserable.

I needed to rededicate myself: to follow my brain instead of my tear ducts, and to stick to cold logic, no matter what. "Come hell or hard water," as Mrs. Mullet had once said.

I couldn't help smiling at the thought, and a minute or so later, everything was more or less tickety-boo. It was a kind of magic I didn't yet fully understand.

By this time I had reached the far boundary of the hockey field which was marked, for the most part, by the walls and fences of adjoining properties. In the middle of a tall hedge, a small wicket gate led to parts unknown. I opened it and squeezed myself through, onto a narrow path which passed between two tall, ragged, and moldy cedar hedges. I turned my body and edged along sideways in crab fashion to avoid being brushed by the dank, unpleasant foliage, which drooped like the ostrich feather wands of the mutes at a Victorian funeral. It smelled like a place in which cats congregated.

At its far end, the path opened out into a paved and boarded area which must, at least in winter, have been flooded and used as an outdoor skating rink. It might once have been a row of tennis courts, but their tarmac was now a cracked wilderness pierced with tufts of wild grass and weeds.

"Watch yourself!"

A metallic roaring behind me caused me to flinch—to

leap aside, in fact—just as a compact cannonball appeared: a uniformed figure on roller skates, its eyes hidden behind ancient black sun goggles and a yo-yo shooting wildly out on a string from one hand.

Nevertheless, I recognized her at once. It was Gremly.

"Sorry!" she shouted, barely missing me as she shot past and rocketed into a sharp right-hand turn, her legs crossing over like scissors, as if she had been born on skates.

"Wait!" I shouted, but she didn't hear me. She roared away, down the length of the old rink, skates and yo-yo flying, across the width, along the far side and into the final turn before passing me again.

"Two hundred and twenty yards!" she shouted as she blazed past without giving me a chance to say a word.

Round she went again, clockwise, a wound-up ball of pure energy completely compressed within her stunted frame.

I waited for the next approach.

"Mrs. Rainsmith?" I called out, trying to put the question mark into my voice as she flew past. Down the long side she raced, across the backstretch, and here she came again.

"Bad medicine!" she shouted back from inside a whirlwind of noise.

On the following lap, I kept quiet and left it to her.

"Pity. First one was nicer."

And she was gone again.

"First what?" I called out into the ferocious roar of racing skates.

I had to wait another complete round for her reply.

"First wife. Francesca. Vanished."

Vanished? Like Brazenose? Like Le Marchand? Like Went-worth?

It seemed scarcely credible. Was Miss Bodycote's Female Academy the last stop on the road to oblivion?

I held up my arm, bent at the elbow, as a signal to stop. But Gremly ignored it.

"Can't," she panted as she came round again. "Hundred penalty laps before lunch."

Again I waited patiently until she came round once more.

"Belching during the sermon," she bellowed as she skated by, her words followed by a whinnying horse-laugh that trailed behind her in the air like a long, flapping scarf.

The sheer defiance of it.

And it was that, I think, more than anything, which made me decide on the spot to confront Miss Fawlthorne.

After all, what could they do to me?

Miss Bodycote's Female Academy was, on a Sunday afternoon, like one of those vast Victorian boneyards such as Highgate Cemetery in London, minus, of course, the tombstones. An unnatural hush hung over the place like a black pall, as if the slightest sound would be a mortal sin. Even the walls and floors appeared forbidding, as if they, too, wanted to be left alone—as if I were an intruder.

I walked slowly along the Old Girls' Gallery, giving no more than a glance to most of the black-edged portraits from the corner of my eye. A more frank stare seemed sac-rilege.

But here was Harriet in her funereal frame. I stopped for a moment, then slowly touched my fingers to my lips and transferred them to hers.

Was she pleased?

I couldn't tell. That was the trouble with being the daughter of a dead woman.

I tore my eyes away and moved on.

A little farther along, toward the end of the gallery—and I hadn't noticed this before—was Brazenose major: Clarissa. I knew this only because her name was engraved, as were all the others, on a small silver plate at the bottom of the frame.

She bore only a passing resemblance to her younger sis-ter. You might have missed it if you weren't looking for it.

I sucked in my breath.

Clarissa was wearing the Michael Award round her neck: that same silver archangel with its upraised wings which was snuggled at this very moment in my pocket.

I pulled it out and compared it with the photograph. There could be no doubt about it. In spite of the tarnish-ing, I could easily see that they had once been identical.

A chill worked its way up my spine and down again. The photograph must have been taken the night of her disappearance—the night, perhaps, of her death.

She had vanished after the ball.

My footsteps slowed as I came closer to Miss Fawl-thorne's study.

Last chance to back out, I thought. *Last chance to let sleeping dogs lie.*

There are choices in life which you are aware, even as you make them, cannot be undone; choices after which, once made, things will never be the same.

There is that moment when you can still walk away, but if you do, you will never know what might have been. Saint Paul on the road to Damascus might have pleaded sunstroke, for example, and the world would have been a different place. Admiral Lord Nelson at the Battle of Trafalgar might have decided he was outnumbered and fled under full sail to fight another day.

I thought for a few moments about these two instances, and then I knocked on Miss Fawlthorne's door. The hollow sound of knuckles on wood echoed ominously from the uncaring walls.

There was no response and so I knocked again.

I was about to turn away (Saint Paul and Admiral Lord Nelson be damned) when a voice said, "Come."

I grasped the cold doorknob, gave it a twist, took a deep breath, and stepped into the headmistress's study.

Miss Fawlthorne was no more than a black silhouette against the brightness of the window. With my gloom-accustomed eyes, she was hard to look at directly because of the dazzle. And yet in spite of that, from her shadowed face there came an unmistakable flash of two moist eyes.

How odd. She had been all right when we walked to the Sunday morning service not two hours ago. Had she caught a sudden chill in the old stone church?

She shoved a bundle of papers into a desk drawer and closed it with a bang.

I stood there awkwardly until at last she said, "Please be seated."

She shuffled some files and red pencils on her desk and I guessed that she was collecting herself.

But for what?

I waited for her to ask me what was on my mind, but she said nothing as the silence lengthened.

"Well?" she said after a while, and left it at that.

I could hardly believe my ears. It was as if the captain of the *Queen Elizabeth* had invited you onto the bridge and then asked you to take the wheel. It was unheard of.

In any conversation with an adult, a twelve-year-old girl is at a distinct disadvantage. The dice are loaded against her, and only a fool would believe otherwise.

And yet here was the fearsome Miss Fawlthorne handing over the conversational reins without so much as a wink. As I have said—unheard of.

Well, I wasn't going to miss an opportunity such as this. It might never come again.

"Mrs. Rainsmith," I said. "The first one: Francesca."

Miss Fawlthorne made no effort to hide her surprise. "You *have* done your homework, haven't you?" she said in a resigned and tired voice. At the same time, she produced a surprisingly workmanlike handkerchief from her sleeve and dabbed at her eyes as if she were dusting them. But she didn't fool me.

"Poor Francesca. Tragic. Absolutely tragic."

I begged with my eyes for her to tell me more.

"She drowned. Fell overboard on a moonlight cruise."

"Oh, dear!" I said. It was the kind of weak remark I despise in others, and I was disappointed to hear such sappy words coming out of my own mouth. I tried to correct the slipup.

"I was led to believe that she had vanished."

"Led to believe" was a clever phrase: the move of a chessman. It implied that someone else was to blame for my faulty belief.

"I suppose she did, in a way," Miss Fawlthorne said. "Her body was never recovered. Absolutely tragic. Ryerson— Dr. Rainsmith, I mean—was devastated."

Pfaugh! I spat mentally. He apparently hadn't been too devastated to prance off to the altar with the dread Dorsey before the remains of Wife One had settled safely on the bottom.

She saw the look on my face.

"Grief takes many forms, Flavia," she said quietly. "I expected that you would have learned that by now."

She was right, of course, and I accepted the little stab in the heart as having been deserved.

"Dorsey was his medical protégée. She was a pillar of strength in his grief."

A pillar of strength, Daffy had once remarked, was a nice way of saying someone was terminally bossy, but I managed to keep that thought to myself.

"Tragic," Miss Fawlthorne said again, and I wondered for the first time what she meant by it.

At the same time, the realization was slowly rising in my

mind, like the water rising round a shackled prisoner in a riverside dungeon, that yet another corpse had been added to the equation.

I had believed—at least until recently—that the blackened body was more likely Clarissa Brazenose, or perhaps the missing Le Marchand . . . or the equally missing Wentworth.

Now, another possibility had presented itself, and an intriguing one at that.

My nerves must have been slightly on edge, as I jumped when a knock came at the door and Fitzgibbon's head appeared.

"Excuse me, Miss Fawlthorne," she said, "but the Veneerings are here for Charlotte."

Charlotte Veneering was a pale, weepy slug in the third form who had, as they put it, "failed to flourish" at Miss Bodycote's Female Academy, and was being sent home at the request of her parents. Being an "FF," as it was called, was the equivalent, so far as the other girls were concerned, to being drummed out of the regiment, and the sad subject was usually whisked away under cover of darkness to whatever FF—feeble future—awaited them.

"Thank you, Fitzgibbon," Miss Fawlthorne said. "Put them in St. Ursula. I'll be there right away."

St. Ursula was the chilly little reception chamber barely inside the front door where nuns had once been permitted— but only under special circumstances—brief glimpses of their families.

With a quick nod, Fitzgibbon was gone. Miss Fawlthorne got slowly to her feet.

288 · ALAN BRADLEY

"A pillar of strength," she said again, and I realized she was still talking about Dorsey Rainsmith.

"Have you finished your report on William Palmer?" she asked suddenly. "I haven't forgotten it, you know."

"No, Miss Fawlthorne," I said. I hadn't the heart—or any other of the required guts, for that matter—to tell her that, with the exception of the few notes through which Jumbo had snooped, I hadn't even begun.

"Well, time is running out," she said, almost reflectively. "You might wish to work on it until I return. You may sit at my desk."

"Yes, Miss Fawlthorne," I said, ever obedient.

I waited until her footsteps were fading in the hall before I got up and resettled myself in her swivel chair.

Now, then, into which drawer had she shoved the papers? Ah, yes . . . here they were. Second drawer from the bottom. I spread them on the desktop. Pink paper, black headlines. Yesterday's edition.

THE MORNING STAR . . .
FOUR STAR SPECIAL

WHOSE HEAD?
By Wallace Scroop,
Morning Star Crime Reporter.
AUTOPSY SHOCKER.

There was a photograph of the said Scroop standing alone on the many steps of what might have been a courthouse, notebook in hand, pencil poised.

The *Morning Star* has learned that the human remains recently found in a chimney at Miss Bodycote's Female Academy in East York have yet to be
identified. An autopsy has revealed that while the
body is that of a woman aged 14–45, the detached
head is that of a mummified male, possibly from
ancient Egypt. "We're at a loss," said pathologist
Dr. Dorsey Rainsmith. "These findings are most
unusual and most unexpected." Dr. Rainsmith
went on to say that anthropologists at the Royal
Ontario Museum had been consulted. "So far,
they're as baffled as we are," she admitted. Officials
contacted at the ROM have declined to be interviewed further. "It's still a police matter," said one
public relations staffer, who requested that his
name not be published.

There was more: much more, but all of it repetitive with
little additional information. The only real facts were
those contained in the first couple of sentences, spun, like
candy floss, into endless threads of speculation, and I
couldn't help noticing that the story was as much about
the *Morning Star* as it was about anything else.

Were they withholding anything?

I knew that certain details likely to be known only to
the killer—and who would believe for an instant that the
body in the chimney was not a murder victim?—were
often held back from the public.

If there was more to be known, the only way I was going
to find it out was from (a) Dorsey Rainsmith, (b) the po-

lice, in the form of Inspector Gravenhurst, or (c) Wallace Scroop.

The choice was an easy one. I reached for the telephone directory.

Ah, yes . . . here it was: the *Morning Star*. *ADelaide* 1666.

Miss Fawlthorne was not likely to be back in the next few minutes. It was now or never.

I dialed the number, which was picked up almost immediately by a surprisingly bright-sounding young woman.

"Newsroom, please," I said, trying to make my voice sound as if I did this every day.

"Who's calling?" she asked.

"Gloria Chatterton," I said. "I wish to speak with Wallace Scroop."

There was a pause, during which I knew she was making up her mind whether to put me through or not.

"Oh, Sister Mary Xavier," I said, half covering the telephone's mouthpiece, "could I ask you to close the chapel door, please? I'm speaking to the *Morning Star* and don't want to disturb the High Mass. Thank you, Sister. It's very kind of you, I'm sure."

"I'm putting you through," the operator said. "Hold the line, please."

She must have been Catholic. I had to pinch myself to keep from exploding.

"Newsroom," said a suitably gruff voice.

"Wallace Scroop," I said sharply, cutting the niceties. "He's expecting my call."

There was a hollow bang at the other end as the phone

was put down and I was left to listen to what sounded like the pounding of a platoon of typewriters.

This was living! My blood was electric!

"Scroop," his voice said.

"We met at Miss Bodycote's," I said, plunging in with no preliminaries. "I have some information for you."

"Who is this?" he demanded. "I need a name."

"No names, no pack drill," I told him. It was a phrase I had heard Mrs. Mullet's husband, Alf, use on more than one occasion.

There was a dry chuckle at the other end of the phone, followed by a rustling, a scratching, and a wheeze. I knew he had just lit a cigarette, and I could almost see him, perched on the corner of a desk, cigarette in mouth and pencil in nicotine-stained fingers, ready to take down my every word.

"Shoot," he said, and I shot.

"Three girls have gone missing from Miss Bodycote's in the past two years. Their names are Le Marchand, Wentworth, and Brazenose."

"Brazenose with a Z or an S?"

"A zed," I told him. This man was wizard sharp.

"Is that it?" he asked.

"No," I said. It was, in fact, only the bit of bait I was using to get him on the hook.

"I'll trade you," I told him. "Fact for fact. You give me one, I'll give you one."

"Tit for tat," he said.

"Exactly," I said. "Your turn."

"What do you want to know?"

"The body in the chimney. Identity . . . cause of death."

"Hard to say. Badly smoke-damaged. They're working on it."

"And the skull?"

"Like I said in the article, ancient, possibly Egyptian."

"Is there an Egyptian skull missing from the Royal Ontario Museum?" I asked.

"Shrewd kid. They're looking into that, too."

There was a bit of a lull in our conversation, during which I could hear him scribbling notes.

"My turn," he said. "What's the scuttlebutt at the school? What are the kids saying?"

"Ghosts," I said, and he laughed, and then I laughed.

"And the teachers?"

"Nothing."

He paused to let my answer sink in. "Bit odd, isn't it?"

And it was.

When you stopped and thought about it, it was odd indeed that there had been no official mention of a death at Miss Bodycote's. There had been no assembling of the girls to reassure, or explain, or even deny. The police had come and gone in near silence.

Which could mean only one thing: that they already had their answers; that they were only waiting to pounce.

It was a chilling thought.

"Still there?" Scroop's voice emerged tinnily from the receiver, and I realized that I had let it slip away from my ear, listening to the sound of approaching footsteps in the hall.

"Yes," I whispered. "I have to go"—at the same time closing the telephone directory and shoving the newspaper back into the desk drawer.

"No! Wait!" he shouted, putting me even more on edge. "Give me something . . . anything. I need more to go on."

"The first Mrs. Rainsmith," I whispered, my lips tight against the holes of the telephone's mouthpiece.

And then the door opened and I was caught.

Miss Fawlthorne and I stood there staring at each other for half an eternity.

"Hello? Hello?" Wallace Scroop's voice was saying, as if from the depths of a well.

"Oh, yes," I said into the receiver. "Here she is now. She's just come back. I'll put her on."

At the same time, I slowly pressed down on the cradle with my left forefinger, disconnecting poor Scroop in the middle of a "Hello?"

"Someone for you, Miss Fawlthorne," I said, handing her the now-dead receiver. "I'm sorry, I told them you had stepped out."

She took the instrument from me and held it to her ear.

"Yes?" she said. She had fallen for it hook, line, and sinker. "Hello? Hello?"

But of course there was no answer.

"Did they leave a name?" she asked, hanging up.

"No," I said. "It was a man's voice."

I added this in case she had heard any of Wallace Scroop's words leaking from the receiver.

"Possibly the police," I couldn't resist adding, watching her reaction. "It sounded official."

She stared at me as if I had slapped her face, and in a way, perhaps I had.

"Sit down, Flavia," she said. "It's time we had a little talk."

·TWENTY-THREE·

WHENEVER SOMEONE TELLS YOU they want to have a little talk, you can be sure they mean a big one.

There's something in human nature, I'm beginning to learn, that makes an adult, when speaking to a younger person, magnify the little things and shrink the big ones. It's like looking—or talking—through a kind of word-telescope that, no matter which end they choose, distorts the truth. Your mistakes are always magnified and your victories shrunken.

Has no one ever noticed this but me? If not, then I'm happy to take the credit for being the first to point it out.

Perhaps only J. M. Barrie, the author of *Peter Pan*, saw through dimly to the truth: that by the time we are old enough to protest such rotten injustice, we have already forgotten it.

I sat, reluctantly, watching Miss Fawlthorne with wary eyes.

"It isn't easy, is it? Being so aware, I mean."

God help me! Here it came again, that whole "Poor, dear, lonely, unhappy Flavia de Luce" business. She had pulled this sudden switch the night I arrived at Miss Body-cote's and now here she was trying it on again.

As it was in the beginning, is now, and ever shall be, world without end, Amen.

Whichever one of the Desert Fathers it was who origi-nally came up with those words certainly knew his onions.

I felt like tossing my toast.

"I've spoken to the Rainsmiths," Miss Fawlthorne began. "They tell me you had a bit of a . . . *contretemps.*"

There it was again: "a bit of a—"

That did it. I was fed up.

"If you call attempted murder a *contre*-whatever-it-was," I shot back angrily. I didn't even know the meaning of the word.

"There is a tendency in some girls," Miss Fawlthorne said, putting her fingertips together as a sign that she was about to say something important, "to overdramatize the commonplace."

I unleashed one of my famous glares. I couldn't help my-self.

"*Quod erat demonstrandum,*" Miss Fawlthorne said, al-most to herself, thinking, I suppose, that I didn't know the meaning of the phrase, when in fact I'd probably written it in my laboratory notebook more times than she'd been kissed.

Q.E.D. As if my glare had proved her point.

Well, she could jolly well suck my salmon sandwiches. I am a calm, cool, and composed person by nature, but when my temper is up, I am a sight to behold.

I leapt to my feet.

"They're drugging Collingwood!" I shouted, and I didn't care who heard me. "They've been giving her chloral hydrate. Now she's gone—like the others. They've probably killed her."

"Flavia, listen to me—"

"No!"

I knew what she was thinking: that I was a petulant brat who ought to be turned over her knee and given a good thrashing. But I didn't care. Collingwood was in trouble and there was no one to rescue her but me.

"Flavia—"

"No!"

"They're on our side."

It took quite a long while for her words to trickle from my ears into my brain, and when they finally *did* arrive, I didn't believe them.

I think my mouth fell open.

"What?"

It was like watching the moment in some ghastly silent film in which the booby realizes that the shoe he has set on fire is his own. Not just disbelief, but horror, shock, dismay, and yet in spite of it all, the urge to let out a filthy great donkey laugh.

"They're on our side," she repeated, her words still seeping like slow honey into my understanding.

"But Collingwood—she's gone. They—"

"Collingwood experienced a very bad shock. She was given chloral hydrate to help her sleep, to help her cope. Unfortunately, she has since somehow come down with rheumatic fever. She needs better and more intensive medical care than we're equipped to offer. Dr. Rainsmith has arranged—at his own expense—to have her moved into quarantine at his own private nursing home. Miss Bodycote's can ill afford an outbreak. It's a dreadful time, Flavia, and the Rainsmiths are doing their best."

The words "rheumatic fever" struck fear into my heart. I would never forget Phyllis Higginson—"Laughing Phyllis," they called her—in far-off Bishop's Lacey, who was struck down so suddenly. There had been panic in the village until Dr. Darby had called a meeting at the parish hall to explain that the disease was not, in itself, contagious, although the streptococcal throat that preceded it was. Phyllis had died on a heartbreakingly glorious day in June and I had attended her funeral in the churchyard of St. Tancred's.

I could still remember refusing to believe she was dead. It was all a dream . . . a joke . . . a fantasy that had spilled over into real life.

Poor dead Phyllis. Poor Collingwood.

Had I been exposed to her contagion? Had anyone else at Miss Bodycote's?

"I'm sorry," I said to Miss Fawlthorne, not sure if I really meant it, or whether I was apologizing under the pressure of fear.

"Do you mean that the Rainsmiths are members of the

Nide?" I asked. I couldn't put it more bluntly than that. Enough of this pussyfooting about with word games, I thought. Miss Fawlthorne and I were both adults—or as near as dammit—together in a closed room, and it was time to say some things that needed to be said.

Did she go a little white? I couldn't tell.

It was, after all, she who had brought up rheumatic fever. Would she have done so if she thought we were overheard?

I knew at once that I had overstepped. This wasn't the way the game was played.

If my own aunt Felicity, the Gamekeeper, refused to tell me whether certain persons—including my own father!— were members of the Nide, what chance did I have of wheedling such information from a relatively low-ranking sub-officer in this far-flung corner of the Empire?

Precious little, I realized. None, in fact.

My thoughts flew back to the dismal day the Rainsmiths had come to Buckshaw. Had there been the slightest indication that they were part of any Inner Circle? That Father had ever laid eyes upon them before?

"Please come in" were the only words I could remember him speaking. I had, in fact, admired the quiet, not-quite-openly-bristling way with which he had met their coarse gushings. That the Rainsmiths could be members of the Nide simply beggared belief, and my expression must have shown it.

"You must learn to trust, Flavia," Miss Fawlthorne said, and I noticed that she hadn't answered my question.

What kind of muddle was this woman's mind? Did she

not realize that her words directly contradicted the advice she had given me earlier?

"What about Le Marchand and Wentworth?" I demanded. "What about Clarissa Brazenose? Did *they* learn to trust?"

These were questions that cut to the bone, and I meant them to.

My whole life had been lived in doubt—doubt about my mother, doubt even about my own identity. I had been brought up not knowing sometimes if I were foundling or changeling, taunted by sisters who were capable of being as exquisitely cruel as those in any fairy tale.

Where identity was concerned, I was a raw sore—an open wound.

I was quickly learning that I couldn't exist in a world of shifting shadows and whispered half-truths.

I needed facts the way a tree needs sunshine. If ever I had met a kindred spirit, it was the hard-hearted Mr. Gradgrind, in Dickens's *Hard Times*: "Stick to Facts, sir! . . . In this life, we want nothing but Facts, sir; nothing but Facts!"

His words seemed to echo in my head, just as they had that winter's night at Buckshaw, with snow falling so beautifully outside the drawing-room windows, as Daffy read aloud to us: "Now, what I want is, Facts. Teach these boys and girls nothing but Facts. Facts alone are wanted in life. Plant nothing else, and root out everything else. You can only form the minds of reasoning animals upon Facts: Nothing else will ever be of any service to them. This is the principle on which I bring up my own children, and this is the principle on which I bring up these children."

How I envied those little Gradgrinds, with their little conchological cabinet, their little metallurgical cabinet, and their little mineralogical cabinet! How lucky they were to have such a hardheaded father.

What I needed, in order to survive, was science—not shadows.

Chemistry—not conspiracy.

"I want to go home," I said.

The silence was long and agonizing.

It wasn't as if Miss Fawlthorne had never before dealt with a girl who wished not to remain at Miss Bodycote's. Hadn't she, just now, seen off Charlotte Veneering, that jellyfish life-form from the third, who had failed to flourish?

Why couldn't I be an FF, too? Why couldn't I be rushed in the night, weeping, bent over and covered with an old mackintosh, to a waiting taxicab? It might even be fun.

I could negotiate my freedom as if I were both kidnapper and kidnapped. I was already planning how I would do so, when Miss Fawlthorne said: "I can't allow you to leave."

Just as flatly and matter-of-fact as that. As if I were a captive.

"Why not?" I asked. "Veneering left."

"Charlotte Veneering is to be pitied," she said. "You are not."

It was a cruel cut. Like one involved in a duel with razor blades, I had to look to see if I had sustained a wound. I was almost surprised to find myself intact.

"If I let you go, I shall have failed," Miss Fawlthorne

said. "And so shall you. But we will not. We are both better than that."

I saw at once that she was appealing to that same tired old court of last resort: my pride—and I hated her for it.

But I let it pass. Why? Because, in a way, I pitied her.

And yet, to my horror, I saw that my left hand, as if it had a life of its own, was slowly creeping across the desktop toward her. Appalled, I jerked it back and held it tightly in my lap with the other—which made things even worse, because it was now perfectly plain that I was restraining these rogue fingers as I might a trained tarantula.

I could feel my color rising.

Miss Fawlthorne said nothing, but sat staring at me as if I were a cyst. The air in the room was so thick that you would have needed a chisel to cut it.

She was not going to make things easy for me, I knew. She was going to wait until I spoke, a tactic I recognized as one from my own toolbox.

We would sit here, then, she and I, glaring at each other in stubborn silence until the cows came home from the pastures of Heaven.

I have to hand it to her: Miss Fawlthorne was good at this game.

But not nearly as good as I.

I waited until it seemed that one of us must surely scream, and then I said suddenly: "Clarissa Brazenose is still alive, isn't she?"

No more and no less. I left it at that.

Miss Fawlthorne blinked but she said nothing.

"And so are Le Marchand and Wentworth. They're all still alive, but they've gone undercover."

I think I was as surprised as Miss Fawlthorne. Actually, the idea had been forming in some back room of my brain for quite a long time, I realized, but had not revealed itself until it was needed.

"If that were true," Miss Fawlthorne said, "—and I'm not for a moment saying that it is—it would be very dangerous knowledge."

I nodded, biting my lip wisely, as if I knew far more than I did. I did not enjoy being on the outs with this woman. She had, as I had noticed from the beginning, an unexpected gentle side that was not just at odds, but perhaps even at war with her role as headmistress.

Hadn't she, after all, doled out to me the so-called punishment of writing a paper on William Palmer? And now, just today, she had sentenced Gremly to skate a hundred laps round the old rink. Gremly! Who loved roller skating as Dante loved Beatrice—as Romeo loved Juliet—and as Winnie-the-Pooh loved honey!

In spite of whatever her grim connections to the Nide might be, the woman was at heart a softie.

And I couldn't help loving her for it in a complicated way.

"All right," I said, getting to my feet. "I understand. I am forbidden to ask and you are forbidden to tell. Neither of us much cares for it, but that's the way things are."

With that, I got to my feet and walked out of the room, and she didn't so much as lift a finger to stop me.

The interesting thing was this: Even before I reached the door, her eyes were dampening.

Back in Edith Cavell, I stood on my head in the bed, my heels against the wall. I needed to think.

I had wondered this before: What if this whole business were a sham, a put-up job? What if my being banished to Canada and the sudden appearance of the body in the chimney were merely part of some gigantic war game— some vast exercise in which all of us were pawns in a game staged by inconceivably remote manipulators for their own veiled purposes?

If so, Miss Fawlthorne might be as much at the mercy of these shadowy masters as I was, both of us in the grip of powers beyond our understanding.

Or—and I shuddered at the thought—was this simply the way life was?

Maybe God was master, Fate the hand that moved us on the playing board, and Chance the finger that flicked us bum-over-boiler into the ditch at the slightest misstep.

Whatever the truth, it was all too much for me, and I fell asleep standing on my head.

I awoke with a fierce headache and a crick in my neck. The room was in darkness. I closed my eyes again and allowed myself to come slowly awake.

There is genuine joy in being alone in the dark inside your own head with no outside distractions, where you can scramble from ledge to rocky ledge, *hallooing* happily in a vast, echoing cave; climbing hand over hand from ledge to ledge of facts and memories, picking up old gems and new: examining, comparing, putting them down again and reaching for the next.

The first thought that came to mind was that the Rainsmiths were on our side—at least according to Miss Fawlthorne. The second was that Le Marchand, Wentworth, and Clarissa Brazenose were possibly still alive.

If that were true, then obviously the body in the chimney could be none of them.

Or was it from a far earlier date? Because Miss Bodycote's Female Academy had once been a convent, was there the possibility that some poor nun in the distant past had been murdered (it was fun to wonder why) and stuffed up the chimney? Fitzgibbon had said that use of the fireplaces was forbidden until November, but that in itself didn't mean that the body hadn't been baking away during the winter months since time out of mind. Arguing against that theory was the fact of the substitute skull, and the fact that the corpse had been clutching a fairly recent Saint Michael Award. It seemed unlikely, too, that a chimney had remained blocked for fifty or so cold Canadian winters without anyone noticing.

I shivered and dropped out of my headstand.

What I needed now was information from the past: information about the first Mrs. Rainsmith—plain facts from someone who had known her personally.

It was obvious that that someone would have to be a member of faculty, and I knew almost instinctively that there was none better than Mrs. Bannerman, who had not only been here for years, but was blessed with an analytical mind much like my own.

I carried the clock to the window and saw that it was half ten: well after lights-out.

Mrs. Bannerman wouldn't be in the lab for hours, and yet I was now too wide awake to go back to sleep. I wrapped myself in a blanket and settled in a chair at the window.

Only then did I remember that I had announced to Miss Fawlthorne my determination to drop out of Miss Bodycote's Female Academy and go home: a resolution that I meant to keep, come Hades or high water.

Mrs. Mullet is quite fond of saying that "Well begun is half done," but I think there's more to it than that. Half done is only fifty percent, but there is a satisfaction in making a firm decision which is surely closer to ninety or ninety-five percent.

Making up your mind brings a relief, which "well begun" can't even come close to.

So, by hook or by crook I *was* going home, but it was still a long way from "Case Closed" at Miss Bodycote's. There were more ghosts here than the ones that fiddled with Ouija boards, or those that walked these haunted halls.

With hours to wait until Mrs. Bannerman would open the laboratory, there was no longer any excuse to delay my report on William Palmer, I thought, so I might as well get on with it.

It made no difference whatsoever that I had no reference materials at hand. Every detail of the Rugeley Poisoner's lurid life, having been burned happily and permanently into my memory, is forever at my fingertips. (*Don't lick them*, a gnomish little voice teases. *They're covered with arsenic.*)

I opened my notebook in my lap and picked up my pen.

Doctor William Palmer, I wrote, *was particularly proud of his soft white hands, which he was perpetually washing . . .*

Time flew by like butter, as Mrs. Mullet once said, as I outlined the life, the crimes, the trial, and the death of that saucy strychnine artist who had the nerve to ask Throttler Smith, the public hangman, as he spotted the trapdoor, "Are you sure it's safe?"

I ended my assignment with that lighthearted tidbit, thinking it would do no harm to provide Miss Fawlthorne with a smile.

How wrong I was.

I was rubbing my tired eyes when a flash of headlights outside in the street caught my attention. A car had pulled up and stopped at the curb.

How odd, I thought, that anyone should be coming or going at such an ungodly hour. Miss Bodycote's was not the kind of establishment that encouraged callers, even during the daylight hours, so that a middle-of-the-night arrival or departure was most likely to be bad news.

Had someone been taken ill? Had someone called a doctor? If that were the case, the doctor was not Ryerson Rainsmith. I knew his car, and this was not it.

The interior light flicked on, and I could see that the passenger was a man: not anyone from Miss Bodycote's, then. He was talking to the driver.

After several minutes, both doors sprang open and two men stepped out. Even in the dim light of the streetlamps I recognized Inspector Gravenhurst and Sergeant LaBelle. As they came up the steps, the front door opened, and a long rectangle of yellow light was cast out into the night. Silhouetted in it was the shadow of a woman, though whose, I could not tell.

And then the door was closed, and the entranceway was once again in darkness.

I crept quietly out into the hall, leaving my bedroom door ajar. Thank goodness I was still wearing yesterday's clothing and didn't have to dress.

At the top of the staircase, I paused, keeping to the shadows, and peeked down into the foyer.

The inspector and Sergeant LaBelle were standing just inside the door. They had not removed their hats, so they didn't intend to stay. Facing them was Miss Fawlthorne, and beside her, stiff as a marble statue, was Mrs. Bannerman.

The two women had obviously been awaiting the police, since they had opened the front door at once.

The inspector stepped forward and said something in a low voice, which I could not quite catch, and then Miss Fawlthorne opened the door for the others to step outside.

Not wanting to miss the least detail, I tiptoed back to my room as quickly as possible without giving myself away, and flew to the window.

Inspector Gravenhurst, with a firm grip on Mrs. Bannerman's elbow, was easing her into the backseat of the car.

In spite of the outward appearance of manners, I knew

that Inspector Gravenhurst was no Prince Charming, and Mrs. Bannerman no Cinderella.

It was no candlelight ball they were off to in a pumpkin coach, but rather a cold car ride to some dank, sour cell in a draughty police station.

Mrs. Bannerman was under arrest.

·TWENTY-FOUR·

I FELT AS IF my heart had been shot down in flames and crashed into the sea. Primarily, of course, for poor Mrs. Bannerman, but also, I must admit, for my own lost chances.

It was entirely my fault. I should have taken the opportunity to question her earlier about all those goings-on at Miss Bodycote's in years past. She had certainly been there long enough to know where all—or at least most—of the bodies were buried, if I may put it in such a coarse way.

Those early morning hours in the chemistry laboratory before the academy was awake had allowed us to form bonds that could never have developed in a classroom or on the playing field.

Squandered, I thought. *Utterly wasted.*

Without putting myself in even more of a jam than I was in already, there was no way of questioning students or faculty.

But that had never stopped Flavia de Luce before.

"Trust no one," Gremly had typed out on the Morse code sender. And Miss Fawlthorne had said the same—at least before she had contradicted herself.

Gremly, at least, was a member of the Nide, or so she had claimed. It was she, also, who had tipped me off about the first Mrs. Rainsmith. But she had distanced herself from me on the bus, and I knew, even without being told, that she did not want us to be seen together.

Who, then, *could* I trust?

Scarlett? I had asked her the cryptic pheasant question, but she, like Gremly, had recoiled with something that could only be fear.

Inspector Gravenhurst, I supposed, but it seemed unlikely he would share the results of his confidential investigations with a mere schoolgirl such as me.

Wallace Scroop came to mind, but I wrote him off almost immediately. He had spilled the beans about the ancient skull, but nothing more. If the truth be told, I had given him more information than he had given me—even if mine *had* turned out to be untrue. If Clarissa Brazenose, Wentworth, and Le Marchand were still alive, the information I had fed him was no more than a load of old horse hockey. I wondered if he knew?

At any rate, Wallace wouldn't likely be in much of a mood to share further confidences.

Outside, it had begun to rain: not a downpour, but a cold drizzle which almost at once, due to condensation and the dropping temperature, began to fog the window.

I breathed heavily upon the glass, obscuring my view of

the street, and creating a blank canvas upon which I could draw a whole new world with my forefinger.

I did it without even thinking: It came from somewhere deep inside.

Here was Bishop's Lacey, and here, St. Tancred's, with its churchyard. I sketched in a couple of little tombstones with my fingernail. Over here was the High Street, and Cow Lane, and Cobbler's Lane, and Mrs. Mullet's cottage.

Lord, how I missed her!

A warm tear ran down my cheek, matching to perfection a racing raindrop on the outside of the cold glass.

Here was her picket fence, and here her old rosebushes, which Alf kept trimmed to military standards. I almost began to sob as I etched in the clothesline, with someone's shirts—Father's, I realized with a shock—flapping wildly, sadly, in the fresh English breeze.

Laundry! Of course! What a fool I had been! I felt a stupid grin crawling like a fly across my face.

I wiped my eyes with the back of my hand and the wet window with my palm. No point in leaving clues behind, even if they *were* drawn in dampness.

Who was it—Daffy would know—that wanted "Here Lies One Whose Name Is Writ in Water" carved on his tombstone? Keats? Yeats?

I couldn't remember—which was precisely what he wanted, wasn't it?

It was Monday morning: washing day. The laundry would be opening early and I would be there—with bells on!

*   *   *

I let myself in and locked the door. In the early morning darkness, the laundry clanked and groaned as if it were a sleeping beast.

Kelly must have turned up late last night, or earlier this morning, to stoke the boilers, which were now hissing like a basket of angry asps. Already, the heat was almost unbearable. By midday, it would be killing.

I took the note I had written and placed it dead center on the table where Marge worked. She could hardly miss it.

It had caused me a considerable amount of thought and a considerable amount of blood. I hoped it was worth it.

Guided by the beacons of glowing pilot lights, I felt my way in the near darkness round the back of the main boiler to the ladder I had spotted on my earlier visits. Putting one hand on each rail and a foot on the bottom rung, I hauled myself up and began to climb.

A false dawn broke as I neared the frosted window at the top of the wall, where the sickly orange glow of a yard light seeped in among the panting pipes. I inhaled the acrid smell of hot steam.

At the top of the ladder I stepped off onto a walkway of perforated metal which spanned the room behind and above the boilers. Great valves—some painted red—sang away to themselves, like colorful barnacles on the hulk of a sunken liner.

An enormous duct, wrapped like King Tut in some kind of insulating material (asbestos, I hoped—otherwise it would be too hot) ran in an "L" shape down and across the laundry. I hauled myself cautiously up onto it, creeping wormlike along its length until I was directly above Marge's worktable.

From this "coign of vantage" (as Shakespeare would have called it) I could not possibly be seen. I was tucked away, safely out of sight, high above my enemies like one of the swallows in the battlements of Macbeth's castle.

> . . . no jutty, frieze, buttress,
> Nor coign of vantage, but this bird hath made
> His pendant bed . . .

And here I would nest.

Daffy would be proud of me.

I tucked myself in and waited. The warm humidity and the gentle hissing of the steam duct made it seem as if I were a baby animal—a hippopotamus, perhaps, or an elephant, tucked up in contentment against her mother's leathery skin, listening to her distant heartbeat and her long, slow breathing.

The heat must have caused me to fall asleep. I was jolted awake by a scream which began as a screech, then rose and fell, wailing in the air.

My eyes flew open, my blood already well on the way to curdling.

"What is it, Marge? What's the matter?"

Sal's voice.

"You look as if you've seen a ghost. Sit down, I'll get a chair."

I didn't risk peering over the edge of the duct upon which I was lying. My uncanny powers of hearing would tell me all I needed to know.

A nauseating scraping of wood on concrete followed by a plump thump told me that Sal had fetched the chair and that Marge had dropped heavily into it.

A rustle of paper confirmed that Marge had handed my note to Sal.

There was a silence in the steam as words ceased, and a low moan began.

I was enjoying this, actually.

I pictured Sal's eyes tracking hesitantly across the page, her lips moving as she read.

"What does it mean? *One of you knows my killer?*"

After hours of pondering, I had decided to crib the message of the Ouija board word for word. I could hardly have bettered it.

"Christ! It's written in blood, Sal." Marge had regained the power of speech.

"Fresh blood, too," she added. "Hasn't gone brown yet."

I rubbed my thumb against the still-raw end of my fore-finger, which I had pierced again and again with one of the despised embroidery needles from the personal kit I had been issued. It's surprising how much blood it takes to write half-a-dozen words.

I had signed the message *Francesca*—a long, smudged signature that leaked horribly off the edge of the page.

"Could it be—*her*—do you think?" Sal again, her voice trembling.

"Has to be. No other dead Francescas around here—not that I know of."

"Put it down, Marge. It's haunted. It's bad luck. Take my word for it."

"Wasn't here Friday when we locked up. Place is tighter than a drum. How did it get in here?"

Sal's voice had begun to develop a quaver. "What's it mean, 'One of you knows my killer'? She wasn't killed, she fell off a boat and drowned—or so they said."

"Never found her, though, did they? Maybe somebody bumped her off."

"Bumped her off?" Sal said indignantly. "Who'd do a thing like that?"

"Beats me. She was like a kid, really. Loved dressing up. Can't imagine anyone wanting to do her any harm. I found one of her famous red socks a couple of months ago behind the sorting table. Made me sad. Remember how she used to sneak us bags of her home laundry? 'The chairman would like a little more starch in his white collars,' she used to say, didn't she? 'The chairman would like to have his cuffs turned and leather patches on his elbows.' Remember? Well, the rich must have their little perks, mustn't they? Lord love her. I wish her well wherever she might be."

"Do you think she's listening to us—right now, I mean?"

"Don't be ridiculous, Sal. There's no such thing as ghosts."

"But what about this note?"

Marge gave out a laugh that was a little too confident. "Dollars to doughnuts it's one of our dear sweet girls. One of our dear, sweet, innocent little darlings that hopes to give us a heart attack. She's probably hiding behind the boiler at this very moment with her fist shoved in her mouth.

"AREN'T YOU, DEARIE?" she shouted. "Hand me the broom, Sal. I'll give her what for."

There came a wild whacking on the wall and I caught a glimpse of Marge's hairnet. I could almost have reached down and touched her, but I thought better of it.

"Come out, come out, wherever you are!" Sal cackled.

It had become a game, and I was the quarry.

"Ready or not, you must be caught. First caught's *it!*"

These two grown women had, in a matter of seconds, reverted to the kind of primitive urge that once made gentle housewives willingly assist in hauling old women off to the village green to be burnt or drowned as witches.

Drowned—was that what her killers did to Francesca Rainsmith? It didn't make sense. My mind was reeling.

For the first time since coming to Miss Bodycote's I was genuinely frightened.

"We're coming to *get* you!" they began chanting, one at first and then the other. "We're coming to *get* you!"

They began banging on the steam pipes, presumably with brooms, or whatever else was handy. The din was ferocious.

Fear, Dogger had once told me, is often irrational, but is nevertheless real because it is generated by the reptile part of our primitive brain: the instinctive part that is designed for dodging dinosaurs.

It was this uncontrollable reflex that caused me to do what I did: Instead of clinging to the duct and trying to hide, I scrambled to my feet and came clattering down the ladder—into their very midst, like a flushed rat.

The effect upon Marge and Sal was electric. They were as surprised as I was.

Marge put her hands on her hips and took a step toward me; Sal put her hands behind her back and stepped cautiously away. Both of them went red in the face like Tweedledum and Tweedledee.

"I told you," Marge said. "I told you she was up there, didn't I?"

Sal nodded wisely.

"What are you up to?" Marge demanded.

I looked from one to the other, pausing as long as I dared so that my words would have their maximum effect. When I judged the moment to be precisely right, I said: "I'm investigating the murder of Francesca Rainsmith."

There are times when truth is the simplest and the most effective weapon, and this was one of them. It's risky, but it sometimes works.

"Investigating?" Sal scoffed—almost spat. "A girl like you?"

I looked her in the eye. "Yes," I said. "A girl like me."

Utter silence.

"I hope you'll be able to assist me," I added, just as a way of oiling the cuckoo. The word "assist" is so much more civilized and lubricating, I find, than "help."

"Depends," Marge said, her voice cracking.

Hallelujah! I was halfway home!

"How well did you know Francesca Rainsmith?" I asked. "Did she come here often?"

"She used to bring her laundry in—his, too. Said she didn't have time, and she used to give us a plant at Christmas—a poinsettia, generally, in colored foil."

"Was she a medical doctor?"

Sal blew out air. "Her? No. I don't know what she did. Nothing, I think. I saw her one time on a Wednesday afternoon—I remember because it was my day off—at the Diana Sweets, having tea in the middle of the afternoon. Shopping bags everywhere, on the chairs, on the floor. She nodded at me, I think, sort of."

"Did they have any children?"

Facts, again. I needed facts. I was trying desperately to piece together out of thin air a detailed portrait of a woman I had only seen once, and even then, dead and decapitated.

She had not been at her best.

"Good lord, no! She hated kids. Used to cover her ears when she came around. Kept well away from them. Said they made her nervous. Wasn't much more than a kid herself, to tell you the truth . . . tiny bit of a thing. Girlish."

"Was she ever a student here?" I asked, in what seemed to me a sudden burst of inspiration.

"What makes you think that?" Marge said suddenly.

"I don't know," I told her truthfully. "It was just an idea."

A cloud had come over Marge's face, as sudden as a summer storm. "Say, is this anything to do with that body in the chimney?"

"Yes," I said, watching her face carefully. "I'm afraid it is."

Marge's and Sal's hands went to their mouths at the

same time, as if they had been stitched together at the elbows. It was obvious that, until this moment, they had not made the connection. I watched as horror crossed their faces.

"Listen," I said, "I'm only telling you this because I trust you. I'm sticking my neck out. If anything comes out I'll be held responsible."

"Who told you this?" Marge demanded. "Was it that Scroop, from the *Star*?"

"As a matter of fact, it was," I said, gilding the lily a little.

"Don't you have nothing to do with him," Sal said.

"Why not?" I asked, all wide-eyed and innocent.

"He's always nosing around, isn't he, Marge? A regular busybody. Miss Fawlthorne said not to breathe a word to him. If he tries to ask you questions, send him packing. That's what Miss Fawlthorne said."

"Send him to *her* is what she said," Marge corrected. "But he's never been back, not so far as I know."

"Mrs. Rainsmith," I said, getting back on the track. "Francesca, I mean. How did she die?"

"Originally, or recently?" Marge asked.

This Marge was a smart cookie. I had to give her credit.

"Originally," I said. "The moonlight cruise."

"Two years ago. Right after the Beaux Arts Ball. Their anniversary. She was all excited about it. The chairman booked it in advance as a kind of treat."

"Dr. Rainsmith?" I asked. "Ryerson?"

"That's right. She *was* all excited about it, wasn't she,

Sal. Said she'd been a bit nervy. Moonlight cruise was all she needed—just what the doctor ordered. She laughed when she said it, 'cause the doctor was her husband, you see, and he *did* order it."

I smiled dutifully. "She told you this?" I asked.

"Stood right where you're standing," Sal said.

"And they never found the body," I said.

"No. They were seen going up the gangplank, and from then on it was all drinks and dancing. They didn't hobnob with the other passengers—didn't want to, really. It was their anniversary, you see. Very romantic. They even wore their wedding outfits. It was in all the papers, you know. A real mystery. Sometime after midnight, somewhere off Port Dalhousie, the chairman told the captain he thought his wife might have fallen overboard. Might have had a drink too many. Captain kept it pretty well to himself . . . didn't want to alarm the other passengers. That's what he told the papers: didn't want to upset the other passengers. If you ask me, what he meant was he didn't want bad publicity. He sailed around in circles in the dark for a while—searchlights, and that—but they never spotted her. Not a trace."

"Not a ripple," Sal added. "I remember they called in the Air Force in the morning: boats, helicopters. No use. It was on the radio."

" 'Course there wouldn't be, would there, if she was in the chimney all along," Marge said, glancing at me knowingly, as if we had just shared a very great secret.

"And the second Mrs. Rainsmith?" I asked. "Dorsey?"

"He knew her for years," Sal said, with an obscure kind of glance at Marge. "Met her at medical school."

"They say she was a great comfort to him in his time of loss," Marge said.

"Who's 'they'?" I asked. "Who said that?"

"Well, *she* did," Marge admitted.

A shadow flitted like a bat across my mind. How could Dorsey, Miss High Muckety Muck herself, ever have happened to come into conversation with the likes of Marge, a lowly laundry lass.

"Oh!" I said, seeming surprised. "Does *she* bring her laundry round, as well?"

"No," Sal said.

"Well, just the once," Marge said reluctantly. "She had a dress—an expensive one. Pure silk, like rippling water on a lake. Bought it at Liberty's, in London. Must have cost her an arm and a leg, I told her. 'More than that,' she said. 'Far more than that.' I remember her saying it."

"And?"

"An emergency. She was called in to handle an emergency. Car crash. Got blood on it. She phoned me at home and asked if I could help her out. Girl to girl. She slipped me ten bucks. Oh, don't look at me like that, Sal. I'll split it with you, if you like."

"Hold on," I said. "Was this after she married the chairman?"

"No, before. A year or so. I'll still split it with you, Sal."

"Was it before or after the Beaux Arts Ball?" I asked, my heart accelerating.

"After," Marge said. "Just after."

"Thank you," I said. "You've both been of enormous help, and I mean to make it up to you."

Marge glowed, and although Sal brushed off my remark with a flick of her fingers, I knew that she was secretly pleased.

"May I ask one last question?"

"Fire away," Marge said.

"How was it that you knew Dorsey Rainsmith *before* her marriage to the chairman?"

"Why, because she was on the board of guardians," Marge said.

My head was like a spinning top as possibilities sparked and glittered off in all directions.

Was Ryerson Rainsmith a member of the Nide? Was Dorsey? Had Francesca been?

Had Francesca's death been an official undercover act? An execution?

Was Miss Fawlthorne in on the secret?

Or was it more sordid than that? One of those Lady Chatterley affairs that Daffy was so keen on reading, and which left me bored stiff?

Time enough to think about those things later. I had suddenly become aware of my hands, which meant only one thing: It was time to say my farewells and make a graceful—or at least dignified—exit.

Dogger had once told me, "Your hands know when it's time to go."

And he had been right. The hands are the canaries in one's

own personal coal mine: They need to be watched carefully and obeyed. A fidget demands attention, and a full-blown not-knowing-what-to-do-with-them means "Vamoose!"

I gave Marge and Sal a grateful smile and headed for the door.

"Oh, by the way," Marge called out, "better get Fitzgibbon to put something on that finger. I think you've cut yourself."

·TWENTY-FIVE·

"NEWSROOM," I WHISPERED INTO the telephone transmitter. "Wallace Scroop."

I was in the shadows of the back hall, hoping my uniform would make me invisible against the dark paneling. It was still early, after breakfast but well before classes, and the sudden departure of Mrs. Bannerman seemed to have cast an invisible pall over Miss Bodycote's.

There was an eerie silence: an absence of joy and youthful voices. The air was a weighted vacuum.

"Scroop." Wallace's voice came clearly through the receiver.

"It's me again," I said. "I need a favor."

"What's in it for the *Morning Star*?" he asked. "More to the point, what's in it for Wallace Scroop?"

He caught me by surprise. I had not expected to negotiate, had not thought it through before placing the call.

I had to make a snap decision, and I did. It was one of the most difficult things I have ever been made to do in my life.

"Everything," I said.

And I meant it.

"All right," he said, when we had agreed on the terms, "tell me what you need."

"The details of Francesca Rainsmith's death. She drowned on a midnight cruise two years ago. I am told by a reliable informant that it was in all the papers. You must have them in the files. I need everything I can get, especially eyewitness accounts, the captain and crew, passengers, and so forth."

"That's a tall order, isn't it, little lady?"

"I'm not a little lady and it's not as tall as what you're asking *me* to do for *you.*"

"Touché, José," he said. "But there's no need to disturb the morgue—that's what we call the files, by the way. Yours truly was on the scene and it's etched into my brain in hot lead."

"Go ahead," I said. "I'm listening."

"Gentleman and lady show up in taxi at harbor two minutes before sailing. Both in wedding duds: tux, tails, boiled shirt, cuff links, bow tie; white dress, veil, lots of lace, bouquet. Tips the purser—tells him it's their anniversary."

"Were they carrying anything?" I asked.

"He was. Big gift box. Fancy wrappings, blue ribbons."

"And her?"

"Just the bouquet."

Somewhere above me, a floorboard creaked. Someone was on the stairs.

"Hold on," I whispered. "I'll be back in a jiff."

I put down the handset and tiptoed to the bottom of the stairs. By craning my neck I could see to the landing and above.

I put my foot on the bottom step and began upward, making more noise than I needed to by shuffling my shoes.

And then I stopped. If someone *had* been listening, they had beetled off.

I went back to the telephone.

"Sorry," I told him, whispering. "Go on. About the Rainsmiths . . . ?"

"They danced. Danced their hooves off till the wee hours. Everyone dog-tired. Drinks. Nobody paying attention. He appears in the wheelhouse, frantic. Out of his mind. Wife's fallen overboard. Tipsy—must've lost her balance. Maybe the bang on the head."

"Hold on," I said. "What bang on the head?"

"Oh, yeah. I forgot to tell you. She conked her head on the door frame getting out of the taxi. There was gore galore. Purser offered to call a doctor. Wouldn't hear of it. Rainsmith said *he* was a doctor. Just a scalp wound. Scalp wounds bleed a lot, you know. Nothing serious. He would patch her up."

"And did he?"

"Must have. Like I said, they danced like there was no tomorrow."

"Did anybody have a look at her?"

"Not much. It was dark, remember."

"Dark? I thought it was a moonlight cruise."

"Bit of a washout there. Cloudy night, cold for June. Rainy squalls, choppy. Not many dancing on deck. Only the foolhardy and the lovesick few."

"And afterwards?"

"Rainsmith was a broken man. Had to be helped off the boat."

"What about the box?"

"Never had a chance to give it to her. Very touching story. *DROWNING VICTIM DUCKS FINAL GIFT*. Tasteless, maybe—but it won me a press award."

"Congratulations," I said.

"Look, kid. I've got to scram. There's been a bank robbery downtown, and they're screaming for Scroop. And listen, don't forget our deal."

"I won't," I said, but he had already rung off, leaving me alone again.

I think it was in that moment, standing alone at the back of the dark hallway at Miss Bodycote's Female Academy, that I realized I was not only on my own, but likely to remain so. Although I had made the acquaintance of several of the girls at the Academy—Gremly and Scarlett, for instance—no deep long-term friendships had grown out of it. We were all of us like the proverbial ships that pass in the night, signaling only briefly to one another before sailing off over the horizon into our own patch of darkness.

At least, that's how I felt. It was sad, in a way.

And yet, if it was sad, why did I feel so exhilarated?

Could it be the challenge?

In my personal experience, the solving of murder mys-

teries had involved the examination of a body, the gathering of clues, the putting-together of two and two, the
unmasking of the killer, and . . . *Voilà! Bob's your uncle!*
Case closed. It was as easy as boiling water.

But this case was an entirely new kettle of fish. The
body had been removed before I'd had a chance to do more
than barely glance at it, and there wasn't the faintest hope
that Inspector Gravenhurst was going to show up at the
door to pile heaps of evidence at my feet with a shovel.
There was no way of gaining access to autopsy results—
short of trying to pry them out of Dorsey Rainsmith, which
would be about as likely as the sun rising in the north tomorrow and setting in the south.

I was going to have to develop a whole new technique:
a new modus operandi, as Philip Odell, the private detective on the BBC wireless, would have put it.

Rather than reasoning from corpse to killer, as I had in
the past, I would now have to reverse the process. It would
be like solving a crime in a mirror.

Which was, perhaps, the cause of my excitement.

I began a mental list that, if written in my notebook,
might have looked something like this:

(a) Who had a motive to murder Francesca Rainsmith?

(i) Her husband, obviously. Daffy says there are
motives in marriage that lie beyond reach of
the church, the courts, and even the ~~front~~
page. Note: The <u>News of the World</u> claims that

most killers and their victims come from the same family.

(ii) Her soon-to-be replacement, Dorsey Rainsmith, whose reasons for wanting her rival dead are as plain as the nose on your face.

(iii) Someone other than above. A stranger, perhaps. Some madman or madwoman.

(b) Who has the capability to behead a corpse?

(i) Dorsey Rainsmith is a forensic surgeon. She certainly possesses the know-how and the medical skill.

(ii) Ryerson Rainsmith is a medical doctor. Not so skillful as his wife, perhaps, but still capable of getting the job done.

(iii) Fitzgibbon is a former nurse, and may well have both the nerve and the stomach required to remove the part in question.

(iv) Some unsuspected brute, such as the Ourang-Outang in Edgar Allan Poe that shoved a body up the chimney: a remarkable parallel to the present case, come to think of it. Remarkable, indeed!

Again I found myself wondering: Could I, by sheer chance, have stumbled upon one of those classic killings, such as those written about by Miss Christie, in which the murderer mocks the police by carrying out killings that mimic nursery rhymes or fairy tales? Was Francesca Rainsmith's killer intentionally reenacting *The Murders in the Rue Morgue*? I would never, as long as I live, forget the wild night that Daffy had read that tale aloud to us, the rain drumming on the drawing room windows, the blood and the hair on the hearth, and the old lady with her head cut clean off. I would try to find a copy as soon as possible to search for further parallels. Miss Bodycote's had a small but serviceable library in an alcove in which nuns had once congregated to pray as they worked away at their invisible mending.

Mending reminded me of the laundry. Edward Kelly, the Human Mountain, the stoker of Miss Bodycote's boilers, was the only suspect who physically fit the bill. With his bulk and his muscles, he could probably stuff a body up a chimney before you could say "Ginger!" To say nothing of the detached head.

All of these things flickered like summer lightning through my mind as I stood in the lower hall, the telephone receiver still clutched tightly in my hand.

One fact stuck out like a septic thumb: that Mrs. Bannerman's name did not appear on my list—and yet Inspector Gravenhurst had arrested her without so much as a la-di-da.

Was it because he knew more than I did? That was possible, I suppose, but I can't say I much liked the idea. Or could it be that, as an acquitted murderess, she had become a perpetual suspect? I didn't much care for that idea, either.

The inspector, after all, had access to all the evidence gathered, to the autopsy findings, and to the statements of all those who had been questioned, whereas I had to be content with the crumbs.

As I have said, I was on my own, and the business of gathering evidence was, and would continue to be, like picking up spilled pepper in the dark.

I was, like poor, homesick Moses in the book of Exodus, a stranger in a strange land.

An outcast.

But there was no point in feeling sorry for myself. It is always better, and far more rewarding, I have observed, to have someone else feel sorry for you, than to do the job yourself.

Which gave me a splendid idea.

"May I come in?" I asked, knocking lightly on the door frame.

Miss Moate looked up from the shelf attached to her wheelchair, upon which she was sorting fossils.

She did not say yes and she did not say no, so I took a chance and stepped into the lab.

"Well?" she asked, in her permanently peeved voice. I could tell that she hated being interrupted.

"I'm sorry to bother you, Miss Moate," I said. If I'd worn

a cap I'd have been wringing it in my hands. "I wonder if you might spare me a few minutes. It's rather a personal matter?"

I was proud of my strategy. It was one I had been saving for just such an occasion as this. Who can say no to a personal matter? Even God is curious about such things, which is why He listens to our prayers.

As a teacher, Miss Moate had presumably been trained in some dim and remote teachers college in how to handle the confidences of her pupils. Appealed to directly, she could hardly say no.

"I'm busy," she said. "Personal matters should be taken up with the head, or with your housemistress."

"My housemistress is Mrs. Bannerman," I said, "and she's been arrested."

"What?" A fossil clattered onto the hard surface of the tray. I could tell by the genuine look of surprise on her face that Miss Moate had not yet heard the news.

"Arrested," I said. "They took her away. In the middle of the night."

Rat-a-tat-tat. Just like that. Shocking news is best delivered in bursts for maximum impact. I was sparing this woman nothing.

"How do you know this? Where did you hear it?"

"I didn't hear it," I said. "I was there. I saw it with my own eyes."

I could see the wheels turning as she lifted the huge padded cozy from the pot and poured herself a cup of tea. Should she gossip with a student, or place herself above idle chatter?

"This . . . personal matter," she said at last. "You may speak. But first, close the door."

I did as I was told, knowing, as I began, that one of us was not good at this sort of thing.

"I'm frightened," I said.

Her eyes considered this, and then she asked, "Of what?"

"The place is haunted," I told her. "Footsteps are heard in the halls, and a girl who died two years ago has been seen coming out of the laundry."

It was a bold opening, and I was proud of myself to have thought of it.

"And have you seen with your own eyes, as you put it, this dead girl? Have you heard, with your own ears, these footsteps in the halls?"

"Well, no," I admitted.

"Science does not believe in ghosts," she said. "And nor, as a budding chemist, should you."

So my special classes with Mrs. Bannerman were no secret.

"Ghosts are most often seen by girls and certain young men with an iron deficiency."

If she was referring to chlorosis, or hypochromic anemia, she might as well have saved her breath. The condition had been described as early as the sixteenth century, and a remedy containing iron, sulfuric acid, and potassium carbonate concocted more than a hundred years ago by Albert Popper, the Bohemian chemist, and it was no news to me.

"I'm sorry to have bothered you," I said, turning toward the door.

"No, wait," Miss Moate said. "Don't take offense."

I let my shoulders slump a little as a sign of defeat.

"You mustn't judge an old woman too harshly," she said, her voice softening. "Look at me."

I didn't want to, and I found my eyes repelled by hers as if they were the like poles of a pair of magnets. By sheer strength of my optical muscles, I forced myself to meet her gaze.

"I was not always like this, you know," she said, her hands fluttering reluctantly to indicate her body. "No, this useless husk was not always as you see it."

She gave a barking, seal-like laugh to indicate the irony of her situation.

"How did it happen?" I blurted, before I could stop myself.

Now that I had locked my gaze with hers I found that I could not break free.

"You are the first person at this academy who has ever asked that," she said.

"I'm sorry," I said, aware, even as I spoke, what a marvelous picklock power was contained in that one little word.

"Don't be," she replied. "Everyone else in the world is sorry. Dare to be something *more* than that."

I waited for the electric charge in the air to settle.

"As you are now, so once was I," she said, the words seeming ancient in her throat. "You'll find that inscribed on tombstones in old graveyards, you know."

I was well aware of it. The churchyard at St. Tancred's had several variations of the verse:

336 · ALAN BRADLEY

Remember, Friend, as you pass by,
As you are now, so once was I.
As I am now, so you must be,
So Friend, prepare to follow me.

It was almost my favorite piece of poetry, as opposed to Keats, say, or Shelley, or someone who wrote less practical verse.

"It was an accident," she said, her voice harsh, the words now suddenly raw in her mouth. "A car accident. . . . a village . . . a valley . . . a picnic . . . a friend. She was thrown clear, but I"—she touched the rubber tires of her chair, almost caressing them—"was trapped among the wheels."

I was going to say that I was sorry, but I held my tongue.

"My only consolation is in being allowed to spend most of my time here, among my *real friends.*"

She brought her hand round in a broad sweep to include the glass cases of stuffed creatures.

"They are trapped, also, you see? Birds of a feather! You may laugh, if you wish."

"It's not amusing," I said. "It's tragic."

I was thinking how I would feel if I were no longer able to swoop like a swallow through a country lane, my feet on Gladys's handlebars as we raced down Goodger Hill and swept across the little stone bridge at the Palings. "Yaroo!" I used to shout.

There was a silence in the room, and I turned away from Miss Moate, as if I had become suddenly interested in the displays in their cases.

I took down a browned skull from a shelf, turning it over in my hands.

I could hardly believe my eyes.

Steady on. Keep calm, I thought. *Poker face, stiff upper lip . . . anything to keep from giving away what you've just seen.*

"Don't touch that!" Miss Moate snapped. "The specimens are not to be handled."

"Sorry," I said before I could stop myself, and returned the grinning head to its place among the others.

"I've done it again, haven't I? But as I said, you mustn't judge an old woman too harshly."

"It's all right, Miss Moate," I said, focusing on trying to appear normal, which is much more difficult than you might think. "I understand perfectly. I have a very great friend back home in England who is confined to a wheelchair. I know how dreadful it is."

I thought of dear old Dr. Kissing, parked in his rickety bath chair at Rook's End, who, in his ancient quilted smoking jacket and tasseled hat, his cigarette ash drooping like an acrobatic gray caterpillar from the leaf of his lower lip, was snug as a bug in a rug. Dr. Kissing had certainly never complained about his lot in life, and I mentally begged his forgiveness for even suggesting that he might have done.

"Very well, then," Miss Moate said abruptly, clearing her throat as if to wipe the conversational slate clean. "Now, back to this personal matter . . . you're frightened, you say?"

"Well, not so much frightened as worried," I admitted. "It's about the Rainsmiths."

I dared not say more.

"What about them? Has one of them done something to you?"

"Not to me," I said, "but perhaps to someone else."

"To who?" she demanded ungrammatically.

"I mustn't say. School rules forbid it."

Although I kept a sober face, I was smiling inwardly. Defending oneself by hiding behind the rules was a clever trick, like using a mouse to stampede the enemy's elephants and causing them to trample him to death. Shakespeare had a phrase for it (as he had a phrase for everything): "hoist by his own petard," which, according to Daffy, meant rousted by the smell of one's own barn burners.

"Forget the school rules," she said. "When a child is at risk, the rules must be set aside."

Who did she think was at risk? I wondered. I had admitted being frightened and worried, but I had said nothing about being at risk—which was actually no more than a weasel word for danger.

"Now, then," she said in a soothing voice, "tell me about the Rainsmiths."

"I think they may have murdered someone."

"Who?" she said instantly. "In particular."

"Clarissa Brazenose."

I could have mentioned the names of Le Marchand and Wentworth, but I wanted to keep things simple. I had already suggested to Miss Fawlthorne that this trio may still be alive, but Miss Moate was not aware of that.

Partial disclosure is a sharp knife that can be used again and again as long as you watch what you're doing.

"That's a very serious accusation," Miss Moate said. "Are you sure?"

"No. I only *think* they may have. But I needed to tell someone."

"Well, I'm glad you did. I shall certainly see that—"

Somewhere a bell went off, and moments later, the halls were filled with the sound of many feet. A babble of loud voices came closer and closer, and suddenly the horde, like a buffalo herd, was upon us.

"Later," Miss Moate said, mouthing the words to be heard above the clamor. "We shall talk later."

Then, her voice suddenly restored, she shouted harshly: "Girls! Girls! Girls! We are not savages!"

I nodded to let her know that I had understood and, like a salmon fighting its way upstream, I muscled my way to the door.

I forced myself to plod doggedly along the halls to my room. No one paid me the slightest attention.

When I reached Edith Cavell, I stepped inside, closed the door, and flattened my back against it. Now that it was safe to do so, my breath began coming in great, ragged gulps. I was becoming light-headed.

The skull in Miss Moate's science lab—the skull I had held in my hands . . .

Before I replaced it on the shelf, I could not help spotting that three of its teeth contained amalgam fittings.

·TWENTY·SIX·

DENTAL SURGERY HAS BEEN around for almost as long as teeth. I had learned this stomach-curdling fact from the pages of a rather sticky journal in the waiting room of a London dentist's office—a dim and ancient chamber of horrors in Farringdon Street whose prominent painted Victorian signs on every window, *PAINLESS DENTISTRY* and *NO WAITING*, had been lying to the public in florid capital letters for more than a century.

Fillings, I had read, had been found in the teeth of some of the skulls in the Roman catacombs, although it was believed that most of the ancient mouths had been plundered by grave robbers who had pried out the gold. The Etruscans and Egyptians also had tinkered with teeth, and it was believed that even our earliest ancestors had stuffed their cavities with beeswax.

I'm no expert in the art of filling teeth, but I've spent enough time hog-tied in the chair, having barbed wire strung from tooth to tooth, to have studied in great detail the large colored posters that illustrate in dripping color the perils of not brushing after every meal. As I've said elsewhere, I adore rot, but not in my mouth and, more to the point, not in the mouths of strangers to whom I have not been introduced.

The fact remained that a skull from antiquity was hardly likely to contain a tidy modern filling, much less three of them, which looked to me as bright and fresh as if they had been installed last Friday morning.

I'd bet my tongue, tonsils, and toenails that these fillings had not been done in any Stone Age cave.

In my mind, a few more pieces of the puzzle snapped into position: *click! click! click!* If this were a jigsaw, I'd now have the border complete.

I reached into my pocket and my fingers closed around my wadded handkerchief.

Of course! I'd wrapped the Saint Michael medallion to protect it from further contamination, which was odd when you stopped to reflect that it was usually the other way round: that while others begged Saint Michael to protect them, I was protecting Saint Michael from others.

Flavia de Luce, Protector of Archangels.

It had a nice ring to it.

My heart was a little lighter for the thought as I descended the stairs.

Today was Monday, and I remembered that I was due for

342 · ALAN BRADLEY

my regular meeting with Miss Fawlthorne. What would she have in store? I wondered, and what kind of mood would she be in?

One could never tell.

Was I early or late? I'd forgotten the time she told me to report this week, but better late than never—or as I had learned as an investigator, better early than late.

But I needn't have worried. No one answered my several knocks at the door.

I opened it gently and peeked into an empty room.

Tiptoeing—for some odd reason which I didn't quite understand—I took a piece of scrap paper from the wastebasket.

Dear Miss Fawlthorne, I wrote. *I was here but you were not.*

Perfect! Brief but informative, with just a pinch of accusation.

Now then, how should I sign it? *Your obedient servant? Yours faithfully? Yours respectfully? Sincerely?*

In the end, I simply put *Flavia de Luce*, and left it on her desk.

The library was probably the only room at Miss Bodycote's where one could be alone without being accused of being up to no good. I could see through the many-paned glass doors that no one was inside.

As I let myself in, my nostrils were filled with musty but pleasant air, as if the books themselves were breathing in their sleep in the unventilated room. I made for the small fiction section and began scanning the shelves.

Anne of Green Gables was cuddled up next to *Huckleberry Finn; The Hunchback of Notre Dame* was wedged tightly between *Heidi* and *Little Women;* and *Nicholas Nickleby* leaned in a familiar way against *A Girl of the Limberlost*.

None of the books were in alphabetical order, which made it necessary to cock my head sideways to read each one of the spines. By the end of the third shelf I had begun to realize why librarians are sometimes able to achieve such pinnacles of crankiness: It's because they're in agony.

If only publishers could be persuaded, I thought, to stamp all book titles horizontally instead of vertically, a great deal of unpleasantness could be avoided all round. Chiropractors and opticians would be out of business, librarians cheerier, and the world would be a better place. I must remember to discuss this theory with Dogger.

Here, on a shelf near the bottom, was *Ben Hur*, and over there was Angela Thirkell: They were what Daffy called "nice novels," with *that* look on her face. Except for a couple of blue-covered novels about a person named Nancy Drew, which had been read to ribbons, most of the books appeared seldom to have been opened.

Ha! Just as I had hoped: *Tales of Edgar Allan Poe*.

I slid it from the shelf. The illustrations were horrific—so horrific that I felt as if a moist snail were crawling across the back of my neck, especially when I turned to "The Murders in the Rue Morgue," where a gigantic Ourang-

Outang, its shoulders scraping the ceiling, hunched over the body of a woman with a cutthroat razor in its hand.

I tucked the book under my arm for bedtime reading.

A shelf marked *Geography* caught my eye. Here were a handful of lonely-looking books: China, Africa, Europe, and so on. And here was Canada: a history of the maritime provinces, a biography of someone named Timothy Eaton, a cookbook by someone named Kate Aitken, an autobiography called *No Star to Guide Me* by Helen Murchison Trammell signed by the author—an old girl of Miss Bodycote's, who, according to her biography on the dust jacket, had married an oilman from Calgary and never looked back—and a *Gray Goose Street Guide of Greater Toronto*, which I pocketed.

A quick trip to the telephone directory told me that the Rainsmiths lived in a neighborhood called Rosedale.

Rosedale was considerably farther from Miss Bodycote's than I had imagined. The streets were laid out among a series of hills and ravines, some of them little more than horseback trails. Estates lay behind elaborate iron gates, with flowerbeds and lawns which looked as though gardeners on hands and knees had trimmed them with manicure scissors and tweezers. A couple of Rolls-Royces and Bentleys were parked in driveways in front of half-timbered houses. It was all very grand: a reflection of England but ever so much less grubby: more new and somehow unreal, as if it were a backdrop freshly painted.

The Rainsmiths lived in an Elizabethan manor house the size of a cricket pitch. To one side of the garden, at the end of a trellised walkway, was a long, low building of yellow brick that looked as if it meant business. It had once apparently been a coach house, but was now all casement windows and gables and climbing vines.

A couple of electric lamps burning inside during daylight hours, and a swinging Georgian sign reading "*Mon Repos*" in gold and black curlicue letters, told me that this was the private nursing home.

Somewhere behind all that glass and ivy, Collingwood was being held prisoner.

Or was she?

There was only one way to find out.

Directly across the street, a neighboring mansion was meant to be modeled on Anne Hathaway's cottage, complete with what appeared to be a thatched roof and what undoubtedly *was* an English cottage garden: one of those little jungles of artists' colors whose owner tries to include every flower mentioned in Shakespeare. Because it was now late in the year, the garden was not at its best, but I still managed to nick a fistful of Michaelmas daisies and chrysanthemums: the daisies because of Saint Michael— and, I must admit, because they were pictured on the dress of one of Jack the Ripper's victims—and the mums because I was in a hurry.

Back across the street, I was already inventing lies as I approached the glass doors of the nursing home. I needn't have bothered: Ahead of me an endless corridor of closed doors stretched off into the distance. There was no one at the desk.

Were all nursing homes, everywhere, alike? I thought of Rook's End, with its bubbling linoleum, where Dr. Kissing sat smoking away in his ancient bath chair. Rook's End, too, had infinite hallways and an unattended entrance, which had always surprised me. It was as if you had arrived at the Pearly Gates only to find a sign saying "Out to Lunch."

With the bouquet clutched in plain sight in my fist, and a look of sad resignation on my face, I walked quietly along, as if I knew where I was going. The occupants' names were printed on removable cards—in case of death, I supposed—attached to each door, so it was easy enough to construct a list of patients.

The place smelled of commodes and playing cards, and before I was halfway to the end I had made a firm resolve never to begin to die. For me it would be all or nothing: no half measures, no lingering on the doorstep.

A metallic clatter made me spin round.

A woman in scrubber's uniform was backing out of a room, hauling a wheeled bucket behind her. She seemed as surprised as I was, and then a grin broke her face.

"Cripes! You startled me!"

"Same here," I said, wiping my brow with my forearm and flinging off drops of imaginary sweat.

We both laughed.

"Can I help you?" she asked. "Looking for someone in particular?"

"No," I said. "I'm with the Girl Scouts. Rosedale Troop

Number Thirty-nine, Scarlet Pimpernel Patrol. I'm work-ing on my charity badge and Brown Owl assigned me to visit as many of the patients here as possible."

I tried to arrange my features into a look of hopeless determination combined with wilting enthusiasm. It was not easy.

"Quota system, eh?" the woman said. "Everything's quotas nowadays, it seems like. So many yards per floor per shift."

She stuck the head of her mop into a mechanical squeez-ing mechanism and gave the lever a fierce pull.

"'Life's a tally board,' my dad used to say, 'where the peg won't stay in.'"

I gave her a slightly conspiratorial grin—not enough to discredit the Girl Guides but enough that she would know that I wasn't born yesterday, either.

"Carry on, then," she said and, cracking my heels to-gether, I gave her a two-fingered bunny salute.

At the end of the hall, the last door on the left had a bilious yellow card hanging from a thumbtack: *QUARAN-TINE. NO ENTRY.*

I had found Collingwood.

But there was no card in the slot: no name to identify the room's occupant.

I pushed open the door.

The room was as empty as the infirmary had been at Miss Bodycote's.

Collingwood had vanished again.

I took the precaution of checking the WC.

It, too, was empty. Where was she? What had they done with her?

I was trying to think what to do next when I heard voices in the hall, voices that were coming closer with every second. As a precaution, I dived into the WC and pulled the door to, leaving it open barely a crack.

Two people came into the room: nurses, I guessed, from their words.

"I suppose now we'll have to burn the bedclothes," one of them said. "*And* the mattress."

I shrank back in horror. What *had* become of Collingwood?

"No such thing," the second voice said. "We don't do that anymore. Fumigation's cheaper. Cost-saving's the name of the game. Mattresses are money. So are sheets and towels. Better check the bathroom. I've already asked Gilda to clean it. God knows what—"

I pushed the door closed the last inch and positioned myself on the toilet seat.

And not a second too soon. The door was flung rudely open by a middle-aged woman in white, whose mouth fell open just before her face froze.

She slammed the door.

"There's a girl in there," I heard her say.

"Who?"

"No idea. Complete stranger."

There was a silence with much muttering as they discussed strategy.

Then there was a knock at the door.

"Who is it?" I asked, trying to sound outraged.

"Staff," came the muffled answer.

I waited for a decent interval to pass—twenty-five seconds by actual count—then flushed the lav and walked out with my nose in the air as if I were the anointed queen of the hoolie-joolies.

"Disgraceful," I said, pointing behind me. "You ought to be ashamed of yourselves."

And I walked out of the room and out of the building without so much as a look back.

Chalk up another Triumphant Exit to Flavia de Luce.

·TWENTY-SEVEN·

GAINING THE UPPER HAND might result in a few moments of pleasure, but it does not bring genuine contentment. I realized this as I stood, suddenly dejected, on the brick walkway between the Rainsmiths' mansion and the nursing home, my bouquet still clutched firmly in my hand.

How foolish I must have looked.

I might have won the battle, as Mrs. Mullet's husband, Alf says, but lost the war. Collingwood was still missing, Mrs. Bannerman was in jail, and I was stuck in some godforsaken suburb of Toronto without two fresh ideas to rub together.

I was not hopeful. I hardly dared even think about poor little Collingwood. The very mention of burning her mattress was enough to suggest that her end had been a tragic one. And as for Mrs. Bannerman—well, any dreams I might have had of studying with her had vanished like so much smoke up the chimney.

And it was in that instant—as it so often is—that a major piece of the puzzle fell into place, as if from the sky—as if the Gods of Deduction had tossed it overboard and let it fall at my feet.

I needed to get back to Miss Bodycote's and the chemistry lab without wasting another minute.

A hissing sound caught my attention. It was coming from somewhere behind the Rainsmiths' house and to my left.

A hissing in the garden is a sound that cannot be ignored by any human female since the time of Eve, and I was no exception. I moved slowly off the walk and onto the grass, craning my neck in the hope that it would allow me to see without being seen.

A pleasant-looking gentleman in uniform except for his shirtsleeves was playing a hose over a blue car: a car I had last seen picking up Miss Fawlthorne on the Danforth with Ryerson Rainsmith at the wheel.

While I was considering my options, my feet developed a mind of their own and began walking toward the man with the hose.

"Hello?" I heard myself calling out. "Is this the Rainsmith residence?"

The man twisted the nozzle and the spray of water choked to a drizzle. He studied me before answering.

"Miss Bodycote's?" he said at last, although it was not really a question.

My school uniform was a dead giveaway.

I nodded glumly.

"And your name is . . . ?" he asked.

"De Luce," I told him. "F for Flavia. You must be Mr. Merton. I was dreadfully sorry to hear about your mother passing away," I told him. "It's awful when that happens. My own mother died in April."

And with that, I handed him the bouquet.

Without a word he accepted the flowers, retrieved his jacket from the stone wall where it had been draped, and beckoned me to follow him into the house.

The interior was dim, and the kitchen, being on the north side of the house, was a room that had never known sunshine.

"Elvina," he called out, "we have a visitor."

A slim, dark woman of middle age came out of the pantry, dusting her hands of flour. Her gleaming black hair was held in a tight bun by a black tortoise-shell clasp and her eyes were like newly polished Whitby jet. She was Spanish, perhaps, or Mexican, although her dark dress gave away nothing.

"Flavia de Luce," he said. ". . . from the academy."

And there was something in the way he said it that put me on high alert.

A fugitive look flitted between them.

"Here," Elvina said, taking the flowers from Merton. "Let me put these in a vase. They're lovely."

"Flavia brought them," he said. "For my mother," he added. "Most considerate."

I hadn't, of course, but I didn't try to correct him. Credit is credit no matter how you slice it.

"Michaelmas daisies mean 'Farewell,'" Elvina said, "and the chrysanthemums 'Cheerfulness in Spite of Misfortune.' You must have put a lot of thought into choosing them."

I hung my head in bashful acknowledgment.

"We were just about to sit down for tea. Would you like to join us?"

I knew that she was fibbing: Merton was washing the car and she had barely begun baking something.

"Yes, please," I said.

Merton pulled out a chair as if I were a lady, and we all sat—at least Merton and I did until Elvina boiled the kettle and joined us at the kitchen table.

Beginning a conversation is always difficult with three strangers who have nothing in common. The usual method is to start with the weather and hope for the best.

But I hadn't the time. I would soon enough be missed at Miss Bodycote's and a hue and cry sent up. I needed to get back to the lab for a crucial test. There was no time to waste.

"You've had a great deal of bereavement," I said. "Your mother, Mr. Merton—and the first Mrs. Rainsmith."

It was a bold thing to say, but I had to take a chance.

"A great deal," Merton said. "A very great deal. This household has had its share of sadnesses."

"It must have been an awful shock to you when

Mrs. Rainsmith drowned," I said. "I mean, not that it wasn't to Dr. Rainsmith, but he's a medical doctor, isn't he, and trained to cope with death. But poor you . . ."

I left the thought hanging in air.

Elvina gave me something of a sharp look, but Merton said, "Flavia's mother died in April."

"I'm sorry to hear that," Elvina said. "Was it unexpected?"

"Yes and no," I said. "She had been missing for ten years and her body was found in the mountain ice."

"Oh! You poor lamb!" Elvina said. "You poor, poor lamb."

And then, as if anxious to change the subject to something less tragic, no matter how little, she said: "It's not that poor Mrs. Rainsmith's death was *completely* unexpected, what with her being so ill before the accident."

"Ill?" I asked, daring to say no more.

"Gastric trouble," Elvina said. "Very bad. But she was a trouper. Never let it get in the way of her obligations."

"Gosh!" I said. "You must have felt awful. It's always the cook that—"

I cut my words off as if I had just realized what I was saying.

"You have no idea," Elvina said. "Most people don't appreciate the cook's position. Gastric trouble is cook trouble. There's always someone willing to point the finger."

"So I suppose, in a way, it was a good thing that she drowned. I know that must sound awful, but—"

Elvina gave off a nervous laugh. It was time to get my feet on firmer ground.

"I know what you mean when you say she was a trouper," I said. "She presented one of the awards at the Beaux Arts Ball the night she was taken ill, didn't she?"

"Nothing to do with me!" Elvina said. "Bit of bad lobster at the ball. That's what Dr. Rainsmith said. I never saw her again, so I wouldn't know."

"Never saw her again?" I leapt on her words like a hound on a bone.

"No, never. Dr. Rainsmith brought her home and had invalid soup sent over from the nursing home."

"Did she eat it?" I asked.

"Must have. The bowls came down empty in the morning and she was off to the cruise on the second day."

My veins were throbbing like plucked harp strings.

"Dr. Rainsmith must have been devastated," I said. "Even though Miss Fawlthorne says that the second Mrs. Rainsmith was a great comfort."

"I expect she was," Elvina said, not looking at me. "Yes, I expect she was."

There fell a great silence, and we all of us sat thinking our own thoughts, each of us cradling our teacups in our hands as if it were a family trait we shared.

For the first time in many weeks I felt at home. I could have stayed here forever in this cozy kitchen. I could have kissed the table and hugged the chairs, but of course I didn't. Instead I offered up a little prayer of thanks to the Michaelmas daisies, and to Saint Michael himself who had brought me here.

"Can I run you home?" Merton asked. "I expect you'll be wanting to get back, and it's a long walk."

How could I tell him that in my heart I was already at home—and that a ride to anywhere else would take me farther from it? That by departing I would be in some way diminished?

"Thank you, Mr. Merton," I said. "I'd be much obliged."

The streetlights were coming on as we drove along the Danforth.

"May I ask you a question?" I said.

"Of course, miss," Merton said.

"What was Francesca Rainsmith wearing the night of the Beaux Arts Ball?"

Merton smiled, and then he laughed aloud. "A Cinderella costume," he said. "Tattered gingham dress, apron, hair in a bandanna, Charlie Chaplin boots with red socks sticking out. She was ever so proud of the getup. One of the girls helped her make it. No more than a girl herself, Miss Francesca was. We miss her."

"I'm sorry," I said. "I wish I'd had the chance to meet her."

We drove in silence for a while.

"How are you finding it?" Merton asked. "Miss Bodycote's Female Academy, I mean?"

"Frankly, Mr. Merton," I said. "Just between you and me and the gatepost—it's a bugger."

And I think by the look on his face that he knew what I meant.

Miss Fawlthorne was, as I knew she would be, livid.

In its proper sense, the word "livid" is used to describe

someone who is black in the face from strangulation, and I wasn't far off. Her countenance was ghastly.

"Where have you been?" she demanded, her voice trembling.

"I went for a walk," I said, which was true, as far as it went.

"The whole academy has been turned out looking for you—do you realize that?"

Of course I didn't. I had only just come in the door.

"We thought you'd been abducted. We—"

She was suddenly speechless.

Why ever would they think that? Did they know something that I didn't?

"I left a note on your desk," I said, but realizing even as I spoke that Miss Fawlthorne was near tears, and that it was no time for childish games.

"I'm sorry," I said, and left it at that. Of course I wanted to tell her about my worrying about Collingwood—my visit to the nursing home—my interview with Merton and Elvina.

But I didn't. The time was not yet right. I needed more facts and more time to gather them.

"I'll go to my room," I said, saving her the trouble.

I lay on my bed reflecting upon (a) my wickedness and (b) the fact that I hadn't eaten all day. Thank goodness for the box of biscuits I was buying on the hire-purchase plan from the grocer's on the Danforth. I had borrowed the down payment from Fabian with the promise to repay, at twenty-five percent interest, as soon as I received my first allow-ance from home, even though my hopes in that direction were beginning to fade.

Dogger's letter was the only communication I had re-ceived from Buckshaw since my incarceration.

Dear Dogger.

I bit savagely into a cream cracker, willing myself to summon him up in spirit, if not in fact. I tried to picture the two of us, heads bent together over a bubbling beaker, nodding wisely as the liquid changed color and another neck was in the noose, but it was no use.

Magic doesn't work when you're sad.

I realized that I had been putting off a visit to the labo-ratory for that very reason, which came as something of a shock. I needed to deal with things head-on.

Someone had pinned a handwritten note to the door of the lab: ALL CHEMISTRY CLASSES CANCELED UNTIL FURTHER NOTICE.

Underneath it, someone else had penciled *Praise be to St. Jude for prayers answered*, and someone else had written, in red ink, DOWN WITH CHEMS.

I looked both ways to make sure no one was coming, and slipped inside.

With the green blinds closed, and dusk out of doors, the room was in near darkness, which suited me to perfection. I would not easily be seen through the window in the door, or from the outside.

I turned on a low-powered light in an alcove and got to work.

Excited as I was, it was still necessary to follow the rules. I turned on the fan which would exhaust any fumes from the hood which covered the work area. More than one chemist in days gone by had, while conducting the Marsh test, sniffed at his apparatus and died in agony.

I pulled the silver medallion from my pocket. Fortunately I had remembered to wrap it in a bit of cellophane for protection before tying it back into a knot in my handkerchief.

As I set up the required glassware, I was possessed by the old familiar thrill. Like the vicar in the run-up to the consecration, I was about to witness a transformation at my very fingertips, to be glorified by the gods of chemistry.

The Marsh test is not only simple and elegant, but also the most theatrical of the chemical procedures. How many sleuths in fact and fiction have hunched tensely over that telltale flame?

It is that hushed moment just before the final curtain when all the world seems to hold its breath: the moment when nothing more than a tiny, flickering, and nearly invisible flame will either send the accused to the gallows or set him free.

It was James Marsh, the ordnance chemist of the Royal Arsenal at Woolwich, who recognized that nascent (meaning newly generated) hydrogen, whenever brought into contact with any compound of arsenic and oxygen, will produce water and arseniuretted hydrogen, otherwise known as arsine, an extremely poisonous gas with the chemical formula AsH_3 and the odor of garden-fresh garlic.

His test is so sensitive that it is able to detect as little as two parts in a million of arsenic.

These days, of course, the idea of newborn hydrogen having superior powers is generally pooh-poohed, and it is now believed that age does not wither its ability to finger a felon.

Oxygen is oxygen is oxygen they say, although Dogger, being old-fashioned, doubts this.

I dropped a bit of zinc into the bottom of the U-shaped tube, then filled it somewhat more than half full with sulfuric acid.

With a small twist of surgical cotton, I wiped off about a quarter of the shiny black tarnish from the medallion and dropped the swab into the left side of the tube, sealing it with a glass stopper. The swab began to char and turn black as it was carbonized by the sulfuric acid.

The zinc at once began to bubble in the acid. Hydrogen was being born!

And, if my hunch was right, arsine.

The stoppered right side of my U-shaped container led off through a slender glass tube which ended in an up-turned tip.

I waited for about thirty seconds . . . lit a match . . . held it to the tip of the exhaust tube and . . .

Poof!

A flame . . . burning red, burning orange, burning blue . . .

I reached for an unglazed pottery dish, flipped it over, and held its underside to the flame, much as a freezing schoolboy home for the holidays holds his bottom to the family fireplace.

A circular dark patch began to form around the outer edges of the flame, brownish at first, but quickly turning black and shiny.

An arsenic mirror, in which, if I were any judge, the image of a murderer would soon be reflected.

This wasn't the end of it by any means. First, I needed to place a few drops of sodium hypochlorite in solution on part of the newly formed mirror. If the sooty deposit was soluble, and vanished, it was arsenic; if it remained, it was arsenic's cousin, antimony.

And then, of course, I needed to repeat the experiment with clean, uncontaminated glassware and a fresh and untreated swab. This would be my control, or reference, and should result in no formation of an arsenic mirror.

I leaned back from the little pool of light to think about what I had discovered: about what it would mean for me—and for several others. Once I made my findings known, Miss Bodycote's Female Academy would never be the same again.

It was at that moment that a voice from out of the darkness behind me said: "Very clever."

·TWENTY·EIGHT·

I SPUN ROUND, MY eyes only slowly adjusting to the darkened room.

From out of the shadows, a figure was moving slowly toward me.

It was Fabian.

"Very clever," she said again as she came half into the light, and I could see the tight-lipped smirk on her pale face.

"How long have *you* been there?" I asked, trying to inject a touch of outrage into my voice.

"Longer than you," she said, fishing a packet of cigarettes from her pocket and putting a match to one, then tossing her hair like French women in the cinema.

"You were expecting me, then," I said, but other than blowing out a dismissive stream of smoke, she did not bother to reply.

"What made you think of the Marsh test?" she asked. "What made you think of arsenic?"

I shrugged. "Just a guess," I lied.

"I'll bet it was," she said.

We could have stood there all night, I suppose, fencing with words, until one or the other of us decided to use something more deadly.

I saw my chance and I went for it. "But you already knew that, didn't you—that it was arsenic."

"Of course I did." She smiled, taking a satisfied puff. "I was there when she swallowed it."

"What?"

"The night of the Beaux Arts Ball, two years ago. I was there."

I must have looked like a gaping loony.

"Some of us were asked to serve at table: Jumbo, Druce, Forrester, myself. A few of the faculty, as well: Miss Fawlthorne, Miss Moate, Mrs. Bannerman, Miss Dupont.

"It's something of a tradition," Fabian went on. "Meant to show up the democratic principles of the old hall—even if it's only once a year."

"Jolly good of Miss Moate to pitch in," I said. "It mustn't be easy for her."

"Moatey's a good sort," Fabian said, flicking ashes on the floor. "Her bark is worse than her bite."

I nodded, even though I didn't agree. I was still trying to sort out where Fabian and I stood, which side we were on, and what was behind this duel in a shadowed room. Which one of us, for instance, was darkness, and which of us was light?

"She's had a hard row to hoe," Fabian said. "Since the accident, that is. Ditched by her best friend."

Ditched? I was missing something here.

Fabian saw my look of dismay. "Run off the road and into the ditch. Car flipped. Moatey flung out through the windshield. Broken spine, broken neck. They practically had to pick up her bits in a basket."

I felt my gorge rising. Those injuries would account for that awful froggish expression into which her face had fallen. The poor woman must have undergone eons of surgery.

"It was positively eerie," Fabian said, echoing my thoughts, "to see her at high table, serving lobster to the very person who put her in the wheelchair."

I blinked, blankly.

"Francesca Rainsmith," she said. "Her onetime best friend."

My throat was suddenly dry. I was finding it hard to swallow. I thought of all those long-gone chemists who had accidentally inhaled a fatal dose of arsine and died with their legs in knots behind their necks. Or had I, without paying attention, taken a drink of water from a contaminated glass?

But no—other than the shock of hearing about Miss Moate, I had exhibited no symptoms.

"Why are you telling me this?" I asked. We were still circling each other as warily as two roosters in a ring, and I had already made up my mind not to be the first to mention pheasant sandwiches. If she was a member of the Nide, she could jolly well bring it up herself.

"Because you need to know," she said. "I've had my eye on you for some time."

I shrugged. What else could I do?

"You say you were actually there when the arsenic was administered?"

"I think so," she said. "I was sitting across from Francesca when Moatey brought her a plate of lobster."

"From the sideboard?"

"Can't say. I had my back to it. Oddly enough, I remember Moatey lifting her beloved tea cozy from the plate."

"She brought Francesca's lobster under her tea cozy?"

"Doesn't make sense, does it? I didn't think much about it at the time, although I do remember thinking that our beloved chairman might have salted her plate with something nasty. He made such a show of breaking up the lobster for her, the claws, the abdomen—she squealed and closed her eyes at the sight of the antennae. Made her feel sick, just looking at them, she said. Funny, isn't it."

"Strange" was more the word that came to mind, but then Miss Moate's oversize tea cozy was big enough to conceal almost anything you might wish to put under it.

Which raised a whole new set of possibilities.

"Which one of them was it, then? Ryerson Rainsmith or Miss Moate?"

"I don't know," Fabian said with a sigh. "I really don't."

"Why didn't you tell anyone?" I asked. "The police, for instance."

Fabian regarded me with a distant eye, and then she said: "I have my reasons."

I could have named one of them on the spot, but I

didn't. I decided to steer the conversation into less personal channels—at least for now.

"We have to be very cautious with seafood poisoning," I said. "Mussels, clams, scallops, and oysters contain organic forms of arsenic. So do crabs and lobsters."

I never thought I'd find myself in the position of defending Ryerson Rainsmith, but it's a funny old world, and when it comes to poisons, it's always best to watch your step.

A hanged man can't be unhanged, and besides, I didn't think I could stand being made a fool of.

"The Marsh test can't distinguish between the various forms of arsenic," I said. "But since no one else died at the Beaux Arts Ball, I think that we can assume, at least for the moment, that Francesca Rainsmith's poison came from somewhere other than the lobster's natural toxicity."

"The lobster was just a cover? Is that what you're saying?"

"It might have been," I said. "And then again, it might not."

Fabian fixed me with a long stare, then shook her head. "You're a strange one, de Luce. I can't figure you out."

"Neither can I," I said. "So tell me more about the night of the ball."

"It was as it always was. Long tables, alternate seating: faculty, student, faculty, student—democratic principles, remember. No hierarchy—everyone equal, that sort of thing."

"Hold on," I said. "How was it that the chairman was seated next to his wife? You *did* say that, didn't you?"

"Hmmm," Fabian said. "I hadn't thought of that. Unless it just worked out that way because of the number of chairs."

"So," I said, changing the subject. "Miss Moate produces Francesca's plate of lobster from under her tea cozy, the chairman breaks it up for her, and she tucks into a hearty meal. Is that it?"

"Pretty well," Fabian said. "I was busy dismembering my own lobster, mind you, and it was a chore. One hates to splatter one's neighbors with melted butter and intestinal juices. One tries to be ladylike."

"And Francesca?"

"Oh, she seemed to be getting on quite well, chatting up the girls, for a while, anyway. She was the center of attention in her Cinderella getup."

"What about the chairman? Was he in costume, too?"

Fabian snorted. "I should say not. He's above that sort of thing."

"What about the prizes?" I asked. "Didn't Francesca present one of them?"

"Yes," Fabian said. "I think so. Oh, yes, of course she did."

"The Saint Michael Award," I said. "For church history."

"Yes."

"To Clarissa Brazenose."

"Yes."

"Who vanished later that same night."

"So they say," Fabian said.

"And what do *you* say?"

Fabian lit another cigarette with the same mannerisms as before. "You mustn't put too much stock in what the younger kids say," she said, blowing out the match with as much force as if it were a forest of candles on the birthday cake of a hundred-year-old. "Their minds are full of nonsense. Ghost stories, fairy tales. They're easily spooked."

"I'm not asking what the younger girls say, I'm asking what *you* say."

"I say, 'Who knows?' People come and go all the time. It's the nature of schools. She might have been sent down. Gated. Failed to Flourish."

"Yes," I said. "She might have."

This whole game of to and fro, this whole game of put and take, this whole game of cat and mouse with Fabian was getting me down, and yet it was somehow strangely familiar. I realized with an almost physical start that it was the same rigmarole I had often fallen into with Feely: a parlor game where persistence paid and only the bold survived.

"About Francesca," I said, with a cucumber-cool expression on my face. "She gave out the Saint Michael Award, and then what?"

"I don't know," Fabian said. "I suppose I noticed she had become more quiet—withdrawn, you might say. Touching her napkin to her lips a lot. She seemed to be growing paler by the minute. Wiped her brow a lot, too. Although it was hot, you know: June, crowded room, stuffy, too many bodies. Not that she wasn't trying to remain on the rails. She asked Clarissa if she could have a better look at the medallion she had just presented—stared at it as if she were trying to remember where she was and what she was doing. Then she whispered to her husband. He helped her to her feet, said something to Miss Fawlthorne and Miss Dawes—"

"Miss Dawes?" I interrupted. "You've lost me."

"Dorsey Dawes. Dorsey Rainsmith, now. She was on the board of guardians at the time."

"Interesting," I said. "Go on."

"Well, they helped Mrs. Rainsmith away from the table and out of the room. That was the last I saw of her. You could have knocked me over with a feather when I heard a couple of days later that she had drowned. The whole school felt like that. We were in shock."

"I suppose you don't know where they took her when they left the table?"

"Oh, but I do. They took her to Edith Cavell. Moatey insisted."

"Edith Cavell? Why on earth—?"

"Because it was Moatey's room at the time. They were renovating hers, and she had moved into Edith Cavell for the summer to get away from the paint fumes."

"And whose room had it been before that?" I asked.

"Mine," Fabian said.

Somewhere in the universe something went "*click*," and then another . . . and another. Like footsteps on the tiles of time.

I wanted to shout out "Tombola!" or "Bingo!" or whatever they call it on this side of the pond, but I restrained myself.

Already there wasn't glory enough to go around and I didn't want to dilute it any further.

"Hmmm," I said instead. This was the moment I had been waiting for.

"And the chairman," I said. "Did you see him again? That night, I mean?"

"Of course. He and Dorsey—Miss—sorry—*Doctor* Dawes—came back and danced for hours."

"With whom?" I demanded, perhaps too quickly.

"With everyone. He danced with students—democracy again—with faculty—"

"With Miss Moate?"

"Of course not! Don't be ridiculous."

"Where was she by this time?"

"I don't know. She was around somewhere, I expect. I remember helping her roll up the paper garlands at the end of the night."

"And the chairman—dancing. Didn't he seem worried about his wife?"

"Didn't seem to be. 'Upset tummy' was the word that went around. After all, he *is* a doctor, and ought to know. Besides, it was his duty to dance with all the girls."

"Yes," I said. "I know: democratic principles. Did he dance with you?"

"Yes. Twice, in fact."

"Why?"

"How do I know, you idiot? Because I was the most beautiful girl in the room. Because he liked the smell of my Chanel. Because he likes tall girls. What a ridiculous question!"

I saw that I had struck pay dirt, but I kept a poker face.

"What did you talk about?"

"Oh, for god's sake, de Luce . . . how do you expect me to remember that? It was years ago."

"I'd have remembered," I said. "I don't often dance with a doctor. Or a man, for that matter."

"What are you getting at?"

"Nothing," I said. "It was just a thought. What did you talk about?"

"The weather. The heat. He said I waltzed well. He complimented me on my corsage."

"Did he bid you farewell?" I asked.

"What do you mean?" Fabian demanded.

"Did he wish you well in your new life?"

"Whatever are you talking about, de Luce? Are you insane?"

"Not entirely," I said. "I thought he might at least have congratulated you on winning the Saint Michael Award . . . Clarissa."

·TWENTY-NINE·

I REACHED OUT AND ran my finger slowly down her cheek. It came away covered with pale powder. Underneath, her exposed skin was the same swarthy shade as that of her sister, Mary Jane.

"Makeup, hair color, and hairstyle can fool a lot of people," I said, "but the underlying facial structure can never really be changed—not in the long run, anyway, and not to the professional eye."

This was a fact I had learned from Dogger one rainy afternoon in the greenhouse as we pored over photographs of criminals in the back issues of *The Police Gazette* he had turned out from under the stairs. We had assumed (incorrectly, as it turned out) that they had belonged to Uncle Tar.

Nevertheless, Clarissa Brazenose's transformation into Fabian had been remarkable, a triumph of the actor's makeup box. Even now, with the light stain on my fingertip, there was only an inch of the real Clarissa showing through.

"You've managed to fool even your own sister," I said. "You ought to be proud. You ought also to be ashamed. Poor kid, being made to think you were dead these past two years. She still doesn't know, does she? And perhaps never will."

Fabian stared at me, not quite defiantly. I had to give her credit.

"How did you manage?" I asked. "The makeup, of course, which you were taught to apply professionally. And you must have worn wigs, changed your posture, re-learned how to walk. I compliment you on a most remarkable performance."

I reached out as if to touch her hair.

She backed slowly away out of reach.

"I haven't the faintest idea what you're talking about," Fabian said, as of course she would. She had been trained to deny even to the death.

And was I, at bottom, any different?

The truth of the matter was that I hadn't the heart to expose her. If I revealed the fact that Fabian was Clarissa Brazenose, then, even though I had won, she had lost. All of her efforts, and those who had trained her, would be for naught.

The point of it all was this: Did I have the generosity to let her get away with it? Could I let her win? Throw the match, so to speak?

"I'm sorry," I said. "I must have been mistaken."

And before she could stop me, I ran out of the laboratory.

I did not need more entanglements.

It was only when I got back to Edith Cavell that I realized I had not completed my experiment. I would return later to clean up.

When Fabian was gone.

Sleep was impossible. I tossed and turned, sweated and swore. By daylight I was a bad-tempered haystack, but I didn't care. I had made up my mind what I was going to do. I would do it and hang the consequences.

Rosedale at dawn was a very different place. The weather had turned cold overnight and left the world brittle. In some of the lower spots, patches of low fog lurked among the hedges, as if the atmosphere there had curdled. Dark trees overhung the frosty grass, and the air was as sharp as knives.

I walked quickly, swinging my arms to generate a bit of heat. A school blazer and white blouse were hardly meant to replace a parka, and by the time I got to the Rainsmiths', my nose was running and I was beginning to sneeze.

I was not a pretty picture.

Smoke was rising from the kitchen chimney as I made my way round the back of the house.

I tapped lightly at the door and Elvina opened it almost at once.

"I'm sorry to bother you," I said, "but I should like to speak with Dr. Rainsmith. It's urgent."

"Urgent, is it?" she asked, beckoning me to come inside. "So urgent that you can't have a cup of hot tea and a buttered scone? You look as if you've fallen off a dogsled."

"I'm all right," I said, resenting both the remark and the way I looked. "Is Dr. Rainsmith at home?"

"Which one?" she asked.

"The chairman," I said. "Ryerson."

Some people are shy about using the forename of an older person, but I am not one of them.

"I'm afraid he's not, dear. He's off to a conference in Hamilton. Won't be home until tonight. Is it something that can wait?"

"No," I told her, perhaps unwisely. "It's a matter of life and death."

Unshaken (and it was only later that I realized that she probably dealt with matters of life and death daily, as others deal with dust) she replied, "Is it something I can help with—or Mr. Merton? He ought to be back from the train any minute now."

"No," I said. "It's personal."

The look on her face told me that she was recalling our earlier conversation.

"Honestly, I'm fine," I said, touching her hand. It was the least I could do.

It was only then that I noticed that Dorsey Rainsmith was standing in the doorway. She had followed me in from the garden with a wicker basket full of flowers. I must have passed her without seeing her. Perhaps she had been bent over with her secateurs.

Was it just my imagination or had Elvina given a little jump? Had Dorsey Rainsmith taken us both by surprise?

"Well," she said, "what is it?"

I had no more than a second to make up my mind. Did I stay or did I go? I thought of Alf Mullet's many talks on military tactics which I had dozed through behind fascinated eyes. "Confrontation is a cannon," he had said. "It's a powerful weapon, but it gives away your position."

"It's about Francesca Rainsmith," I said.

No going back now. I had fired my shot and could only wait for the consequences.

"You'd better come in," Dorsey said, placing the basket of flowers on the kitchen sink and leading the way through into another room which turned out to be her study. The walls were lined with medical reference books that I'd have given my eye teeth to read, but this was hardly the time or place.

She took a chair at the desk without asking me to sit, then swiveled round to face me.

"I'm very busy," she said.

"Good," I said. "So am I. Let's get on with it. Francesca Rainsmith."

"What about her?" Dorsey said. "She died in tragic circumstances, and I'd prefer you to respect my husband's privacy, and mine."

"She died of arsenic poisoning at the Beaux Arts Ball," I said. "A few days later, in a wedding dress and veil, you impersonated her on a moonlight cruise."

"Quite preposterous," she said.

"Yes, it is," I replied. "Inspector Gravenhurst will find it even more so."

I paused to let her guilt get to work. "He'll find the results of the autopsy particularly interesting, especially in view of the fact that you've been in charge of the body since it was discovered."

"What do you mean by that?"

"I mean good morning, Dr. Rainsmith," I said, and turned toward the door, an effect that was largely spoiled by my being convulsed with a sneeze.

"Flavia—wait."

Reluctantly, I turned to face her again.

"Dr. Rainsmith and I—Ryerson, I mean. We're on your side, you know. Pheasant sandwiches."

She bared her teeth in a ghastly grin that was meant to be friendly but which, to me, looked more like a corpse in a comic book.

I said nothing. I was not going to let on that I recognized the phrase.

"Pheasant sandwiches," she said again, smiling horribly . . . plaintively.

Again I gave her a barn-door stare.

"Listen," she said. "What do you want?"

"The truth," I said, and I must admit that those two words, as brief as they were, were as sweet in my mouth as milk and honey. "First of all, Collingwood. What have you done with her?"

"She's been sent home to her parents. She suffered a bad shock at Miss Bodycote's, then contracted rheumatic fever.

378 · ALAN BRADLEY

We brought her here for a while, but she's now been released."

That much, I thought, was probably true.

"And Francesca Rainsmith?"

Dorsey Rainsmith got to her feet and locked the door.

Was I terrified?

Well, yes.

"I wish you'd wait until Ryerson comes home," she said. "I'm sure he could make it quite—"

"He won't be home until late tonight," I said. "He's away at a conference."

"Oh, of course he is—I'd forgotten."

"So it's just you and me," I said. I resisted the urge to add "Sweetheart," like Humphrey Bogart.

"Talk," I told her, and she did.

I could hardly wait to tell Inspector Gravenhurst.

"So you see," I said, pacing up and down the room, "believing she was suffering from no more than indigestion, they took Francesca to Edith Cavell. A good sleep would do her good. They left her there and went downstairs, where it was said that they danced for hours.

"Toward the end of the evening, when they finally got back to Edith Cavell, they found Francesca dead on the floor. Her throat had been cut. They were appalled. They panicked. After all, it had been implied that they had much more in common than medicine, if you see what I mean.

"He needed to return to the ball to keep up appearances,

Ryerson decided. He made his excuses, left instructions that his wife was not to be disturbed, and drove Dr. Dawes home. He'd deal with things himself. It was while driving back that he came up with a plan. He remembered that Francesca had wanted to go on a midnight cruise: to renew their vows. He'd already booked the tickets. There mustn't be a breath of scandal, he decided: not about him and Miss Dawes and certainly not about Miss Bodycote's Female Academy.

"When he finally got back to Miss Bodycote's, although it was quite late, there was still laughter in the ballroom. He went quietly up to Edith Cavell, and found . . . nothing! Francesca's body was gone. Not a sign of her. The room was untouched. Wiped clean.

"What to do? There was scarcely time to think. He told Fitzgibbon he was taking his wife home. No, no need to make a fuss. Carry on. He'd see to it.

"Two nights later, they carried out their charade with Dorsey wearing a wedding dress and veil. The gift box, of course, contained her ordinary clothing, and while Ryerson alerted the captain that his wife had fallen overboard, Dorsey was packing the wedding gear in the box and putting on a dark suit, after which she mingled with the other passengers on the deck until they returned to port. No one paid her the slightest attention; no one, remember, because of the veil, had previously seen her face.

"How did I discover this? Well, in the first place, Ryerson's wife banged her head getting out of the taxi at the pier. Francesca Rainsmith was tiny: Had it been she, it never could have happened. That was what first alerted me. And then the taxi: Why had they taken a taxi instead of having Merton drive them to the ship? As for the rest of it, I got it straight from Dorsey Rainsmith's mouth."

I waited for this to sink in.

"Now then: Did they kill Francesca? The answer is no. They foolishly plotted to conceal her death, but as for murder, you will find them not guilty. Francesca died of arsenic poisoning. You will almost certainly still find traces of it in her body.

"What made me suspect arsenic? I'm glad you asked. As you undoubtedly know, arsenic, heated, produces arsine gas. A body permeated with arsenic, wrapped in fabric, such as a flag, over time, will give off fumes that tarnish silver. I subjected a sample of the tarnish from a small silver medallion—which was clutched in the corpse's hand—to the Marsh test, which confirmed my suspicions. I'll be happy to turn it over to you so that you can verify my work. Yes, of course I ought to have handed over the medallion when you first arrived. I realize that now. But, like poor Collingwood, I must have been in shock. I hope you won't think too badly of me.

"And now the flag. Why was the body wrapped in a Union Jack? To absorb the blood, of course, of which there was a great deal. The flag was easily at hand, being stored in a trunk in the hall. It was flown over the academy every twenty-fourth of May, Victoria Day. Mr. Kelly will probably confirm that it was missing last May, and that he had to requisition a new one. No, I haven't asked him myself, but I *have* observed that there is presently a quite fresh Union

Jack in the trunk: one which can't have been flown for more than a couple of days.

"Who, then, killed Francesca Rainsmith? The deduction is an easy one. Who held Francesca responsible for the car crash that condemned her friend to a life of torture in a wheelchair? Who has hated Francesca with every moment of her waking life?" (I'll admit I was being a bit dramatic here). "Who is it that keeps a museum of taxidermy specimens, who has the ways and means to decapitate a dead body? Who had the upper body strength to shove a pitifully little body up the chimney? Having seen the killer run a wheelchair up and down steep banks and ramps with my own eyes, I'm satisfied that we need look no further.

"And why decapitate? To avoid identification if the body were ever found. The skull which is presently in the morgue was formerly on the shelf of the natural history museum, here at Miss Bodycote's. And as for Francesca Rainsmith's skull, I expect you will find it on that same shelf in the same position, dyed with tea, in order to age it.

"How do I know that? Why, I smelled it, of course. There is a definite odor of orange Pekoe.

"Have I missed anything? Well, I suppose someone might ask how Francesca Rainsmith's killer managed to get her severed head from Edith Cavell to the museum, and the replacement skull from the museum back to Edith Cavell, without being spotted on the night of the Beaux Arts Ball, when the place was simply crawling with people. Don't quote me on this because I'm not absolutely positive, but I suspect it has to do with an oversized tea cozy.

"And now, thank you for your time, Inspector. I am happy to have been of assistance."

These were the things I *might* have said to the handsome Inspector Gravenhurst had I been given the opportunity, but of course, I hadn't. I had made a bargain with Wallace Scroop that he was to get the credit for figuring out the Rainsmiths' moonlight cruise deception, and I meant to stick to it. I have to admit that I've never regretted anything in my life so much as giving up that glory. But choices are choices, and there's no going back.

I didn't much mind not being able to tell the inspector that Fabian was Brazenose, but then, it's not my place to be doing his work for him, is it? Let the police carry out their own investigations. It will keep them on their toes.

Fabian had, of course, given herself away by admitting that she had been at the Beaux Arts Ball, and had witnessed the poisoning of Francesca Rainsmith. Rather a bad slipup on her part. She *had* been present, but in the character of Clarissa Brazenose. "Fabian" had not been created or enrolled at Miss Bodycote's until a year ago.

I hadn't mentioned in my summary her transformation into Fabian. It had puzzled me for a while why Fabian had been forced to appear without her disguise, the night Scarlett had spotted her outside the laundry. I'd speculated that she might have had a bank account from which she could not withdraw funds without appearing in person, but that idea proved to be a bust when I remembered that Scarlett had seen her at night; the banks closed at three o'clock.

As it turned out, the solution was a simple one. The Brazenose sisters have an elderly great-aunt who suffers from a form of senility which they call "hardening of the arteries." Clarissa sometimes risked sneaking out at night to visit the old lady, who lives, as it turns out, just a block away from Miss Bodycote's. Miss Fawlthorne is apparently aware of this bending of the rules, but chooses to overlook it.

Poor Mary Jane. She still believes her sister is dead. Will they tell her the truth one day? I don't know, but one thing's certain: *I* won't.

Le Marchand and Wentworth will, I suppose, haunt me forever: phantoms of Miss Bodycote's, never seen but ever present. I wonder who they are and what they are doing, and sometimes the very thought of it makes my blood run cold.

I looked at myself in the mirror in which I had been rehearsing my speech to the inspector: a speech which I knew I would never deliver. What I saw staring back at me was a plain, ordinary, somewhat dowdy schoolgirl in black tights, blue blazer, white blouse, and a panama hat.

I was dressed that way because I had been ordered to report to Miss Fawlthorne's study, and full kit was the rule.

I turned, and marched out the door to meet my fate.

· T H I R T Y ·

"COME IN," MISS FAWLTHORNE said.

She was seated at her desk behind a pile of papers, among which was my report on William Palmer.

"Please be seated."

I sat primly on the edge of a chair, my knees together and my hands folded in my lap, leaning forward eagerly, as if I could hardly wait for my next assignment.

"You'll no doubt be happy to hear that Miss Moate has been arrested," she said, "and Mrs. Bannerman released."

I nodded sagely.

"I don't know what part you have played in these matters, and I'm not sure I want to know. If you have been instrumental in bringing the right person to justice, I congratulate you. I must say that I am relieved to learn that a person from the *Morning Star*, Wallace Scroop, is being commended for pointing the police to a solution. He was apparently on the scene two years ago, at the time of Francesca Rainsmith's death, and has never ceased making extensive private inquiries.

"But in doing so, he has dragged the name of Miss Bodycote's Female Academy into the public press. The headlines are shocking. The chairman and his wife are being questioned. Our board of guardians is a shambles. The work that we do here has been seriously compromised, if not damaged beyond repair.

"Fortunately for us, this Scroop cannot be made to reveal his sources, but I suspect you know nothing about that, do you?"

"No, Miss Fawlthorne," I said.

"If you and Collingwood had not broken the rules at the outset, this would never have happened."

I couldn't believe my ears! Was this woman suggesting that it would be better if Francesca Rainsmith had remained shoved up the chimney for all time, and her killer never brought to justice?

"You must understand that reputation is paramount. There are things which, even though they be wrong, are best kept quiet for the greater good."

The greater good? Did such a thing exist? And even if it did, who was in charge of deciding what it was?

Not knowing these things was like worshipping a god whose name and home address were a secret.

"I feel that we have failed, Flavia. I have failed and you have failed."

A slight chill had come upon me. Was it the room? Was it Miss Fawlthorne? Or was my cold returning in full-blown form?

I stifled a sneeze. Miss Fawlthorne waited until I found my handkerchief.

"We have done our best for you, but it has not been enough. You have broken the rules again and again, as if they didn't matter. I needn't enumerate; you know what they are."

I hung my head a little because she was right.

"Consequently," she said, dragging it out the way people do when they want to deliver an invisible blow, ". . . we are sending you home."

I was numb for a moment.

"You will be escorted by Mrs. Bannerman, who has been granted a compassionate leave to compensate for her ordeal. I have cabled your father, and he will be expecting you."

Now my mind was reeling like a wobbly spinning top that has lost its velocity.

Was this another one of Miss Fawlthorne's famous punishments?

I knew that I could never know.

But the thought—the very thought!—of Buckshaw was already pouring, like a river that has breached its banks, into my mind and into my heart.

"Thank you, Miss Fawlthorne," I said.

EPILOGUE

I WAS STANDING AT the bow, the wind whipping my hair and what might have been sea spray wetting my face.

Banished! I thought. *Banished again!*

Was I doomed, like the Flying Dutchman, to spend all eternity sailing the seas in search of salvation?

I had asked that question of Mrs. Bannerman—in somewhat simpler form—last night in the ship's lounge.

"Good heavens!" she had said. "You've passed with flying colors. Don't you realize that?"

"I'm an FF," I said. "Failed to Flourish. Sent home in disgrace like Charlotte Veneering."

"On the contrary." She laughed. "Your photograph will be hung in the gallery, like your mother's. You will become part of the legend."

"But the rules," I said. "What about the broken rules? Miss Fawlthorne told me that reputation is paramount."

"Ah, yes," she had said, this once-convicted murderess, staring thoughtfully into her pink martini and giving it a stir, "but she also probably mentioned that there are things which, even though they be wrong, are best kept quiet for the greater good."

I had to admit she had a point there.

"I'm sorry you had to be arrested," I said. "I'd have spoken up sooner—"

"Shush!" she said. "Not a word of it. I told you I helped the police with their inquiries from time to time. Ambiguous, I know, but I mustn't say more. If you want to feel sorry for someone, feel sorry for poor little Collingwood. It was she who helped Francesca make her costume, and of course she recognized the red sock. I'm assured that she'll recover in time, but a couple of little prayers will do no harm."

And with that she bowed her head and so did I.

I keenly regret that I was unable to use either the spectrophotometer or the electron microscope in solving the case: that in the end it had been the plain old everyday Marsh test that had done the job.

Perhaps there was a lesson there.

There had been no good-byes at Miss Bodycote's. No little parties, no little gifts. I was there and then I was gone. To the other girls, I would be just one more of those who had vanished. My name would be added to those of Wentworth, Le Marchand, and Brazenose.

My spirit would be summoned in darkened rooms by Ouija boards, and used to frighten little girls who were away from home for the first time.

I smiled at the thought and lifted my head to the breeze.

An unexpected wave dashed cold water into my face, but I didn't care.

Somewhere ahead of us, to the east, lay England. Somewhere, still over the horizon, lay Buckshaw.

ACKNOWLEDGMENTS

WHENEVER I BUY A book, I usually flip first to the back pages to read the names of those who helped. Contrary to popular belief, no book is written in isolation, and this one is no exception.

My editors, Bill Massey at Orion Books in London, Kate Miciak at Delacorte Books in New York, and Kristin Cochrane at Doubleday Canada, have been the supports that hold up this bridge of words.

My agent, Denise Bukowski, is always there: my literary guardian angel.

Brad Gossen and Russell Eugene "Bud" Gossen have patiently answered my questions about policing Toronto in the 1950s, and Carol Fraser has loaned documents and precious family treasures to help get some of the historical details straight.

Again, Robert Bruce Thompson, whose *Illustrated Guide*

to Home Chemistry Experiments has taught hundreds to do forensics tests without even having to leave the house, has saved me from the pitfalls of poisons, as well as providing a number of excellent suggestions.

Special thanks to Maija Paavilainen, editor in chief of *Bazar Kustannus Oy* in Helsinki, for inviting me to visit that beautiful city, and to Vilja Perttola for getting me everywhere on time in spite of a hectic schedule.

And finally, as always, to my wife, Shirley, whose love makes it all worthwhile.

Isle of Man, June 28, 2014

ALAN BRADLEY is the internationally best-selling author of many short stories, children's stories, newspaper columns, and the memoir *The Shoebox Bible*. His first Flavia de Luce novel, *The Sweetness at the Bottom of the Pie*, received the Crime Writers' Association Debut Dagger Award, the Dilys Award, the Arthur Ellis Award, the Agatha Award, the Macavity Award, and the Barry Award, and was nominated for the Anthony Award.

alanbradleyauthor.com
Facebook.com/alanbradleyauthor

ABOUT THE TYPE

THIS BOOK was set in Goudy Old Style, a typeface designed by Frederic William Goudy (1865–1947). Goudy began his career as a bookkeeper, but devoted the rest of his life to the pursuit of "recognized quality" in a printing type.

Goudy Old Style was produced in 1914 and was an instant bestseller for the foundry. It has generous curves and smooth, even color. It is regarded as one of Goudy's finest achievements.

If you enjoyed

As **Chimney Sweepers Come** *to* **Dust,**

read on for another
enchanting Flavia de Luce mystery in

The **Curious Case** *of the* **Copper Corpse**

A Flavia de Luce Story

BY ALAN BRADLEY

In which eleven-year-old Flavia de Luce, chemical connoisseur, is immersed in her element.

I WAS PEERING THROUGH the microscope at the tooth of an adder I had captured behind the coach house that very morning after church, when there came a light knock at the laboratory door.

"Excuse me, Miss Flavia," Dogger said, "but there's a letter for you. I shall leave it on the desk."

And with that, he was gone. One of the things I love most about Father's jack-of-all-trades is his uncanny sense of decency. Dogger knows instinctively when to come and when to go.

Curiosity, of course, got the better of me. I switched off the illuminator and reached for the butter knife I had pinched from the kitchen, which doubled for crumpets and correspondence.

The envelope was a plain one, with no distinctive markings: the sort sold in any stationer's shop at eleven pence per hundred. There was no postmark—there wouldn't be on a Sunday—which indicated that it had been shoved through the letter slot at the front door.

I sniffed it, then sliced it open.

Inside was a letter written in pencil on lined paper. That and the horrid scrawl suggested that the sender was a schoolboy.

Murder! it said. *Come at once. Anson House, Greyminster, Staircase No. 3*, and it was signed *J. Haxton* or *Plaxton*. The writer had pressed so hard that the pencil had snapped in the middle of his signature, which seemed to have been hastily completed with the broken bit of graphite squeezed between a grubby thumb and forefinger.

Murder, urgency, frenzy, fear: Who could resist? It was my cup of tea.

Gladys's rubber tires hissed happily along the rainy road. My rapid pedaling had transformed the inside of my yellow mackintosh into a superheated tent, and I was now so soaked with perspiration that I might as well not have bothered: The rain would have been cooler.

Greyminster School was shrouded in mist. Acres of green lawns produced a ghostly, floating fog which gave only brief, unnerving glimpses of ancient stone and staring windows.

Father's old school seemed to exist simultaneously in both past and present, as if all of its Old Boys, back to the year dot, were hovering somewhere in the wings. More dangerous than phantoms, however, was Ruggles, the nasty little porter who had accosted me on my last visit. I had not forgotten him, and it was unlikely that Ruggles had forgotten me.

I parked Gladys beneath a sign that said *Faculty Bicycles Only*, and went round the end of the building. The staircases, I remembered, were also accessible from the rear.

Staircase No. 3 was at the farthest corner of the building: a dark, narrow climb with black paneling and no windows. I made my way upward, trying to ascend in silence. The studies on the first landing were marked with white cards in holders: *Lawson, Somerville, Henley*. A fourth door revealed a cramped WC and bathtub. On the second floor, the doors were marked *Wagstaffe, Baker,* and *Smith-Pritchard*.

Up I climbed, into an increasing cloud of smells: boots, jam, ink, and unwashed shirts mingled with the unmistakable odors of brilliantine, leather dressing, and mislaid bits of baking, all with an underlying whiff of tobacco smoke.

The staircase ended at the top in near darkness. Only by putting my nose to the doors could I read the names of the last three occupants: *Cosgrave, Parker,* and *Plaxton*.

I had found my man—so to speak.

Before I could knock, the door came open just enough for a reddened eyeball to look me up and down. "Flavia de Luce?" a cracked voice asked, and I nodded. The opening widened to allow me to squeeze inside, and the door was closed instantly behind me.

I've seen frightened people in my life, but never one so terrified as the boy who stood before me. His face was the color of mildewed bread dough, his hands were trembling, and he looked as if he had been crying. "Did anyone see you?" he demanded.

"No."

"Are you sure?"

"I said no, didn't I?"

He nodded in obvious misery, and we were right back where we had started. Murder is not an easy subject to broach, and I realized that I needed to take it easy on this boy. He was, after all, not much older than me. "Where's the corpse?" I asked.

He flinched, then brushed past me into the hall. The WC on this landing had a hand-printed note pinned to the door: *OUT OF ORDER! NO ENTRY!* which seemed excessive for a busted loo.

Standing well back, Plaxton mimed that I was to open the door. I held my breath and turned the knob.

The room was dim, lighted only by a small stained-glass window, whose diamond-shaped panes of violet and yellow gave to the scene a curious carnival air. Directly under the window was a bathtub, and in it was what I took at first to be a statue. "Is this a joke?" I asked. But the look on Plaxton's face, and the way he covered his mouth with his hand—not to hide a mischievous grin, but to keep from vomiting—gave me my answer.

The thing in the tub was not a statue, but a man—a *dead* man, and a naked one at that. Save for his face, he seemed to have been carved out of copper.

"I'm sorry," Plaxton whispered, averting his eyes. "This is probably no place for a girl."

"Girl be blowed!" I snapped. "I'm here as a brain, not as a female."

Plaxton actually took a step backward.

"Who is this?" I asked, still scarcely able to believe my eyes.

"Mr. Denning," he replied. "The housemaster."

I opened my mental notebook and began recording the scene.

The deceased reclined in the tub, as if—except for one remarkable detail—he had dozed off during a long, comfortable soak. Several inches from the top of the tub was a regular ring of blue scum, and at the foot, a cracked rubber stopper was still jammed into the drain hole. Whatever liquid had filled the tub had leaked out, and the porcelain was now completely dry.

I touched a finger to the residue and sniffed it. *Copper sulfate:* $CuSO_4$. *Unmistakable.*

A look round the back of the tub showed me what I was already half expecting to see: an automobile battery. One of its lugs (the positive) was connected to a black rubber wire, its farther end bared and coiled in the bottom of the tub like a sleeping snake. The other lug (the negative) was connected to a similar length of wire, terminating in a large crocodile clip, which was clamped firmly to the corpse's nose.

The chemical and electrical action had electroplated the man. Electrodeposition, to be precise.

Although I knew it was useless, I felt with two fingers for a carotid pulse, but there was none. Mr. Denning was decidedly defunct.

"Give me a hand," I said, seizing the shoulder and pulling the body away from the back of the porcelain. It crackled, and a few chips fell into the bottom of the dry tub. A glance at the expanse of flesh, plated as it was with copper, told me that there were no bullet holes or knife wounds.

Plaxton hadn't moved a muscle.

"Is he dead?" he asked, almost blubbering, his lower lip trembling terribly. I could have made any number of witty retorts, but something told me to control myself.

"Yes," I said, and left it at that.

"I thought so," Plaxton said. "That's why I wrote you." Which seemed an odd thing to say until you considered that the boy was still in some degree of shock.

"But why me?" I asked. "Why write instead of telephoning? For that matter, why didn't you call the police?"

Plaxton went even pastier, if possible. "They'd think I killed him. I needed someone who could prove I didn't. That's why I wrote to you."

"And did you? Kill him, I mean?"

"Of course I didn't!" Plaxton hissed, getting a bit of color in his cheeks at last.

"Then who did?"

"I don't know. That's why I sent for you."

Plaxton was beginning to sound like a broken phonograph record. I took one long, last, lingering look at the body in the bathtub.

"Can we talk in your room?" I asked. Fascinating as it might be, discussing the details of its own murder within earshot of a corpse seemed to me not in the best of taste. Besides, I wanted to have a discreet peek at Plaxton's study.

"Tell me," I said, when I was seated in his best basket

chair, "about the other boys on Staircase Number Three, beginning with Parker and Cosgrave."

"Cosgrave's all right," he replied. "He's the captain of the first eleven. His father's a professor of chemistry, at Cambridge."

"Not Harrison Cosgrave?" I asked. "The author of *Sidelights on Thiocarbanilide?*"

The book had a permanent place on my bedside table.

"It could be, I suppose. He's a queer old duck. Comes up for Founders' Day."

"When's Founders' Day?"

"It was yesterday. The seventeenth."

"And Harrison Cosgrave was here?"

"Yes."

Confound it! I thought. I'd have given my liver to have met him.

"And Parker?" I asked.

"Keeps to himself. Plays American jazz on his gramophone in the middle of the night."

I made a mental note that gramophone music might well mask the sounds of murder and its aftermath.

"Whyever would they think *you* killed Mr. Denning?" I asked, hoping that a question out of the blue might startle the truth out of him.

"Because of the flaming great row we had a couple of days ago."

"Yes," I said. "I'm listening."

"I threatened to kill him," Plaxton blurted.

"Good lord!" I said. "Did anyone hear you?"

"Everyone on Staircase Number Three, I expect. We were making the most frightful uproar. It ended in his slapping my face. I'm afraid I lost my head for a moment."

"What was the row about?" I asked.

Plaxton wrung his hands so hard that I was expecting water to dribble out. "The bath," he said. "Rather than using his own facilities, Mr. Denning preferred to come up here, away from it all, and soak in silence. He'd put a sign on the door and stay in the tub for hours, reading."

"Did he place the *OUT OF ORDER! NO ENTRY!* sign on the door, or did you?"

"I did," Plaxton admitted. "Although it was the same wording as the one he always hung out. I thought he might take the hint."

"Ha!" I said. "And now, because it's in your handwriting, you think the police will suspect you posted it to keep anyone from discovering the corpse."

"Something like that."

"Why didn't you remove it?"

"Because it's evidence," Plaxton said. "And no matter what you may think, I am not a killer."

"All right, then," I said, as if it didn't matter. "Who is?"

Plaxton had a habit of furrowing his brow when he was thinking intently, and he furrowed it now.

"Well," he said at last, "Lawson's father is a chemist, in Leeds. He could easily get his hands on copper sulfate. Besides, he's the biggest boy at Greyminster. His biceps are like farm fence posts. He could easily lift someone the size of Mr. Denning."

"What makes you think copper sulfate was involved?" I

asked casually. To tell the truth, I was a little peeved that he was getting so far ahead of me.

"It's a required subject here," he answered. "We grow blue crystals in hot water and do another experiment with carbon rods and a battery. I say! You don't think—"

"Who's your chemistry master?" I asked.

"Mr. Winter. He's a good sport, old Winter is. Lets us drive his Jaguar at speed when he's in a good mood."

"And when he's not?"

"He's a right tartar! Squabbles with everyone."

"Including Mr. Denning?"

Plaxton furrowed his brow again. But before he could answer, there was sudden thunder on the stairs and the room was filled with shiny red faces and blue blazers.

"What's this?" one of them cried, a portly lad whose sheer size hinted of the sweet shop and regular picnic baskets from home. "A girl in your room? You surprise us, Plaxton!"

A general uproar followed. Surrounded by his nudging schoolmates, Plaxton looked at me helplessly. The place had suddenly become a boy's world and I needed to speak the language.

"Oh, grow up!" I said loudly. "I'm his cousin Veronica."

The portly one stuck out a hand. "I'm Smith-Pritchard," he said. "But you may call me Adrian."

I ignored the hand. "I've heard the name before," I told him. "On the wireless, perhaps. Isn't your father something or other in the government?"

"He's in Parliament—the member for—"

"No point in telling me," I interrupted. "I have no head

for that sort of thing. I'd rather hoped he raced Aston Martins, which would at least be worth talking about."

"I say!" said the tall, good-looking lad on Smith-Pritchard's left. "Are you keen on cars?"

I recognized him at once: He was the spitting image of his father, George "Taffy" Wagstaffe, the celebrated Battle of Britain pilot who had shot down an enemy aircraft as it attacked Westminster Abbey and, after taking a direct hit himself from the rear gunner of the doomed bomber, parachuted into the Abbey's garden and stayed for tea with the dean and chapter. He was now, five years after the war, the director of his family firm, Wagstaffe Chemicals.

"Dead keen," I replied. "I live on petrol fumes and swill motor oil for breakfast."

There was a silence.

"What do you think of the Maserati 4CLT/50?" someone else asked in a quietly menacing voice.

I recognized that I was being tested.

"Not such a bad car," I said, offering up thanks that I had kept my ears open while hanging round Bert Archer's garage in the village. "Though not quite up to the Alfa 158 in the ferocity of its engine."

My questioner was a slender boy, so pale that he looked almost like a photographic negative. A whitish cowlick covered his forehead. I squirmed inwardly at his spectral stare.

"Who's that?" I whispered, turning to Plaxton.

"Wilfrid Somerville," Plaxton whispered back. "They say he dabbles in the occult."

"Does he?" I asked.

"I don't know. I keep clear of him anyway."

"Is there anything else?"

"Not much. His father's a clergyman in Hastings and a keen amateur photographer. That's all I know."

"What are you whispering about?" Somerville demanded, shoving the others aside with his elbows and moving menacingly toward us.

"Veronica was just telling me," Plaxton said without batting an eye, "that her pater's going in for the Grand Prix at Monza this year."

"Eh?" Somerville said, startled. "What's his name?"

"It's a name with which you're not yet familiar," I said airily, "but one with which you soon will be, I assure you."

An outbreak of laughter eased the tension.

"Good on you, Veronica." Wagstaffe laughed. "That's giving him the old what for. You've met your match, Somerville. Time to retire the side."

Somerville, scowling horribly, turned away and fell into a pretended and overly animated discussion with Smith-Pritchard.

A slightly embarrassed silence fell upon the rest of the boys. I shrugged, hauling my shoulders up to my ears, and turned my hands palms out, as if to say *Who gives a fig?* I wasn't frightened by the likes of Wilfrid Somerville. He was a bully, and it was written all over him.

I was about to make a joke when the door burst open again and another boy elbowed his way into the already crowded room.

"Hullo, Plaxton," he said, jerking a thumb toward the landing. "Old Denning's holed up in the jakes again. He's hung his rotten great sign on the door. What say we roust him? Come on, Lawson—you're the son of a chemist. Surely you can raise a decent stink bomb on a minute's notice?"

Lawson licked his lips, looked round the room as if searching for another exit.

"Leave the old fellow alone, can't you, Henley?" he asked. "Don't you think he's been ragged enough?"

"Oh, don't go all pi on us," the newcomer said. Presumably this was the Henley whose study shared the first floor with Somerville and Lawson. "Come on, then—who's in for a lark?"

"I am," Somerville said loudly, as if being first to volunteer would make up for my shaming him. "Come on, lads . . . Henley, Cosgrave, Smith-Pritchard—what say. Let's give old Denning a rocket up the rear that he won't forget!"

There were several nods and a general movement of bodies toward the door. I couldn't allow this to happen.

Before anyone could stop me, I shoved my way through the pack of boys and out onto the landing. I flung open the door of the WC, darted inside, slammed the door behind me, and rammed home the bolt.

I turned round to see if Mr. Denning was still dead in the tub, which he was.

The door rattled, and from outside in the hall came a murmur of voices, Somerville's louder than the rest.

"I say, open up, Veronica," he called. I did not reply. A minute passed.

"Put her out, sir," Somerville said, apparently addressing

the deceased housemaster. "She has no right to be in this house. Please remember that it's off-limits to females. Just put her out the door, sir, and I'll see her off the premises."

Again I kept silent, only gradually realizing that here was a God-sent opportunity for a closer look at the crime scene. Somerville and his cronies could howl all they wanted at the door: There wasn't a schoolboy on the planet—or a man, for that matter—who would dare disturb a female locked into a WC. I knew that for a fact.

Perhaps they would tire and call in someone with authority: some roving housemaster, or even the headmaster himself.

But in the meantime, I had the late Mr. Denning all to myself.

Tucked knees-up in the tub, he reminded me of one of Mrs. Mullet's least successful poultry courses, brought cold and naked to the table in the *bain-marie* in which it had been steamed.

A closer look revealed that several small, irregularly shaped chips of copper had broken away from the body and fallen into the bottom of the tub—perhaps when I had moved it earlier. Small patches of the corpse's skin had been revealed: most of them fish-belly white, but one or two an angry red. And oddly enough, the copper around the red spots had rather a rough, raised surface, like little craters, while that around the white spots was quite smooth and flat.

I was reluctant to touch the corpse—not out of any fear of handling the dead, mind you, but because I didn't want to leave further signs of my examination. In due time, the police would need to see for themselves this copper-plated curiosity with an electrical cable clipped like a crab to its nose: surely one for the record books.

Using a washcloth to prevent fingerprints, I pried open Mr. Denning's mouth with a handy wire soap dish. As I had suspected they would be, the mouth and palate were ulcerated and the tongue and gums tinted a greenish blue.

A quick unclasping of the crocodile clip and a look up the nose showed old lesions and extensive erosion of the mucous membranes. I replaced the clip, taking great care to line up its teeth with their previous impressions.

It was then that I noticed for the first time the clothing draped over the sink behind the door: trousers, jacket, and waistcoat, all of navy serge; shirt and linen underthings all neatly laid out. On the floor beneath them, a small military kit bag of khaki color. Without unfolding the trousers, I worked my hand into each pocket and removed its sparse contents: a large ring of keys with a rabbit's foot charm and a change purse containing a few small coins, including a shilling, a sixpence, and a bent coin marked C. *20*, with a female Italia on one side and bearing, on the other, the head of a mustachioed gentleman, *VITT. EM. III*, whom I took to be a king. The rest of the markings had been obliterated by a fierce fold in the coin, as if it had stopped a bullet.

Next was a worn black letter case that was coming apart at the seams. The contents were few. It was obvious that it belonged to a man of frugal habits. There was a five-pound note, a creased black-and-white snapshot of an Irish setter with "Brownie x/ix/39" penciled on the back, a prescription for Pentostam written by a Harley Street specialist, several prewar postage stamps bearing the image of King George V, and a worn newspaper clipping with a photo of the British Eighth Army landing on Sicily in 1943. The photograph had been handled so much that it looked like a hole-riddled snowflake cut by a child from a sheet of repetitively folded paper.

Overtaken suddenly by an inexplicable sadness, I glanced at the man in the tub as I laid aside the letter case.

Steady on, Flavia, I thought. *Keep your mind on the business at hand. Harsh as it may seem, in detective work there's no place for feelings.*

Right, then: now for the kit bag. I removed the contents one at a time, a little squeamish at handling a man's personal belongings, even if he *was* dead. Fortunately, they were pitifully few: hog-hair shaving brush, pewter mug, shaving soap, tin mirror, double-edge safety razor, nail scissors, toothbrush, tooth powder, and a tube of theatrical greasepaint makeup, Number 12 rouge.

I've always been amazed by the ease with which a stranger's life can be reconstructed by simply snooping through their belongings. Art and imagination combine to tell a tale that's more complete than even a fat printed biography could ever hope to equal. And Mr. Denning was no exception: His secrets were laid so bare that I felt I ought to be apologizing.

But I didn't, of course. The man was dead and I needed to get on with my investigations.

Somerville and his herd were still shuffling and mumbling on the landing. I could not let them in to trample on

414 · ALAN BRADLEY

the evidence. All but one of them, or two, perhaps, were still in ignorance of Mr. Denning's death.

They would not break down the door—of that I was certain. The British schoolboy may be many things, but he is not a beast. In spite of his outward shell of highly polished indifference, he is at heart a gentleman and a jellyfish. I had learned this from years of close observation of my own father, who was himself an old Greyminsterian.

By the time the door was opened, I would be gone. I smiled at the thought of the looks on those boyish faces.

The window above the bathtub was like all the rest at Greyminster: diamond panes in a lattice of lead strips. It was but the work of a moment to haul myself up on the edge of the tub (begging the corpse's pardon, of course), lift the latch, and swing the opaque panes outward.

Scaling the exterior of the school was nothing new to me: Because I had done so during a previous investigation, I knew my way around. After a quick look outside to see that no one was in the quad, I squeezed through the open window and scrambled onto the network of vines which clung everywhere to the old stones.

My descent was ridiculously easy: I felt a bit like Tarzan of the Apes as I swarmed hand over hand to the ground as a choir of angelic voices came floating from the chapel. Borne on the tide of the mighty organ, their words provided a perfect and cinematic musical score for my bold escape:

"Praise to our God; the vine he set
Within our coasts is fruitful yet;

On many a shore her offshoots grow
'Neath many a sun her clusters glow."

Whistling along with the hymn, I strolled nonchalantly off toward the far end of the building.

I remembered that the housemaster's study was located just inside the west door. Taking care to avoid the porter's lodge, I made my way along the back of the building.

Sundays, I decided, are perfect for detective work. Everyone expects that Justice is set aside—at least until church or chapel lets out—and their guard is let down.

I met not a soul, and slipped as easily into Staircase No. 1 as if I were invisible.

The study was precisely where I had remembered it, with the name *W. O. G. Denning* lettered neatly on a card.

I suffered a brief pang as I realized I should have brought the keys from Mr. Denning's pocket. Perhaps, though, a man of such authority would have no need to secure his doors: Respect would serve as its own lock and key. Even if he had shot the bolt, I could always count on my powers of lock-picking, for which I am eternally grateful to Dogger. A bent fork from the dining hall or a bit of stout wire from a stovepipe was as good as a Yale key in the right hands. As it turned out, though, I needn't have worried: The door opened at a touch, and I had locked myself into the housemaster's study before you could say "Spit!"

My stealth was wasted. The room was as empty of personal belongings as a tomb. Save for a foxed Christmas card from four years ago, propped open on a windowsill, addressed "Dear Mr. Denning," and signed "Norah Willett (for the Battersea Dogs' Home)," there was nothing but a bed, a desk, and a shelf of dusty schoolbooks. The desk drawers were empty except for a red pencil, a ruler, scissors, an India-rubber eraser, a box of drawing pins, and a spoon.

It was as if the man had no more needs than a phantom: as if he scarcely existed.

Although I checked under the mattress and pillows and inspected the undersides of drawers and the insides of rolled-up socks, my heart was not in it. I expected to find nothing, and nothing's what I found.

I let myself out.

In order to reach the stairs, I had first to run the gauntlet of staring, black-framed faces that lined both sides of the hall: those Old Boys of Greyminster, students and masters, who had graduated into death "That Others Might Live," as it said on each of the frames. I kept eyes front as I passed in review before these now-dead eyes, trying with all my strength not to break into a run before I reached the staircase.

At the back of the next floor up was the chemistry lab: a shameful jungle of unwashed flasks, stained beakers, and soiled petri dishes which showed clearly that Mr. Winter, the chemistry master, was more obsessed with Jaguars and speed than with cleanliness. I could have swatted him!

The blackboard was covered with equations, as well as a list of test results, upon which the names of Somerville and Plaxton led all the rest.

The chemicals were stored on shelves in a long, dim, narrow anteroom, and were arranged more or less alphabetically, although not always, since zinc sulfate came before sulfur. I could see, even before I came to it, what I was looking for. An empty space between calcium carbonate and hydrochloric acid showed that a large jar of copper sulfate was missing. I had no doubt that it would turn up sooner or later in one of the rubbish bins at Anson House. The question was this: Who had moved the jar from here to there? Fingerprints might or might not come to light, but all of that was still in the future.

For now, there was only one thing left to do before I took my leave. I erased a few of the chemical equations on the blackboard and, taking a stub of chalk in my left hand so as to obscure my handwriting, I wrote on the board in large letters: CLEANLINESS > GODLINESS, which could be read in several ways. Actually, I was quite proud of myself.

As I emerged into the quad, a stream of boys and masters came spilling out of the chapel's open mouth. The sun had made its appearance, promising a fine day after all. I drifted slowly over to an old oak, where, after shedding and spreading my mackintosh, I sank demurely and sat with my hands folded in my lap, my placid face upturned to the sunshine in a slight smile. Somebody's sister, up for Sunday tea and biscuits: no more, no less.

How easy it is, on the whole, to pull the wool over the eyes of men and boys.

As I waited for the worshippers to disperse, I began to review the facts and possibilities in the case.

First and foremost was the evidence of the tub itself, and the copper-plated body that remained seated in it, looking like nothing so much as an oversized motor-racing trophy.

Not that it wasn't tragic, and so forth, but still, in its own way, it was a spectacle second to none, and I was grateful to Plaxton for having called upon my services.

There was no doubt that the body had been copper-plated by one lead of the automobile battery having been dropped into the tub—filled at the time with a solution of copper sulfate—and the other clipped to the nose of the deceased like a clothes-peg.

The ring of sediment left behind was remarkable for its regularity: another clue that needed to be considered.

Identifying the culprit was going to be no easy task, I thought as I reviewed the suspects.

First of all, and top of my list because of his attitude, was Wilfrid Somerville. His father was an avid photographer, according to Plaxton, so it seemed reasonable to theorize that a certain awareness of chemicals would be inevitable in the son. Even the most careless observer would likely know that copper sulfate was sometimes used as a reversal bleach in the photo lab.

And then there was Lawson, whose father was a chemist in Leeds.

"Taffy"—Wagstaffe's father—after his glorious career in the RAF, had taken up a hereditary post at the head of Wagstaffe Chemicals, a position into which the boy would likely someday follow him.

Henley, if my deductions were correct, came from a family made wealthy by plumbing supplies: a profession in which the use of copper sulfate to kill tree roots in sewer lines is known to every scullery maid. A medallion head of Henley senior—the family resemblance was remarkable—

was stamped on every tin of their patent product, including the one that Dogger kept in the greenhouse at Buckshaw for emergencies, and I had recognized the son at once.

The chubby Smith-Pritchard, by contrast, seemed to have no obvious connection with the metal salts. The son of a member of Parliament, he appeared to be far more interested in stuffing food into his face than in fungicides.

That, except for Baker, was the first and second landings accounted for on Staircase No. 3, leaving only Cosgrave, Parker, and Plaxton himself, who had called me into the case.

Cosgrave was, of course, the son of Harrison Cosgrave, the noted—not to say famous, in certain circles—author of one of the standard works on chemistry.

Parker was the dark horse: the quiet one, the one who kept to himself and played American jazz on his gramophone in the small hours of the morning. Plaxton had said nothing about Parker's family connections and it was quite clear that I needed to question Plaxton again.

One of these boys, I was certain, had had a hand in what I was already coming to think of as The Curious Case of the Copper Corpse. (It is no longer enough simply to solve crimes: We modern private detectives must also be able to come up with catchy names for our cases.)

My train of thought was interrupted by a footstep beside me. I looked up to see Plaxton steadying himself with a hand on the tree. He was breathing heavily, and even from a yard away I could almost hear his heartbeat.

"The jig is up," he wheezed. "The head has sent out a

420 · ALAN BRADLEY

search party for Mr. Denning. He was supposed to be at a housemaster's breakfast at half-seven. He's never missed in all his years."

"Sit down beside me," I said. "Don't attract attention."

Plaxton sat.

"Now, then," I told him, "time is short. There are several points that need clarifying. What can you tell me about Baker?"

Baker was the only one of the nine students on Staircase No. 3 whom I had learned nothing about.

"Sandy Baker? He's the little chap with glasses. Quite frail and a little hunched. You must have noticed him in my study."

In fact I hadn't, and I wasn't proud of my slipup.

"He's studying art and sculpture."

"And his parents?" I asked.

"His father's a veterinary surgeon somewhere in the west country. I'm afraid that's all I can tell you."

It was enough. I recalled that veterinarians commonly used a footbath of copper sulfate to treat foot rot in sheep.

How remarkable, I thought, that six of the nine students on Staircase No. 3 had, in one way or another, direct connections to and perhaps some personal experience in the use of good old $CuSO_4$. Knowledge or experience did not, of course, necessarily imply guilt, but it helped greatly in the process of elimination.

"Is Parker the son of a baker, a bookbinder, or a manufacturer of straw hats?" I asked Plaxton.

"Not so far as I know," he said. "A music publisher, I believe."

"And your own father?" I asked. It was a question I had been fearing to ask.

"He's a Fleet Street journalist," Plaxton answered. "He's in jail for refusing to reveal his sources in the government pension scandal."

"Of course," I said. "I'm sorry." I had seen the sensational stories in the illustrated news magazines: the fist-shaking crowds, the handcuffed prisoner.

"Tell me about Mr. Denning," I went on, trying to get past the awkward moment. "Was he in the Service?"

"As a matter of fact, he was," Plaxton replied. "He waded ashore at Castellazzo, in Sicily, in 1943, with the Eighth Army. Poor chap—he never really got over it. That's why I felt so dreadful about—"

A great flare went off in my brain, and in that instant, everything became suddenly clear.

"Did he always wear long sleeves?" I interrupted.

"Funnily enough, he did," Plaxton said, with an odd look. "Even in summer."

"Then," I said, "the only question left to ask is this: What did you do with the empty bottle?"

Plaxton's face collapsed as if it were rubber.

"You know, then?" His voice was that of a ghost.

"Of course I know." I tried my best to sound matter-of-fact. "The poor man was suffering from the Sicilian strain of sandfly fever."

It was, I knew, a recurrence of kala-azar, or dumdum fever. Dogger, who knew at first hand a great deal about tropical diseases, had told me tales of the dreaded ailment caused by the bite of the phlebotomine sandfly, which feeds upon the blood of rodents. The fever, common in the Mediterranean, could manifest itself even after twenty years. The sores and lesions in the dead man's nose should have alerted me at once, as should the prescription for Pentostam.

"You found him dead in the tub," I told Plaxton. "He had suffered a heart attack while soaking himself in a bath of copper sulfate, whose crystals he had pinched from the chemistry lab to alleviate his sores. He may already have absorbed enough of the stuff to cause poisoning. An autopsy will tell.

"The evenness of the blue ring showed that there had been no thrashing around. The ring around his neck was constant and his face had not been immersed. Therefore, he either died in the tub, or was already dead when he was put there.

"You should have left the empty bottle, Plaxton. It was a careless oversight.

"Because of the god-awful row you'd had, you were still in a rage. You decided to hook him up to the battery, which you removed from Mr. Winter's car, to make it look as if someone else—some unknown person, some passing stranger—had murdered him."

"They'd never have believed me!" Plaxton blurted. "But how did you know?"

"By your irritated eyes," I answered, "to begin with, and the hoarseness of your voice when you opened the door. Exposure to the steamy fumes of copper sulfate. You were there *before* the bathwater cooled."

I didn't feel any need to tell Plaxton about the theatrical greasepaint which Mr. Denning had been using for years to cover up his awful scales and lesions. In death, the poor man surely deserved at least a pinch of privacy.

"The police will soon be here," I said. "I advise you to be straight with them. You needn't mention my name."

"Big help you've been," Plaxton said, his voice dripping sarcasm.

"Thank you," I replied, pretending not to notice. "As you requested, I've at least given you and your playmates excuses why you shouldn't be charged with murder. You might be asked some awkward questions about interfering with a dead body, but that's your problem—not mine."

"No—look," Plaxton said, coming to his senses. "Here, take this."

And he pressed a five-pound note into my hand. I let it flutter to the ground, but he scooped it up and shoved it into my pocket.

It simply boggles the mind the way in which some people can turn on a sixpence. Or perhaps it was that I had misjudged Plaxton from the beginning. Pity is not always the best basis for trust.

As I got to my feet and began walking away across the grass, toward the old stone of Anson House, the new banknote crackled crisply in my pocket. It was, I realized with a secret thrill, the first pay I had ever received for professional consultation.

Gladys would be happy to see me. We would stop at Bert Archer's garage on the way home and buy a fresh tin of bicycle oil.

It would be my treat.